The

UNDENIABLE
POSSIBILITY
BY
CHIP POLK

Dedication

For
Dad, Mom, Don
Jeff
Randy
&
Fig

PROLOGUE
Today

• • • •

THE SPRING STILL FED the old fountain, just like he said it would. Water spilled over the scalloped edge of the upper bowl to the larger second tier, and then to the lowest one, before emptying into the shallow walled pool around the base. From there, it coursed down the hillside in a meandering brook that fed the cold, fresh water into a sparkling lake.

Andrew Pembrook could see his wife wading along the edge of the lake below, identical little golden-haired sprites clinging to each hand as they danced on tiptoe, squealing and laughing as the soft mud squished between their toes. He remembered Macy doing exactly the same thing. His four-year-old daughters often reminded him of his sister when she was their age.

Andrew sat on a stone bench beside the fountain and looked down through the break in the trees that lined the pathway up the hillside. He watched his wife and daughters, a smile playing across his lips, while a wisp of melancholy clouded his clear green eyes. His grandmother's eyes, Grandpop had always said. He'd told his only grandson that he would never be a poker player with those eyes.

Today, this place, and what they were here to do, combined to make Andrew's eyes a kaleidoscope of emotion.

It was as though all the times of his life were stored in this place, and it was here where he could clearly look at them, and remember in vivid detail, whatever crisis or possibility had dominated his thoughts during his visits. He could look around and almost see Grandpop, Macy, Uncle Arnie, all of them doing the things they always did together here—fishing, playing cards, dominos, pitching horseshoes, sitting together in the evenings on the broad porch of the big cabin as Grandpop grilled burgers.

Most of his memories of the times when his grandmother had been with them had dimmed over the years. It saddened him, but at least he could cling to those he had. Treasure them.

An image of his father's face flashed across Andrew's mind, and the cloud it produced within showed clearly on the finely chiseled features that so very nearly matched those that he forced away from his thoughts. As soon as Macy and her family arrived, he would have to face those painful feelings again. Just not now. Not right this moment. He needed this time in this special place to shore himself up with memories of happier days.

1

1991

• • • •

IT WAS HALF FULL BEFORE Mason realized he was pouring coffee in the turquoise cup. He stopped. It washed over him again like a wave, tumbling a hundred images over in his mind before he could regain his footing.

Mason Crewe, sixty-five years old, still fit, still vital and creative, still interested and interesting. And still, he was deeply in love with the girl of his dreams. He dumped the half-filled cup of coffee into the sink, rinsed it out and put it away.

It had been weeks since he had done that. It happened all the time early on, and the impulse was there every morning, but usually he caught himself when he picked up her cup, and unbidden memories of a thousand other mornings struck him. He would reluctantly put it back. It made him feel almost guilty now, having those rare moments when he forgot the terrible truth. Arnie said he should throw the cup away, but he couldn't. He just couldn't. And Arnie knew that. His brother-in-law knew him better than anyone, except Annie.

But Annie never got to know him. She just knew him. She strolled right into his heart one day, took stock of what made him tick, probably rolled her eyes and laughed, but for some reason decided to stick around for the long haul.

"Not long enough," Mason muttered to himself. "Not long enough for me."

He picked up his own cup, the brick red one, and headed out to the patio with the morning paper in his other hand. Settling into his chair, his eye fell upon the raised beds that bordered the flagstone terrace, the dappled morning sunlight catching every color of the rainbow in the flowers that Annie had babied through decades of summers.

Gone. That word is just gentle self-deception, Mason thought. *Like she is gone to Chicago. Gone to market in Atlanta.*

But Annie wasn't just gone. She was dead, and reminders of her were there in every nook and cranny of his world. It hadn't been long enough for them to become a comfort. He didn't think they ever would be.

Something flashed in his peripheral vision. It startled Mason from what was quickly becoming another bout of the depressing reverie that had engulfed him so often over the past nine months.

"Well you're back," he said, being very still. The cardinal perched on the rim of the concrete birdbath Annie had placed just outside the kitchen window. She loved to watch the birds gather and vie for a turn to jump into the water, then ruffle and flutter themselves dry, perched along the rim. She hadn't been a bird watcher in the traditional sense, but she had identified the various species that frequented her little avian spa, and kept a camera handy to capture their antics. Annie had loved watching them from the kitchen, and would get excited when she recognized a returning guest.

This one had returned often enough that Mason had grown to expect its visit when he went out for his morning coffee on the patio. He had come to expect it, and strangely, look forward to it.

As he sat quietly watching the brilliantly colored bird, it hopped to the rim and turned to face him, cocking its tufted head to one side, as it appeared to look directly at Mason. It then looked nervously from side to side, fluttered back into the water and out again, flapped its wings and shook itself, sending water droplets flying in all directions. Then stopped once more, and just looked at Mason again, cocking its head to the side.

"So what are you looking at?" he said to the bird.

"Looking at you."

The gruff voice from behind him startled Mason. Annie's brother was her twin, but they were as different as night and day. Arnold Warner, always "Arnie" to his sister's family, his only family, settled into the chair next to Mason. He had helped himself to coffee. Not in the turquoise cup.

This had become a frequent thing since Annie died, Arnie stopping by on his way to work. Mason wondered if it was for his benefit, or that the house allowed Arnie a bit of comfort. He had taken his sister's loss awfully hard.

"Why don't you come in with me today?" Arnie suggested. "The gang would like it, and I'd like to have your thoughts on a couple of things."

"Nah, I have some things I want to do here today," Mason replied evasively." After a moment he added, "I appreciate what you're trying to do, Arnie, but I just don't have the heart to come back. Not Yet. Honestly, I don't know if I ever will."

Arnie had tried several times over the past few months to get Mason to become involved in the company again. Mason, Annie, and Arnie had built the business from scratch together. It had been the bachelor's entire life, and he felt like it was well past time that Mason put his energy and creativity back to work. He thought it would be good for his brother-in-law and best friend.

Arnie was an operations guy, and a masterful one. Mason and Annie were both artistically gifted, and though each had their strengths on the business end, it was Arnie Warner who made everything work. He was in command, not merely in charge of manufacture, marketing, distribution, and personnel. He had been responsible for taking Warner & Crewe from startup to a multi-million-dollar household name.

They could have taken the company public anytime, and the three partners would have instantly become wealthy beyond reason, but Annie, Mason, and Arnie had no desire to change the ingredients in the recipe for success the company had enjoyed. Arnie in particular was a relentless advocate for the small army of employees that he had so conscientiously trained, motivated, and compelled to reproduce, market, and distribute the Warner & Crew collection.

He, Annie, and Mason had all been equal partners in Warner & Crewe from the beginning. They each owned one third of the company and had equal say in any major decisions. Their relationship had been as perfect as any business partnership could be, between committed, opinionated, creative, obstinate people who love and respect one another.

What Arnie had not fully realized until Mason's recent absence, was that his brother-in-law had been a crucial part of the equation on the operations side as well. More specifically, Arnie had realized that with Mason by his side, providing a slightly different perspective on whatever issue that happened to be at hand, he had a measure of confidence and decisiveness that he now lacked.

And yet, this was the new equation. Mason had abandoned all interest in the company. And Annie was gone. It was surprising to Arnie that Mason didn't feel drawn to remain at the company, if only for Meredith's sake. His daughter had to face the absence of not only her mother every day, but Mason as well. She had done so with a kind of grim determination that was hard to watch.

Arnie couldn't help but think that Mason had begun to be self-indulgent in his grief, particularly considering the reality of his responsibilities at Warner & Crewe. And with regard to Meredith. Nevertheless, he also felt a keen sense of duty to support his brother-in-law unconditionally.

"See that cardinal?" Mason asked.

The red bird had returned to the birdbath, having darted away at Arnie's approach. Now it hopped along the edge of the basin, looking up warily at the intruders every few seconds.

"Pretty," was Arnie's offhand reply.

"Annie always loved it back here. She would sit out here and sketch. Those were her favorite," Mason said, nodding toward the bird. Then he added, "Doesn't it kind of remind you of her?"

"Remind me of Annie?"

"Yeah," Mason answered, watching Arnie's face, which bore a somewhat apprehensive expression at the moment.

"I mean, the quick way it moves and tries to look at everything at once. Annie was always like that. Like she was always totally absorbed in the moment, and not wanting to miss anything that was going on."

"Well, that was her alright," Arnie muttered with raised eyebrows as he sipped his coffee.

"And that cardinal... doesn't make you think of her?" Mason asked.

"You two sculpted hundreds of birds over the years. The cardinals have always been a great seller. I guess birds will always make me think of you and Annie," Arnie answered. The strangeness of the conversation was making him uncomfortable.

"If Annie could be anything, she would want to be a cardinal," Mason said quietly.

"Have you seen Meredith and the kids in the past few days?" Arnie said, abruptly and obviously changing the subject.

Mason continued to look at the cardinal, and it appeared to Arnie that he smiled at it and shook his head slightly, then cut his eyes back at him, as though sharing a joke with the bird. A joke on him.

The bird flew up into one of the trees and Mason turned to answer Arnie's question, "Yeah they came by on Sunday. That Andy is growing like a weed. He's a pretty sensitive kid, and I think it depresses him to come over here. He and Annie were big pals."

Glad to have the awkwardness about the bird over with, Arnie said, "Have you been down to the lake since—"

"Not yet," Mason answered, not wishing to hear the rest of that sentence. "But I've been thinking I would go soon. It might be nice if we all went down one weekend. It'll sure be different without her, but I need to get out of the house. Maybe I'll go down by myself first, putter around the cabin. There's always stuff that needs to be done there. Maybe fish a little."

Arnie encouraged him. Mason had seldom left the house since Annie's death, other than to go to church on occasional Sundays. After some small talk about some of the Warner & Crewe personnel, and recounting the recent humorous escapades of Meredith's children, Arnie made his excuses and left, leaving Mason still on the patio scanning the treetops for birds.

• • • •

THE BUZZARDS DRIFTED in lazy circles over the dump. Six of them today. The boy lay spread-eagle on the roof of the house and looked at the sky. The sun felt good on his swollen cheek, and the heat of the asphalt roof always seemed to soak in and soothe the ache within.

Up here he could see nothing but the sky and the birds, and he liked that. He didn't have to work to shut out the squalid confines that had been his whole world for the twelve long years he had been alive. Up here he could forget where he was. Forget who he was.

Freddy Finger, that stupid, stupid name. It wasn't enough to be sired by the drunken piece of trash. He was going to have to live with his name, and perpetuate the joke. The Moron loved their name. He introduced himself by flipping his middle finger to everyone he met, until one surly biker in a bar one night took offense, whipped out a razor-sharp blade and took it off right at the knuckle. That was the only thought about his father that ever made the boy smile.

As he lay there watching the buzzards circle above him, he wished that he had more than shards of memories of his mother left, but he didn't. He would like to think about her, but almost all that remained of her now was sad eyes and black hair hanging in lank curls over thin shoulders.

But he did remember that she had tried to teach him to read. He could recall the warm feeling that she was proud of him when he would sound out a word. That had been a good feeling. She had called it "going to school" and it was his best memory. He still had the book she had used to show him the sounds the letters made, and he had stayed at it after she was gone.

He would pretend that she was still there with him through the long days he spent alone in the house. He would imagine that she was still listening to him read, and still feeling proud of him. Over time he discovered that he could make out most of the words in the newspapers the Moron would occasionally bring home.

He once heard his father call somebody a *moron*. He'd asked what the word meant. That was before he learned to keep his questions to himself.

"It means a stupid idiot, just like you. Now shut your mouth."

After that the boy always used that word when he thought about his father. He didn't believe his mother would have left him there with the Moron. He thought the Moron hit her too hard, too many times one night. He thought he remembered it sometimes, but then it slipped away.

He didn't mind that.

The twelve-year-old watched black wings silhouetted against the shifting shapes of the clouds beyond, and imagined again what it would feel like to fly up there among those billowing peaks and shaded valleys in the sky. He had always liked watching the buzzards fly and imagine himself soaring there among them, but after he'd come upon a couple of them picking at the spilled-out insides of a dead dog over at the dump, he had changed his mind about wishing to be one.

Imagining himself a hawk became his choice. Hawks soared above the dump as well, but they were more rarely seen than the ever-present buzzards. They were predators that would search for their prey, then dive down and snatch it up in their talons. He had read all about hawks.

As the boy watched the birds circle, he found himself thinking again about a family he used to watch on the television. At the beginning of that show you could see the farm where they lived from high above. He imagined it was like a hawk would see it from up in the air. Almost everything the boy knew about the world beyond the house and nearby junkyard, he learned watching the old television in the corner of the front room of the house.

In that black and white world, a family all lived together, the mom and dad and all their children living with the grandparents in a big house on a farm. He had liked the grandparents most of all. The television didn't work anymore, and he missed those people. He still thought about them often.

He pretended to believe that his mother had gone to live with her parents on a farm like that, and would one day come and take him to live there with them. They would have Thanksgiving dinner together. The television family had Thanksgiving dinner once, and the grandfather said a prayer before they ate. The kid wondered who the old man was talking to.

He knew it wasn't true about his mother. If he really had grandparents, the boy had no idea where they lived. He didn't even know his mother's name, first or last. The Moron had referred to her only by obscenities when he bellowed in a drunken rage about her saddling him with a kid to take care of.

Nor had he ever heard his father mention his own parents or any other family. Junkyard dogs, most likely. That's what the Moron reminded him of more than anything, the dogs that roamed the city dump a quarter of a mile beyond the Finger place. There was always the stinking bloated carcass of one or two amid the piles of garbage. He could smell them from the house when the wind came from that direction, and he liked to imagine it was the Moron out there like that, stiff and bloated, the buzzards all around him.

That's where the boy thought his mother really was. That's why he was terrified of the dump. He was afraid of finding her there.

Every week or two the Moron would make him go along to dig through other people's filth for scrap metal, and old appliances and such that he could repair and sell. He always thought he was going to lift a piece of cardboard, or push over a piece of discarded furniture and see her sad eyes staring up from the piles of garbage beneath.

The only thing that made those dreaded trips tolerable for the boy was the chance of happening upon magazines that he could take home and read. One time he had found a cardboard box with seven volumes, from an old set of *Compton Pictured Encyclopedias*. It was like discovering treasure. He still pored over those seven volumes, absorbing everything, from A to G-H.

Had he ever been enrolled in school, his teachers would have discovered that the boy had a startling intellect, insatiable curiosity, and could retain virtually everything he read. Unfortunately, he rarely found discarded books at the dump, though he scoured the trash piles for them at his own peril. The Moron was not interested in books.

Freddy Finger Jr. never attended school. He was seldom beyond the confines of the house and junkyard. What the boy didn't know, was that his father made an occasional belligerent remark at the bars in town and to customers in his garage, about his wife leaving and taking their son with her to live somewhere in Kansas. He insinuated that the boy came down for visits from time to time. That was enough to explain the rare occasion when anyone caught a glimpse of the child. No one wanted to engage the surly Freddy Finger in conversation, much less inquire about his family situation.

Freddy Finger wasn't stupid. He was calculating, methodical, thorough, and he could fix anything. He was a good automobile mechanic, and everybody knew it. He made good money off of anyone who would put up with his foul-mouthed guff. He worked when he wanted and quit anytime he felt like it. It might be later rather than sooner, but he would always get the work done.

Everyone in Slaterville and thirty miles around knew if you could stomach dealing with Finger and didn't get in a hurry, you'd never have a reason to complain about the work. He was good at it.

Finger's Garage did a lot of work for the oil field service companies and hands. The drillers, roustabouts and roughnecks could hand his garbage right back, and then some.

The other paradoxical thing about Freddy Finger, was that he was good with money. But that wasn't hard for him. He never bought anything. He spent nothing to improve or even maintain his house. He and his son wore their clothes until they disintegrated. He bought just enough food to survive. The only thing he ever spent money on was booze, and even that he budgeted.

When his daily *hooch stash* was deposited with whichever bartender he hated least that week, he stumbled out to his pieced-together tow-truck and weaved a mile and a half south of town.

Just beyond the city limits was a sign that read *City Dump*, with an arrow pointing left, where he would turn and cross the railroad tracks onto the caliche road that led back to his shack, and the runt that he said reminded him so stinking much of the kid's worthless mother that he would just as soon throw him through the wall as look at him. And if the boy wasn't prudent enough to be out of his way when he got home, it often felt to the boy like he was trying to do just that.

When the kid started showing signs of getting his growth, Finger knew a day of reckoning was coming. He could see the look already. Just like his mother. He began to make a special effort to forego any thought of defiance from the kid.

The boy knew that his father had some money stashed. The Moron bragged about it, but only within earshot of his son. When he came home drunk he railed about how surprised the fine people of Slaterville, Oklahoma were going to be when they heard Freddy Finger had built a big, fine house with a boat dock down on Lake Texoma. To hear Finger tell it, the cost and responsibility of dealing with a useless kid seemed to be the only obstacle between him and his dream of living on fish he'd catch from his boat, and not having to put up with the *ignernt oil field trash* for another second.

The only visible step Finger had taken toward realizing his dream was a 25-horsepower outboard boat motor, which he had overhauled and mounted on the side of a 55-gallon oil drum that he had cut the top out of and filled with water. He would go outside, back behind the well-house where he had placed the barrel, and pull-start the old outboard motor, then stand there and gaze down toward the submerged propeller as it churned the water in the drum, muttering to himself something lost in the drone of the blue and silver Big Twin Evinrude.

When the boy would hear the backdoor screen slap shut as the Moron went out, he would count down from 58 to 1 and mutter, "Blast off." The motor would pop and then roar to life as Finger twisted the throttle.

Freddy Finger was nothing if not predictable. That was just one of many countdown games his son had invented, perhaps just to have a glimmer of victory somewhere in his dismal young life. The only times he lost the game was when the Moron stopped in the yard to relieve himself, or if he decided his motor needed fresh water in the drum.

Every few weeks Finger would take the motor off the side of the drum and tip it over, the water gushing down to pool at the bottom of a shallow, weed-choked ravine behind the well-house. Then he would carefully replace it with fresh water, remount the motor on the side, and crank it up, standing there chuckling and talking to himself as he watched the water thrashing.

It was plain to the boy that his father cared a lot more about that stupid boat motor than he did about him. Watching him out there, he wondered if the old man wasn't crazy. Who stands and watches a boat motor running in a barrel of water?

• • • •

MASON HAD FORGOTTEN what it felt like to be excited by an idea, and he had spent his whole life being excited about ideas. The feeling was completely foreign to him now. Annie died, and with her, the ideas, and certainly the excitement. Or so he had thought.

He took a stack of typewriter paper from the tray on his desk and dug in one of the drawers for a fine-tipped felt marker. The ink in the first two he tried was dry. The third pen worked and Mason sat at his desk and began to capture what he had envisioned in quick, sure strokes.

When he finally stopped sketching, he realized he was hungry. Glancing at the grandfather clock opposite his desk he understood why. It was a quarter of four. He had been sketching and planning for close to five hours. It surprised him that he felt alive for the first time in such a long time. Then immediately he felt a twinge of guilt.

Mason shook his head at the notion that he was somehow being unfaithful to Annie's memory. That was the last thing she would want him to feel. He knew that. Annie would be as excited about this idea as he was. If only he could tell her about it.

With sudden resolve, he snatched up the stack of sketches and headed out to the back patio, grabbing a banana from a basket on the counter in the kitchen on his way out.

When he got outside, he scanned the trees hopefully, but when he saw no flashes of color or movement among the leaves, he whispered to himself, "Well, I guess not today."

Sitting down in his patio chair, he peeled the banana and thumbed through the drawings for a moment before peering again into foliage that shaded the patio. He sat for a time chewing absently on the banana. Then hearing a rustle of movement above and to his left, he turned and he saw a blue jay settle and squawk intrusively on a high branch in the canopy, its crested head turning abruptly from one side to the other.

Mason shuffled through the paper and rearranged them in some order, then looked again at the bird. He watched it for a long time, and it seemed to be watching him, warily fluttering from branch to branch with an occasional abrasive squawk. Although he didn't realize it, a small smile played across Mason's parted lips.

"You always did look good in blue," he said, smiling up at the bird, "But I think the red suits you better."

This had been going on for weeks. At first, Mason thought the grief was taking a toll on his mind. It loomed over him from the moment he awoke every morning, until long after he turned out the light at night to again attempt to sleep in the big bed alone. Reality wasn't that great anymore, as far as Mason Crewe was concerned, so why not indulge himself in a little fantasy, if it gave him a moment of comfort?

That was his logic, anyway. And it turned out that it had indeed given him comfort. Coming from the bleak state of mind he had been in since Annie died, those occasional, unexpected moments of respite had become tiny glimmers of the joy he had always had with his wife. As small as this was, it was something. Mason looked forward to it, and he hadn't looked forward to anything in a long time.

He knew if Meredith or Arnie should catch him talking to a bird like this, they would surely think he was losing his mind. And especially today. This was the first time Mason had come outside, intentionally, to have a conversation. Now that he was actually doing it, he felt a little embarrassed, and worried that either Meredith or Arnie might happen by, and hear him.

But taking a breath, Mason looked up and deliberately addressed the bird that had now settled onto a low branch of the maple tree that shaded the patio. He spoke quietly at first, almost in a whisper.

"Annie, uh..." It took him a moment to continue, "I just wanted to tell you about this. I'm really excited by it, and how am I supposed to do anything with it, if I can't tell you about it? You know how it works. I have to talk it through."

Mason could see the scene just as it had played out untold hundreds of times. Annie would come into his study, bringing him a cup of coffee after she had her morning shower, and find Mason sketching something, making notes, paper scattered across his desk, and on the floor under his chair.

"Must be a good one," she would say.

"Oh, I don't know. It might be junk, but I'm kind of excited about it," Mason would answer.

"Well, show me what you've got," she'd say, her eyes alight, always ready to be carried away in her husband's whirlwind of enthusiasm.

Mason would hand her the most complete sketch he had, and then watch her face. He would know almost immediately if he had struck on something that was going to work. Her eyes gave it away, good or bad.

Then she would say, "What's the story?" And Mason would tell her.

As the story behind the idea unfolded, he would reveal the progression of drawings and notations that he had used to arrive at the final sketch. He continued to watch for the sign that she was catching the vision and her own creative fire was beginning to ignite.

When she said, "Give me a pencil," it began.

This was the magic that had spawned the Warner & Crew Collectibles line. Their porcelain figurines were collected worldwide, and almost every piece had begun with some variation on this same scene.

"This story is a little different," Mason began, glancing at the jay, as though he truly believed the bird was listening. "I need a change. Everything here..." Before continuing, Mason looked back toward the door into the house to assure himself that he was alone, and then again glanced up to the bird that was still sitting on the same branch, "Everything here reminds me of you, and that isn't bad. But yeah, honey, it kind of is. At least it is right now. See, it isn't only that I've lost you. It's like I've lost myself too. If I don't do something..."

Mason stopped himself, looked down at the stack of paper he held in his hand, and said, "I just have to do something." He laid a sketch on the patio table. The bird made a short series of clicking noises and shot to another branch.

"There's something I think I want to build down at the lake." Mason glanced down at the sketch and saw that, unconsciously, he had turned it so that it would be upright if the jay should look at it.

"Maybe I am losing my mind," he said. Then looking up at the bird he added, "That wouldn't be the worst thing that could happen."

The lake was a three-hour drive southeast on a secluded wooded Ozark property that Warner & Crewe had purchased thirty years back. Annie and Mason had frequently gone down over the years to ramble through the woods photographing and sketching birds and other wildlife that would eventually end up depicted in their figurines.

In the early years, they camped out on the shore of the lake. After Meredith came along they decided to build a cabin. Eventually, a second cabin was constructed nearby that Arnie used, and occasionally offered to select employees for vacations.

"You know, it would help if you would do something. Come down here and land on your chair maybe."

Mason actually chuckled and said, "I guess you could crap on the drawing if you don't like it." And for just a moment he felt just a flash of that rare chemistry that he and Annie had shared from that very first night they had talked in the art lab back in college. It was more than love.

And the laugh ended with an unexpected wrenching sob as Mason's face contorted and the tears came before he could check himself. He covered his mouth with his hand and the jay became a blue blur among the leaves above.

It only lasted a moment, but Mason felt drained as he heard himself saying, "I'm sorry. That was embarrassing. Hasn't happened like that in a while. I thought I was past that part. Caught me off guard."

He pulled a handkerchief from his back pocket, wiped his face, blew his nose, composed himself. Between sniffs, he waved a hand toward the sketch and managed to say, "It's a fountain."

He didn't look up, but plowed on into his idea, and as he spoke, he began to lose his self-consciousness. For the first time in a long time, he sounded just like Mason Crewe again.

"I want to put it in that clearing up above the cabin where we had the fire pit, remember? And I've been thinking maybe I want to move up to the cabin and live there, or at least spend a lot of time there like we always planned to do together. Who knows? Maybe Meredith and Adam will eventually want to build their own cabin, you know, for weekends. And shoot, Arnie will be ready to retire before too long. He might. Well, we can't predict what's going to happen. We sure know that now, huh?"

He picked up the sketch again, and continued, "But I want to start with this. You remember that spring on the north side up the hill from the cabin, right? Remember how we used to put our sodas in it to chill? Well, that will be the water source."

Mason's pencil pointed, jabbed, and marked up his sketch as he went on, "I'll run a pipeline down the hillside from the spring and if I compress the piping toward the end, it should create enough water pressure to pump a constant cascade from the top bowl of the fountain, and the water would spill down from each tier, and then there'd be an overflow down here that would drain on into the lake from this walled pond around the base. It should run from now on." He smiled broadly and looked up through his eyebrows and added, "Forever."

The jay was no longer where it had been in the maple tree. He didn't see it anywhere as he looked among the leaves of the other trees surrounding the patio. He looked back down at the fountain sketch, and with a slight gesture of resignation, gathered up the other drawings and got up to go back toward the house.

Just as he was reaching for the door he heard a sharp repeated chirp, followed by a second series in a more melodic sound. And then again. Turning slowly, Mason smiled when he saw a beautiful red cardinal land on the birdbath. After a nervous reconnaissance of its surroundings, the bird quickly dipped its beak in the water, then it flew up to a high branch on the maple tree and issued another chorus of the staccato call.

Mason slowly returned to his chair, watching the cardinal as he walked, hoping it wouldn't be frightened away, and spoke gently, "Did you change just for me, because I said red suits you better?"

Again, the call rang out across the yard. Mason chose to believe it was an answer. And if it was indeed a response to his question, this was no ordinary bird at all. In that brief space of time he marveled at the difference it made to be having this conversation. Even if it wasn't real, if he was merely imagining the whole thing, it was comforting. How could there be anything wrong with that?

Mason dove back into his explanation. "Now do you see these? These three birds? Let me tell you about these three. This one here is Poofannie, of course. You can tell. And this impatient fellow over here is Poofarnie. And this good looking one...well he's Poofernando."

For 35 years Mason had been dreaming up adventures for Poofannie, Poofarnie, and Poofernando as part of their design regimen. Virtually every figurine Warner & Crewe released had a hidden, mysterious back-story that had given each one an element of intriguing substance, which their competitors' ceramic collectibles seemed to lack.

Mason and Annie had never revealed the stories. Not even to Arnie. They were afraid it would somehow take the magic away from the pieces, if everyone knew. And besides, it had been their secret ingredient, and theirs alone.

The stories were just silly little adventures, but that had been enough. It had all begun the very first time Mason and Annie had met just before he graduated from college.

4
1951

• • • •

MASON CREWE STEPPED back from the table and looked at his work, turning it slowly, his blue eyes scanning the details of the clay sculpture for any gratuitous contrivance. The last thing he wanted his work to be, was *obvious*. No true artist wants his work to be so pedestrian that the whole thing could be absorbed in a casual glance.

Satisfied that this piece was, if not extraordinary, close enough for jazz, and certainly close enough for an A on his final grade, Mason stood up, stretched his stiff back, and sauntered over to the sink to wash the clay off his hands. He glanced again at the only other person left in the art lab. He thought he remembered that her name was Walker or maybe Warner. He'd noticed the TA, who impersonated a teacher in this class, flirting with her. Mason's table was in the back of the room, so he'd never really looked at her, but his vague impression was that she was cute. Or at least the aide thought she was.

Mason glanced at her piece from across the room. A glance was enough. It was a graceless representation of a bird stuck on a branch with some unidentifiable flowers winding up from beneath. It looked like one of those god-awful plaster ornaments people would buy to paint and sit on a crocheted doily amid the other tasteless clutter that decorated working class homes across America. It certainly wasn't art. But the aide would take care of her.

"Are you finished?" the girl asked, startling him with the notion that she had read his mind about her project.

"Uh...well maybe. I never really know," he gathered himself to reply. "How's yours going?"

23

The girl turned on her stool and gave him a look that made Mason think she really might have read his thoughts and agreed with his assessment. And she was cute. More than cute. Way more.

"Sculpting is not my thing. I love color. This is mud...it's so one dimensional," she said with a little laugh.

"Well, it's actually not. I mean it's three...dimensional," Mason replied, regretting the remark immediately.

"It was joke."

"I knew that," Mason said as though he had, then smiled, not so much about the joke, but because she really was miles beyond cute. Especially when she smiled. Those emerald green eyes just danced, and he actually thought he felt a little short of breath.

How could I spend a whole semester in this room with this girl and never see her? Those eyes, my gosh. And that smile?

Mason's eyes stole a glimpse down at the over-sized, clay-smeared apron that covered the answer to another question he had. It was just a glance, but almost as if responding to his unspoken curiosity, she untied the strings and slipped it off, carelessly discarding the stiff-fronted apron, along with a pair of peeled-off latex gloves, onto the table beside her uninteresting sculpture. She turned away and walked to one of the sinks mounted in the counter along the wall and washed her hands.

Mason liked the answer very much, and again wondered how he could have missed noticing her before. It dawned on him that this project was the final for the class and he might not have another opportunity to get to know this girl.

She spoke as she dried her hands. "I need a break...and a hamburger. How 'bout you?"

"Well I don't know if I should. I mean I don't even know your name."

"So I was right then," she retorted, picking up a purse from the floor beneath the table and absently picking off flecks of dried clay.

Mason asked, "Right about what?"

"Right, when I told myself that you didn't even know my name."

"What question were you asking yourself?" Mason responded.

She stopped and turned around, cocking her head to one side, narrowing her eyes and gazed steadily at him through long lashes, and after a moment said, "Why should I be interested in that guy?" Then extended her hand, which Mason took automatically, even taken aback as he was. She smiled and added. "I'm Annie."

"Annie," he repeated softly.

"And you're Mason."

They stood there looking at each other, her grip on his hand firm, and his tender on hers until it began to feel a little awkward.

"See, I already knew your name," Annie said, then asked as she released his hand and retrieved her purse, "So, is there any hope?"

"Well I don't know yet. Let's see how this first date goes, and you know, go from there. I want to take it slow, though. I mean, I know I may not appear to be, but I'm really an old-fashioned kind of guy," Mason answered, straight-faced, happy to have finally regained his footing a little.

"My sculpture. Is there any hope for my sculpture," she answered, and before he could respond she added, "And you're calling this a date?"

"You asked me out to dinner. I said yes, so I'm counting it," Mason replied.

Annie looked at him for a long time, suppressing a smile that tugged at the corner of her mouth. She started to say something about him bragging to their kids about how their mother lay in wait in the art lab to make her move, but instead simply said, "Yeah, well, about my sculpture?"

"Oh. Oh, this bird thing. Uh, well   "

"Okay. Okay, you don't have to say it. But I seriously don't know what I'm going to do with it, Mason," Annie grimaced.

"Mace," he said. "I go by Mace."

"Mason suits you better. Do you have a middle name, Mason?"

"I think I'll save that for the second date. Or maybe the third," he answered. "Gotta keep the mystery stoked, you know. But as for your piece, what are you trying to say with it?"

"I'm trying to say I need to keep my scholarship. Give me a good grade," she answered.

"Doofus, or whatever his name is...the TA, he'll take care of you on the grade. You don't have to worry. He can't stay away from you."

"So you have noticed me," she said.

"Actually, I was watching the TA. Taking notes. I'm graduating in May. Next year maybe I'll have his job and be the one getting paid to put the moves on hot chicks in my classes."

"Now that was smooth, Mason. You get points for that. And for what it's worth, his breath is terrible and he stares at my chest when he talks to me."

"Well that apron of yours doesn't reveal much. Not that I was staring," he said holding up a pious finger. "As for your work, you really have some nice technique. The play of textures is interesting. The proportions are perfect. These feathers have a delicacy that makes it...very realistic."

"That's like saying she's got a great personality," Annie responded. "You hate it."

"No, it's just that it doesn't seem to *say* anything, and if it doesn't communicate something, or evoke something, it's just sort of going to sit there. It's only going to be decoration. Figure out a way to make it engaging. Maybe it doesn't need to evoke anything more than a question."

"A question?"

"Like what's going on here?" Mason asked.

"Good question. I'm not sure yet," she answered with a sly grin.

Mason missed it and went on, "The communication doesn't have to be a deep psychological reality-altering connection. It just needs to be a reason for someone to take a second look and maybe draw a conclusion. Now, when they can't immediately draw that conclusion, but are sort of mysteriously beckoned toward something deeper, yet it still continues to evade their grasp, well now that...that is when you have something that's going to hold up."

"I think I agree," she said. "But what about my sculpture?"

Mason looked a little befuddled and finally said, "Why is this bird standing on this branch? That's the question."

After studying the piece for a moment, she answered, "You're going to be a good teacher."

"Oh I'm not going to teach," Mason said flatly. "I'm an artist. A sculptor. It's all I've ever wanted to be."

"But you're going to graduate school. That's so buttoned down and pragmatic. I thought most real artists went all Bohemian, rejecting college in disgust just before graduation, renting a loft in New York where they live in sin with an exotic woman who doesn't shave her underarms," Annie said.

Mason grimaced. "No, I'm not attracted to that Georgia O'Keeffe hairy armpit thing, although I love her work," he said walking Annie toward the lab door, which Mason opened for her as he continued, "I want to do large scale sculptures. That means corporate commissions, hopefully for large office buildings, universities, banks. So I'll be dealing with businesses, whether I like it or not. I just figure the decision-makers will be from the academic and business ranks, so I need to have the credentials they'll be looking for."

"You sound like my brother," she said. "He's a business major. He keeps telling me I need to take some business classes. But accounting, statistics...yikes."

"Why should creativity and business be mutually exclusive?" he answered. "I personally believe there's a certain level of creativity in building a business."

"You're still sounding like Arnie."

"Arnie's your brother? Is he going here?"

"He's my twin brother, and yeah. We share an apartment. And before you stop impressing me by asking a stupid question, no we're not identical twins. In fact, we are so not alike it's funny."

"Then, I'm impressing you?"

"I'm an art major. That's sort of lowered the bar."

"Isn't it kind of, I don't know, restrictive sharing an apartment with your brother?"

"Sharing the womb, now that was restrictive. The apartment? No, Arnie is great. And you ought to taste his cooking. For awhile he considered becoming a chef. He would have been a great one. You'll like him."

"So, I'm going to meet Arnie." Mason said, smiling at this girl's freshness and already regretting every day he had missed knowing her.

"If you pick me up at our apartment you will," she answered.

"Then I am impressing you," he repeated.

The feisty banter continued, punctuated by brief touches on religion, politics, the state of the art department, and the American family as Mason drove them to a place that she enthusiastically claimed made the best hamburgers in town because they grilled the onions. It turned out they agreed about that, and almost everything else.

Mason sort of loved that she seemed to possess such unpretentious self-confidence that she would order extra onions on her burger on a first date. If she was also counting this as a date. As for himself, he was a little worried about his breath.

Annie studied his face and Mason drank in hers as they talked, their food was ordered, brought to their table, and they ate. A burger and fries later, there was no doubt in either of their minds, although neither dared to say it then.

When Mason and Annie returned to the art lab, both were aware that they were at the threshold of a major change in their lives, even though it was only two hours before that they had spoken to each other for the first time. Until now, both of them had believed that love at first sight, or in this case, love at first conversation, was wishful thinking.

Before they were through the door, Mason started trying to beg off, "I don't want to do this, Annie. I really don't. Seriously. I mean I'm hoping that you'll go out with me again, and if I say something that hurts your feelings, then it'll get all weird and you might say no," Mason said. He was genuinely hoping to discourage Annie from her insistence that he give her an honest critique and help her rescue the sculpture.

"I already told you I want to go out with you. I said I want you to meet my brother when you pick me up at my apartment. Did you not get that? It's a done deal. Now hush and tell me how to fix this piece of crap."

It was a phrase she would repeat a thousand times in their life-time together. It became a joke between them that defined an extra-ordinary marriage of two very different creative temperaments.

Mason sighed in resignation, "Okay, okay, but you have to promise not to get your feelings hurt," he said before turning to take a long appraising look at the piece.

"So, you're this bird," he began.

"I'm the bird?"

"Of course you're the bird. Now what's the question?" he asked, receiving only a squint of luminous green eyes in return.

He tried again, "Annie, imagine that you're this bird."

"Then what am I doing on this stupid branch?"

"Okay, there we go! Now what's the answer?"

Annie thought for a moment, then said, "I'm going to play a trick on the cat that lives in that house over there."

"Oh really? Why do you want to torment that poor cat?"

"Poor cat? He's tried to eat me no fewer than a dozen times. He found my nest and killed my babies. And ate them! He's a monster cat. I'm going to lure him to his doom," Annie laughed wickedly.

"You're a bird. You're going to lose and become cat food."

"Oh no. Not this time, Mason Crewe. Look down there under this branch I'm sitting on. That, I'll have you know, is..." Annie hesitated for a moment as she searched for the right name. "That, is *Cat-Tastrophe*!"

"Cat-Tastrophe?" Mason repeated, laughing uncontrollably at the lame joke as only a young man in the throes of losing his heart can do.

"You betcha mister. Cat-Tastrophe, the most efficient cat eradication device ever devised by God or man. A relentless chaser of felines of every size and description. His bark is definitely not worse than his bite. This is going to be brutal. Guaranteed."

Her eyes, her face, her hair, the clothes she wore, and above all, the smile seemed to reveal everything he needed to know about Annie Warner. It was all etched in Mason's memory in that one brief moment. He would recall every detail of it a thousand times over, through the years to come.

"Okay, now get to work," Mason said, standing up abruptly.

"You're leaving? I thought you were going to help me," Annie said, surprised.

"I did. Now you've got work to do, and I have a final to study for. Now about that date...seven o'clock Friday good?"

"Morning or evening?" she joked.

"Do have you any tests on Friday?" Mason asked.

"My last final is Thursday," she answered.

"Morning then," he said with a grin as he turned to leave. Over his shoulder he added, "Good luck. Oh, and don't show us the cat...or Cat-Tastrophe. I'll look forward to seeing what you come up with."

He was gone before Annie could reply. She just sat dumbly staring at the closed door. Then turning to her sculpture, she picked up a knife and neatly sliced off the bird's head. She then repositioned the head as though it was peeking slyly back toward an unseen predator, and moved the body to appear poised to streak away in the next instant. As she worked, she unconsciously assumed the pose of the wary, but conniving bird, and smiled to herself as the face of Mason Crewe played across her mind's eye.

"Cat-Tastrophe," she muttered to the clay bird as she raised a delicate wing away from its body. "I'm sure that goofy story really impressed Mason Crewe." She puffed her cheeks and blew out air, stepping back and looking critically at her clay sculpture.

"I'm the bird, huh? Bird *brain* is more like it," she said to herself with a chuckle. Then to the bird, "Oh no offense. I meant me. I'm the birdbrain. I just made a date for 7 o'clock Friday morning."

5
1991

• • • •

MASON LOOKED UP TO see if the cardinal was still in the tree. "Cat-Tastrophe," he said aloud with a smile. "You remember that?" The bird flitted among the branches.

"It's hard to talk to you if you're not paying attention," he said. "But I remember the rules of poofing. I get it. You can't do anything that would make it obvious that you are you. You've got to be the bird. Well, sweetheart, you're great at it. And why should I be surprised. You've always been great at everything. But, you do know that's a male you've poofed into, right?" And he sat smiling, watching the bird, reflecting on this strange idea that had been such an important ingredient of his and Annie's life together.

Poofs. Which one of them had come up with that name? He couldn't remember, but as he thought back on the way it had all begun, in those first months after he had returned from serving in Korea, it occurred to Mason that it had been *Poofs* that had helped him find his way back then, too.

He had come back from Korea feeling nothing like the artistic, idealistic kid who left. His ROTC obligation had taken precedence over graduate school plans, and over the budding romance with a vibrant green-eyed art student who had filled his thoughts from the first smile. He graduated and was immediately commissioned. It was 1951 and Korea was hungry for fresh-faced officers coming out of college.

In the war, Mason had witnessed suffering and death face to face. His own hands had inflicted both. He had known stark fear and given himself over to unbridled rage. He had learned to survive by living in the moment, following his orders, and seeing that the men in his platoon followed theirs.

Arriving in Korea, he had reasonable confidence in his training. But his first encounter with the enemy made Mason think that he had absorbed little more than rudimentary military assault. Point your weapon that way and fire. It was absolute chaos. He believed it was luck or God that kept him, and the men under him, alive long enough for Mason to gain enough experience to become genuinely competent.

What his men saw was something different. They followed with confidence and growing respect for the courage of their young leader.

Day followed day. Lieutenant Mason Crewe didn't allow himself to think about the life he was missing, or might lose. Annie's letters had been following him from base to base since he had been called up, and in them, she said everything Mason should have wanted to hear. She wrote about her dreams for their future together, and confessed her love without reservation. He attempted to write back to her with the right words. At least they were words that would convey the emotion that he knew he was supposed to have. He wrote with as much feeling as he could muster, but receiving and answering Annie's letters jolted him out of sync with time. Out of sync with reality it seemed.

The letters he received weren't just from another place, but it was almost as though they were written to another man. Not to him, but to some idiot kid who thought color, form, and abstract communication of some insipid message through anemic metaphor was somehow important. It embarrassed him that he had ever been so shallow.

Mason had been stationed there for eighteen months when he received the last letter Annie Warner would send to him in Korea.

"Lieutenant Crewe," the clerk called out. Mason retrieved the envelope and shouldered back through the tent to his bunk, tucking the letter inside his shirt. No time to read it now. The truck was being loaded and he and his men were to pull out immediately after brief-ing.

Crewe checked his equipment one final time, and left the tent along with several other platoon leaders who were also leading missions that day. They assembled for a routine briefing with the C.O., and fifteen minutes later he was in a truck headed out of the camp. Another day, another hill.

That much Mason could remember. Arriving at the drop-off point, moving into position, the advance under fire, the impact of the round tearing into his side, his body being raised and driven backwards, his right kidney being obliterated, the sky and earth spinning before his wide-open eyes, tumbling, caroming off rocks and plummeting over a craggy precipice were all a blur of disconnected images when, sometime later, he began to regain consciousness.

Mason tried to open his eyes and couldn't. It felt like his face was somehow tied to the ground. He couldn't see the long brown grass that was stuck to the dried blood that covered his face. He tried to move and very nearly passed out again. He lay there in the rocky bottom of a dry ravine, face down, alone, his blood soaking into the ground around him.

Time passed. The guns fell silent.

"Got one here!" he heard from somewhere behind him, followed by fingers pressing the side of his neck, and an urgent voice close to his ear, "Sir, can you hear me? We're gonna get you out of here."

Mason mouthed something into the sand, but the soldier couldn't make out what he was saying.

There was excruciating pain as the medic first began to field-dress his wounds, but the morphine he was given took effect and Mason began to drift in semi-consciousness.

Mason Crewe knew that his father had lived through a terrifying experience during the first World War. That experience had resulted in him naming his only son in an unknown soldier's honor. Mason's trauma, blood-loss, and the morphine apparently combined to create a curious mental aberration during the time the injured lieutenant was being transported to the field hospital. Or perhaps it was something more.

His father's horrendous experience in the war, which had forever changed his life and faith, became strangely interwoven with Mason's own. In that dreamlike fog, he believed that he was actually living through the events of his father's story.

Mason was there. He was no longer in Korea, but in the final days of the great Meuse-Argonne campaign, the division under heavy German artillery fire. It was he, rather than his father who was struggling to will himself to consciousness. Trying to remember. Feeling himself trapped under something, unable to move his legs, and blind, fighting to breathe. He had no memory of the battle, nor any idea where he was, whether it was day or night, if he was alone or still among his comrades.

He could feel the rising blisters on his face, neck, and hands, but he felt and discovered that his clothing was intact. He had not been burned, but gassed. His eyes were swollen shut, the clusters of painful boils being the effect of mustard gas shells lobbed amid the German artillery barrage. And although the pain was searing, the corporal took hope from the realization, knowing that if he lived, he had a chance of recovering his sight.

His throat and lungs were on fire, and every ragged breath whistled through the passage that he knew could close completely at any moment, covered within, as he knew it had to be, in the same blistering that he could feel on his hands and face.

He also knew that he had been unconscious for quite some time, because the blisters from the gas that covered his exposed skin seemed to be half the size of hen's eggs. Such an effect took some hours. He had seen the gruesome result of mustard gas.

Blind, his legs pinned under some unknown object, he could hear the sounds of battle some distance away, but in what direction? The forest concealed and confused the sounds. Corporal Crewe knew only that he heard nothing nearby. He was alone.

He discovered that his rifle, had fallen beneath him, and he felt along the barrel and found the bayonet still attached. Fumbling to release and remove it with great difficulty, the blistering of his hands rendering movement of his fingers almost impossible, he nevertheless managed to grip the handle and push the long slender blade into the soft earth under his right leg. If he could dig himself out from under whatever was on his legs, he thought perhaps he would be able to walk. He felt no pain below, only the pressure from the weight of the immovable unseen object. He could feel that it was cold, hard iron, but could gain no sense of what the thing was. It was heavy enough that Crewe knew the soft dirt he lay in had spared him his legs. At least he hoped so.

He dug, the exertion sending him into a fit of excruciating coughing, and he thought as he teetered on the edge of unconsciousness once again, that the abyss beyond might well be death.

It was some time later, he had no sense of how long, that he rallied, and managed to dig a bit more, until he again fainted from another spasm of coughing. And again, and again. With each episode, his strength and hope waned a little more.

Hours later, Crewe had no idea how many, he felt strong hands under his arms, dragging him. The muffled sound of a voice under a gas mask. He knew the sound.

"Can you walk?"

It was an urgent voice. It was English, but with an accent. Brit? No, something else, but Crewe was sure, and thankful, that it wasn't German.

"Can you walk?" the voice repeated.

Can't feel my legs," he croaked. Even he couldn't understand the words.

"I don't think you're injured, other than the gas. Perhaps just lost circulation. You'll be alright. Don't try to speak."

Crewe felt the sensation of being jostled below and realized that the unseen hands were rubbing his legs, trying to restore circulation. He welcomed the ache and sting that signaled that his legs were intact. After a moment he moved his feet, and found himself hoisted upright, his arm slung over the shoulders of his unseen rescuer.

His legs were rubbery at first, and he was being half carried, half dragged somewhere. He finally gained his footing, but blind, he was still a burden on the man. A fit of coughing halted their progress.

"Here, can you drink this?"

He felt a canteen being pressed to his lips, and the cool liquid coursing through the constricted passage in his throat was exquisite relief, abruptly ended by a choking cough and a stream of bloody, yellow pus the corporal spat onto the ground.

"Where am I?"

"Not far from my unit. We have a medic. You'll be alright. But now we have to go. Quickly. There was a German patrol just behind me when I found you. Come." An arm was slipped under his own and they were off again.

Crewe tried to control the impulse to cough as they scuttled through the unseen forest. He tripped and fell, was picked up, tripped again, and doubled up in a racking coughing fit. He could taste the blood in his mouth, but got to his knees and was pulled up and away again.

The corporal had no idea how far they had come when he heard the sounds of men and equipment. He was exhausted, blind, and in pain, but he was alive, and thankful. Thankful to be with allies and not captured. Thankful to the unseen man who had risked his own life to save him.

"Fernando, is that you?" a clipped British voice spat with authority.

"Yes, Sergeant-Major," said the man at his side.

"We thought we had lost you, Corporal."

"I found this man. American. He's been gassed, but he was lucky. I found no other survivors."

Medic!" the Sergeant-Major shouted, and then with typical British decorum "Good work, Lance Corporal Fernando. The Ceylon Light Infantry commends your courage."

"Thank you, sir."

Other hands took Crewe's arms and turned him away from the voices.

He turned back and croaked hoarsely, "Fernando?" He had not known the man's name. "Fernando...thank you. You saved my life."

"He's gone, soldier, but from the look of you, you're quite right. Now let's finish the job he started."

"Fernando," Mason muttered. He heard a quiet metallic noise somewhere close-by and managed to open his swollen eyelids until just a slit of light appeared in his sight.

"Ah, you're back with us. You had a rough go, Lieutenant, but you're going to be fine," a raspy, but feminine voice said, drawing him suddenly into the moment and back to reality. Back to himself.

Anticipating the question, looking at the confusion in the lieutenant's eyes the nurse said, "You were injured. You're in a hospital. A pretty lucky guy."

"Yeah. Yeah, I feel lucky," he said hoarsely, then coughed and a wince of pain shot through his back. "Am I okay? I remember the mustard gas."

"Mustard gas? Well I don't know anything about that, but you're going to be fine. The bad news is, you lost a kidney. The good news is, you have a spare, and judging from what I see down here," she said checking a bag attached to the cot, "It's working just fine. You've been sedated pretty heavily for a couple of days.

"Throat's parched," he said.

"Here, she said producing a cup of water with a straw from somewhere beyond his vision. "Just a sip."

He realized there was tape across his cheeks and over his nose, and gingerly touched it, asking, "What's this?" just as she guided the straw to his lips.

"Broken nose. Suppose you broke it when you fell. And your arm. You're bruised from head to toe, so I'm guessing you took quite a tumble on top of everything else. Lucky the doctor went ahead and set your nose. Usually they don't bother with that kind of thing. Yours must've been pretty severe. Probably pointing to your left ear. You still look a little like a raccoon, but at least now your eyes aren't swollen shut. Glad to see those baby blues."

She took the cup away and continued to prattle on, "So who's Fernando?"

"I'm sorry, what?"

"Fernando," she repeated, "You were mumbling that name before you came around. Just wondered who it is."

"That's..." and a whirlwind of images flashed through his mind before he finished the answer with, "That's my middle name."

"Funny thing to be fixated on," she answered. "Usually it's a girl."

"Oh, that reminds me..." the nurse said, reaching again to an unseen table somewhere beyond his field of view. "This was with your things, and it's still unopened," she said, holding up a blood-stained, crumpled envelope. "Hope it's still readable. You want me to open it? It's hard to open a letter with one arm in a cast."

"Sure. Thanks," he said.

The nurse opened the letter and unfolded it as she handed it to Mason. A creased photograph fell onto his blanket.

"Oh, there is a girl. And a pretty one," she said, picking it up and flattening the picture. "What's her name?"

"Annie," he said as he glanced at the opened letter. The blood hadn't soaked through too badly, thankfully.

The nurse handed him the photograph and said, "Call me if you need anything else, Lieutenant." Then added, "Enjoy Annie's letter," as she made her way to her next patient.

He held the picture up, and saw everything he needed. Everything he would ever need. Nothing mattered but that beautiful face. Those eyes. That smile.

6
1965

• • • •

THE IDEA STARTED AS a glimmer of hope, then it grew in his mind until the kid decided that it was the only thing that mattered. He had to discover the hiding place for the money the Moron claimed he had stashed. After he began to imagine what life could be like without Freddy Finger, finding the money became the only thing he could think about. He began a systematic search that started every day when the tow-truck roared out of the yard and down the dirt road toward the garage in town.

The boy knew time was short. His father had mentioned more than once that he was finally getting old enough to start earning his keep. He would be at the garage all day with the Moron before long. He had to find the money, and he had to find it soon.

As he searched, he planned. It was more than a fantasy. He was envisioning his life as he intended it to be. He had seen the way other people lived on television, which, back when it still worked, had been practically his sole contact with the outside world. Over time that life was more real to him than his present circumstances. If he could find the money, the boy was convinced that he could make that dream a reality. He was willing to do whatever it took.

He thought of ways he could rid himself and the world of Freddy Finger. He never thought about the idea being evil, or even wrong. He just worried if he would be strong enough to do it when the time came.

He was sure the money was hidden at the house somewhere. The Moron would never put it in a bank. He was convinced the government was searching for him, and banks were nothing more than an extension of the Internal Revenue Service.

Long before the boy understood what the IRS really was, he imagined that it was something like the FBI, and his father was a criminal in hiding. He had read about the FBI in his encyclopedia, but he only had volumes up through G-H.

Over time, listening to the old man's drunken tirades against *them stinking Yankee bureaucrats up in Washington*, the kid pieced together that his father had never paid a nickel in income taxes. He didn't even have a social security number, whatever that was.

Finger had been an auto mechanic all his life, and would accept only cash payment. He'd lived his life under the radar of the federal government.

"The finger! That's all they're ever going to get from me," Finger would wave his remaining middle digit vaguely toward the northeast and tramp out into the dark, either to relieve himself or fire up his boat motor.

The kid made a thorough search of the place. He even crawled, flashlight in hand, under the house through the scuttle hole in the foundation. The fine, sifted dust and spider webs were undisturbed. No one had been under there in years. He dragged himself a good ten feet, the sagging floor joists brushing against the top of his head, and the smell of putrid urine and rot filling his nostrils. A fat black widow that caught the light a few inches in front of the kid's nose sent him scrambling backward out of the scuttle hole, convinced that the money was not there.

The boy tried to think where else the Moron might have put it. He was always imagining that someone was trying to break into his garage to steal his tools. He'd never leave it there. It had to be somewhere around the house.

And then, as if someone slipped the thought into his mind, the boy could suddenly see the Moron going out and dumping the water out of that drum every few weeks. And then he knew.

It had taken over fifty trips carrying a rusted paint can full of water out into the weeds behind the house, being so careful not to spill a drop anywhere close by. The whole thing could have been over before it started when the big oil drum careened over, without the weight of the water as a counter-balance, sending the Evinrude crashing to the ground.

The boy could scarcely breathe for a full five minutes. There was a circle of rubber where the drum had been sitting. It looked like it had been cut out of the inner tube of a truck tire. The boy carefully removed the rubber.

There was a square plate of thick iron that lay flush with the ground around it. He carefully lifted one side up, then with a surge of adrenaline he lifted and tossed the heavy plate aside. It had been covering a square hole cut into the earth, the sides and bottom bricked and mortared. Sitting in the hole, side-by-side on another piece of rubber, were two identical steel boxes.

He'd seen one of these boxes before. He remembered, because he liked the way the latch worked. It was at the Army Surplus store in Ardmore. He'd only been to Ardmore twice that he could remember, and he'd loved the Army Surplus store.

It was a steel U.S Army issue ammo box, nearly the size of two shoe boxes stacked one atop the other, painted olive drab. The boy very slowly lifted one up and out of the hole. His eyes darted around to see if anyone was watching, though he knew his father wouldn't be home for hours. He stayed at the bar until nine o'clock almost every night, but this was Friday. He never came home until later on Fridays.

The boy's hands trembled as he struggled to pull up the big cantilevered latch on the end of the container. Finally it popped open, ripping up the ends of three fingernails. Normally it would have hurt like crazy, but the kid didn't even notice.

It was there. Money. More money than he ever dreamed the Moron could have stashed. The big steel box was filled with four stacks that reached to within an inch of the top. He reached down and took a single bill from the first stack with a shaking hand. Benjamin Franklin stared up at him with a sardonic, chiding smirk. He carefully replaced the bill. There were fifties, twenties, and tens in the other three stacks. Surely it was enough to buy a real boat. Maybe even enough to build that big house on Lake Texoma.

He pulled up the other box. This one he opened almost effortlessly, his adrenaline surging and his heart pounding now. It was completely full, packed to the top, arranged identically to the first box, four stacks, side-by-side. He couldn't imagine how much money was there.

The boy fought the urge to take the boxes and leave right then. After all, if the old man noticed even a scratch, or anything else wrong with the boat motor, which still lay on the ground attached to the overturned oil drum, he would never find it again.

He imagined the scene that would follow such a discovery, but quickly realized that he wouldn't have time to lament not taking the money and running away when he had the chance. The Moron would surely beat him to death. So the kid decided to take only what he thought he would need to set his plan in motion.

He thought it would be smarter to take the money from the full box. The Moron wouldn't be opening it to add more. There wasn't room. He gently extracted one of the hundred-dollar bills. He held the cash between grimy fingers for a moment, then thrust it into his pocket and looked around, almost certain that someone was watching.

Satisfied that the stacks of money appeared undisturbed, the boy closed the boxes and struggled again with the cantilevered latches. Each snapped closed with the force of a bear-trap. He lifted the full one first.

He had a moment of panic as he tried to remember how the boxes had been positioned in the hole. *Had the full one been on the left?*

The boy willed himself to calm down and remember. The first one he had taken out was the one that wasn't quite full. It was the one on the right.

Suddenly doubting which box was which, he re-opened the one he thought went on the right side. Reassured, he snapped it closed and gingerly replaced the ammo box in the hole, precisely in the indentation it had made on the rubber that covered the bricks in the bottom of the hole. And then did the same with the other one.

Covering the hole with the steel plate, and then the circle of rubber just the way it had been when he found it, he stood to survey the situation with the motor and empty drum.

It took every shred of strength and fear the boy had to raise the motor up off the ground, but after he got it up a little past his knees, the drum began to function as a fulcrum and the barrel came up almost in its original spot. A little careful nudging, lest the thing decide to crash to the ground again, and the bottom rim was back in the circular impression the barrel had permanently etched in the hard-packed dirt, covering the circle of rubber.

He had gotten the greasy-handled shovel from the well-house. Wedging it at an angle between the motor and the ground, he went and pulled a water hose from across the yard and fed in into the gaping mouth of the drum. He turned the faucet on full force. It seemed to take forever for there to be enough water in the bottom that the barrel seemed stable again.

As the oil drum continued to fill, the boy inspected the motor, brushing away dirt. There were scratches, but he had never paid close attention to the motor, so he had no way of knowing if they were there before. There were no rocks where it had fallen, so perhaps the scratches were already on it. Nothing appeared to be bent or broken, but how could he really know? He found a rag and wiped what appeared to be oil off one side of the motor, and continued watching the water filling, he pulled the bill from his pocket and looked at it again, going over his plan in his mind until the water reached the mark he had made with a small, chalky stone on the inside the drum.

A hundred dollars. He had never held anything larger than a five, and that was just long enough to go into Pembrook's Grocery now and again for a loaf of bread or a pound of hamburger, while the Moron sat swilling a beer in the truck. He thought about walking into town and going straight to the candy display he had lingered over at Pembrook's. As much as he'd wanted to, he'd never dared buy a bar of candy, knowing that the Moron would slap him across the room if the change was short twenty-five cents.

He suddenly wished that he'd taken the money in smaller bills. If he showed up now at Pembrook's with a hundred-dollar bill, the grocer would know something was up. Old Mister Pembrook knew who he was, and might say something to the Moron. He was one of the few people in town the kid ever saw, and one time he had even asked him if he was Freddy Finger's boy.

He would never forget that, because when he had nodded in answer to the old man's question, Mister Pembrook had told him to pick out a bar of candy, anything he wanted, and it would be his treat. The kid hadn't been able to believe anyone would do something like that. When he had just stood there staring, unable to decide which one to choose, Mister Pembrook had suggested a Hershey's chocolate bar, telling him it was his personal favorite.

When he got back in the truck the Moron had cuffed his ear and badgered him about what took so long in the store, but it was worth it. He'd never tasted anything as wonderful as that chocolate.

Of course, he didn't tell the Moron about it. He waited until that night when he heard snoring from the other room, then he very carefully unwrapped one end and just inhaled that delicious aroma for a long time. Even that smell was etched in his memory, and it always would be. At last he had broken off just one small rectangle of the chocolate, and ever so slowly savored the delicious sweetness of it. Then he wrapped it up carefully in its fragile foil. Watching the door and listening for any change in the Moron's gurgling snore, he tucked the ends of labelled wrapper around it. Determined that the mice wouldn't get to it, he put it in a Mason jar he'd found at the dump, screwed the lid on tight, and hid it in a hole that the Moron had kicked in the sheetrock by the boy's mattress.

He took twelve days to finish it, allowing himself just one bite every night, and he had never forgotten it. A Hershey bar was the first thing he planned to buy with that money, but only when the time was right, and not before. He had to be careful.

After he'd turned off the water and tossed the hose back across the yard the way it had been before, he pulled a leafy branch off a low limb of the elm tree that grew up alongside the foundation of the house and brushed lightly around the drum to hide his tracks and the marks that the drum and motor had made when they fell over. He'd seen that one time on a TV show. An outlaw covering his tracks. He hoped it would be enough. Now that he had seen the money, the boy experienced something he had never felt, even one time in his life. Hope.

He tried to imagine how much money was in that box. Thousands and thousands of dollars. There was no telling how much. He stood rooted to the spot, looking down into the water that filled the barrel, thinking he could almost see through the steel bottom of the barrel, through the round piece of inner tube rubber, the iron plate, and through the green steel boxes that contained his future. His whole life. He could see the money stacked in the boxes. It was more money than he could ever spend.

Now he had to get serious about the next step. He knew he couldn't just take the money and run away. The Moron would find him. There was only one way, and he had always known it. The question was how to do it.

On television, they made it look easy, but the kid knew it wasn't that easy to kill somebody, because the Moron hadn't killed him yet. He had often been struck hard enough to send him flying across the room, crashing into furniture. The Moron's fist, or the edge of a chair or table had knocked him out often enough, but he always came to. Broken ribs, cuts, bruises, and burns had all hurt. He was pretty sure his left arm had been broken at least twice. Both times the Moron had later held him down and pulled on it until the pain was so intense that the boy had lost consciousness. When he woke up, his arm was wrapped in tape with a stick to keep him from moving it. It had ached for weeks, and it wasn't really straight anymore, but he hadn't died. Every time the Moron really went off on him, the boy thought he might, and sometimes wished he could, but he never had.

The boy knew that if it was that hard for a grown man to kill a kid, it was going to be a lot harder the other way around. But he had to do it. He knew there was no other way.

Lightning suddenly streaked across the afternoon sky, followed by a bone-rattling crack of thunder. The scrawny boy jumped, startled to see that the sky had grown thick with menacing dark, low clouds while he had been intent upon his work. Rain, driven by a sudden wind, began to buffet the boy. He dashed across the yard, the rain, as cold as ice ran in rivulets over his hot skin, etching white lines in the accumulated grime on his face, neck, and arms, and plastered his thick greasy hair to his scalp.

He stopped before he got to the house, turned slowly and walked back out into the open, stripping off his tee-shirt, steeling himself against the chill, he spread his scrawny arms wide, and turning in slow, deliberate circles, just like a hawk soaring high above the muck below, he let the water wash over him. And as it did, grim, gaunt, frightened little Freddy Finger, Jr. melted into the leak-stained sheetrock ceilings and molded stink of that shack beside the road on the way to the dump. And disappeared.

• • • •

BEING WOUNDED HAD BEEN Mason's ticket home. He decided that he wouldn't see Annie until he was healthy again. He wanted to be, not only physically healthy, but sure that he had both feet on the ground in other ways.

The strange experience Mason had after he was wounded had continued to recur in his dreams, and would invade his thoughts with no apparent trigger. And there was more. An increasingly distressing montage of memories, experiences that he had taken in stride as part of the job he had been sent to Korea to do, he now found himself looking at, not as platoon leader, Lieutenant Crewe, but simply as Mason.

His medical discharge and recovery gave him time to spend back in his hometown with his parents. He talked to Annie on the phone, and although he was aching to see her, he thought he needed this time with his folks first. He needed some time with his dad in particular.

He and his father watched ball games and fished together. Their relationship had always been close, but now they had more in common than before, yet for some time the subject was left alone.

Mason had left home a confident young twenty-two-year-old, whose most challenging life experience had been college finals. He returned changed. Profoundly changed.

His father waited. He remembered his own homecoming. Walter Crewe sensed, and respected that his son was working to cope with those moments of internal assault that every soldier returning from war faces.

The elder Crewe wished that he could tell his son that the visions would end. But that would be a cruel lie. Moments of reliving and being appalled by, and yes, glorying in the terrifying extremes of his own capabilities, were to come over Mason when he was most vulnerable. Reverend Walter Crewe knew all too well that war delivers into hands of the enemy of God and man, a vast array of weapons to cast into the path of the brave.

The injury was, in its way, fortuitous. It gave Mason time to decompress. Time to take those things he had endured, sort through them, and then very deliberately box them up and put them away.

If Mason needed counsel, or just needed to talk, Walter Crewe hoped his son would be able to come to him. That moment came as they stood on the bank, casting their lures into a favorite of the several ponds where Mason had grown up fishing alongside his dad.

"Daddy, I want to tell you something," and he fell silent for a moment as he reeled in his line before continuing, "Something that...well it's kind of hard to explain, but I just want to thank you for giving me Corporal Fernando's name. I think I know now what it meant to you."

Tears filled Mason's eyes, the sudden emotion taking him by surprise, and he turned away. He finally managed to say in a choked voice, "Wow, I don't know where that came from."

Walter just remained silent, but tears welled up in his own eyes as he watched his son struggle with the tide of emotions that he could see threatening to burst through the walls that had them contained.

Regaining his composure, Mason turned back with resolve to face his father and asked, "Do you remember when I was about seventeen, I can't recall exactly when it was, but I said something to you about my middle name? Something stupid. You sat me down and told me why you had given that name to me."

"I remember," his father answered.

"You told me everything that happened to you, and I remember feeling so bad about what I'd said. The story really made an impact on me, but I didn't really grasp what it meant to you. Not really. Not then."

"You were a kid."

"Yes sir, but the thing is, even after that, I still didn't like the name. I was embarrassed about it. I would try to avoid telling anybody."

"Well, I understand that. If his name had been Fairbanks or Gable or something, I'll admit it would have a better ring to it," Walter said with a smile.

"But see, I wouldn't want another name now," Mason said, turning to look out over the water before continuing in halting sentences, pausing and reflecting as he tried to put the experience into words.

"When I was wounded, Daddy, I thought I was going to die. Thought maybe I had at first. Then they found me. It was the strangest thing. The doc said it was probably a reaction to the morphine the medic gave me. I know this is going to sound crazy, but it was like...like I was you."

"You were me?" Walter asked gently. "I'm afraid I don't understand."

"Dad, I experienced, or thought I experienced everything that had happened to you. Everything you had told me about was happening to me. I was blind. I could feel my legs trapped. I felt the blisters on my skin from the mustard gas. I actually thought I was there, alone. I thought it was happening right then, to me, just the way you told it."

"This sounds crazy when I say it out loud, but it was so real, Dad. Not just the physical sensations, but the desperation. The hopelessness!"

Mason shook his head and continued, "I remember Corporal Fernando pulling me out from under whatever it was pinning my legs. I remember him pulling and guiding me through the forest for hours. Tripping, falling, blind, choking, and scared to death. I remember it! And Fernando, he just kept picking me up guiding me, encouraging me."

Walter said quietly, "Yes, I remember too."

"Daddy, did you ever wonder if..." Mason took a deep breath and went on, "If Fernando was...was an angel?"

"Of course. Often."

"I don't know how you made it through that."

Walter Crewe was baffled by what he heard his son saying, but it was obvious that the experience had affected him powerfully.

He answered carefully, "I suppose, son, the same way you did. With God...and Fernando's help."

"Well, I just want you to know, that I am so proud to bear his name. I can't begin to make sense of all that, but that much I know. Thank you, Daddy, for giving me such an honor."

Walter tried to smile, but his mouth belied the emotion that gripped his throat. He was eventually able to say, "I've spent a lifetime being thankful to God, and to Fernando, for all the blessings I would have missed if he'd not been willing to do what he did for me. I've never seen either of them, but I've felt both their hands guiding me. Now that's something we can share." He patted his son's chest for a moment, then gathered himself and added, "That's all we can do with it, son...be thankful. Be thankful that we were two who got to come home healthy and whole. So many didn't. So many don't."

"From both sides," Mason said, looking down into the gentle little waves that slapped the stones along the bank of the pond, but he was seeing a place a half a world away. "Dad, when I was there, I did things that—-" Mason began, but couldn't finish the sentence.

Walter Crewe said, "Son, you're going to remember a lot of things. They'll come at you right out of the blue. I want you to try to remember this when they do," he said, speaking very deliberately, and looking directly into blue eyes that mirrored his own. "You did your duty with courage and with honor. You gave your country what your government required of you. The Word of God says that is what we are to do. You were willing to lay down your life for your brothers. Jesus himself said there's no greater love than that."

Walter chose his words carefully, "Thankfully, that season of your life is over. If you think there's something that you need to be forgiven for doing when you were serving your country, you're forgetting the sermons you heard me preach when you were growing up. There is nothing you or I have done, or will ever do that God did not see when His Son died on that cross for the sins of man."

"We were doing our duty. You did, and so did I. But even if what we were ordered to do were acts of sin, Mason, those sins are as far removed from you, and from me...and from God, as the east is from the west. That's what Jesus did for us. Don't let the enemy drag those things back to you as accusations."

The old preacher's eyes bore into his son's. The scars were less visible now amid the lines and creases of age in his face, but Mason saw them clearly.

"Remember who you are, son. I was there the day Christ made you a new creation. I saw you born, and I saw you born again. The two greatest blessings of my life."

Walter leaned in close, and with strong hands, also bearing the marks of the corrosive gas that had so nearly taken his life, gripped his son's battle-hardened shoulders, "When you see those things, it isn't God's doing. It is Satan's. Remember who you are. You are a beloved child of the Living God, forgiven, sanctified, and glorified by the Holy Spirit of Jesus who loves you and is proud of you. Even more than I am, if that's possible."

He patted his son's cheek and added with a smile, "Now, let's catch our supper...Mason Fernando Crewe."

• • • •

MASON SAT IN HIS CHAIR on his patio, his thoughts of his father, who had been gone for so many years, bringing tears to his eyes as he remembered the gentle, deep voice, and the wisdom of his counsel. He still missed him every day.

And then Mason was struck by a memory. It had been his father's death that added a new dimension to the Poof story. He looked up and saw that the cardinal was still among the branches of the maple tree.

Mason was again marveling at the comfort that gave him, when he heard a soft cooing sound. It drew his eye down to the birdbath, where two gray doves were perched on its rim. Lost in his thoughts, he hadn't noticed them landing there. Mason's parents came to mind immediately, and again he experienced the comforting sensation of being in their presence.

If this was imagination or madness, Mason didn't care. He allowed himself to enjoy the notion and gave himself over to it completely.

"Well hey, look who joined the party," and he added gently, "I've been missing you two."

As he sat there on the shaded patio, the soft cooing of the doves punctuated by the staccato chirp of the cardinal, Mason felt at peace for the first time since Annie's death.

He didn't talk aloud to the birds, because it seemed like just being there with them was enough. As though his thoughts were as clear to them, or clearer, than speech would have been.

He reminisced about their times together, times when he and Annie went home for holidays and birthdays when they were first

54

married. He thought about the meals his mom cooked, and the early morning fishing with his dad. And how they had fallen in love with Annie, just as he had.

It had been when he was there with them after Korea. Mason didn't know she was coming. It was something she and his mom cooked up one afternoon when Mason and Walter were out fishing. Mason's mother thought that the surprise would be just the thing for her son.

Annie had met Mason's parents when they came for his graduation, and both were immediately taken with her. Then, throughout his time in Korea Annie had sent cards and notes by mail, and always received warm replies in return.

She and Mason had so little time together before his induction that Annie felt a little awkward and presumptuous the first time she wrote to his parents, but Edith Crewe's response had been welcoming. As time went on, and the tone of Mason's letters became increasingly wooden, her correspondence with his mother gave her a connection to Mason that was comforting.

Annie didn't realize it, but Mason's parents were similarly comforted by her attentiveness. They looked forward to receiving her letters, which Edith would open and read aloud to Walter as soon as one arrived. They had become fond of Annie Warner, and it was obvious, when they had seen the two together at Mason's graduation, that she was different from any other girl their son had dated. And he was different from the moment he had met her.

Then when Mason had been wounded, Walter had been the one who telephoned Annie to tell her the news. In one of her letters she had mentioned that she was going to work for her father after graduation. He ran a factory in Kansas City that produced insulators for electrical lines. Walter remembered the name of the company and managed to find a telephone number and called for her there.

Annie was touched that the Crewes would be that thoughtful toward her. Walter had been so gentle when he broke the news of Mason's injury that Annie's affection was forever won.

Mason's transfer from the hospital in Tokyo to a stateside veteran's hospital, and subsequent medical discharge from active service took several weeks. Annie kept in touch with his parents throughout that time.

He called her from the military hospital in Washington state. His voice had gained a more mature timbre than she remembered. Although he reassured her that his hope was for things between them to take up where they had left off a very long two years before, Annie was understandably disappointed and a little confused that Mason had clearly not wanted to see her as soon as he arrived at home.

Two weeks later, she had been thrilled when Mason's mother had telephoned. "Annie, now I know Mason has said he wants to wait until he's completely well to see you, but if he's fit enough to go fishing with his father, he's in good enough shape to see you. He may be a grown man, but his mother still knows a thing or two," Edith Crewe had told Annie, who could hear the smile on the other end of the line.

"Walter and I have been dying to spend some time with you, and if that son of mine believes he can string us along like this, well he has another thing coming. I'll make up the spare room, and we'll meet you at the train station Friday afternoon," and then her put-on bossiness softened and she continued, "Because I think you will be the best medicine he could possibly get."

On the other end of the line, Annie was all smiles.

"Now if you talk to him, don't tell him you're coming. We'll make the whole thing a surprise. And you can trust me, Mason is going to be thrilled," his mother said.

A few days after that, Mason's mother set him to work dusting the living room. She'd gone on a sudden cleaning binge, and enlisted both Walter and him in the work.

"Mom, where'd you get this?" Mason asked. He was studying a colorful figurine on a side table in the living room.

"Oh, I forgot to show you that," she said, coming out of the kitchen drying her hands on a cup towel. "Annie gave that to me last Mother's Day."

"Annie gave you a Mother's Day gift?"

"She told me you helped her make it," his mother said, admiring the colorful bird perched warily on a branch, looking as if it were just about to dart away. "It's just beautiful. I love it."

Mason picked up the ceramic sculpture and turned it slowly, observing every detail before saying quietly, "Well I'll be."

"Don't you remember it?" Edith asked. "She said you helped her on it."

"Oh I remember it, but I never saw it after it was painted and fired. It really is beautiful, he answered. And then somewhat incredulously, he asked, "And she gave this to you as a Mother's Day gift?"

"She said since you weren't where you could do anything special for your mother, that she decided this should be my gift, since you had helped make it."

Mason continued to gaze at the piece, and said, "All I did was make a suggestion. She did all the work. Wow, this is really...really beautiful. I can almost see her in it. Isn't that something?" Mason said as he sat the figurine back on the table and stepped back to look at it from a distance. "I can't believe I hadn't noticed this."

"Oh I had it in the hutch. It's so fragile looking, I keep it in there so it doesn't get knocked over. Your father is a wonderful man, but he's clumsy as an ox. Always has been," she said, laughing and turning to go back to the kitchen.

"Did Annie come here to bring this to you?" Mason asked, still somewhat amazed that a relationship seemed to have sprung up between his girlfriend and his mother.

"Oh goodness no, silly. She shipped it to me. I thought it was very sweet of her to do it."

The telephone rang at that moment, and Edith scurried to the hallway table to answer it cheerily, "Hello? Just arrived? Well I'll send my son, Mason, right on in. Thank you for calling. Bye-bye."

As she returned to the kitchen his mother called over her shoulder, "That Mister Coggins, you remember him, don't you, he works at the train depot? I told him I was expecting a package today, and I said I didn't want it sitting at the depot over the weekend. It just came in on the four o'clock."

"I remember Mister Coggins," Mason said offhandedly, still thinking about the figurine. It had taken him back to the night he had met Annie Warner, and suddenly he wondered why on earth he had not rushed to Kansas City as soon as he got out of the hospital.

From the kitchen, "Well, would you run out to the depot and pick it up for me?"

"Right now?" Mason called back, remembering the little story Annie had made up to help her rescue the sculpture from banality.

"Cat-Tastrophe," he muttered to himself, picturing her wide green eyes sparkling as she made up the tale. It had worked. It added just the right nuance to the piece to make it interesting. Even intriguing. The bird seemed poised to fly, but not from fear. It seemed to be baiting its prey.

"If you don't mind, sweetheart," his mother called from the kitchen.

Annie had managed to convey that with beautiful subtlety. And Mason was genuinely taken with her use of color. The reds of the bird were not just red. She had taken an almost impressionistic approach, juxtaposing colors to trick the eye.

"Not easy to do with fired glazes," he mumbled. "Impressive."

For just a moment, and for the first time in a very long time, he felt a creative spark stir.

His mother called back from the kitchen, "Go ahead and run over to the depot. No telling who might decide to pick it up and walk off with it. This may be a small town, but we still have rascals," Edith answered. Walter had come into the kitchen through the back door and they stood there looking at each other with conspiratorial grins.

"Sure, Mom," Mason said, his mother's banter finally breaking through. "Need anything else while I'm out?"

"I don't think so," she answered gaily amid the clatter of dishes. "Dinner at six."

"Don't think it'll take me three hours. Depot's just at the edge of town," Mason laughed. "Back in a minute."

She was standing outside the door at the old depot holding her suitcase when a man pulled up and got out of a pickup truck. He just stood there staring at her, and it startled her at first.

The man was thickset and broad-shouldered. A dark shadow of heavy afternoon stubble covered the lower part of his suntanned face, his hair was coarse and close-cropped over a creased brow.

But when he smiled, his blue eyes alight, and said softly, "Annie," she knew it had to be Mason.

He rushed to her and caught her up in a crushing embrace. Held there against his broad chest, Annie felt small and young, and a little scared because the boy that she had carried in her mind and in her heart for those many months had vanished.

She looked out over his shoulder into the afternoon sky, felt the rough stubble against her cheek, and saw the fresh young face of Mason Crewe with that crooked wry grin and dark curls that fell over his forehead. Annie's chin quivered and a tear coursed down her cheek as the man released and pushed her back, holding her slender shoulders in strong hands covered by wiry black hair.

"Annie," he said again. "It's you. You're here."

The next day, Mason and Annie sat facing each other across the table of a booth in the soda fountain of the old downtown drug store. They had spent the morning wandering around the old town and surrounding countryside. Annie had tried. She tried to find Mason in the face, in the voice, anywhere in this sober, quiet man who led her around the world of his youth.

Only when he smiled could she catch a glimpse. Then his eyes had that same look she remembered, but this man who called himself Mason Crewe just didn't smile much.

"I used to eat in here every day when I was in high school. Tuna sandwich on toast, chips, and a Coke every day. Must've eaten about five hundred of these," he said, holding up a half-eaten sandwich. "Doesn't taste the same anymore," he added, looking pointedly into Annie's eyes. "I can't figure out if they changed the recipe, or if it's me, but it's just different."

"It's still good though," Annie said, blinking back the sudden threat of tears and finding it hard to meet Mason's eyes.

"You've changed, Annie. You're even prettier than you were before. I didn't think that was possible, but you are," he said, and when Annie looked at him and attempted to smile in response to his compliment, her eyes still brimming, he changed the tone.

"And this thing with my folks, how'd that happen? You met them once and I come back and you have this thing going. Last night at dinner, it was like you three are old friends. They know more about you than I do," and the smile was there for an instant. "Oh and Mom showed me the gift you sent her for Mother's Day. That was really sweet of you to do that," I never saw it after you did the glazes and fired it. It really is beautiful. I can't imagine how you got that effect. I'd like to look at it with you when we get back to the house," Mason said.

"Thank you," Annie replied, still trying to realize that the man across from her was the boy she had met that night in the art lab. The boy she had fallen in love with.

"That was really, really something for you to do that. It meant a lot to her. And she loves it."

"I told her you helped me with it," Annie said.

"Well, as I recall, I just said a couple of things. You did the magic. I was just trying to impress you so you'd go out with me again."

"You did," she said, smiling, remembering.

"Annie," Mason looked at the table for a moment, then continued somberly, "The past two years are a blur for me. I hope it stays that way. There's nothing about any of it that I want to remember. I so wish we could just go back to that night."

Annie simply said, "Me too," but the tone conveyed a sense of loss that both had felt, but had been trying to ignore from the moment she had arrived. Now it loomed between them.

Mason pulled out his wallet, placed a few bills on the table to cover their ticket and said, "There's one more place I want to show you."

9
1953

* * * *

IT WAS A SHORT DRIVE to the church that Mason's father had pastored for many years. It was postcard picturesque, with white shiplap siding and a steeple that was the tallest structure in the town. The door wasn't locked.

"What I want to show you is in here. I did it when I was in high school," he said. It's what convinced me that I wanted to be an artist. It's the first time I really tried to convey anything with art. Up to then I was just showing off," Mason said.

He watched Annie as she realized that he was talking about a high arched stained-glass window, framed by an alcove above the pulpit in the back wall of the old church.

"It also convinced me that stained glass, and color in general is not what does it for me," he added, looking back at the intricate design of colorful leaded glass.

"You're crazy, Mason. That is gorgeous! You did this when you were in high school?" Annie said, not taking her eyes away from the piece. "The dove is just amazing. You've made the whole piece create...my gosh, Mason, it looks like it's moving. Like it's just blazing across the sky, or the universe. The urgency...I love that."

Mason watched her and his heart ached. This was the first glimpse he had gotten of the unbridled spirit he remembered. She had been subdued since she arrived. Disappointed. Almost grieving it had seemed.

"I should have brought you at sunset. The light changes it. It's pretty dramatic."

"So tell me the story," she said, turning to him her eyes alight.

"What story?"

"The story. The story that makes me want to know where that dove is going. I've seen a lot of stained glass windows, and photographs of hundreds more in class. Some of them are truly magnificent, just for the sheer labor involved if nothing else, but yours is different. And the dove represented in religious art is usually so...I don't know, passive I guess. Gentle. Yours is like it's on a mission."

"Wow. That's interesting that you put it that way," Mason said, smiling, appreciating her response.

"So tell me the story."

"Well now if I tell you the story, it takes away the magic," he answered. "You won't ever look at it the same way."

"So we don't tell anybody else," she answered.

"Okay," he relented, hoping that what he was feeling was their hearts being woven back together. Hoping that Annie was feeling the same thing.

They sat down on the front pew together. "My dad was in the battle of the Meuse-Argonne in France in the first World War. Not long before I did the window, he told me some things about his experiences there," Mason began. "It was really hard for him to tell me. I never understood why he didn't talk about the war. I get it now. Talking about it...thinking about it calls up images that you just want to forget. It's like an album of snapshots. Scenes that—-"

Mason fell silent for a moment and Annie reached over and placed her hand tenderly on his.

He took a deep breath and shook his head, then continued, "My dad named me after a man who saved his life when he was serving there. He would have died, or been captured, which was almost worse during the first war. You wouldn't believe some of the things those men went through.

Mason didn't speak for a time, then gathered himself and continued, "My dad heard this story when he was in the field hospital."

"So he was wounded in battle too?" Annie said.

"He was mustard gassed. I'm sure you noticed the scars on his face and hands. He was fortunate not to have lost his eyesight permanently. Dad was the only one of his squad that survived. There was fellow from the Ceylon Light-Infantry that found him and rescued him. Germans all around them. He got Daddy through the forest and back to his camp.

"And he's the one you were named after. His name was Mason?"

With a small laugh Mason shook his head. Annie caught a look in his eyes that colored that gesture with a note of reverence.

"His name was Fernando," Mason said, "And that's my middle name...I'm honored to say."

"I love it," Annie said. "I love Mason too. It's such a solid, manly name," then lowering her voice she pronounced it gravely, "Mason." Then with an affected accent she drew out, "But Fernando...now that's an artist's name. It's perfect for you, because you truly are an artist," she said turning again to admire the stained glass. "I still can't get over that you did this when you were still in high school. So now tell me the story."

"Well, it's a story about a battle that went on for over a month. During the assault, for five days there was a battalion from the 77th, close to 500 men, that got cut off and surrounded by the Germans."

"The Lost Battalion, right? I've read about this," Annie said.

"So you've heard about Cher Ami?" Mason said, then added, "The carrier pigeon?"

"Oh yeah, I do remember reading something about that. I think it was a story in Life Magazine. What was it? A pigeon got out with a message?"

"Yeah, these five hundred men, or what started out as a battalion of five hundred, had been surrounded and were being picked off by the Germans, and on top of that, the Allied artillery was pounding their position, not knowing that our soldiers were trapped out there."

"Between the enemy fire and artillery, over half the battalion was killed. The only way they had to communicate with Command was by carrier pigeon. Messages attached to the leg. The commander of the battalion sent two pigeons out when they discovered they were surrounded. Both of those were immediately shot out the air by the enemy."

"My dad said the story about this circulated all over the front in no time, but he actually heard it from one of the survivors of the 77th...one of the guys who was there. The fellow said he was standing right there when they released the pigeons."

"He said their situation was worse than desperate. They were pinned down by the Germans and the artillery barrage was falling directly on them. Nowhere to run, and no shelter from the shelling. They didn't even have food. The only shred of hope they had was the one pigeon remaining...Cher Ami."

"She was finally released with a message canister attached to her left leg. The message was a desperate plea to call off the artillery. By that time over half the men had been killed or wounded. The bird was literally their last hope, and as soon as she flew up, the Germans started shooting. For a minute it looked like she might make it, but then she was hit and fell. They could hear the cheer that went up from the Germans when she went down."

"They knew they were lost. But then the most amazing thing happened. Cher Ami is suddenly back in the air again. And this time she makes it."

"What the guys on the ground didn't know, was that she had been shot through the breast, lost an eye, and her right leg was almost blown off when she was hit. Cher Ami flew in that condition for twenty-five miles back to Command and delivered the message in just over an hour. There were fewer than two hundred men that survived, but every one of them knew they owed their lives to Cher Ami."

"Did she survive?" Annie asked.

"For a little while. They say that Black Jack Pershing himself carried her onto a ship that brought her to the states."

"So this is Cher Ami?" Annie said, looking back at the stained-glass window.

"Well, I was thinking about the story when I was working on the design, and it just didn't seem...natural. I know that's obvious, but I mean, why would a bird demonstrate that kind of devotion, or tenacity? It had to be in horrible pain, and bleeding. Weak."

"And that was your question?" Annie said.

"Exactly," he answered.

"And did you find an answer?"

"My answer is..." Mason hesitated looking as though he might reconsider telling her, but finally went ahead, speaking softly, "My answer is that Cher Ami looked like a bird, and acted like a bird, but she was more than what she appeared to be. She was woman. A woman whose son was there, wounded in the battle and needing help. A mother who had died when that son was a child, and she had to watch him grow into manhood, still loving him just as much as ever, just as much with him as any mother would want to be. Just unseen, but always right there."

"And so now here he is, her boy, caught in this desperate situation. Well, God gives her a way to help him, and her spirit somehow manifests itself as a bird. I mean, God can do anything He wants to do, right? He did the same thing Himself when Jesus was baptized."

"When they release her with the message attached to her leg, there's no way she is going to fail, but it can only be that she has nothing more than the ability that a carrier pigeon would naturally have. She experiences the awful pain of being wounded and plummeting to the ground. But then with that desperate determination of a mother trying to save her child, she fights through the pain and rises into the air again. And she does it. She saves him."

Annie's eyes had been transfixed on the intricate depiction of the bird in the stained glass throughout Mason's story. She hadn't seen it before, but there was the blood, the wounds, the forest below, the bullets. She could see the explosions and smoke of the artillery shelling.

She turned and looked at Mason, who was also looking at the window, and beyond. Tears now streamed down his cheeks and he was struggling to control his emotion. She moved closer and placed her hand on his shoulder.

"I'm sorry. This is embarrassing," he managed to say.

"No, it's not. It's an amazing story, and it doesn't take away the magic. Not for me," Annie said tenderly.

"When I did this, I had no idea. I was just a kid. I'd never seen a mother—" he was unable to speak for a time, and Annie could feel his body convulse as Mason fought to suppress the roiling emotion he was experiencing. After a time, he managed to say, "That was before I had ever seen a mother die trying to protect her child." A sob escaped from deep in Mason's chest and he suddenly stood, turning to walk a few steps away.

Annie sat quietly, her heart aching.

"When I was working on the piece, I thought about my dad being there too. He wasn't part of the Lost Battalion, but he was in the Argonne at that same time. His situation was just as grim. Maybe worse, because his whole squad was killed, and he was alone, blinded, suffocating, his legs pinned under something he couldn't see, unable to move. I couldn't begin to imagine his desperation. At the time when he told me the story, I wasn't able to appreciate how miraculous his rescue was, and what an honor he had given me by naming me for that man."

Pointing to the stained glass, Mason said, "They're there. Down there in the forest, the Germans right on their heels, surrounded by all that noise and chaos, blood, pain, and fear. You can't imagine what it was like. I couldn't. Not then. I was just a stupid kid trying to show everybody how creative I was. How *talented*." He spat out the word in a mocking tone. "Sculptures, pictures...none of it means anything to me now. I can't imagine how it ever did."

"Annie, I feel like I lost so much over there. While I was there, I couldn't let myself think about who I was, or what I believed. Or what I wanted. What I was missing. I lived one moment at a time. That moment was all that mattered. I think that's the only thing that kept me alive. And kept me sane. But now...I don't seem to remember how to be me again."

Watching Mason made her heart ache for him. She had read his letters and sensed the detachment he described now. She had thought it was his feeling toward her that had changed, and wondered if she should release him from their promises to one another. Annie really had little time to get to know Mason before the war, but she knew he was not one to walk away from a commitment.

"I thought some time here at home would help, and it has, but..." he turned again and gestured toward the stained glass, "just like showing this to you, and talking about the story behind it, it feels like I'm talking about someone else's life, just pretending it was mine. It feels like I've lost myself, and being here, even seeing you makes me feel..." he turned and walked away, and stood with his back to her, shaking his head in frustration, "Makes me feel even more like a phony. Like an imposter who's stolen someone else's identity."

"Annie, I'm sorry, I know probably none of this makes any sense."

"Of course it does. I can't possibly imagine how it feels to fight in a war, and then come home and try to pick up your life where it left off, but this helps me to see it through your eyes."

She walked to him and put her hand gently on his shoulder, "I'm trying to find you too, Mason. When you came to pick me up at the train depot," she hesitated before admitting it, "You got out of that truck and...and I didn't recognize you. I didn't know it was you. And even after I realized it was you, you have just changed so much. You look so much different, I mean."

"But you are Mason Crewe. I finally saw you when you were talking about your beautiful work. It is you. You're here. You're back. This is what I've prayed for every day since you joined the service. Now we can start to build our life together." A sudden thought caught Annie off-guard and quietly, uncertainly she added, "If that's still what you want."

"Annie, I don't know anything else. I don't know what I want to do. I don't have any idea about where, when, how. But I do know one thing...the only thing that matters. I want to spend every minute of the rest of my life with Annie Crewe."

"Annie...*Crewe*? You sure about that, Fernando?"

When she had arrived, Mason had put his arms around her and held her for a long time. Perhaps he had subconsciously sensed the bewilderment she had experienced when she failed to recognize him. For whatever reason, after he had gathered her in his arms, then when the moment came to kiss, it had been strangely awkward for both of them, and the moment had passed. Now it came naturally, and perfectly, and it never ended.

10
1953

• • • •

MASON'S FOLKS SAW THEM off at the train station. When Mason and Annie had come back to the house after their afternoon together, it was obvious to Walter and Edith Crewe that the awkward wall between their son and this girl who had so completely stolen his heart, and theirs, had crumbled. More than that, Mason was more himself than he had been since he came home from the war. It was no surprise when he told them he would be returning to Kansas City with Annie.

The next day Mason sat between his mother and Annie on the second pew from the front, as his father delivered his sermon. Annie envisioned church as it would be, just over three months later as it turned out, when he would be performing their wedding ceremony, with the late afternoon sun filtering through the brilliant colors of the stained glass above them.

Sunday dinner was pot roast with potatoes and carrots, a tossed salad Annie helped Edith prepare, big yeasty rolls that had been rising since dawn, and Mason's favorite, a cherry pie. They savored the meal together, and the time, all of them marveling at how naturally they had already become a family, and each one privately thanking God for answered prayers.

The next day when they got settled on the train to Kansas City, Annie said, "I'm really hoping you and Arnie can become friends."

"I haven't gotten to be around him much, but he seemed to be a good guy. If he's anything like you, I'm sure we'll get along great."

"Well, he's nothing like me."

Mason had met Annie's twin brother when he first dated Annie back in college, but because they didn't start dating until after finals

70

his senior year, and Mason was inducted into the Army right after graduation, there had been little time to get to know Annie, much less her brother.

"I think Arnie feels guilty about not joining the Army. He's afraid you'll think badly of him because of it," Annie said in her direct way.

"I wouldn't wish Korea on anybody. I don't hold it against anyone who wasn't there. Especially someone who had a definite plan for his life and was here working toward something...and keeping an eye on you."

"Well Arnie feels a sense of obligation, I guess. Anyway, he is hoping that you two can hit it off. I keep telling him I'm afraid I'm going to be the odd man out in this deal," Annie said.

"You are sort of an odd man, all right."

"Funny," she answered, rolling her eyes.

They talked off and on between lapses of comfortable silence, during which Annie snuggled against Mason's shoulder and watched the countryside drift by.

"I think I like these new muscles," she said as she awoke from a short nap. "And you're all manly and hairy now," she added, brushing the black hair on his arms against the grain, giving him a chill.

"What was I before? Girly?" he laughed.

"Compared to the other guys in the art department, you were King Kong. It's just that you were, I don't know...boyish. You had curls. I miss those," she said as she ran her hand over the military style buzz-cut. "Now they're all down here," she said, coyly fingering the soft black curls that filled in the vee at his collar. "How much more of this is there down there?" she said, suddenly pulling out the collar and peeking down the front of his shirt."

"Annie!" he almost shouted, giggling and looking around the train car to see who might be watching.

Mason Crewe giggling. It was a sound utterly foreign to his own ears, but strangely healing. The two playfully flirted, and for the first time in so long that Mason had forgotten the feeling, he rested in the comfort of thinking that everything was going to be alright.

After a time, the two of them settled into one another's arms and Annie dozed off again. Mason just watched her sleep and stroked her tousled curls, thinking that their kids were almost certain to be curly-headed. He hoped they would have her happy-go-lucky personality.

"I dreamed about your dove," she yawned, awakening and stretching from her nap.

"The one in the stained glass? That's a homing pigeon," Mason answered.

"It was a lady."

"But it's not a dove. It's a pigeon. They look similar, but a pigeon is larger."

"Is this how it's going to be, Fernando? You are way too much like Arnie. It's kind of weird," she said with a squinty-eyed look up through drawn brows. "Now I'm serious. I mean it *was* a lady, not a bird at all. Just like you said. I dreamed about it, and I could see her there watching her son in the battle, and you were right, he was wounded. He couldn't see her, or feel her touch, but she was stroking his face and telling him to be strong. To not give up. To have faith in God."

"And she wasn't the only one there. There were hundreds of other people there. There were more of them than the men who were fighting. They were everywhere...on both sides, but none of the soldiers could see them or hear them." Annie's eyes were wide and her face animated as she related her dream.

"The lady who was with her son reacted, like she heard someone speak. I couldn't hear it, but it was obvious that she was listening to someone. I'm pretty sure it was God. And then just...poof! And she's in this cage in a different place. She's the carrier pigeon! And they're taking her out and attaching this little canister to her left leg."

"Poof."

"Yeah, just...poof!" Annie said. "So you were right."

"It was just a dream. You were just thinking about the story I told you and you—"

"I don't think so, Fernando."

"What's with this Fernando stuff all of a sudden?" Mason asked, shaking his head and smiling. "That's sort of a secret, you know."

"Good luck with that one...Fernando. I like the way it just rolls off the tongue." Then lowering her chin and raising an eyebrow she said in her best, most seductive Spanish accent, "Kiss me, Fernando."

"You're a little nutty. I didn't know that when I was saying all that *every minute for the rest of my life* stuff," Mason said.

"Fernando...why haven't you kissed me yet?"

A hundred miles later, "What about kids?" Mason said.

"Want some," Annie answered off-handedly, as she shaped a fingernail with a nail file. "Not a houseful, but two maybe."

"I was an only child and I always wanted a brother, so yeah, two or even three," Mason said, falling silent as he watched Annie file her nails, suddenly struck once again by the reality that the two of them would actually be spending a lifetime together. He smiled at the wonder of how life could turn on a dime.

"So did Arnie," she said.

"So did Arnie what?"

"Wanted a brother," Annie answered. "Now you're both going to get your wish. I sure hope that's the way you feel about each other. I think you will."

"What about your work? Do you have any idea what you want to do?" Annie asked.

"You know what I'd love? I'd love it if you and I could work together. My folks always have. Every church he pastored, she took care of the church office, and they worked on everything else side-by-side. When I was a kid I thought all parents did that. Eventually, I'd love to have something we could do together like that."

"I'm going to have to work? If I'm going to have to get a job, why do I need a husband?" Annie asked in astonishment.

Mason was taken in, and aback by her mock outrage, and he stammered, "Well no. I mean, of course not if you don't want to. I can—"

He was interrupted by a peal of laughter, "You are so funny. I was joking. I didn't go to college so I could find a husband to support me, although I think I was the only female I met there who didn't," she said. "I've always wanted to work. Growing up I loved going to my dad's factory and watching the way everything happened. It was like magic to me when I was little. It's still a little astounding, and I'm there every day."

"His company makes, what was it? Insulators for electrical lines? Things like that? Am I remembering that right?" Mason asked.

"Yes, high voltage power line insulators like those," she said, pointing to the electrical high lines that ran alongside the railroad track. "Those probably came from our factory, in fact."

"How is it, working with your dad and your brother?" Mason asked.

"It's been a little stressful lately, to tell you the truth. I told you, Dad is in the process of selling the business to a Japanese company. If it works out, he will actually go over there and set up their manufacturing operation. He and Mom will be living in Japan for awhile."

"What about Arnie?"

"Arnie is against the whole thing. Adamantly against it. He has always thought he would take over operation of the company. He's worked there every summer since he was a kid. He worked on the line, learning every aspect of production. Now he feels like Dad's pulling the rug out from under him. But it's Dad's decision. It's his company."

"So all three of us may be a little at loose ends, it sounds like," Mason said.

"What about sculpting? I remember you had a very definite plan about doing large scale work."

"I don't know. That's part of this whole thing that's been going on since I got home. I don't even remember what it felt like to want to be an artist. I put that away when I left for Korea, and I don't know if it'll ever come back. Right now art seems meaningless," Mason answered.

"Well you haven't been home very long. It may just take awhile for you to get your bearings," Annie said. "But what you said about us working together...I love the thought of that. And there may be something we could do together right away."

"Really, what's that?"

"Well, Arnie and I have been talking about something, and it may be sort of a long shot, but he's been doing a lot of research, and he seems to think there's potential," Annie began, but then seemed hesitant to go on.

"Okay...and?" Mason said.

"I don't know, Mason. You were so serious about your art before, and what we're talking about is creative, and I think maybe even artistic, but you may think it's..." and she made a sour face that completed her sentence.

"Look Annie, the only thing I am serious about now is you. It wasn't just Korea that changed me. Meeting you, falling in love with you, changed everything. If you and I could make a living weaving baskets together, that sounds like heaven to me."

Annie smiled and took his hand in hers, "Well, be careful what you wish for, that's not too far off the mark," she began, "I've been working on a few ideas...bowls, platters, pitchers, cups, teapots, stuff like that, but not traditional, boring, bland serving pieces. Instead, I mean whimsical, colorful, but useful...and maybe even collectible," she said. "Hopefully," she added, watching Mason's eyes, hoping for a flicker of excitement.

He could see that she was wanting some response, and finally said, "So you're talking about designing and manufacturing these things? I guess you're thinking ceramic, right? Porcelain?" He tried not to look skeptical as Annie nodded and he added, "Finding someone to pour and fire the quantities you would need if you were going to try to sell these...that has to be expensive. And to try and get set up to do it yourself on that scale..."

"That's the thing," she interrupted, "We already have the factory. My dad's factory. Those insulators he manufactures are porcelain. He's selling the name and his contracts, designs and processes, but the factory isn't going to Japan. They're building a new one there."

"The equipment is already here. And the people who know how to operate it. Arnie thinks with a little re-fitting we should be able to be in production in no time. And he's convinced that it could be a viable business."

"The three of us would be working together then?" Mason said, suddenly intrigued.

"Partners, she said. "*Warner and Crewe* has a nice ring to it, don't you think?"

11
1966

• • • •

THE RAILROAD TRACK was a quarter-mile away from Finger's house, and the sound of the trains roaring through, and blowing the whistle as they approached the crossing so nearby would have been unnerving to anyone unaccustomed to it. It was such a routine part of his life that the boy hardly noticed it. Until that night.

The urgency of the whistle and the shrill scream of metal braking against metal punctuated by the hollow boom of impact sent him bolting out the screen door and to the road.

He could see the train still moving, the brakes still shrieking, sparks flying, the diminishing speed measured by the clanging couplings of the passing freight cars. The boy ran. He was there before the train finally drew to a stop. It was dark, but there was enough moonlight to make out the heap of mangled steel that had been his father's wrecker off the road in the brush at the base of the embankment. He could smell the spilled diesel and hot metal. He knew it was the Moron's truck, because the twisted shape of its a-frame towing mast jutted up from the mass of wreckage.

Soon, men with flashlights were scrambling down the embankment and shouting to each other over the drone of the idling locomotive engine, now more than a hundred yards down the track. They couldn't see the boy, and he couldn't move from the spot.

One of the men reached the remains of the truck, shined his flashlight into what remained of the cab, then immediately whirled and vomited between his feet. Two others joined him and the boy could hear their words plainly enough as their flashlights scanned the wreckage and the surrounding ground. They weren't talking really, but just shaking their heads and blurting foul epithets...coupled with the repeated word *dead*. He heard the unmistakable sound of a man throwing up again.

The boy was surprised by how easy the rest of it was. He had planned so carefully, and everything that didn't work the way he thought it might, only worked out better. He had been managing for twelve years to stay in one piece by staying one step ahead of a short-tempered, mean-drunk father like Freddy Finger. If nothing else, that hardscrabble life had made the kid resourceful.

He had been smart. Smart enough to be patient. The money was still right where it had always been, safe and secure until the time was right. And now was the time.

The boy was certain that the whole thing was somehow meant to be. The Moron was dead. A boy was supposed to be sad when his father died. He didn't feel anything but relief. Freedom. He had wanted him to be dead. He had thought he would have to do it himself. He had planned how to do it. Exactly how to do it. But now it had been done for him. The Moron was down there in that pile of debris, his body so mutilated that those men had thrown up when they saw it.

He had to move fast. He had seen it on television. People would be coming to the house, and if they found him there, they would take him somewhere, and someone would eventually move the drum and find the money. His money.

He turned and ran, and a grim smile broke across his face in the moonlight.

Early the following morning after the accident, the boy watched through a crack in the door to the well-house as the Coffey brothers slowly drove by the house twice in their beat-up truck.

They had thrashed the engine in that truck a couple of summers back, and had hiked out to talk to the Moron about Floyd Coffey working off the cost of repairs. It was one of the few times anyone had ever ventured out to Freddy Finger's house.

One other time was a Sunday afternoon, and the Moron was out there revving the boat motor when they drove up. He didn't hear them until they followed the sound and found him back there. It was two men he called *Baptists*, but he called them a lot more than that. He cussed a blue streak when they surprised him. The boy had enjoyed seeing him caught unaware like that.

Floyd Coffey turned out to be decent help. He had worked for the Moron off and on ever since.

The third time he heard the truck's engine, he watched between the cracks as the Coffey brothers turned in and drove straight back around the house and stopped right beside the oil drum. The kid almost cried out, certain that they must have somehow known about the money hidden underneath.

Floyd jumped down out of the driver's side door, and his brother, Len slid across under the wheel. The brothers were talking through the rolled-down window, and he had to strain to hear what they were saying over the throaty rumble of the engine.

"You give me twenty minutes then come back. If it's here, I'll find it," he heard Floyd say.

"You're sure his kid ain't in there?" Len Coffey answered.

"No, I told you, Finger said he's living with his mother off somewhere. Besides Barstow would've took him somewhere last night if he was here anyway. Now you get out of here before someone drives by and sees the truck. Twenty minutes we're gonna be rich, little brother. Now go!"

"The Moron told him about the money," the boy muttered under his breath as the truck backed out of the yard and headed toward the highway.

He didn't breathe while he watched, his face pressed against the crack in the door, as Floyd dashed straight in through the back door of the house. The boy's eyes never left the crack, worried that Floyd Coffey would come out any minute and turn over that barrel.

An eternity later he heard the rumble of the truck, and again, Len Coffey drove right around to the back and stopped right by the well-house and the oil drum beside it. The boy's heart was pounding out of his chest.

Floyd burst out of the house, stomped around to the driver's side, ripped the door open, shoved his brother over and got in. He gunned the engine and started backing out. The boy was just blowing out the breath he had been holding, when Floyd suddenly stopped and pulled back up even with the well-house.

He jumped out, leaving the engine running and went straight to the oil drum. A small sound escaped the boy's tight throat as Coffey started loosening the mounting clamp that held the motor to the side of the barrel.

Floyd bellowed out, "Len, get out here and help me with this! Get the tailgate."

His brother jumped out and ran to the back of the truck, looking around furtively in every direction while he unhooked the chains and lowered the tailgate. Then he scurried over to Floyd's side and helped lift the big Evinrude up and out of the water, its shiny propeller catching the sun and reflecting it right into the kid's eyes through that crack in the well-house door.

The Coffey brothers shuffled to the rear of the pick-up carrying the motor between them, jostled it into the back and raised the tailgate.

The boy was certain that they were about to turn over the oil drum, but instead both brothers jumped back up into the truck, and Floyd once again gunned the big engine and they tore out of the yard, the boat motor sliding and crashing against the wall of the pickup bed and the tires sending a spray of rock and a cloud of chalky dust as it fishtailed onto the road, the water from the motor streaming out under the tailgate.

After he was sure they were gone, the boy ran across the yard and went through the same back screen. The place was a wreck. Kitchen cabinet drawers dumped out in the floor, the old couch and the Moron's recliner cushions were ripped open and the furniture over-turned. The mattresses were cut open. The pillows too. Floyd Coffey had destroyed the place, but he hadn't found what he was looking for.

Two days later, the assorted remains of Freddy Finger were buried. No one cared enough to even show up at his funeral, such as it was. The boy had never been to a funeral, but he had seen them on TV shows. He knew people were supposed to come and say nice things about the deceased loved one. The Moron was nobody's loved one.

The boy hid in the scrub beyond the weedy south edge of the cemetery and watched as the backhoe operator lowered the box that contained what remained of Freddy Finger Sr. into a long, deep rec-tangle that the man had just gouged out in the ground with grim and singular purpose. The operator got out and removed the harness that had cradled the coffin. He looked around, then took off his ball cap and looked down into the grave and spoke a few words the boy couldn't make out, then shook his head, climbed back up into the seat of the big yellow tractor, lowered the rectangular bucket and be-gan to push the pile of soil he had removed back into the hole.

That was the end of Freddy Finger. Neither he nor his son would ever answer to that name again. The boy thought it would be appro-priate if someone would haul the big oil drum and boat motor down here to mark the grave. But the motor was already gone.

The gravedigger finished up his work, raking away the small humps of excess soil by hand. Tossing his tools and the coffin harness into the upturned bucket, he clambered back up into the seat and revved the throaty diesel engine as he deftly pivoted the big yellow machine, leaving a swirl of black smoke floating above the fresh grave. The tractor lumbered off toward the cluster of low tin sheds that surrounded the caretaker's modest white stucco house, and it disappeared from view in the gathering dusk.

It had been hard for the boy to figure out where to hide two steel boxes crammed full of bills. He had thought it through carefully, and knew it might be five or six years that the money would have to remain hidden. It had to be a place where no one would accidentally discover it. It had to be a place that he could find when the time was right. A place that couldn't burn down, or be paved over. A place that wouldn't change.

The boy emerged from his hiding place. He walked and ran in jerky spurts awkwardly, the metal handles of the heavy green ammunition boxes sawing against the joints of his fingers. One end of a long greasy handle was clamped under a skinny arm and the shovel at the other end skidded along the ground behind him. A folded piece of inner tube rubber was clamped under the other arm as he stumbled across graves and dodged headstones.

According to the police report typed up and filed away by Police Chief Aubrey Barstow of Slaterville, Oklahoma, Freddy Finger died suddenly and violently in a collision between his truck and a train. There was a notation in the paperwork that Finger was thought to have a surviving son living with his mother, name and address unknown, possibly in Kansas. Barstow had made a half-hearted inquiry with the state about records of a child support agreement or anything that might give him some notion of how to reach the woman to inform her of Finger's death. Nothing came up referencing a marriage, divorce, or birth of a child. Nothing at all.

The Police Chief had only a vague notion that Finger had a kid. Someone, he thought it had been one of the Coffey brothers, said the boy lived with his mother up in Kansas.

Barstow was the only law officer in the one-stoplight town, and the closest thing to a government official. All he knew was, he didn't have time to figure out what to do with the son of a foul tempered drunken ingrate, and if one of the Coffey boys said he lived with his mother in Kansas, that was good enough for him. There was no telling how many forms he would have had to fill out to get a kid into a home or something. It was out of his hands, and if there was a kid, he was bound to be better off without Freddy Finger in his life.

Barstow made only a cursory investigation of the accident that killed Finger. The man was drunk according to Hank Fulbright at the Pit Stop Bar, but that was no surprise. According to the engineer, Finger's tow-truck was hit on the driver's side just as it straddled the railroad tracks that Finger crossed over every night, turning off the highway onto the dirt road that led out to his house. The engineer stated that the idiot was racing to cross in front of the train that came through at 9:30 pm. The collision had turned the truck and a good deal of Finger, truth be known, into scrap.

12
1956

· · · ·

IT HADN'T BEEN EASY to get started. Arnie was grieved watching the Warner Insulator Manufacturing employees who had lost their jobs leave the factory parking lot with their final paychecks. It was a memory he would carry with him from then on.

Eventually, Arnie was able to bring most of those same people back to work at Warner & Crewe. It was a commitment he made to himself, and Arnie Warner took commitment very seriously.

The three of them had an easy working relationship right from the outset. Mason and Arnie had an immediate rapport. Although Arnie knew the manufacturing process for insulators, there were some challenges to adapting the equipment and technique for producing the more delicate, colorful serving pieces that Annie was busy designing.

Mason learned through that process, and found that he enjoyed operating the kilns, and the working atmosphere on the factory floor. He, Annie, and Arnie worked long hours together those first years, and would look back on them as the hardest, and some of the best times.

Mason and Annie turned out to be a good sales team. Neither had a clue what they were doing when they began to call on area department stores, but they figured it out, and one store at a time they began to gain some ground.

Annie's designs were different from anything anyone had ever seen, but they began to catch on. Eventually colorful and imaginative Warner & Crewe bowls, tea sets, and dessert serving pieces became familiar wedding gift options in a growing number of regional stores. It wasn't long before they were shipping to several states.

"Okay, I need you to look at this," Annie said, leaning into Mason's office.

Mason looked up and laughed. The gray apron she wore had a big smiley face smeared in clay over Annie's very round tummy.

"You're going to give him a complex before he's even born, decorating his room like that," he said. "That's what you wanted to show me?"

"No, come here," Annie said, shaking her tousled curls and heading back down a short hallway to her studio. "I need to know what to do to fix this piece of crap," Mason got up and followed, laughing to himself. Annie had always been plain-spoken, but this last month of her pregnancy, she had become even more blunt and saucy than usual. He and Arnie had both laughed at the wrong time more than once when she was being dead serious.

"I can't imagine that it's that bad," he said soothingly.

She just looked up through her eyebrows at him, then did an exaggerated presentation gesture with both hands as they turned into the studio door.

Mason had a flashback to their first meeting as he looked at the clay figurine on the worktable. It was a bird on a spiral of grapevine, its wings raised, and head turned almost backward.

"Oh honey, this is not crap," Mason said.

"Yeah, that's what I was after. I wanted it to be not crap," she said sourly.

Mason gave her an indulgent look. The pregnancy had been uneventful physically, but Annie had seemed to struggle with her work almost from the beginning. She had lost interest in designing yet another teapot or gravy bowl, regardless of the growing demand for her serving pieces.

Warner & Crewe was beginning to show signs of really becoming an established brand around the country, with potential for longevity, but the creative burden rested on Annie's shoulders. She asked

Mason for his opinion of her work routinely, and his input always seemed to add that missing spark that made every piece work, yet he had never been inclined to design anything on his own.

Mason seemed to be content in his sales role in the company, and he genuinely thought he was. He and Arnie worked together seamlessly, and genially. He got to be with Annie throughout every day. The three of them took their lunches together, and as often as not, Arnie joined them for dinner on the way home in one of their several favorite restaurants.

Home life was pretty much non-existent in those early years. The company was their life, and all three savored the work. Annie fretted over Arnie finding a wife, but he seemed resolved to being single. There were women whose company he enjoyed on occasion, but as time went on, his work, and being the de facto patriarch of the Mason & Crewe family seemed sufficiently fulfilling to Arnie Warner.

When Annie announced that she was pregnant, any void of fatherhood in the bachelor's life vanished. Arnie staked a claim on the baby that surprised and delighted Annie, while it gave Mason just a twinge of irritation that he would have never admitted to anyone.

"So how do I fix it?" Annie asked irritably, after watching Mason study the clay sculpture for a time.

"Before we talk about that, why don't you tell me what's bothering you," Mason said gently.

"What's bothering me? Mason I'm carrying around a twenty-pound bowling ball all day and it's sitting square on top of my bladder. My back hurts, my feet hurt," she blurted in a flurry of frustration, "And what happens when it's a baby that needs to eat and be changed and cries, and Lord knows what else. How am I going to take care of a baby and get anything else done? I don't want to be at home by myself with it." Annie put her hands on her hips and arched her back with a grimace.

"And I'm sick of looking at cups and saucers and bowls and teapots, I just wanted to do something interesting for a change. Arnie says I should be thinking about things for babies. More cute crap. I want to do something that isn't cute. I hate cute."

"Really, I wish you'd open up and tell me what's going on," Mason said with a smile. "You shouldn't hold it in."

Annie rolled her eyes as Mason stepped over to her worktable and ran his fingers through a pile of moist clay she had left under a wet cloth. He turned to Annie and with a few strokes he had turned the smiley face that had decorated her apron into a wicked-looking imp with pointy teeth.

"Not helping," she said, punctuating the words with a put-on sharp look that dissolved into laughter when Mason held up the mirror she used to test the composition of her designs.

"That's the most artistic thing you've done since we started the company, you know," she said. "There's an amazing artist in there, Mason. You need to let Fernando out of the bottle. Come in here and roll up your sleeves and work with me."

"One of these days, maybe. I love everything that you've done, but it's just not..."

"Art?" she finished his sentence for him.

"Stop that. You know what I mean," he said. "But that," he said as he pointed to the sculpted bird on the table, "Could be."

"Isn't yet?" she said.

"Close. Very close," he answered, leaning down to study the piece. After a moment he turned and said, "You really have a remarkable touch, honey. I'm not kidding. This detail is really extraordinary."

Both of them thought it at the same time, but Annie said, "I'm suddenly hungry for a burger and fries."

"With grilled onions?" he asked.

"Absolutely," she answered with a playful smile. "I'll tell Arnie we're going to sneak off for a little date. Just what the doctor ordered."

"Which reminds me, you didn't tell me what the doctor said about the pains you were having last night. You did call him like I asked, didn't you?"

"I called," she answered. "He asked me a couple of questions, and said it was probably nothing to worry about. He wants me to come in next week."

"Have you had any more?"

"A twinge earlier. No big deal," she said dismissively as she went out to find Arnie.

As she left, Mason looked after her with a worried squint, then turned to study the piece again. It was mounted on a turntable, and he slowly rotated it, stepped back a few paces and studied it. He had his back to the door and didn't notice Annie return and exchange the apron for a long raincoat.

"Are you just trying to make me feel good, or do you really think it's interesting?" she asked.

"You know it is. Or it will be," and then Mason asked, "What's the story?"

"No story. Just a bird on a vine," she said. "Do you have your umbrella? It's raining again."

"That's why it's just a bird on a vine," he said, then asked, "Where's the Polaroid?"

"It's over here," Annie answered as she picked up the big camera and took it over to Mason. "What do you want to take a picture of?" she asked.

"Your piece," he said as he pulled out the accordion-like lens of the camera. He took the shot of the sculpture, and pulled the undeveloped photo out of the camera and held it by its paper tab. He checked his wristwatch as the film developed. After sixty seconds of

Annie leaning against the doorframe, holding her purse and tapping her foot, he peeled off the gooey backing and studied the result.

"Ready to go?" Mason said after a moment.

"Been ready for awhile now," she said as Mason handed the still wet photo to her and went to get his raincoat and umbrella.

Thirty minutes later, experiencing some chagrin that she'd had to wedge herself into the booth, Annie said, between bites of her cheeseburger, "This isn't as good as that place we went on our first date, but it's not too bad."

Mason had eaten only a few fries. He still studied the photograph of the bird sculpture.

"Your burger's going to get cold. And if you're still trying to make me feel good, it already worked. I feel great. Appreciated. Fulfilled." Looking down at her rounded belly she added, "And Mommy's sorry she called you a bowling ball."

"All it really needs is a story," he said, picking up the burger and peeling back the paper wrapping. "I was thinking about when I was working on that stained-glass window for the church when I was a kid. Remember how I told you about Cher Ami, the homing pigeon?"

"Of course. Don't you remember the dream I had about her...that lady there with her son, and she just poofs into the bird?" Annie answered. "I've never forgotten that dream. It was so real to me."

"Okay," Mason said, "So what if we imagine this bird...is it a blue jay?"

"No, a cardinal"

"Okay, this cardinal is somebody like that."

"You mean a dead lady poofed into my cardinal?" Annie asked. She leaned down to the photograph of the clay bird, put her hands behind her ears imitating gills and sang with tone-deaf gusto, "Or would you rather be a fish? A fish won't do anything but swim in a something, da-da-da-da-bum-bum..."

"Let's say it can only be birds," Mason said, laughing at his wife's animated rendition of the old Bing Crosby tune, and looking around self-consciously to see if anyone else in the café was listening. "And let's say this cardinal is no cardinal at all, but a person."

"A dead person," Annie interrupted.

"Yes. Well, departed. One who has shuffled off the mortal coil and stepped through the veil. And let's say this person has some compelling reason to have returned in this form."

Annie, beginning to warm to the idea, said, "Like the mother who poofed into Cher Ami."

"Or maybe it doesn't have to be some life-threatening ordeal. Maybe it's just someone who wants to be around someone they loved in this life. I mean, if I croaked, I would still want to hang around with you," Mason said.

"Creepy," Annie said around a mouthful of cheeseburger. "But don't you say people in heaven can see us here already?" Annie asked.

"Oh I absolutely believe they can. There's a passage, I think it's in Hebrews, that says there is a great *cloud of witnesses* watching our lives, and it talks about them being people of faith who have died," Mason answered.

"Then why should anybody poof into a bird or something, other than to do something that saves the life of their loved one, like Cher Ami, or some other big deal like that?"

"What if they just want to be seen? Mason asked. "If I died, even though I could see you, I think I'd sometimes want you to see me too, even if I was just a little bird sitting on your windowsill. Can you imagine how it would feel to be right here with me, and me not look at you? Not acknowledge your presence?"

"Happens every time you pick up the sports page, babe," she said blandly.

Mason answered with a smirk.

"And why only birds? Why not squirrels? Or fish...or how about cats?" Annie mused.

"Because there's actually another verse of scripture that talks about people who hope in the Lord *soaring on wings as eagles*," Mason said. "Soaring on wings as eagles," he repeated. "It's in Isaiah. And what kind of person would want to be a cat anyhow?"

"Yeah, but that's figurative, right? A metaphor for finding strength in faith and stuff like that."

"Maybe that's all it is, but it's a passage that starts off talking about how no one can fathom all that God can do, because He's the everlasting God and Creator of everything, and He can basically do anything He wants," Mason answered, "And since live people aren't often seen poofing into a bird and taking wing, it must be a promise for life beyond. And it's in the Bible, so I'm saying it's a possibility...an *undeniable possibility*," he added with comic emphasis.

"Okay, you're the preacher's kid. My family went to church on Easter and Christmas Eve, so what do I know?"

"Well you're probably never going to hear a pastor claiming that when we die we get to come back and hang around with the people we love. Especially not in the form of a bird or something," Mason said.

"Preachers have to color inside the lines, or they'll find themselves selling shoes door to door. The Bible doesn't offer a lot of description of life in heaven, so it's all pretty much conjecture. That kind of thing can open a whole can of worms for a pastor."

"But I remember asking Dad about that passage in Isaiah. I was probably twelve or so, and he had used it in a funeral," Mason said. "My grandfather's funeral. Mom's father."

When he didn't continue, Annie looked up from her burger to find a distant look in Mason's eyes.

"What are you thinking about?" she asked.

"I loved my grandfather, and had a really hard time with his passing. It just occurred to me, that the day after his funeral, I asked Dad if Grandpa really had wings now, like the Bible said. That was when I realized that I had this feeling of, I don't know, I guess it was being drawn to profess my faith in Christ. I just wanted to be sure that when I died, I would go wherever Grandpa was."

"Dad told me that there are wonders God has prepared for us that we can't possibly imagine," Mason recalled with gentle reverence in his voice. "And of course, he explained what Jesus had done to make it possible for us to be with Him, and those we've lost, when we die. How to become a child of God."

"But we're all God's children," Annie said.

"The way Dad always put it was, we enter the world *unborn* children of God. We're not truly His children, fully alive to Him, until we are born into the family of God. Just like that little guy in there," he said.

"Little girl," Annie said, around a mouthful of cheeseburger.

"Whatever it is, it's our child, we already love it, and we have all kinds of things planned for it. But until it's born, we can't truly experience a relationship with it."

"Oh, I think I'm experiencing a pretty close relationship. With *her*." Annie said pointedly. And then looking down, she added, "Daddy didn't mean to call you an *it*, Meredith dear."

Mason just rolled his eyes and took a bite of his burger.

Then Annie smiled and said, "You know, you'd have made a pretty good preacher, Fernando."

He laughed, "No, I wouldn't have, because I would have preached the same sermon every Sunday." Then, in a bad attempt at a Billy Graham impression, waving a French fry for emphasis, he said dramatically, "There is a dividing line in this Bible."

"Uh, that's a French fry."

"Okay, then," Mason smiled, again holding up the fry, "There is a dividing line in human history. Before the cross and after the cross. We live here...after the cross."

"Again, that's a French fry."

Mason scowled in response, "No heckling the preacher please, Sister Crewe."

"Amen. No more heckling. Preach on, brother!"

"Let me ask you, have you ever even read the apostle's letters to the Gentiles?"

"You're asking me? Of course I have. Romans is my favorite."

"I'm asking them, my congregation, Sister Crewe, and I'm going to forget my sermon if you don't stop interrupting me."

"You were at *the apostle's letters to the Gentiles.*"

"Correct. Those are God's letters to us! If you would read those, maybe you would understand why Jesus came. And what He did. And what He changed. And then maybe you would stop being so stinkin' obsessed with everything that happened before the cross, the Old Testament, the Jewish Law, the Jewish history of the Jewish people. And realize, that what *we* have, here and now in Jesus, after the cross, after the resurrection, is so much better than what they had! A better covenant, founded on better promises, written, and signed in the precious blood of Jesus." Mason said, concluding his impression, by popping the French fry into his mouth. Then added, "And after a few Sundays of that, they would have fired me."

"And defrocked you for doing that terrible impersonation."

"What? It was spot on. Billy Graham."

"Sounded more like Foghorn Leghorn, babe."

Mason just scowled at her again, and grinned from behind his burger." Then turning his attention back to the photograph, he said, "I just think it's interesting how that particular passage in Isaiah struck me when I was a kid, and it still seems to be sort of tugging at my mind, thinking about your piece."

"Isaiah? Old Testament? Before the cross? Jewish prophet?" Annie asked playfully.

"Yeah, yeah, yeah," Mason laughed.

"But Fernando, I've got to say, that was a pretty good sermon."

He fell silent for a moment, then said, "So let's come up with her story."

"Okay, this dead person has poofed into this bird. What are the rules?" Annie asked.

"Rules? Rules for what?"

"Rules for poofing. There's got to be rules." Annie said, "Otherwise all these birds that used to be people...these *Poofs*... would be doing all kinds of crazy things, perched on their favorite chair watching *Ed Sullivan* and stuff." Then she added, "And hey, since we're the ones making the rules, I say they ought to be able to poof into anything. Anything they want. That's way more fun."

Mason laughed, "Alright, so they can poof into anything. Any living creature, fish or fowl, mammals, reptiles, frogs, you name it. And it's obvious that they can't do anything that would be uncommon for whatever creature they've poofed into. They can't overtly reveal themselves to be anything other than a regular bird or whatever."

"What if they poof into a parrot and can talk?" Annie asked.

"Well they can't say, '*Honey I'm home! What's for dinner?*' can they? It has to be '*Polly want a cracker!*' or something a parrot would normally say," Mason answered.

"But what's to keep them from breaking the rules?"

"God," Mason said.

"Yeah, that works so great for people. Why not for Poofs?" she said rolling her eyes.

"But it would. See these are departed saints. People of faith. They're no longer hindered by the temptations of the flesh. They are in perfect harmony with God. Whatever they do is going to be fine with Him," Mason said.

"So only the people who go to Heaven get to poof? Well that takes all the fun out of it," Annie joked. "I was thinking these Poofs could wreak all kinds of havoc. I didn't know they were going to be Sunday School Poofs."

"If you were a Poof, I'm pretty sure you'd find a way to create a little mischief. Being free of the influence of evil won't take away your personality. You'll still be you," Mason said, picking up the photograph of Annie's sculpture again. "In fact, let's just say this *is* you. *Poofannie*. What's she up to?"

"So you're saying I'm dead," Annie said.

"For the sake of the story, yeah."

"Then I want you to be dead too. And Arnie."

"Okay, we're all dead," Mason agreed. "You, Arnie, and me. But this is you. Now what are you up to?"

Taking the photograph from Mason's fingers, Annie held it up, studied the clay bird for a moment, then said, "And so begins the adventures of Poofannie, Poofarnie, and Poofernando! But I've got to get my hands dirty to think. Are you through eating yet? Let's go back to the studio," she said, already beginning to wedge herself awkwardly out of the booth.

13
1956

• • • •

ANNIE'S STUDIO ALWAYS made Mason think of his first-grade classroom. It was about that size, with the same tall ceilings and rows of white-globed drop-down light fixtures. The same tall windows ran the length of the north wall, with roll-up canvas shades. She even had a chalkboard that covered most of an adjacent wall, and a heavy old oak desk and chair.

Where the students' desks would have been, there was a tall, square worktable. In the center of the table Annie had a turntable that contained a variety of tools for working with clay. Around the perimeter of the table there were four other similar turntables, and she often had projects mounted on each.

Today there was only the bird. Annie had been working hard to get ahead, so she could take whatever time she needed when the baby was born. Everything was in order and ready. The studio was even less cluttered than usual. Annie seemed to work best in a state just on the edge of chaos.

She came in with Mason following, and flipped on the overhead lights. The heavy gray skies outside cast a strange muted light over the normal cheerfully sunlit space. The clay bird sat perched as they had left it, but both looked at it with different eyes, as they mulled over what the story might be that would give life to its static form.

Annie traded her raincoat for the clay-crusted apron she had worn earlier. "I'm putting on some coffee. Want some?"

Mason was standing, head cocked to the side, studying the piece. "Sure," he answered offhandedly. "You know, if you're dead and poofing into this bird, and Arnie and I are both dead—"

"I don't like that. I mean I don't like saying it that way, because we're not dead-dead," Annie said. "We just poofed out of our bodies one day, and now we can poof into any form we want, except people. We can't poof into people, that's another rule."

"Okay, so are we poofing into an existing bird or something, or are we just sort of materializing out of thin air?" Mason asked.

"Thin air. The other way is too creepy. We're still people, we just look and act like birds or whatever," she answered.

"Okay, then what about bugs?"

"You want to be a cockroach?" she asked with a grimace.

"How about a butterfly?" Mason said.

"Aw, yeah. A butterfly," she answered with a smile.

"The point is to be seen. To be with someone important to you, and have them acknowledge that you're there with them, without exposing yourself as anything more than a normal creature," Mason said. "I think butterflies are a natural."

"Okay, we have enough to start, so what's the story with Poofannie here?" Annie said.

"What I was just thinking was, here we are with all the wonders of Heaven to enjoy, but there is some compelling reason to poof into something and visit someone. The only reason that makes sense, is love," Mason said. "And if the three of us are all dead...I mean, if we have poofed out of these bodies for some reason, then whomever it is we're here to visit has to be someone we love. Someone we love, who has outlived us."

Annie looked down at the round form under her apron. "Oh no, our poor sweet baby is an orphan?"

"Well, how about this? Driving back over here I was thinking how great it would be to believe that my grandpa had been stopping by from time to time throughout my life. So instead of it being our kids we're poofing in to check on, how about making it our grandchildren?"

"I'm already a grandmother?" Annie said, feigning chagrin.

"Well, yeah but you're dead."

"Well, there is that, but I like it better. That way it isn't so morbid. We're imagining grandchildren we won't have for another thirty years, and putting them in situations that Poofannie, Poofarnie, and Poofernando have to do something about."

Mason nodded and shrugged, "We won't know if it works until we try it out."

Annie went to her tub of clay, removed the cover and pulled out a softball-sized lump. With her clean hand, she snatched her spare apron off a hook on the wall and handed it to Mason.

Putting the clay on one of the turntables, Annie said, "Those slacks have to be dry-cleaned. You don't want to get clay on them or that tie. Better roll up your sleeves, Fernando, and start poofing."

"Wait a minute. This is your territory, Annie," he said.

"Teapots and cake stands are my territory. Figurines are a brand new thing. If they are going to be as special as I think they can be, it's going to take both of us. Fernando, you're the artist."

"But Annie..." Mason began.

"What? Porcelain figurines can't be art? Let's just see about that," she said before he could object.

"That's not what I was going to say. I have to admit that the idea of sculpting again is appealing, which sort of surprises me, to tell you the truth. It's just that I don't want to invade your studio."

"It's our studio. It always has been. I've wanted you in here with me from the beginning, but I knew cute little pitchers and bowls were a waste of your talent. What I love is the color, and you're an amazing sculptor. Together we'll be magic," she said, putting the apron around his neck and pulling him toward her for a kiss.

"Okay then," Mason said, tying the apron around his waist, then rolling up the sleeves of his dress shirt, picking up the lump of clay and starting to knead it as he studied the clay bird Annie had crafted. "Poofannie, who are you looking in on?"

Squinting and kneading, sounding like a fortune-teller, he said, "I'm seeing our grandson. He's out in the yard playing with a ball, and having a fine time. He's about seven I think."

"Does he look like me?"

"No, he's boy. He looks like me."

"What about the girls? Surely they look like their grandmother."

"I don't see any girls," Mason answered, his eyes closed, his face upraised in the dreamy expression of a mystic.

"Our grandson is an only child?"

"Oh! No, the girls are in the house playing with the tea set their grandmother made for them," Mason answered.

"Before I kicked the bucket," Annie said with mock dismay.

"Yeah, back when you were alive and kicking everything but the bucket," Mason answered. "I think Poofannie sees our grandson about to get into trouble. Come here, you do this. I don't want to mess with what you've already done," Mason said.

"It's okay, Mason. I know it's too static. I'm not emotionally invested in this thing. Not yet anyway. Do whatever you think it needs," Annie said.

Mason cleared his throat and said, "Okay, I don't like it, but okay. Do you have some paper and a pencil? I'll show you what I'm thinking." Annie answered by pulling out a drawer under the tabletop that contained a sketchpad and several charcoal pencils.

Mason flipped to a blank page and began to sketch as he continued, "Well, here's the deal. Our grandson is about to kick that ball into the street. Now Poofs, you see, sometimes have an awareness of things that are about to happen. Poofannie here knows that her grandson is about to be placed in terrible danger."

He fell silent as the sketch progressed, and looking at what he was drawing, Annie took a cutting tool and carefully cut the connection between the bird and the vine and laid the bird aside.

Turning the sketch so Annie could see it, Mason explained, "See I think the vines here are beautiful, but they're too sweet for this story. We need something that communicates the threat. Something like a jagged branch coming out up here, and then jutting out toward the danger. Like a finger pointing, see?"

As she looked, he picked off a sizeable piece of clay from the lump he had kneaded and began to form it in into a thick column, fashioning the form of the branch. Looking up and receiving an approving nod, he added it to the piece.

"So what's the threat?" Annie asked, seeing the tone of the sculpture changed already by the spiky branch Mason had created.

He stepped back and said, "Here, why don't you do the texture of the branch. Rough bark, don't you think? I'm going to do something else," Mason said, taking up another bit of clay.

Rolling it into a ball, he began to tell the story. "There's a man who lives down the street from our grandson, and this guy is very reckless. He drives fast. He doesn't pay attention to anything around him. He's actually sideswiped cars in the neighborhood because he was fiddling with his radio driving down the street. He's a menace."

"And our grandson is by himself out in the yard with this maniac on the streets?" Annie said dramatically. "What kind of woman did our son marry?"

"Maybe his mother is our daughter. You said it's going to be a girl," Mason answered. "Well anyway, this knucklehead is blasting down the street in the direction of our little guy and his ball. Poofannie knows what is about to happen, and she knows she has to do something fast."

"What can a bird do to stop a madman in an automobile?" Annie posed.

"Exactly the problem," Mason said and then added, "Which is why Poofannie here is frantically calling in her fearless companions, Poofarnie and Poofernando!"

Mason held up two roughly formed, but recognizable bumble-bees between his thumbs and forefingers.

Annie laughed, and said, "I love it."

Mason continued, "Now I think if you put Poofannie back, maybe here," he pointed out a place a bit lower down on the branch, and maybe open her mouth and change the position of her head to make a more urgent posture like this," he said using a few quick stokes with the charcoal to sketch what he meant. "What do you think?"

"I think I love this," Annie answered, picking up the delicate clay figure of the bird. With careful cuts and nudging the clay with a wooden shaping tool, she succeeded in opening the bird's mouth and arching the neck upward. Raising some leaves of clay to represent ruffled feathers at the neck gave it an attitude of urgency, just as Mason had envisioned.

In the meantime, Mason more completely fashioned the bees as he resumed the story, "You see, Poofs can make only the sounds that whatever they've poofed into would naturally make, but they're able to communicate with one another in thought...telepathy you know. Across vast distances, of course. But in an excited state like this, Poofannie would obviously be inclined to shriek as well as call out to the others with her mind."

"Obviously," Annie smiled.

"The maniac is flying down the road, tuning his radio and lighting a cigarette, driving at breakneck speed, steering with his knees and elbows," Mason continued as he positioned the bees.

He placed one of the bees near the tip of the jagged branch, looking as though it was just lifting in flight. "Poofarnie here takes off first and flies right down beside the road toward the car. The guy's driver's side window is down, of course, and Poofarnie zips right in behind his head and lands on the back of his seat to wait for just the right moment."

"In the meantime," Mason added, delicately mounting the second bee on a lower fork of the branch, similarly seeming about to take off, "Poofernando zooms off and flies down the road right behind him."

"Then Poofannie here takes off and watches as old Poofernando peels off and hovers just to the side the road. Now they're down a few blocks away from our grandson's yard, and here comes his big blue sedan, dust and rocks flying up all around, and behind it clouds of gray exhaust blowing out of the tailpipes. The guy's still trying to light his cigarette, and still changing stations on his radio."

Mason squinted his eyes and curled his lip as he described the villain. He had a mischievous twinkle in his eye that reminded Annie of the much more boyish Mason she had admired from across the room during his last semester at college. It made her smile, seeing him so animated as he told the story.

Mason continued, "Now the first assault is up to Poofannie. She gathers as much speed as she can and dives, pulling up barely in time to avoid being smashed on the front grille," Mason said. "Close enough that a couple of red feathers are left floating in the cloud of exhaust and dust behind the car as it rockets on down the road. The guy never even notices Poofannie. Wouldn't have hit his brakes or swerved if he had. Poofernando knew her idea wouldn't work, but what are you gonna do? Poofannie's always had a mind of her own."

Mason got an elbow in the ribs for that remark, and he resumed with a grin, "Now about this time, our grandson kicks his ball, and it's a good one. The kid's probably going to be a place kicker for the Kansas City Chiefs when he graduates with honors from college, and before he goes on to become a famous brain surgeon. That ball flies right out to the edge of the yard and rolls right into the middle of the street. Of course, he blazes after it. And he's a fast runner. Something he inherited from his grandfather," Mason said.

"Of course. You run like the wind," Annie said with a smile. "Now get on with the story, Fernando. "I'm risking my neck and you're hanging out watching from the sidelines."

"Actually, Poofannie, who needs to recover her breath after that close call, has perched herself up on a high-line wire, so she has a bird's eye view of the real action."

"Ha-ha," Annie scoffed. "You just couldn't wait to use that one."

"Shhh, we're getting to the climax," Mason said, still working on the bee's fragile connection to the branch. "By now he's just a block away from our little guy, who has made it to the curb and almost out into the street. That's when Poofarnie shoots up and lands on the guy's neck. He buries his stinger in deep, and about the time the man lifts his hand to slap him, which is not going to go well for my brother-in-law, here comes Poofernando, with my plump little yellow and black striped body aimed right between the numbskull's eyes...and splat!"

"No! Poofernando can't die!" Annie exclaimed in amused horror.

"Of course not, I'm already dead. But wait, I'm not finished with the great climax of the story," Mason chided.

"Poofernando is everywhere. The guy can't see a thing. He flips on his windshield wipers. Bad idea. He hits his brakes, skids to a stop, jumps out of his car holding his hand over the big lump rising on his neck. Right out in front of the bumper of his car, his eyes as big as saucers, so terrified his knees are knocking is our little grandson. The ball he's holding falls out of his hands and bounces off into the gutter."

Annie's eyes were wide. "Oh my gosh, this is a terrible story!"

"It's a wonderful story. We saved our grandson's life, and he never runs out in the street like that again," Mason answered. But it's not over. You keep interrupting."

"Sorry, but I don't like it anyway. You got smashed on the windshield."

"It's okay. It just stung for a second."

"Good," Annie said.

"Well this guy starts yelling at our grandson for being in the street, and the kid's crying and he turns to pick up his ball, when here comes Poofannie! You're not about to let this jerk get away with making your grandson cry, after he's almost run him over. You come zeroing in and nail the guy right on top of his head like a dive-bomber! It's big and it's runny."

"Oh Mason! That's disgusting!"

"Well it teaches the guy a lesson," Mason said. "You mess with Poofannie's grandson, and she's gonna crap in your hair."

Annie burst into peals of laughter, holding her swollen belly. "You are awful! I love it! But I still wish you hadn't gotten smeared."

"All part of the plan. Poofannie, Poofarnie, and Poofernando are a force to be reckoned with.

With the story in mind, they fell to work, and the figurine took on a new dimension that would become the inimitable element of Warner & Crewe collectibles. There was a mysterious, almost magical element that the stories imparted to every piece that Annie and Mason crafted, and their creative partnership became legendary among collectors of porcelain figurines.

The work added a new dimension to Annie and Mason's life together as well, and to the Warner & Crewe bottom line, which of course delighted Arnie. They spent more and more of their time in the studio together, conjuring their enigmatic creations from the tales Mason would spin. The Poofs remained their magic, and their secret.

14
1978

• • • •

ARNIE WARNER HAD HIRED hundreds of people over the years. He had developed an efficient interview process, and trained others to winnow the grain from the chaff, leaving only the best prospects. But until Arnie Warner *took a read* on an applicant, no one was hired. He had been wrong only a handful of times. Even if they passed Arnie's internal radar, people hired for high-level positions were routinely vetted by Joe Kitchens, a friend of Arnie's, a retired FBI agent that did background investigations for a small corporate clientele.

Arnie's read on Adam Pembrook had been thumbs down the first time he met him, but he knew neither Mason nor Annie wanted to hear it. Meredith, their daughter and only child, was head over heels in love with the boy. So, Arnie had made a call to Joe, without telling his sister and brother-in-law. He knew he was overstepping his bounds, but Arnie Warner loved Meredith as his own, and there was something about this Pembrook kid that just didn't ring true.

Two weeks later, to the day, the receptionist called Arnie's office to let him know the investigator was there to see him. After instructing her to send Joe in, Arnie stood up and came from behind a worn, round oak table that occupied one corner of his office. The table, rather than his desk, was where Arnie did most of his work. Foregoing pleasantries, Kitchens merely shook hands with Arnie, then sat down in one of the chairs at the table and began to peruse the loose pages he had assembled in a manila file folder that he had placed on the table.

Arnie closed his office door and returned to his chair and took up a yellow legal pad and pen, an ever-present fixture in any meeting with Arnold Warner. He immediately started laying out a sort of diagram. He would be jotting notes, circling some and connecting them with lines as Kitchens delivered his report. Arnie reduced everything to a schematic like this. Everything had to connect. Had to make sense. It was the way he thought, and the way he had built the business end of Warner & Crewe.

Looking through a pair of reading glasses perched on his nose, the imposing ex-special agent seemed mildly bored as he began reciting his assessment to Arnie. "The kid's an orphan. No known relatives," Kitchens began. "Grew up in Carthage Creek Children's Home outside of Tulsa, Oklahoma. He was placed there when he was twelve or thirteen years old. I've got to tell you, Arnie, it's a pretty remarkable story."

Kitchens filed the first page to the back of the stack and went on, "He graduated from high school at the top of his class. Valedictorian. Received a boatload of scholarships. This kid's S.A.T. scores were pretty much off the charts. Came up here to college. Same story. Magna Cum Laude when he got his Bachelor's degree, and he's tracking to do the same when he gets his MBA this May."

Kitchens looked up over the top of the glasses, and the offhand manner receded a bit as he continued, "See the thing is, this kid's not just smart, he's driven, and he has been since the day he appeared."

Arnie looked up, from the notes he had begun to scribble on the legal pad, his lips pursed and brows drawn into a look of concentrated suspicion, "Appeared?"

"Appeared," Kitchens confirmed. "Adam Pembrook was born twelve years old."

"What do you mean?"

"He didn't exist before then. No school records, no birth records. Nothing until age twelve."

He let Arnie absorb that for a moment, then resumed, "I was lucky though. I tracked down a social worker in Tulsa who remembered his case. A pretty grim one, and bizarre enough that she recalled a lot of details.

Arnie continued his cryptic outlined notations as he listened.

"This kid shows up in Tulsa. Just shows up. He's been beat all to crap, old bruises, new bruises, and says he was abandoned. Left there because he wouldn't steal anymore. Says he had been with these people as long as he could remember, but they were not his family. He never knew his parents."

"This is Adam Pembrook you're talking about?" Arnie interjected in disbelief.

"Yeah, but not yet. The kid doesn't even know what his real name is. Says the people that he traveled with just called him Moron. He doesn't even know how old he is. The social workers just guessed at his age. He can read, but he can't write. Never been enrolled in school he says, claimed he was taught to read by another kid with this family of gypsies or whatever they are. Like I said, the kid is smart." Kitchens then looked around and asked, "You have any coffee, Arnie?"

Arnie stepped out and asked the receptionist to make some fresh coffee, and bring a couple of cups to him and Kitchens. That was unusual, because Arnie was adamant about appearing to be just one of the team. The receptionist had never, as far as she could remember, been asked to make and bring coffee to her boss. And it was very rare that he closed his office door.

Arnie knew that if Mason or Annie happened to see Joe Kitchens they would ask questions. It would be natural for either one of them to be curious about who it was that Joe was checking up on, and he would have to answer. And then he was pretty sure it would hit the fan.

"The social worker couldn't remember much more," Kitchens continued. "They sent out all the usual alerts and such, but it wasn't as easy to share information as it is now. No kids were missing that fit his description, or at least no agencies responded."

"They had a doctor check him out, and x-rays were consistent with his story about being beaten over the course of years. Apparently, the kid had some old fractures or something. I haven't been able to get the actual medical records yet." Kitchens stopped to shuffle through his papers.

Arnie looked skeptical and asked, "You're saying he was supposedly living with a roving band of thieves? That sounds pretty far-fetched, Joe. Like something a kid would make up. Does that kind of thing really happen?"

"Not as far-fetched as you might think. When I was with the agency there was a gang that worked the Midwest. Momma, Daddy, about a dozen grown kids and some little ones. Quite a little organization. Weird stuff happens out there, Arnie," Kitchens answered. "The kid was twelve and pretty bunged up when they found him. Maybe he made up the story, but even if that wasn't the truth, he'd run away from somebody who had been abusing him for a long time."

Arnie sat staring at his legal pad shaking his head, finally asking, "You have anything else?"

They named the kid *Adam*, because it was sort of like they were creating a new person, and I guess he liked that better than Moron."

The receptionist knocked on the closed door and brought in two mugs of hot black coffee, some sugar packets and wooden stir sticks.

"Appreciate it, Maureen," Arnie said, as the receptionist was turning to leave.

Maureen just smiled and glanced a little nervously at Kitchens. Arnie was pretty sure that Kitchens could have told him the brand of perfume and what Maureen had eaten for breakfast that morning. The man was like a sponge, absorbing the most minute details of every encounter. He seemed to see right through you. It was intimidating. Arnie thought absently that he would not have wanted to be a suspect in one his friend's cases back when he was active FBI.

Kitchens continued as the door closed behind the receptionist, "This social worker didn't know where the *Pembrook* came from. The boy had heard it somewhere maybe, and liked it. Maybe it's his real last name, or some family connection, but not likely, since that's the name he chose. He was doing his best to run away from his past connections."

"Regardless, after a few weeks or maybe a month of legal foot-dragging and form filing, a Tulsa judge finalized the name change, or name assignment in this case." Kitchens started to take a sip from the coffee before continuing, then thought better of it and allowed it to cool for a moment more.

"I've already told you the rest of the story. Once Adam was enrolled in school, he made up for lost time in nothing flat. He caught up with, and then left his classmates behind, choking on his dust.

Kitchens, glanced through the notes in the file on the table before going on, "I interviewed his last house parents. The home he was in is a church-funded deal. The kids live in cottages, four or five to a house, with a couple. Pretty nice set-up really. I still haven't talked to the first couple that had him when he got there. The ones I visited with, had him when he was in high school."

The investigator stopped, took a careful sip of the coffee, and with an appreciative nod looked over his reading glasses at Arnie and went on, "They say he was a machine. He had an after-school job at a supermarket, then straight home and got on the books. This kid never even got a B throughout junior high and high school. Never went out. No drinking, partying, none of that. Didn't have any close friends, and never was close to any of the other kids in the home. He had one date and that was for the senior prom. That's about it as far as his life goes before he showed up here."

Kitchens closed the file, took off the reading glasses and took another slow sip of the coffee then said, "It's a pretty inspirational story, to tell you the truth. I'm sort of looking forward to meeting this young man," Joe paused, then added, "And when I do, I just have one question I want to ask him. It's the part of this boy's story that doesn't fit, and it really has me puzzled. It's a pretty big part. A real mystery."

Joe Kitchens enjoyed making Arnie Warner wait. He had known the C.E.O. of Warner & Crewe for a long time. Kitchens thought he was a good man. He was a man who knew his strengths, which was not unusual among fellows who had made something of themselves. But Arnie Warner also knew his weaknesses, and would waste little time before reaching out to a resource that could fill in that gap. Kitchens respected him, and was glad to be one of those trusted resources.

He had done enough work for Warner & Crewe to know that Arnie was not a patient man, and Joe was just mischievous enough to string him along just a little. During his twenty-five years at the FBI, Kitchens had been pretty much all business. It was nice to have a little fun with a client when it wasn't a life and death issue.

Kitchens took a long sip of coffee and said, "This is really good. Is this some special blend you guys have made up or something?" And he took another sip, closing his eyes and savoring the aromatic brew.

"This reminds me of the coffee I used to get at this little joint in San Francisco when I was assigned there. I had an apartment down on—-"

"Good grief, Joe! It's coffee. What's the question, man?" Arnie exploded right on cue.

Kitchen's smiled over the rim of the cup, and waited just a few seconds before saying, "Where'd all the money come from?"

"Money?"

"Yeah. Quite a lot of money, I'm thinking." When Pembrook shows up here to enroll in college, he didn't appear to be some poor kid coming out of an orphanage. He drove up in a brand-new Corvette Stingray convertible."

Arnie mused, "Well, maybe he had a benefactor. Someone heard about his past and his grades and all, and decided to give him a leg up. Sure sounds like he deserved a break. If I heard about a kid like that, I think I could be moved to do something for him. Good Lord, what a story." Arnie shook his head, still trying to square what he was hearing with his impression of young Adam Pembrook.

The truth was, Arnold Warner had been just such an anonymous benefactor to a number of people over the years. Family members of Warner & Crewe employees, and occasionally others with special financial needs that Arnie became aware of, would find that arrangements had been made to accommodate their situation, often with life-changing results. No one other than his attorney, not even his sister and brother-in-law, knew.

Joe answered, "No benefactors according to the social worker or the house parents. He got scholarships for school. Deserved them. And the house parents say he was frugal, saved almost everything he made working at the supermarket, but none of that comes close to accounting for the money he's been throwing around since he got out of high school and showed up in Lawrence to enroll at KU."

Retrieving the file, Kitchens slipped on the reading glasses again, flipped through the pages and began, "I tracked that Corvette. He drove it three years and traded it in on the Porsche he's driving now. He bought the Stingray at a Chevy dealership in Ardmore, Oklahoma."

"I guess that's near Tulsa?"

"No, that's the funny thing. Ardmore is a pretty small place south of Oklahoma City. It's over two hundred miles southwest of Tulsa. The kid left the children's home right after graduation. The house parents took him to the bus station themselves, and everything he owned was in a suitcase. They thought he was headed to Lawrence to try to find a summer job before classes began in the fall. Ardmore is not on the way to Lawrence from Tulsa. It's the opposite direction."

"Maybe he just decided to take a vacation. A road trip before starting college. Kids do that," Arnie suggested.

"To Ardmore, Oklahoma? I doubt it. I went there. Not a vacation spot. No, I think there was a reason he went there. Maybe some family connection or something. I'm still digging. But let me tell you about the Corvette. The guy who sold it to him still works at the Chevrolet dealership in Ardmore. Been there something like eighteen years."

Kitchens referred back to his notes and continued, "He couldn't remember the day, but vehicle registration records say it was the 28th of May, which was just four days after the kid graduated from high school. He walks into the dealership with his suitcase in his hand, and there's this red Corvette convertible there on the showroom floor. The only Corvette the dealership had received. The guy remembered because everything about the deal was weird."

"Everything about Adam Pembrook is weird it seems," Arnie interjected.

"So this eighteen year old kid walks straight over to this Corvette and gets in. The salesman goes over to him, mainly to keep an eye on him and be sure he doesn't jack up anything. The kid asks how much the thing costs and the salesman tells him the sticker price, which is more than my house cost. The kid gets out and picks up his suitcase and asks where the restroom is. He goes to the restroom and after a few minutes, comes out and hands the guy fifty-eight one hundred dollar bills."

"You're kidding."

"No, that's why the salesman remembered the deal so clearly. Nothing like that had ever happened before. And it's even stranger than that. The guy says this cash smelled funny. Said it reminded him of his grandmother's root cellar. The money had a musty smell. And after the kid drove off in his car, they got to looking at the cash, and some of the bills were fifteen, twenty years old."

"You're saying this kid had a stash of money buried somewhere around Ardmore, Oklahoma?" Arnie asked, mouth still agape.

"I'm thinking he had a very sizable amount of it stashed. He went there, or somewhere around there, to get it before he went off to college. And when he got to college and enrolled, he had invented a whole new life story."

"I'm eager to hear that. All my sister told me was that he had no family," Arnie responded.

"He came to college with a story about his parents dying when he was a kid. Killed in a private plane crash on their way to a ski weekend in Aspen, Colorado, where the family had a vacation home. Left him to be raised by his mother's parents in Tulsa. No other living relatives. The grandfather had died some years before, and the grandmother had recently passed away when Adam left to come to school, leaving the boy with a fat trust fund, and no living relatives." Kitchens looked up over his glasses, "And every word of that is pure fabrication of course."

"Well that's one word for it," Arnie muttered. "How'd you get that information?" Arnie interrupted.

"Pretty easy really. Freshmen are required to live on campus. His first roommate, a boy named Everton, graduated and went back home to work with his father, who's a building contractor in Wichita. It wasn't hard to track him down. That's the story Adam Pembrook told him, as he remembered it," Kitchens answered.

"Are they still friends? Is there any chance he'd call and tell Adam that someone's checking up on him?" Arnie asked.

"Nah. After the first couple of weeks at school, Everton said the kid hardly gave him the time of day. It wasn't that they didn't get along, but apparently his roommate didn't have what Pembrook was looking for in friends. Everton said he was a committed social climber. Before that first semester was over, he'd found his way into one of the more prestigious fraternities on campus. He hasn't spoken with Everton since the day he moved into the frat house."

Arnie frowned as he studied the notes on his legal pad, started to say something, then just shook his head and tapped his pen on a word that he had written on the paper. *Money* was the word. Arnie jotted three question marks after the word and circled it.

Kitchens watched him, then continued, "He's good looking, well spoken, charming, and seemingly pretty well fixed financially. It didn't take him long to become a popular figure among the campus social upper crust, where I think it's safe to say, he encountered a certain young lady that has, it seems, eclipsed all the others he's had on his arm these past few years.

"Sounds like he was almost a recluse in high school, and then he's suddenly *Mister Socialite* when he hits college. It's like he completely changed personalities," Arnie said, again shaking his head. "It doesn't add up."

"Yeah, I know," answered Kitchens. "He seems to reinvent himself every few years."

Arnie sipped his coffee then pondered aloud, "I can understand him making up some story about his life, I suppose. Whatever he went through before he went to the children's home, who could blame him for wanting to forget all that and make a new life for himself? But now he wants this new false identity to include becoming the husband of my niece."

"Are they engaged?" Kitchens asked.

"Not yet, but it's being talked about. Meredith has never been this way about a boy. And she's never brought one here to meet me."

"She did that?"

"Yes, about a week before I called you. There's already been some talk about him coming to work here when he finishes up his degree."

"Arnie, just to round out my investigation, I did a little digging around about your company," Kitchens said.

"Our company? I would have told you anything you wanted to know."

"But I wanted to find out what I could discover on my own. What anyone else might be able to find out, if they were reasonably resourceful," Kitchens said.

"Well?"

"You've done well for yourselves. Warner & Crewe generates a multi-million-dollar annual gross in collectible porcelain figurines, with distribution across the U.S. and Canada, and even some significant trade in Europe. I have a good approximation of the annual income," he said, pushing a page of figures over to Arnie.

"It's a closely held company. A limited partnership in which you, your sister, and her husband are each equal thirty-three percent shareholders. The general partner is a corporation that holds the remaining one percent, and you three own equal shares of that as well. I suppose that's some business structure that makes sense to someone above my pay grade," Kitchens said with a self-deprecating shrug.

Arnie just sat thinking that there was no such thing as privacy anymore, and that there wasn't much that Joe Kitchens didn't understand, regardless of what he might claim.

"You and your partners are very, very wealthy. At least on paper. Neither you, nor they, take an exorbitant salary, compared to most corporate officers, so I'm guessing you plow everything back into the company. Your wealth is here," he said, "But it is significant nonetheless. And there's only one heir, or should I say *heiress* to all this, and she's dating an enigma who calls himself Adam Pembrook."

"Do you think I have a reason to be alarmed?"

"Aware," Kitchens said. "You have a reason to be aware of how this kid right out of high school, with no family connections whatsoever, and zero evidence of any other benefactor is suddenly flush with cash. Enough cash to fund a pretty lavish lifestyle, for a college student anyway. And he's kept it up for almost six years now."

"Do you think you can find the answer?" Arnie asked.

Kitchens didn't answer, but stood up and collected the papers back into the manila folder. "I have to tell you, Arnie, this kid is pretty impressive. The money I don't know about yet, but the rest of it, the grades, and the scholarships, he earned. I almost hate to go digging into this thing, but if I do, yes, I will find the answer."

15
1978

• • • •

JOE KITCHENS FOUND himself driving back into Ardmore, Oklahoma just a week after he'd been there the first time. Arnie Warner had wanted the whole story, and Joe was convinced there was still some smoke in Ardmore.

It had been twelve years since the boy who became Adam Pembrook had shown up in Tulsa. Twelve years in a metropolitan city was forever, but in a town the size of Ardmore, twelve years could still leave a warm trail.

Kitchens located the public library and settled himself in front of a reasonably serviceable Microfiche, prepared for a long afternoon, and the headache he knew would follow hours of scanning the Ardmore newspaper, backtracking through the weeks leading up to July 21st, 1966. That was the day the boy had been located in Tulsa. Kitchens started looking at the July 20th edition, wishing he knew what he was looking for.

Slogging through mundane news and obituaries of octogenarians, he finally found one item that he scribbled on a notepad. On the 18th there was a headline about a train collision near Slaterville, Oklahoma. One man killed, name withheld pending notification of next-of-kin.

Kitchens assumed Slaterville was nearby, since the story was carried in the Ardmore paper, and it wasn't exactly a national disaster. He reloaded the July 20th edition, thinking he must have missed it in the obituaries of the following day. After scouring the 20th and finding nothing there, he loaded the July 21st edition of the Ardmore News & Eagle, where he found a small article indicating that the name of the victim of the July 17th collision of a tow-truck and

117

freight train was Freddy Finger, 35, of Slaterville, OK. He was the owner of Finger's Garage there. He was survived by his wife and one son, Freddy Finger, Jr., place of residence unknown. Local authorities would appreciate any information regarding their whereabouts. Freddy Finger was interred at the Slaterville City Cemetery. No funeral home was listed.

Kitchens re-read the cryptic notice, trying to fill in the blanks. No one knew where the wife and kid were. The wife's name was unavailable, and there was no funeral service.

"Loose ends and no friends," Kitchens muttered, as he loaded another edition of the newspaper, and continued his search.

The following morning Joe Kitchens drove the eighteen miles from Ardmore and took a slow drive down Main Street in Slaterville. His search of the two weeks' worth of newspapers leading up to the day the boy had been found had yielded nothing more promising than the train accident in Slaterville, and that only because the guy's wife and kid were nowhere to be found.

Kitchens thought he had come up with a fairly workable approach to questioning the local law enforcement. It was always tricky working with the locals when he had been with the agency, and now that he was on his own, it was usually worse.

The police station was easy to find. He pulled in beside a lone police cruiser parked in front, and walked in with the air of a fellow professional law officer.

There was a cork bulletin board on one wall covered in several layers of state and federal notifications, photographs, scraps of paper with phone numbers and addresses, and other indecipherable information that dated back no telling how many years. Under it was a cluttered shallow table with a dust-covered, scratched-up two-way radio, a yellowed copy of the ten-codes taped to the top of it. Stacks of other pamphlets, notices, and bulletins, plus various magazines, newspapers, and paperbacks covered the rest of its surface. A clipboard lay on the floor with the rest of the spillover, around the legs of a gray metal folding chair.

A single wooden desk sat in the middle of the room, its top scarred and gouged in the few places where it was visible through similar clutter. An old oak office chair that should have been replaced a decade ago, sat empty, and cocked to one side, with what looked like a bed-pillow molded into its seat.

His eyes swept the room once and Kitchens concluded that Slaterville would probably be a pretty safe place for a criminal to live and work.

A muffled toilet flush sounded from within an adjacent room, immediately followed by the door swinging open, and Chief Aubrey Barstow wedged himself through the narrow opening and out to face Joe Kitchens.

Either because he was startled by the unexpected visitor, or the big man was just habitually rude, Barstow blurted, "Who're you?"

Joe, not minding that he wasn't offered a handshake, having heard no sound of a lavatory faucet after the flush, answered, "My name's Joe Kitchens. I'm trying to locate a young man who lived around here about twelve years ago, I believe. His name is Freddy Finger, Jr.

"Well good luck."

Kitchens asked, "Do you remember him?"

"Remember his daddy. I don't remember ever even seeing the kid. Just heard Finger had a boy. Why are you trying to find him?" Barstow asked, slack-jawed and sounding like he had to labor to exhale every breath.

"I work for the family in Kansas City," Kitchens replied, not liking Barstow's belligerent tone, but not surprised by it. "They hired me to locate him."

Barstow said nothing in reply, and the two big men just stood looking at each other, Barstow's ragged mouth-breathing was loud in the long silence between them.

Finally, Kitchens said, "Look Chief, can you help me out here? This boy has had a rough time, and I'm just trying to figure some things out about his past that might help his family deal with him today. I've been on your side of the table. Law enforcement for twenty-six years," Kitchens said, purposely omitting that he'd been FBI, then adding, "I just need a place to start."

"I doubt you're going to find anything helpful here," Barstow answered, his tone losing a bit of its surly edge. "You want some coffee?"

"Sure."

Barstow picked up a white foam cup from his desk and another from a stack beside the percolator that occupied a folding TV tray against the wall behind it, and began to talk as he poured their coffee, "Freddy Finger, this boy's daddy, was a mechanic here. He lived out by the city dump. There used to be a house out there between the tracks and the junkyard. The town let him live in it rent-free in exchange for running the bulldozer in the dump."

He handed Kitchens a cup across the desk and said, "Pull up a chair," indicating the dilapidated folding chair in front of the two-way. "You know Finger's been dead for...I can't even remember when it happened. Years ago."

"Sixty-six," Kitchens replied. "You were chief then, right?"

"I was," Barstow answered. "That was a grisly deal, I'll tell you. Nastiest thing I ever saw. Train hit his truck broadside. Idiot was trying to beat it over the crossing. The engineer said he made that run routinely between Oklahoma City and Wichita. Said he'd barely missed that same truck a dozen times or more. Finger drove this old tow truck all the time. That time of the night he was almost always drunker'n Cooter Brown. I guess it was a game for him or something. Like Russian Roulette." After a sip of his coffee, Barstow added, "Fool."

Kitchens was glad Barstow was finally willing to talk, and he sipped the bad coffee and led the chief along, "Do you know what happened to his son when Finger was killed?"

"Folks told me the mother had left Finger some time or other before that. Took the boy with her from what I understand. But I'm sure you know more than I do about all that."

Kitchens said nothing and let Barstow believe his assumption was correct.

"I asked around when it happened, trying to find out how to get hold of her. There was a guy that worked for him some at the garage, Floyd Coffey. He's dead now but his brother's still around. In fact, he runs Finger's old garage over on South Peach. I think it was Floyd told me that Finger said she and the boy lived up in Kansas somewhere or other with her folks. Floyd didn't even know her name. Nobody did. I couldn't find anything in public records that gave me a clue how to find her to let her know Finger'd been killed."

"The boy wasn't here when it happened?" Kitchens asked.

"I'd think you'd know he wasn't. Didn't you say you work for the boy's family?" Barstow said, suddenly suspicious. "What made you think you might find out something about him here after all this time?"

Kitchens took a sip of coffee to give him time to come up with a believable reply, "The family hasn't had contact with the boy's mother," Kitchens replied. "I discovered that a few years ago, the boy bought a car over in Ardmore. Too close to his old hometown to be a coincidence. Thought it was worth checking out. Anything you might recall would be helpful, Chief."

Barstow raised his bushy eyebrows and seemed about to dismiss him, but Joe Kitchens held his gaze until the chief finally said, "Well it's been too long for me to remember much about it, but I think somebody or other told me the mother let the boy visit Finger from time to time. Stuck with me because I couldn't imagine any mother in her right mind letting her kid be around Freddy Finger if she could help it."

"I guess, he was around here some, but I never saw him that I recall. I didn't find anybody at home when I went over to the house after the wreck, and nobody knew where he and his mother lived. That's about all I can tell you," Barstow said, standing up and reaching over to retrieve a white straw Stetson from a rack on the wall behind him.

Kitchens stood too, and left the half full cup of coffee on Barstow's desk. Obviously, the interview was over. Barstow walked to the door, flipped off the fluorescent lights and held the door open waiting for Kitchens to follow.

Kitchens came to the door, but was not quite through questioning the suddenly less cooperative Barstow. He asked, "The kid was twelve or so at that time. Were there any toys or anything, a bicycle, kid's clothing, anything to indicate that maybe the boy still lived there?"

Barstow's neck stiffened, but he relented and answered, "Nothing like that that I saw. Lots of junk around the place. Finger fixed up and sold stuff he'd dig out of the dump. But I do remember that the house was torn to shreds. The guy was a drunk, had a terrible temper. Something must've set him off. His furniture was turned over, he'd taken a knife to most of it.

Drawers had been pulled out and dumped in the floor. It was a hellacious mess."

"That looked a little suspicious, didn't it? Kind of sounds like maybe someone was in there looking for something," Kitchens replied.

"Freddy Finger didn't have anything anybody would want. The way some people live, and the crazy things they do...after thirty-six years of doing this job, Mister Kitchens, I'm not surprised by much of anything."

Kitchens was surprised. Surprised that Barstow had held onto his job for thirty-six years.

Barstow added, "You might want to talk to Len Coffey. Him and his brother and Finger were pretty thick. Peach is about six blocks down," he said, gesturing to the east. Turn right and go until you're almost on the edge of town. I don't think Len's ever changed the sign. Finger's Garage is still painted on the side of the building."

"Well thanks for your help, Chief," Kitchens said, extending a hand he would be sure to wash at the first opportunity.

Barstow gripped the hand briefly and expelled, "Good luck," and turning away he lumbered toward his cruiser.

* * * *

KITCHENS THOUGHT HE needed another cup of coffee to get rid of the taste of the burned mess Chief Barstow had given him. He knew there had to be a local diner somewhere. He got back to his car and drove just a couple of blocks down Slaterville's Main Street glancing at signs and the storefronts, when a sign at the end of a side-street caught his attention.

Pembrook's Grocery was a store from another era. Kitchens pushed open the screened door, its faded red metal Coca Cola promotional push panel bringing back a fifty-year-old feeling of familiarity. A bell tinkled above the door as it opened. The worn hardwood floor creaked and popped as he stepped inside.

Kitchens immediately caught the precise, strangely comforting aroma of a corner grocer from his childhood. He drank it in with a nostalgic smile, knowing he was not likely to happen upon a place like this again. Stores like this were becoming scarce even in the smaller towns. Seeing one that had survived this long was a rare treat.

The single check-out counter at the entrance was empty, but he caught a glimpse of a bald head ringed by a neatly trimmed rim of snow white hair bobbing up and back out of sight a few aisles over. A plump little man wearing a long white apron was arranging cans of turnip greens on a lower shelf. Kitchens had to speak before the elderly grocer was aware that he was there.

"Good morning, sir."

"Oh my, you sneaked up on me," the man said pleasantly, looking up over wire-rimmed glasses and squinting at Kitchens as though trying to recall his face, before he added the obligatory, "Could I help you?"

"I hope so. My name's Joe Kitchens," he answered, extending his hand.

"Marvin Pembrook, Mister Kitchens," the grocer answered as he quickly wiped his hands on a towel tucked under the tie string of the apron, and shook the hand warmly.

"You don't see many stores like this one anymore, Mister Pembrook, and that's a shame. How long have you been open?"

"We opened on May the first in 1919. But I expect it won't be too long before I throw in the towel. I am eighty-five years old after all," he said with a proud squawk of laughter, then continued, "The wife passed a little over a year ago. Hasn't been the same since. Of course, she was ill for some time. She hadn't been able to work here for three years before she passed. Stroke you know."

Mister Pembrook looked down and shook his head, sniffed and pulled a handkerchief from his hip pocket and wiped his nose.

Kitchens said, "I'm sorry for your loss. You two worked here all those years together though?

"Worked here side by side for fifty-six years. Those years just flew by. Now the last few have been kind of dragging on. It's just not much fun anymore without Mattie. Now you probably can't imagine that it would be fun, I guess. Little grocery store in a piddly town like Slaterville, but Mattie and I had fun. This was like our living room, and we had company every day. Weren't blessed with children, so this store was pretty much our life, and the people of Slaterville have always been good to us," the talkative old gentleman said, smiling as he reminisced.

I wonder if I might buy a soda-pop, Kitchens said, the nostalgic atmosphere suddenly changing his mind about coffee.

Mister Pembrook ambled to a glass-fronted refrigerated box. Kitchens followed, and was pleased to see it stocked with glass bottled sodas, in addition to the more popular pull-tab aluminum cans. He chose a Coca-Cola in the glass bottle.

"We have a bottle opener up at the counter," the old gentleman said as he headed that way. "Glad they haven't gotten rid of the bottles yet. To me, they just don't taste the same in the cans."

As they neared the check-out counter, Mister Pembrook pointed to a rack of packaged nuts and said with a knowing smile, "Now you'll want some of those peanuts to go in that."

Kitchens took a bag.

At the counter, the old man rang up the Coke and peanuts on a cash register that looked like it was probably original equipment. The bell rang as the cash drawer popped out, and Mister Pembrook deftly made change from the five Kitchens gave him, and counted it back into his hand.

"Now that's becoming a lost art," Kitchens commented. Seeing Mister Pembrook's questioning look he clarified, "Making change and counting it back like that."

"Oh goodness yes. Been doing that for all these years. Do it automatically. Never even have to think, which is good at my age. My thinker isn't what it used to be," he said.

Then with a quizzical look that told Kitchens the old grocer had probably lost little of that particular ability, Pembrook said, "I'm pretty sure you didn't just come in here for a soda, Mister Kitchens. "What is it that you need?"

"Well sir, I'm checking a few facts about someone that's been gone from here for quite a long time. Just a boy when he lived here."

"You're a police officer?"

"Used to be in law enforcement. I was with the FBI for twenty-six years. I've been hired by the boy's family."

"Who is this you're looking for?" Pembrook asked.

"His name is Freddy Finger," Kitchens answered.

"Well he died some years ago, Mister Kitchens.

"It's his son I'm interested in. Do you remember the boy?"

"I do. But, my goodness, it's been years ago. We didn't see him in here very often. I seem to remember Mattie hearing that Freddy Finger's wife left him and took the boy with her. But I supposed he came for visits from time to time, because we would see him every now and again. Until his father was killed, and of course, there was no reason for him to come back here after that. His father's people had been gone for some time."

"Moved away?"

"Both died as I recall. Freddy had a brother, but I understood that he was killed in the war, if I'm remembering right."

"Can you tell me anything about the boy? Anything you remember?" Kitchens asked.

"Is he in trouble?"

"No, nothing like that. As a matter of fact, he turned out to be a pretty remarkable young man. And it's a good family. There are just some blank spots about his life here that I'm trying to fill in. Anything you might could tell me would be helpful."

"I'm just glad the boy's got someone who cares. Whatever he's done, Mister Kitchens, that would end up with his family hiring you, I can guarantee you the problem started with that father of his," Pembrook began.

He looked over his shoulder before resuming in a confidential tone, "I don't like to speak ill of people, more especially of the dead, but Freddy Finger was worthless and everybody knew it. And the thing was, he didn't have to be. He was a bright fellow. A really good auto mechanic. He could fix anything, in fact."

"Poor Len Coffey can't hold him a candle. Floyd was good. That was Len's brother. He wasn't as good as Freddy Finger, but pretty competent, although I never trusted him. But since Floyd died, anything serious, everybody takes into Ardmore if they can. Len's a good boy, just not a good auto mechanic."

Kitchens waited patiently for Mister Pembrook to finish, and at length asked, "Can you tell me anything about the boy?"

"Well, like I said, no one saw him much around here. Just now and again. But it's a small town and people talk. Not much else to do," he laughed and scratched his head, appearing to be trying to recall something, then began again, "I do remember one time, maybe the last time he was in here. Seems like it wasn't long before Freddy was killed. I guess you know about the train wreck and all."

Kitchens nodded, "Yes sir," hoping the old fellow wouldn't get off track again.

"Well the boy came in, and I heard Finger's truck outside. He had loud mufflers on that thing like the boys used to run back in the fifties. You could hear him coming three blocks away," Pembrook said, collecting himself to remember what he was telling and continued, "Well the boy comes in and picks up something. Bread maybe. I don't remember, but he slows down as he goes down the candy aisle. Every kid does, but there was a difference about the Finger boy. Reminded me of those children we would see in the war. I was in Italy in the great war, 332nd Infantry. Kids would come up to us, because they knew some of us had chocolate bars. We carried them in our packs. The eyes of those children, who had precious little to be joyful about over there at that time, well, sir, I'll never forget that look."

Mister Pembrook cleared his throat and retrieved his handkerchief and dabbed at his nose again. "The Finger boy had that same look. Empty. Like a child that had never had a moment of joy in his life. It was hard to see. It wasn't just his clothes and such. The boy always looked and smelled like he never bathed, but so did his father," Pembrook sniffed and looked somberly toward the candy aisle.

Kitchens shifted from one foot to another and took another sip of the pop, chewing the peanuts that came with it.

"He just glanced at the candy, almost like he was afraid to look right at it. Afraid he would want it too much if he did, I guess," Pembrook said. "That was quite a long time ago, but it's stuck with me. Haunted me a little after what happened to his father. It wasn't long after that he ran out in front of that train."

Pembrook paused again for a very long moment, and Kitchens could resist no longer, and finally asked, "What was it that happened that day, Mister Pembrook?"

"Well something just told me I needed to do something for that little boy, and I said to him, 'You're Freddy Finger's boy, aren't you?' He just nodded. I don't guess I ever heard the boy say a word. "And then I told him to pick out one of those candy bars for himself. It'd be my treat. Well sir, it was like those children I told you about in the war. I swear I thought no one must have ever done that boy a kindness. He didn't know what to do. He just stood there looking at that candy. Finally, I went over and picked up a Hershey bar and told him that was my favorite, and I was making it a free gift for him.

Mister Pembrook had walked over and picked up a bar of candy as he told the story, now he shuffled back toward the soda box and chose one for himself. Kitchens followed and the old man continued the rambling tale.

"It struck me that he never smiled like most kids would have. He never said thank you. He just stuffed that candy bar down deep in his pocket and paid for whatever it was he came in to get, and hurried out. I thought then, it was like giving that candy to him made him feel even more desperate than he was before. That's the word I would use to describe that boy. He was desperate."

"Didn't his school teachers ever look into the conditions he was living in? I would think they would have."

"No, he never went to school here, was what I understood. Like I said, he lived with his mother somewhere else. I can't remember where she supposed to live now, it's been too long. And to tell you the truth, I don't remember ever seeing the woman. And Mattie, that was my wife, she passed three years ago...stroke. Well Mattie said there was a rumor around town that the wife, if she and Freddy ever were really married, must have run off and left the boy here. Finger just never enrolled him in school and kept him shut away out there at that shack by the junkyard where they lived. She thought that, because people would see the boy when they would haul junk to the dump during the week when he should have been in school."

"And no one checked into that?"

"Freddy Finger was someone nobody wanted to deal with," the old man replied. "He was mean as scratch, and drunk every night from what I heard," Pembrook said. "But obviously his boy did live with his mother somewhere off down the country. He never was around here after Freddy was killed, and you're telling me it's his family you're working for. His mother's people?"

"Actually, it's his fiancé's family that I'm working for," Kitchens answered.

The old man looked vaguely suspicious, and Kitchens thought it would be best to come clean with the good-hearted old gentleman. He had been very forthcoming, and even though his stories were rather roundabout, he now had a clearer picture of Freddy Finger Junior's dismal life.

"The boy has done well for himself, Mister Pembrook. He graduated at the top of his class in high school, and in college. As a matter of fact, he's just about to finish up his master's degree in business administration, and he'll graduate magna cum laude."

"He's a brilliant young man," Kitchens said as he reached into the pocket of his jacket and pulled out a photograph, "And Mister Pembrook, he may not have thanked you that day, but I know for a fact that he never forgot your generosity. That's the reason I came in here to speak with you."

Mister Pembrook smiled, sniffed and looked at the floor, "It was nothing," he said. "Nothing but a Hershey bar."

"I'm just doing a thorough background check on the boy, because he's about to marry into a very wealthy family, and be offered an important position in that family's company. They're good people, and this is their only daughter, so they're being cautious. That's why I was hired." And without any further explanation he handed the photograph of Adam Pembrook to the old grocer.

The grocer unconsciously wiped his hands on the towel tucked under his apron strings, then took the photo and studied it with squinted eyes, looking through his bifocals.

After a moment, he shook his head and said, "Well I'll be. He might have been worthless, but Freddy Finger always was a handsome devil. If he'd ever bathed, this could be him when he was younger. That's his boy for certain."

17
1978

• • • •

KITCHENS HAD ONE MORE stop to make. The big question was still unanswered. But, he had made progress. Joe was satisfied that Adam Pembrook was indeed Freddy Finger, Jr.

The boy had taken the name of a gentle old grocer who one time gave him a bar of candy. The old man might have shown him the only act of kindness he had ever received.

"Poor kid. Just a lousy bar of candy," he heard himself say out loud. Joe Kitchens was almost afraid to find out the last piece of this puzzle, but he had to know.

"Where'd you get all that money, kid?"

The pavement ended four blocks off Main, and South Peach was a dirt road for the remaining two blocks. Pickups and cars from two and three decades past were strewn along the side of the road at various angles, and in yards with no grass in front of low ramshackle houses. A squat steel building surrounded by twenty or more similar cars sat at the end of the road. From the look of them, they comprised Len Coffey's parts warehouse.

"Finger's Garage & Towing" had once been painted across the side of the building in large block letters. The sign, its once black paint bleached and weathered, like the building and its squalid surroundings, fit the grim image Joe Kitchens had formed of Freddy Finger. Everything he had seen and heard made the life that Adam Pembrook had built for himself seem all but miraculous.

"Somebody was looking out for you, kid," Kitchens muttered to himself as he pulled up to the gaping cavern of a door, and peered into the darkness within.

A decrepit dog, some German shepherd in its lineage, pulled himself up from the oil-stained concrete floor at the mouth of the garage and ambled out listlessly to smell Kitchens' pant leg. Kitchens wondered if anything in this godforsaken town was not half dead.

"Can I *hep* you?" Kitchens heard called from somewhere inside the building.

He walked in and threaded his way among engine blocks, transmissions, tires, and discarded unidentifiable grease-caked mechanisms probably left where they lay when the current owner, or even Finger himself removed them, no telling how long past. Tools littered every flat surface, and the whole mess stank of diesel and motor oil.

A younger man than Kitchens expected scuttled out from beneath a reasonably new Ford, wrench in hand, and grinned up at him from a wheeled creeper.

"Hey," the mechanic said cheerfully. "What could I do you for?"

"I'm looking for Len Coffey."

"That'd be me," Coffey said as he put the tool aside and reached back under the truck to retrieve a greasy rag.

"Joe Kitchens, Mister Coffey."

Standing up, Coffey still had to look up to Kitchens, standing maybe shoulder high to him at best. He wiped his hands on the rag and said, "I'd shake your hand, but..." he held up the still greasy palms and simply grinned again, and stood there expectantly.

Coffey was probably in his early thirties Kitchens surmised. He was small, but had the lean, wiry look of a man who regularly did heavy lifting, and an open, genial face. His mouth seemed to naturally hang slightly open, with a perpetual half grin. Joe's first impression was that the man might not be the sharpest knife in the drawer.

"I'm not here to get a vehicle repaired," Kitchens began. "If you've got a minute, I'd like to ask you a few questions about the former owner of your shop, Freddy Finger."

"Old Freddy. Sure, but why would you want to know about him? He's been dead a long time. He got killed a couple years after I got out of high school. Train hit him when he's on his way home from the bar one night," Coffey said. Then he added in a confidential tone, "Men who saw him said it tore him clean in two." Coffey shook his head and blew out air as he slathered his hands in hand-cleaner jelly, its citrus smell blending into the rank odor that permeated the shop.

"Do you remember his son?" Kitchens asked.

"Yeah, I knew he had a boy. I seen him every once in awhile when Floyd and me would haul something out to the junkyard. Freddy always said the kid lived with his momma up in Kansas, but I know he was around here quite a bit. Floyd and me went out to the dump pretty often, and I seen him there at that old shack. He'd always try to hide, but I seen him. Floyd and me, we done odd jobs around town. Hauled off trash and junk and such for people."

"Floyd was my brother, you know. And after he started helping Freddy at the shop here, we stopped by his house a time or two and I caught a glimpse of the kid then too. Skinny, dirty, looked like he'd never had a bath in his life. Never heard him talk. I don't know, old Freddy Finger was a strange cat. I'm sorry, what was your name again?"

"Joe," Kitchens answered, amused that Coffey seemed to be able to talk without taking a breath.

"Well Joe, Freddy Finger, he was different. Him and my brother Floyd got along. He worked here for Freddy for awhile, and then Floyd and me ended up taking over the shop after Freddy was killed. Floyd's dead now too, you know, but I'll tell you, I myself, I was always kinda scared of old Freddy. He had a bad temper and he was, I don't know what you'd call it. Kinda paranoid I guess. He had secrets Floyd always said." Coffey tossed the rag aside and asked, "How come you want to know about him?"

Kitchens thought that a little subterfuge might help him get the information he was after, so he answered, "I'm actually trying to track down the boy."

"Is he in trouble? Wouldn't surprise me, him being Freddy Finger's kid."

"No, nothing like that. He turned out alright," Kitchens answered.

"Well I always wondered what happened to him. I always kinda felt sorry for that kid. I wouldn't have wanted Freddy Finger for a daddy."

"Was the boy around here when Finger was killed?" Kitchens asked, since Len Coffey was obviously willing to talk.

"Well, I never saw him that next morning when Floyd and me went out there. We were there pretty early the next morning after it happened. I was wondering about where the kid was. Floyd told me if he was around, Barstow probably took him in. They wouldn't have left him out there by hisself."

"Freddy always claimed his kid was up there in Kansas living with his momma, but like I said, I saw that kid all the time out there at the house, or wandering around in the junkyard. Always made me sad to think about him out there, but I didn't see him again after Freddy got killed. I don't guess there was any reason for him to ever come back to Slaterville with his daddy dead and all."

"You were at Finger's house the morning after the accident?" Kitchens posed it as a question, but it sounded a little like an accusation. Just enough.

Coffey suddenly had a look that Kitchens had seen a thousand times. He was trying to think up a lie to explain what had just slipped out. The man's eyes darted left and right and his mouth looked like he was trying to hold the words back.

Joe Kitchens was an imposing presence in any room, but particularly so in the squalid confines of the garage, looking down at the wiry little mechanic. He didn't have to say a word, but unconsciously Kitchens still exuded the intimidating aura of the intrepid FBI special agent, and battle-hardened commanding officer he had once been.

After an uncomfortable moment, to Kitchens' surprise, Coffey blurted, "I might as well confess."

Kitchens still said nothing, as Coffey continued in a guilt-ridden voice, "Let me show you. It's back here," and he started picking his way through the rubble to the back wall of the garage.

Raising a dust-laden cardboard box and tossing it over onto a stack of tires nearby, Coffey said, "Floyd and me, we stole that. It was Freddy's."

Kitchens looked down at a rusted old boat motor leaned up against the wall, and then back at Coffey.

"It was actually Floyd that took it. I just drove the pickup. Well, he made me help him carry it, but it was his idea. I always thought it kinda made it okay that it ended up right back here in Freddy's garage. Sort of like giving it back to him. We never even fired it up. We didn't have a boat. But neither did Freddy. He just had that motor. He kept it mounted on the side of an old oil drum filled with water. We drove up one time and saw him standing out there by that old well-house just revving it up and watching that water churn. Freddy was a strange cat, like I told you."

Joe Kitchens watched the mechanic study the old motor and sensed that there was more to the story. Coffey was working his mouth again and shaking his head. Kitchens just waited.

At length Coffey said quietly, "I never told anybody about that before. I always felt bad about it. Floyd never had no trouble stealing stuff, but I couldn't help it. It bothered me, and I told Floyd that. But he told me old Freddy himself was the biggest thief in the county. Maybe in Oklahoma, not counting the politicians."

Kitchens had a hunch, and decided to take a little gamble. He asked, "Did your brother know about the money?"

Coffey's mouth hung open as he turned and looked up at Kitchens, and stammered, "You mean there really was some money?"

Kitchens continued the ruse, "Oh yeah," he said nodding his head and smiling. "Oh yeah, a lot of money. That's why I'm trying to track down his son. It's rightfully his."

"That's what I told Floyd, but he was dead set on finding that money."

"That's why you were out at his house that next morning?"

"Yessir, Floyd said we had to get out there before anybody else had a chance to find it. He figured Aubrey Barstow would be nosing around out there sometime up in the day. Aubrey stays at the café all morning, no matter what. He always has. So we got up early and went, but Floyd couldn't find nothing. I think he even went back out there two or three times without me, because I told him I didn't want any part of it. He wanted that money bad, and I know he was my brother and all, but Floyd didn't think much about what was right and what was wrong. He never found it though. And then they bulldozed the whole place down. It wasn't nothing but a shack to begin with."

"How did your brother know about the money?"

"Oh he was here at the shop with Freddy one Saturday and they's doing some welding on Freddy's tow truck. Something on the rig had broke. They were having a few beers. Likely more than a few, seeing as it was Floyd and Freddy," Coffey began.

Kitchens was following as Coffey made his way to the back corner of the shop to a pile of paper and magazines that appeared to have some kind of long-buried desk beneath it, and a grease smeared percolator and a similarly grimy mug on a filing cabinet alongside.

He picked up the mug and asked jovially, "You want a cup of joe, Joe?"

"Never heard that one before," Kitchens smiled, and declined with an upraised palm and a shake of his head. "You help yourself though."

Pouring himself a cup, the mechanic said, "Everybody says I should open me a coffee shop and call it Coffey's Coffee," he said with a grin as he pulled out a couple of folding chairs from the other side of the filing cabinet, pushed one toward Kitchens, and sat on the other.

"Hey you and me could go in business together and call it Kitchens' Kitchen and Coffey's Coffee. That'd be even better."

"It would be a genuine greasy spoon," Joe answered, ruefully looking at the grease in the chair and figuring he was about to sacrifice a pair of slacks, but he knew the informality was important, if Coffey was going to supply anything more. He was clearly orchestrating the break to give himself time to think about what he was going to divulge.

Coffey chuckled, "You know I think about how it'd be to do that sometimes. I'm always by myself out here. I mean, you know, I like being around people, and if I had a little coffee shop and maybe had donuts or pie or something, I think I'd like that. The only time I really get to be around folks is at church."

Then without seeming to take a breath he asked, "Are you a Christian, Joe?" surprising Kitchens with the question.

"Well, as a matter of fact, yes I am, Len," he answered.

"So am I! Now, I wasn't always. Floyd and me, we wasn't raised to go to church or nothing like that. Momma always said she didn't have the clothes for it, and Daddy, he didn't care nothing about the Lord or the Bible or anything like that. Anyway, after they died it was just me and Floyd. And then Floyd got killed. I guess when I die there'll be no more Coffey in Slaterville," he said. Then after a second he added with a grin, "I guess they'll just have to drink tea."

He took a sip of his coffee and said, "After Floyd was gone I was pretty much by myself. Floyd wasn't good company most of the time, but at least he was company."

"Neither of you married?" Joe asked.

"Nah, all the girls in Slaterville knew better than to be interested in the Coffey brothers."

Joe had a suspicion that it was Floyd Coffey who had earned the reputation. His little brother seemed to be a pleasant enough guy.

Old Mister Pembrook, he runs the grocery store downtown, he invited me to church one day when I was in there. He's been teaching Sunday School for a hundred years I guess. Just such a good old guy," Coffey said.

"I met Mister Pembrook," Joe said. "And I agree, he is a good man. Nice old fellow."

"Well he's sure been good to me. But he's good to everybody in this town," Coffey said. "One Sunday I was in his Sunday School class. There was just three of us and him. There's never more than five or six. Anyway, Mister Pembrook was talking about how it feels to know, that every minute of every day of your life, you are acceptable to God no matter what, because Jesus became unacceptable in our place. I'd never thought about that. I didn't even know He'd done that. Did you?" Coffey spoke with a clear note of awe in his voice.

"Well I've not heard it put just like that," Kitchens replied, uncomfortable with the surprising turn the conversation had taken.

"You see, God had to turn his back and forsake His own Son, because Jesus had took all of our sins on Himself," Coffey said, his voice raising and then cracking with emotion as he continued. "I mean there He was. He had nails through His feet and His hands. Men and women were staring at Him, and He was naked and bloody up there on that cross. They were saying all kinds of things about Him, spitting at Him and cussing Him, and making fun of Him."

Coffey stopped, the scene playing before his mind painfully, as though he had been among those people. Tears welled up in his eyes and spilled over, tracking down grease smudged cheeks.

"And He was going through all that for them. He was doing it because He loved them. And then on top of all that, His own Father...God turns away, and the Holy Ghost left Him, and for a minute Jesus can't understand that. He's asking God why...why He is being left there like that on that cross alone to die. And then, you know I think it's like He remembered that was exactly what He'd come here from heaven to do. And it was done. His work was finished. And that's just what He said. Them were his last words. *It is finished!* And that was that." Len Coffey looked into the distance as though he could see it happening. Then shook his head slowly, and with grave finality said, "That's what Mister Pembrook told me that day, and I tell you, whew, that was something."

Kitchens just nodded and replied, "Well, yes sir, it was."

"I understood about being left alone, Joe," Coffey said, "But I haven't been alone since that Sunday. Mister Pembrook and them other men helped me find my way to Jesus, and He's been right here ever since," Coffey said, bumping his fist on his chest.

There was an awkward silence while Len Coffey stood looking up at the big ex-FBI agent, unashamed of the tears he continued to blink away. Kitchens was touched by the sincerity and passion of the man's testimony. He was also somewhat bemused by the realization that he was no longer the one in control of this conversation.

At length Kitchens said, "Thank you for sharing that with me, Len. Not everyone can share their feelings about the Lord that openly, especially with a stranger."

"Some things are easier to tell a stranger. Just like telling you about that motor, and this stuff about trying to find Freddy's money. I've been wanting to tell somebody about that for a long time. Don't know why I didn't. Everybody but me's dead and everything."

Kitchens let Coffey continue, still a bit awed by the little me-chanic's impromptu sermon, but now he tried to gently bring him back to the question he had asked. "You were saying that Freddy and your brother were having a few beers and that's when he told Floyd about his money?"

"Yeah, I guess Freddy got to braggin' to Floyd that he had more money than anybody in Slaterville. Maybe more than anybody in Ardmore. Said nobody knew about his stash. Not the government, not the banks, not nobody. He said one day he was going to up and build a big house down on Lake Texoma with it."

"Where'd he get the money?" Kitchens asked.

"I don't know, but I imagine a lot of it he earned right here in this shop. He did a bunch of work for the oil companies and such, and did real well. And you know he'd only take cash. Not even a check. Didn't even have a bank account. He always paid Floyd in cash mon-ey. If you'd seen how he lived, you knew he didn't spend any of it. That money had to be somewhere, Floyd always said."

Coffey raised his cup to take a sip, but first added, "And when Freddy got killed, Floyd was determined to find where he hid it."

"I didn't like the idea of stealing Freddy's money, even if he was dead and all." Then looking toward the door, as though someone might be listening, he went on, "But Floyd said it wasn't even Fred-dy's money. He said there was a lot more to it than that."

Coffey pointed to several sets of keys on nails along the edge of a shelf over the desk. He reached over and got one set.

"These are Mrs. Richardson's keys. That's her car I was under when you came in. I'm changing the oil and tuning it up today. I'm betting one of these other keys here is the key to her house. One time or another I've had the keys to all kinds of places in Slaterville. Somebody just wants their oil changed, spark plugs, belts or some-thing checked before they go on vacation, they'll just drop off the car, leave their keys in it, and get a ride home, and come back later for it or something. It doesn't happen real often," Coffey said, "But often enough. Freddy had a machine and key blanks. You get the picture?"

"Think maybe I do," Kitchens said.

"Over the years he'd collected a lot of keys to a lot of houses, and even some businesses around here. I guess he must have said something to Floyd about it, because Floyd told me Freddy Finger had something going on, and he wanted to get a piece of it. All I know is, when Floyd took over the shop he found them keys. All labeled with names and addresses."

"If Finger was using their keys to break in and rob people's houses and businesses, which I guess is what you're saying he was doing, I'd think people would have put two and two together. Surely Barstow would have," Kitchens said.

"Aubrey Barstow?" Coffey laughed, shaking his head. "I don't think so. Freddy Finger was smart as a whip. If he was using those keys to get into people's houses, nobody ever knew it. He was a whole lot smarter than anybody ever gave him credit for being. He's a whole lot smarter than Floyd. It was those keys that got Floyd killed right off."

"How was that?" Kitchens asked.

"Not long after he found them, he broke into Shorty and Evelyn Burnett's house, south of town off ninety-nine. He tried to get me in on that deal, but I wasn't having any of it. I didn't stand my ground too often with Floyd, but I did that time and I'm glad of it. I'd probably have got killed too, or got sent to the pen."

Coffey took another sip of the coffee, then wrinkled his nose and said, "Got cold while I was jawin." Standing, he poured a bit more into his cup. "You sure you don't want some of this. It's not bad. My name's not Coffey for nothing," he smiled.

"No thanks, I've had my limit," Kitchens replied, then steered the conversation back to the robbery. "You were saying your brother broke into someone's house?"

"Floyd heard that the Burnetts were going to Norman to a football game. People around here are crazy about OU you know. Sooners were playing Notre Dame that week, and ever since Notre Dame put the quietus on their 47-game winning streak back in '57, playing Notre Dame is a big deal. Everybody knew Shorty Burnett was a die-hard OU fan, and he'd be at that game."

"I suppose there was a key to the Burnett's house in Freddy's collection?" Kitchens surmised.

Len Coffey nodded, eyebrows raised, "But it turned out it was Shorty and his son-in-law, Ricky McDaniel, that were going to the game. Evelyn and her daughter were spending the weekend canning."

Coffey sucked in a deep breath, blew it out with rueful whistle and continued, "Floyd goes out there late Saturday night and lets himself in. I guess Evelyn Burnett heard him, and Evelyn Burnett, she was a feisty old country girl, you know. She caught him right square in the chest with the Sweet 16 Shorty kept loaded under their bed."

Shorty and Ricky pulled in right after it happened. Notre Dame had beat us 38 to nothing and Shorty Burnett was so mad about it that he just drove straight back home a hundred and twenty miles, and he was still mad. So if Evelyn hadn't have already woke up and shot Floyd dead, Shorty surely would have when he came in and found him prowling around their house. Either way, the temptation of them keys was bound to get Floyd killed, and it did."

"I'm sorry. It's hard to lose a brother, no matter how it happens."

"I throwed them keys away the very next day, but every time someone leaves one on their ring, it brings it back to mind. It brings Freddy Finger back to mind."

Coffey raised his shoulders and shivered. "You know, since I'm telling you every secret I got anyhow, I might as well tell you this too." The little mechanic looked around the dark recesses of the shop as he continued, "You know, I don't believe in ghosts, but if I did, I'd think old Freddy and Floyd were still hanging around this old shop," he said as another shiver ran through him.

"Sometimes I'll just be working on something right in the middle of the day, and suddenly the hair'll stand up on my arms, and old Freddy'll come to mind. And Floyd's right behind him. Like they're looking at me."

"And I'll just say. *Lord Jesus!* And I'll say it right out loud. I'll say, *Lord Jesus, thank you for saving my soul and thank you for never leaving me and never forsaking me!* Mister Pembrook told me that's what I should do, and I'm telling you it works every time. That feeling's gone after that, and then I just get back to work. I don't think I could survive the rest of my life out here without Jesus, Joe."

Kitchens said, "Maybe you should open Coffey's Coffee, Len. I'll bet you wouldn't get those feelings near as often if you weren't out here in this old place. Not a very cheerful spot to spend a life." He stood up and continued, "You're a pleasant fellow to visit with. I'll bet you'd do a good business. I enjoyed meeting you, and you've been very helpful. I appreciate it." Kitchens extended his hand.

Len Coffey stood up and gripped his hand firmly, and giving it a vigorous shake he said, "Well I pretty much told you my whole life story. I don't know how much help that could be to anybody, but I'll tell you, Joe, it felt good to tell somebody about all that. I've always been glad Floyd and me didn't find that money."

Then he added, "You know, I remember thinking, after some of the things Floyd had told me about Freddy Finger, I wondered if maybe something had happened to that little boy, and maybe Freddy felt so bad about it that he let that train hit him. Freddy had a bad temper all the time, and when he was drunk..." Coffey looked away for a moment. "Well I just always figured that kid got the raw end of things pretty often. Thought maybe Freddy just took it too far. I always kinda wondered about that. I'm glad to know I wasn't right. But I never saw him again. I hope you find him and give him old Freddy's stash. That little old boy sure didn't get nothing else. I'd see him out there at that shack by the dump, and I sure wouldn't have wanted his life for nothing. He deserved something good to happen."

"He's got a good life now, Len. I'm beginning to think He had a lot to do with that," Kitchens said, pointing a finger upwards. "Just one more thing you could tell me. How do I get out to where Finger lived."

"Sure thing, but there's nothing out there anymore. They bull-dozed the whole thing. I think all that's left is the well-house. I don't know if the city uses that well or what, but that's all that's still there."

He gave Kitchens the directions and the big man thanked the mechanic and left the shop with a smile, thinking that Len Coffey really shouldn't spend his life so isolated from people. He was a pleasant guy with a good heart. He had genuinely enjoyed their visit. Kitchens drove back up the dusty side street musing about the way Len Coffey had talked about Jesus, just as though he knew Him.

· · · ·

KITCHENS SCANNED THE side of the road as his car rattled over the railroad tracks where Freddy Finger had lost his miserable life. The place was supposed to be just a short distance down on the right, roughly halfway between the tracks and the entrance to the city dump. The caliche road dipped down from the embankment and then back up to a bald hill. He saw the small structure that he supposed was the well-house Coffey had mentioned.

Joe Kitchens wasn't sure what he could hope to learn. It had been over twelve years since Freddy Finger and his son lived here. It was obvious that a bulldozer had cleared off the house, although they didn't go to the trouble of hauling the remains the short distance over to the dump. They'd just left the rubble to rot in a pile. Enough remained that he could get a good idea of where the house had been as he pulled off the road onto parallel dirt tracks that ran through the weeds toward the well.

He stopped at the well-house and got out of the car, and was struck immediately by the rank smell of the city dump, visible just at the bottom of the hill.

"Charming locale," Kitchens muttered as he surveyed the dismal site. There were a couple of scraggy, half dead trees and some scrub around where the house had been. He carefully opened the well-house door peering down at the floor, thinking about rattlesnakes, but it was an eruption of wasps around his head that made him leap back as the door slapped shut again.

He spied the rusted remains of a 55-gallon oil drum laying on its side a few yards down the hill in a slight depression. The top and most of the bottom were missing. He guessed it might be the same one that

Coffey had said Finger had the boat motor mounted on. He walked down and looked at the shell that remained.

Kitchens found that a puzzling part of Coffey's story. A boat motor mounted on a barrel. He could understand testing a motor that way. He could see how that might make sense, but Finger didn't have a boat. Apparently running the motor in that drum was just something he liked to do. It was just sort of an anomaly though, and it bothered Kitchens. But like Len Coffey had said, Freddy Finger was a strange cat.

Resigned that there was nothing else to see, and tired of smelling the dump, he turned to go back to his car. The blast of a train whistle startled him. He'd been caught up in his thoughts and didn't notice the approaching roar of the locomotive. He stopped and watched it speed through the crossing below, thinking about Barstow's comment that Finger made a game of racing to get across in front of the train.

"Idiot," he said to himself. He had nothing but contempt for a man like Freddy Finger. He was smart, and capable, and could have done something with his life, but he had deliberately chosen to be a worthless piece of human debris.

Between the roar and clatter of the train, the stink of the dump, and the picture that he had formed of Freddy Finger as a father, Kitchens could only sympathize with the bright twelve-year-old who somehow managed to seize an opportunity to take his future into his own hands. He had erased this miserable life and started over. And he did it at twelve years old. Kitchens' admiration for Adam Pembrook was growing by the minute.

He was still looking at the train below when he took another step toward the car and his foot plummeted into a deep hole. Kitchens shin scraped against the edge of brick that lined the hole and he winced as he caught himself from falling flat on his face, both palms planted in a huge patch of goat-heads.

"Good grief!" Kitchens growled between his clinched teeth as he pulled his foot out of the hole, stood up and started plucking the stickers off his hands. Little beads of blood sprang up with every one he pulled out. His knee hurt, his shin was scraped and the blood had finished the job on the pants that Len Coffey's chair had started. He thought there was no use in ruining a good handkerchief as well, so he wiped his hands off on them too.

Then he looked at the cause of the problem and muttered, "What in world?" He squatted down to take a closer look. His knee protested, as Kitchens inspected the hole. It was about 16 inches square, and easily that deep. It had mortared brick sides. The bottom was filled with dirt, and wondering if it was covering a buried water valve, he got up with some effort and limped around looking at the ground for something he could use to dig out the dirt. He figured there had to be something he could use nearby. The ground was littered with random pieces of metal and wood.

He spied a large square of rusty iron, overgrown by weeds and grass, but it was too big. He needed something smaller. He spied what looked like an old bicycle fender in the weeds and took it back to the hole. In a couple of minutes he had discovered that the bottom was also bricked. There was no valve.

It was a curiosity for sure. One that had cost him a good pair of slacks, and he had a suspicion that his knee would remind him of it for some time to come. Nothing healed as fast as it used to. He stood up and tossed the fender aside and was just about to get into the car, when that big piece of iron he'd seen came to mind.

Kitchens limped over to where he'd found it and picked up the heavy plate. He carried it the six feet or so to the hole and put it down over the brick opening.

It was a perfect fit.

———

Then on sudden impulse he walked down and managed to work the remains of the barrel out of the weeds and dirt. It was rusted enough that it weighed next to nothing.

Kitchens carried it easily, and came back up the hill and sat it upright over the steel plate.

Looking down through the rusted-out bottom of the drum, there was the square of steel, perfectly within the circle.

"Just like it was made for it," Kitchens said, and then envisioned the drum filled with water and the big blue and silver Evinrude motor clamped to its side. He smiled as he said, "Freddy Finger's safe, with a six-hundred-pound door made of steel and water."

19

1991

• • • •

ADAM PEMBROOK SAT IN his office tapping a Monte Blanc pen on the leather blotter that covered only a fraction of the oversized mahogany desktop. The tanned jaws clenched, giving his otherwise arrestingly handsome face a pinched, grim look. His own reflection caught his eye in the large mirror mounted in an ornate gilded frame above the leather sofa at the opposite end of his office. He stood and walked straight to the mirror, looking like a man about to throw a punch.

He stopped and glared into the penetrating blue-gray eyes in the mirror. Unbridled, naked hate lay thick between the eyes of the man and the unblinking eyes staring back. Pembrook didn't see the groomed hair or the perfectly tailored suit. It was the face of his father that glowered back in contempt from within the glass, and across time.

"I never saw your face that clean, you filthy moron." The sound of his own voice brought him back to the moment, and Adam glanced up to be sure that his door was still closed. He chanced another glance at the mirror, but now the image was his own. He turned his back on the reflection and walked back to his desk. Adam didn't even remember what the Moron's hair had looked like, covered as it always was in a grease-stained ball cap. Sweat. He always seemed to be sweating. Likely sweating out the previous night's booze.

In Pembrook's mind, that banged up piece of junk 40-something model flatbed tow-truck, with the noise of its loud mufflers and the chains of the towing harness clanging, roared out of a cloud of chalky dust from the road and rattled to a lurching stop in the square of hard-packed, oil-soaked dirt and stickers they called the front yard.

The Moron's voice rasped out yet another in a relentless string of foul threats directed at the scrawny boy standing behind the sagging screen door of the stinking hovel, where Freddy Finger returned like a dog to its vomit every night.

20

1991

• • • •

AS MEREDITH TURNED off the pavement and began to nego-
tiate the two miles of winding road up to the lake, she thought, as
she always did, that time seemed to stand still down here. It always
had. She wondered if they had lost that too, when her mother died.
Would the lake and the cabin have that abandoned feeling that her
folk's house now had? Would it have the sad vacancy of their studio
at Warner & Crewe?

Since he had come up here, her dad was sounding more like himself when she had talked to him on the phone, so maybe there would
be something of the old feeling left here for her too. It had always
been a place of sanctuary, and more than anything right now, Meredith Pembrook needed a peaceful respite where she could sort things
out.

At the first water crossing Macy woke up. She had been asleep before they left the city, stretched out on the pallet Meredith had made
down for her in the back of the Wagoneer. Now she bounded over
the back of the seat to plop down on top of her brother, who was
sprawled across the back seat reading a comic book.

"Macy! Gah!" Andy bawled at his sister. "Get off me!"

"Kids, knock it off," Meredith said, glancing into the rear-view
mirror and seeing the gleeful face of her seven-year-old bouncing as
her older brother tried to pitch her off into the floorboard.

"She's messing up my stuff," Andy groused. "You've got the whole
back, Macy! Get back there and get off me!"

"We're almost there, guys. Settle down. No fighting," Meredith
said mildly. "Macy, get off of your brother right now." In the mirror

she glimpsed her daughter's tiny bottom and flailing legs as Macy dived over the back of the seat and onto her nest of blankets.

Meredith rolled down her window and inhaled the woodland air. At least that hadn't changed. It brought back a hundred images of rattling up this old road, watching the treetops from her own pallet as a little girl, and listening to her mom and dad talking and laughing together in the front seat.

Uncle Arnie had come along sometimes, and those were her favorite memories, because the four of them would play cards and board games, and Uncle Arnie would row out onto the lake with her. They would fish together, or sit on the wide porch and read side-by-side while her parents hiked and sketched in the woods and along the lake.

Meredith had a special connection with her uncle. Neither of them was remotely artistic. Arnie certainly had an appreciation for the work her mother and father did, but like her, he was baffled and disinterested in the thought of trying to do it. Instead, Arnie reveled in the business side of Warner & Crewe, and in his way, he was just as innovative as were her parents on the creative side.

She couldn't appreciate that until she was grown. Really not until she graduated and took a position in marketing at Warner & Crewe, working directly under her uncle's supervision. Arnold Warner was a unique hybrid of hard-nosed intolerance, and unequivocal support. Every person who gained admittance to his domain was the recipient of both sides, the carrot and the stick.

Everyone except Adam, Meredith thought, as again she found herself replaying the conversation she so wanted and so dreaded to have with her uncle.

Uncle Arnie, why do you refuse to trust my husband? Don't you realize how that makes me feel? There is nothing Adam wants more than your approval and support. He has done everything you have asked him to do. Everything! But you just refuse to give him even a hint of encour-

agement! Why? What has he ever done that would make you so pig-headed about my husband, when you will give glowing accolades to any-body on the line, or any sales rep?

She willed herself to stop the internal tirade against her uncle as she topped the hill and the lake came into view below. But it was all true.

After thirteen years of working to earn Arnie Warner's trust, and in spite of some brilliant successes negotiating manufacturing and distribution contracts that had opened the door to great expansion of the Warner & Crew brand, Adam Pembrook remained on the outside looking in. There were many things about her husband that troubled Meredith Pembrook, but his business acumen and passion about his work at Warner & Crewe were not among them.

Adam had developed a daring and innovative proposal for the future of the venerable company that was exciting to imagine. He had been immersed in his research for months. Meredith too, had made a significant contribution to the project, with exhaustive testing of the business model her husband designed, throwing herself into the work in the wake of her mother's death.

But when Adam had made the presentation to Arnie, he seemed to take the whole thing as an affront, and dismissed it out of hand. He was brusque, and even seemed defensive when Meredith tried to get her uncle to reconsider the possibilities. For the first time, Meredith had a personal taste of what Adam had dealt with from day one at Warner & Crewe. It had crushed her.

Adam was brilliant, there was no doubt in anyone else's mind, but Arnold Warner seemed determined not to see it. Now she was caught in the middle. With her mom gone and her dad having turned the operation of Warner & Crewe fully over to Uncle Arnie, everything had changed. It felt like everything, the company, her marriage, her whole life was under assault. Meredith hoped, as she caught the first glimpses of the cabin through the trees, that this weekend would be a much-needed respite.

The sign hung above the gate as it always had, but it looked recently varnished. The relief carving that her dad had done to frame the ornate lettering of the Latin word caught the dappled sunlight, and it shone brightly in the muted light beneath the trees.

Reviresco...I grow strong again. Just what I need, Meredith thought as she turned off the engine and soaked in that first chorus of a thousand birds carried on a gentle Ozark breeze through the dancing canopy of oak and sycamore leaves.

It was a short-lived reverie. Macy's delighted squeal, "We're there!" and Andy's predictable, "Gah, Macy! Scream in my ear why don't you!" ended the delicious moment of serenity. Meredith smiled and waved as her dad stepped out of the cabin onto the wide veranda that surrounded the front and sides of the log structure.

"Oh my gosh! A beard?" Meredith laughed as she got out of the Wagoneer and met Mason with an embrace. "Whatever possessed you to grow a beard?"

"You like it?" he answered. "I didn't shave for a couple of days and thought, oh what the heck."

"Might take a little getting used to, but yeah, I think it suits you. And you're all tanned. You look great, Daddy! Healthy," she said.

"Reviresco," he answered.

"I saw the sign. Looks new again. It is a magical place, Dad. I need some of that right now," she said.

"You look like Santa Claus, Grandpop," Macy said as Mason swept her up in his arms and looked with concern across the little shoulders at Meredith's pinched expression, while Macy wrapped her arms around his neck, the hug accompanied by heartwarming noises of childish delight. Then she drew back, hunched her shoulders and wrinkled her nose. "Sort of like hugging a big puppy."

"A big puppy? You crazy little monkey," Mason laughed as he put a giggling Macy down to give Andy a squeeze and said, "I hardly have to lean down to give you a hug anymore, Andy. It's only been a few months and I think you've grown a foot."

"What can I carry?" he asked Meredith, who had opened the back of the Wagoneer and started pulling out backpacks and bags and distributing them to the kids.

Taking her own suitcase toward the cabin she said over her shoulder, "The groceries. I brought a few things so we wouldn't leave your cupboard bare. Oh, and those fittings are in a hardware store bag right here by the tailgate. Hope we got the right things. I gave your list to Adam and he picked them up."

The next morning, Mason was up early as usual, making the morning coffee, and moving quietly, hoping not to wake Meredith and the kids. This had always been his favorite time of day at the lake, and he liked to savor it.

The cabin was a constant, in an ever-changing world, it seemed. Even with the void left by Annie, Mason had found a measure of solace there. He had wondered whether it was his renewed sense of purpose, or the place itself with all the vivid memories it evoked. Either way, *Reviresco* had done its job, or had begun to, and Mason felt, for the first time in a long time, like he was standing on solid ground.

He realized that having Meredith and the kids here seemed to validate his confidence in this newly discovered normalcy. Even as he thought it, Mason acknowledged to himself that *normalcy* might be a bit of a stretch.

Part of his feeling of well-being, he knew, had been his ongoing...what was it, a fantasy? Mason didn't care if that was all it was. It had helped. It felt like having Annie with him, and it had been pleasant. Almost joyful compared to the months of dismal existence he had endured since his wife's death.

Here, without the concern he had about Arnie or Meredith dropping in unexpectedly, as they were inclined to do at his home in the city, and possibly finding him engrossed in a conversation with a bird in the back yard, Mason had enjoyed freely indulging himself in the possibility—*the undeniable possibility of Poofs*. That is what he and Annie had always called it. Now he had truly begun to entertain the notion that their speculations about Poofs were true. Or at least, the part about departed loved ones being able to make themselves visible as very natural-looking creatures. Birds in particular.

Mason justified it with the biblical account of God doing exactly that when Jesus was baptized by John. Of course, He was God and He could do anything, but Mason took it as evidence of truth in what he and Annie had talked about through all those years of sculpting the Warner & Crewe figurines together.

Of course, they had made up wild stories about the Poofs rescuing their future grandchildren from all sorts of danger, by great feats of coordinated chicanery. What Mason had decided could be the more likely reality of Poofs, was experienced simply in fleeting moments of reassurance. It was a palpable, encouraging feeling that seemed to be communicated on a level apart from thought, at the appearance of a bird, landing on a nearby branch, or outside the kitchen window.

It didn't happen every time, but when it did, there was a sense of recognition and connection that Mason could not deny. Now that he was deliberately embracing the possibility, it seemed that he was almost constantly looking up and seeing a bird, a butterfly, or one evening in the kitchen, even a housefly, and sensing that same brush of contact.

It was as though Annie was taking every opportunity to say it so clearly that he could almost hear the words, *"I'm right here, Fernando! I'm just one step away. Do you think that body I left was me? Look at me! Just look at what I can do! I can be anything I want to be. We were right! I'm a Poof!"*

Mason was sitting in a rocker on the porch, looking out over the glassy surface of the lake as the day came alive to the surreal colors of the sunrise. A cacophony of calls came from the woods that surrounded the water. He and Annie had photographed and sketched hundreds of different kinds of birds here over the years. They all seemed to gather to raise a chorus to the morning, and Mason smiled at the thought of Annie blissfully joining that glorious choir, just for the sheer joy of it.

21
1991

· · · ·

THE SCREEN DOOR CREAKED open and Meredith came padding out quietly in a robe, carrying a blanket over her arm, a cup of coffee in one hand and the pot in the other.

"Mind some company?"

She leaned down, kissed Mason on the cheek and refilled his cup as he said, "Love some. Did you sleep well?"

"Better than I have in weeks. I've always slept like a stone up here," she answered, dropping the blanket on the porch swing and putting her cup on the cedar railing before going to take the pot back inside. "Do you want some toast or anything, Dad?"

"Not now, just the coffee, thanks sweetheart," Mason replied.

His relationship with Meredith had always been easy. It was a curiosity to him that he could see so little of himself in her, nor much of Annie. Instead, she was very much like Arnie in so many ways. She had his pragmatic, forthright nature, and although not humorless, and always pleasant, Meredith had, since childhood, tended toward a somber disposition.

Since they had arrived the previous afternoon, Mason had sensed that she was even more subdued than normal. He thought it could be just being there without Annie. Meredith and the kids had often joined them at the cabin for weekends.

Adam had never appeared to enjoy the place, or perhaps it was being in such close quarters with his in-laws that he didn't enjoy. They worked together, and took lunch as a group several times a week. Mason could understand him wanting to have a break from them. For whatever reason, Adam always seemed to find a conflict that prevented him from coming along. He had been to the lake only a handful of times over the years that they had been married.

Meredith reappeared through the screen door, and wrapping herself in the blanket, sat in the porch swing and sipped her coffee looking out over the lake, "I hope it never changes up here," she said after a moment.

"Me too," Mason answered, "But we know things change."

"It seems to have done you good to be here. Has it been hard?" she asked, leaving off the *without Mom* that both of them knew she meant.

"It's been okay," he answered lightly, almost as if it was a surprise to himself. Then without thinking about it long enough to reconsider he said, "I've found something that's really been a help dealing with missing your mom. It's a secret she and I have had for a long, long time. I think maybe it's time I told you."

"A secret? Really? That's kind of intriguing. So what is it?" Meredith answered.

"Well it may sound sort of out there, unless I told you how it all began, but here it is," and Mason told her. He began with the story about the time he showed Annie the stained-glass panel and told her the story of Cher Ami. Then he told her about the Poof stories behind all the figurines that he and Annie had created over the years.

Mason was more animated than Meredith had seen him since her mother's death, and it delighted her to see him talking and laughing about their times together.

When he finally stopped to refill his coffee, Meredith said, "That's incredible. And you never even told Uncle Arnie about these...*Poofs*?"

Mason leaned back and sipped his coffee. "No, never did. You're the only other person that's ever known about them. We were afraid that if we told anyone it would take away some of the magic or something. And it was just fun keeping the secret. So many times we would almost slip and say something about *poofing* into this or that when we kicked the bucket. In a family business, you don't have too many secrets, as you well know."

There was a long pause. Uncomfortable for Meredith, because she was thinking that he was alluding to the problems between she and Adam, and trying to imagine how he found out. For Mason, it was uncertainty about how Meredith would take it when he told her that he thought Poofs could possibly be real.

At last he chose to just say it. "The thing is, I think we might have been right."

"Right about what?"

"Right about Poofs. I think maybe your mom and I had it right. Or at least partly right."

"What do you mean, Dad? You're saying you think people really do *poof* into animals when they die? That's pretty weird, you know," she said, trying to be delicate, but failing. She punctuated the comment with a little laugh, which didn't help.

"I know it sounds strange, honey, and I don't want you to think I'm off my rocker. I'm not saying that this is absolutely the way it works, but for years your mom and I have talked about the possibility, and now that she's gone, there have just been some things that have convinced me that maybe it really is true."

"Things...like what?" Meredith asked.

"Little things. A bird will light on a branch nearby when I'm out here in the morning and it'll be perfectly natural, but I'll just get this feeling. I don't know how to explain it, but it feels like she's out here with me. I'll find my eye drawn to the bird, and it's like there's this...moment." Mason stopped, feeling a little dismayed because the words sounded far-fetched even to him. The look on Meredith's face left no doubt that they did to her.

But he went on in spite of her expression, "It's only a momentary sensation. Like I get just a glimpse. Just a tiny glimpse of your mom.

It's not like I see her, but more like, I don't know, like a whiff of her perfume might be. It's like this sweet glance, just between the two of us, like we shared a million times when we'd have some inside joke between us in a room full of people. Or I'd say something stupid and look up and she'd catch my eye. That kind of glance, you know? And sometimes when I'm missing her so badly, that glance is...well, it's just everything."

Mason was quiet for a moment and Meredith's eyes filled with tears as she saw the sadness return that had clouded his once jovial face. All of her life she had thought her dad's face always appeared to be just on the brink of a laugh, as though he was anticipating every conversation to end in a punch line. And if it didn't, he was likely to supply it. She had missed that. Seeing it there again when they had arrived, and this morning as he had been talking about these *Poofs* he and her mother had invented, she had realized how much she had longed to see the corners of his mouth slightly turned up, the creases around his eyes, looking as though he was the only one getting the joke. She could see that her reaction had taken that away again.

She couldn't bear that and said, "Daddy, I'm sorry if I sound skeptical. It isn't that I don't believe what you're experiencing. It's just a little...different, you have to admit. But I loved hearing about the Poofs and how you and Mom used that idea to make the pieces you created so magical. I just want to look at every one of them again now, and hear the stories."

Mason, unable to help being a little dismayed that she was trying to deflect what he was telling her, said, "I know it's weird for you, honey. I don't want you to think I'm delusional or anything. It's just that your mom and I talked about the possibility of Poofs for so many years that it feels like they've always been part of my life."

He looked across the lake and squinted as the morning sun reflected off the water, "And I'll tell you, right at first, when I started getting these sensations, I pushed the idea away myself. I thought maybe I was losing my marbles, but then I decided that even if it was all in my head, and I was just inventing this way I could imagine that she was stopping by to check in on me…it comforts me. It really does, honey. So why would I not just embrace it, and be thankful?"

Meredith found herself wanting to believe her dad's *undeniable possibility,* in spite of her innate skepticism. If anyone's love could transcend the barrier of the grave, it would be theirs. She had no doubt about that.

Meredith measured her own marriage by their example, and found it lacking in every respect. She and Adam were so different from her folks, in personality and every other way. They were both intense. Adam far more so, but both were inclined toward focused work, whereas Meredith's impression of both her parents, growing up, was that they *played* for a living.

Not that they were unproductive, because their creative output was prodigious, and exquisite. And it wasn't just that they always tended to *cut up* as her dad liked to put it. But it did seem, as he had mentioned, that there was always a running joke, or some continuing dialogue on a frequency just between them, that made it appear as though the two of them were never disconnected, even when separated by a room full of people.

It was no surprise to her at all that they would have a secret like *Poofs* that they enjoyed keeping, even from their daughter and their business partner.

Meredith and Adam had nothing like that. Nothing remotely like that, Meredith acknowledged sadly. She wondered if they had anything at all, aside from the kids and the company.

In the small hours of the morning, lying beside Adam and staring into the darkness, Meredith would try to remember the thrill of falling in love with him. She would try to remember what it felt like for him to be everything she had ever wanted. Her tears were the only proof that what she had felt for him was still dear to her.

It was there, when they were close enough that each could feel the heat of the other's body, and remember, that Meredith knew she and Adam were both lying there alone.

"Does it really trouble you that much, honey?" Mason said.

"What? Oh no, Daddy. I was just thinking. It always makes me sad to talk about Mom, and I guess I especially miss her right now. Some things have been going on that I just really wish I could—" Her chin quivered and she pressed her fist against her lips, trying to quell the sudden rush of emotion.

"Mommy I'm hungry," a small voice interrupted. Macy's pixy face, framed in a frizzy nest of blond hair was pressed against the inside of the screened door. She held a stuffed bunny against the front of the pink polka-dot footie pajamas she wore.

Standing up and putting his face down against the outside of the screen, Mason answered for Meredith as she composed herself, "Hungry? Hungry? You want me to catch you a fish?"

"Not fish! Not for breakfast, Grandpop."

"How about...turtle soup? I saw a big turtle out on a rock this morning, and I bet I could catch him and make some soup out of him."

"Yucky!" Macy answered.

"Frog-legs it is then. Frog-legs for breakfast always puts a spring in my step," Mason said. "I'll just go catch a few frogs!"

"No, Grandpop. Not frog's legs. How could they jump if we eat their legs? I don't want any," Macy said with an exaggerated shake of her tousled head.

"Okay then, how about a stack of Grandpop's signature pancakes, you little fuzzyhead?"

A pink blur whirled and whizzed away into the dim light inside the cabin yelling, "Pancakes! Grandpop's making pancakes!"

A distant, *Shut up, Macy! Gah! I was asleep. Get off my bed!* followed by a fit of giggles, and the sound of little feet running around the hardwood floors inside the cabin, signaled time to get up and start breakfast.

As they started to go inside, Mason turned to Meredith and said, "Honey, I know it's not the same as talking to your mom, but whatever it is that's going on, I wish you'd let me help if I can."

"Thanks Daddy, maybe we can take a walk later and talk about it. I don't want the kids to overhear. And don't worry. It's just a rough patch that Adam and I are going through. I'm sure it'll pass."

It was the middle of the afternoon before Mason and Meredith had a chance to take that walk. Macy was taking a nap and Andy had an assortment of comic books scattered over the dining table and was hunched over a big sketchpad, pencil gripped tightly in his fingers, intent upon copying a fierce-looking dragon from one of the books.

Mason was pulling on a sweater as he walked into the main room of the cabin. Noticing his grandson's concentration, he quietly looked over Andy's shoulder at his drawing, raising his eyebrows in approval. "I think you're getting it, Andy. Wow, you really have a talent for drawing, you know. Not everybody can do something like that."

Andy didn't look up, flipped the pencil in his hand and applied the eraser to a large piece of what he had just drawn. "Thanks, but I can't make the fire coming out of his mouth look right. And my smoke looks stupid. It's kind of pointless to draw a dragon if you can't draw smoke and fire."

"Yeah, fire's hard. Can I show you a trick? I don't want to mess up your drawing. Let me show you on another page."

While Andy was flipping to a new page of his sketchbook, Mason went to an old roll-top desk in a small nook off the main room and rummaged through the little drawers and cubbies. He returned with what appeared to be a plastic prescription bottle.

Holding up the bottle and popping off the plastic top Mason said, "Now this is my own invention, so you have to keep it a secret," as he tipped over the small brown plastic bottle and tapped on its side. Fine dark gray powder spilled out onto the paper. Mason produced a small cotton ball that he held between his thumb and finger, and gently rubbed the powder across the page, creating a light gray tone over that area of the paper.

"This is graphite, just like your pencil lead. See inside the bottle, I glued a piece of sandpaper, rough-side out. I've always used this to sharpen my drawing pencils. The sandpaper grinds off the graphite and gives you a nice sharp point, and you capture all this magic graphite powder that you can use like this," Mason said revealing a small piece of kneaded eraser that he'd found among his drawing supplies.

He flattened the eraser, and with a few quick, light strokes he had created some very realistic flames and smoke within the toned area of the paper.

"Then you can go back in with some darks, like this," he said, holding the pencil sideways and making broad black swirling lines. "And here is the magic," he added, holding up a small white block of another type of eraser, "Will give you some even cleaner highlights." And he touched the drawing here and there, which resulted in an animated response from his grandson.

"Gah, Grandpop! That's great! Mom, look at this smoke and fire Grandpop drew!"

"Shhh! Your sister is asleep," Meredith said. "Your Grandpop is an amazing artist, Andy. Didn't you know that?"

Andy was already trying to copy the effect, "Yeah, but I didn't know he could draw fire."

"I was so good at drawing fire it almost got me killed once," Mason said.

"What?" Andy said, whirling around in his chair.

"That's right, and I've still got the scars to prove it. But that's a story for another day when you're a little older." Then directing Andy back to his drawing, he said, "Now don't rub the graphite in too hard. Just very lightly with the cotton. There you go, that's right."

Mason took a hat from among an assortment on the rack by the door. Several were Annie's, and he hesitated for a wistful moment before turning with a gray tweed Irish walking hat in his hand. "Sweetheart, I want to show you what I've been working on. Andy, can you hold down the fort while your mom and I take a little walk?"

"Sure, Grandpop."

Meredith picked up a sweater and slipped it on. She pulled a couple of tissues from her purse. If the conversation with her father went the direction she thought it might, she knew she would need them.

22
1991

• • • •

IT USED TO BE JUST a trail up through the trees, but Mason had widened it, and laid paving bricks. There were two or three steps at intervals that made it an easy climb.

"You've done all this by yourself?" Meredith asked as they walked up the path arm in arm.

"Not by myself. Otto's been giving me a hand with it. You remember Otto Ericsson, of course. I've really enjoyed working with him. His boys are grown now. They were all three little when we met Otto."

Meredith looked rueful, "Grown? I remember them. They were such cute little boys."

"They're still good looking, just not so little," Mason smiled. "They brought out the brick and unloaded it, and did most of the shovel work too."

The path had several switchbacks as it ascended, with little bridges over a small brook that snaked down the hill to the lake. The walk up was pleasant under the dappled sunlight. Meredith soaked in the tranquility of it as she listened to her dad prattling on pleasantly.

"Otto's been worth his weight, all these years of keeping an eye on things out here. No telling how many things he's fixed that he never even charged us for. I think he and Lucille love the place as much as we do."

Meredith said, "I'm glad there's someone up here you can call if you ever—" Then she realized how what she was about to say would sound, and stopped. Since her mother's death, he had seemed to age. Until then, she had never thought of her dad as *old*. It would have never occurred to her that he might need someone to look after him.

He had always been so obviously capable of doing anything he set out to do.

"If I ever fell and broke a hip or something?" he chuckled, completing her thought. Well, I'm still pretty solid, and this work I've been doing with Otto has been good for me. I've enjoyed every minute of it. But, yeah, it's nice to have someone close-by that I could call if I needed to."

They rounded a final turn, and a clearing opened in the trees. Meredith caught her breath. "Oh my goodness, Daddy, it's beautiful!"

It was a large three-tiered fountain, surrounded by a low walled pond. Two concrete benches flanked the pond on either side.

Mason walked around pointing out various areas as he spoke, while Meredith stood admiring the fountain.

"It isn't finished, of course. There will be plantings here and over on that side, and along the path up I'm planning to make some beds of perennials." He seemed a little nervous as he talked about his plans.

Meredith was still studying the fountain. "You sculpted this? My gosh, Dad, it's just gorgeous. This is bronze?"

"Yeah. It's definitely a one of a kind."

It was more like a large sculpture than a traditional tiered fountain. It had the appearance of a sinewy tree, but its trunk was actually three thick intertwined vines that rose gracefully to divide into a canopy of cascading clusters of leaves and flowers. The vines cradled three descending basins. Water flowed from one basin to the next, and into the pond, and it trickled down from the flower clusters creating the effect of a gentle rain.

"It's a wisteria vine, like in the back yard at home," Meredith said, looking at the detail in wonder.

It was a stunning piece of work. A large bird, beautifully rendered in bronze, was mounted on the rim of the top tier. It looked out from the shade with a quizzical, expectant posture.

"I love the bird. A dove, right?"

Mason answered, "Yes, I went back and forth on what kind to make it. I wanted to make it a cardinal, but chose the dove because of the size, mainly."

"You mean because of the scale of the piece?" Meredith asked.

"No, because of its capacity. Its function."

"Function?"

"Have a seat," Mason said, as he sat and patted the bench beside him. "I'm sure you realize that the dove represents your mom."

"Mom *poofed* into a dove. Yeah, I got that. I mean, I wouldn't have if you hadn't told me the story, but I see it."

"Well, there's a little more to it than that. I've done two more doves that will be mounted on the fountain sometime later. One for me, and one for Arnie, if he agrees to it."

"Agrees to it?" Meredith asked.

Mason fidgeted for a moment, then decided to go ahead and just say it, "I sealed your mom's ashes in the dove."

Meredith turned to look at the dove with an expression Mason couldn't quite interpret. He had been worried that the whole idea might sound macabre, but it had seemed so perfect when it first struck him. He really hadn't considered how Meredith might take it.

She was just staring at the dove through the droplets of water that glistened as they gathered and fell with a melodic patter from the clusters of flowers into the pond below. Mason saw a tear course down her cheek and her lip tremble as a gentle sob caught in her throat.

"Daddy...it's perfect."

Mason's own eyes spilled over as Meredith turned and put her arms around him, "I know she would love it."

"I think she does," he whispered.

They sat there quietly for a time, both enjoying the feeling of serenity that the soft pitter-patter of droplets seemed to cast over the place. A few birds fluttered in and landed here and there on the sculpture, hopping in and out of the basins and shaking themselves before plunging back into the water.

Mason pondered something that he had noticed many times before. These birds did not strike him as anything but ordinary birds. It was this total absence of any kind of impression or feeling of connection that had most convinced him that Poofs might be real. It was obvious, although in no consciously discernible way, that most birds were merely birds.

It was a strange subtlety when he saw a bird that he thought might be Annie...or his dad, mom, or grandfather. Mason had experienced two distinct and sudden thoughts of his father as he had been working on the fountain, only to look up and see, on the first occasion a large thrush, and on another a dove perched on a nearby branch. Nothing like goose-bumps ever occurred, although it had struck him that the term was a little ironic.

It was as natural for him to be there with Mason in this form, as it would have been when his father was still alive. When the dove appeared, it was a day when Otto was not helping him, so Mason had actually indulged himself in stopping his work, pouring a cup of coffee from his thermos and sitting on one of the benches and chatting out loud about his progress on the fountain.

He glanced often at the dove as he talked about how the water from the spring above was being routed into the fountain to create sufficient pressure, and explained how the network of hidden tubing would create the overall effect of a gentle spring shower.

There was nothing unusual in the way the dove behaved. It made a typical cooing sound from time to time, turned its head from side to side, but it seemed content to sit there on the branch as Mason spoke.

And then it flew away as naturally as any other bird might, or as naturally as his dad might have gone off with his fishing pole and tackle box in hand. Mason had smiled after him, and again experienced that distinct feeling of comforting reassurance.

He said with a laugh as the bird flew out of sight, "Nice of you to stop by, Dad. Of course, your son may be officially losing his marbles now, but I really enjoyed the visit." Then after a moment Mason had felt his eyes tearing up as he added, "I hope you'll do it again soon. I sure miss you, Pop."

Meredith was marveling at the absolute peace of the place. She looked through the glittering droplets at the sculpture of the dove that contained her mother's ashes, surrounded by an assortment of birds frolicking in the water. It felt like a perfect culmination, seeing her mother actually become part of this beautiful creation.

She blinked away tears as she thought about a time when her dad and uncle Arnie would join her mother as part of the sculpture. And it occurred to her that she would love to think that she also might be included when that time came. Each of them, one by one.

"It's your masterpiece, Dad," Meredith said, squeezing his hand. "Just perfect."

After sitting a few more moments in comfortable silence, Meredith gathered her courage, and brought up the real reason she had wanted to come up to the lake. Once she began, it all came out in a gush.

"I told you that Adam and I have been going through a rough patch. Well, Daddy, it's really more than that, and I honestly don't know what the outcome is going to be."

"The thing is, it all seems to be centered around the company. Our life is so entangled with things that go on at work, and the problems there. I think it's getting to the point that..." She felt her throat constricting and she struggled to say, "My marriage may be over."

Shocked, Mason said, "Honey, I had no idea you and Adam were having this kind of trouble. How long has this been going on?"

And as he said that, Mason realized that he really had no idea about what was going on in anyone else's life. He had been so consumed by his grief that he had simply walked away from the world. Even from his daughter.

If both Meredith and Arnie hadn't made the effort to routinely stop by the house, he knew that he could have easily sat alone, lost in his memories of Annie, waiting to join her. That had been all he wanted to do. Everything else was just going through the motions.

He felt suddenly guilty for indulging himself in such weakness, and not even knowing that Meredith was in trouble.

Her voice broke through the wave of self-recrimination that Mason was feeling. "He's so frustrated with Uncle Arnie. You know how he treats Adam. He always has. I feel caught in the middle and I try to explain Uncle Arnie's position, but I really can't, because I don't get it either. But then Adam feels like I'm taking sides against him."

She stopped and caught her breath. "It's just all changed so much without you and Mom there, Dad. It isn't the same company, and Uncle Arnie has his hand in Adam's face constantly. He's never liked him. He's never trusted him. When you were there, it seemed like Uncle Arnie at least gave him the benefit of the doubt. But he sure doesn't anymore."

Mason took in what Meredith was saying, and had no doubt it was true. Arnie had seemed to take a dislike to Adam before the kids ever married. He had not seemed enthusiastic about bringing Adam into the company, but he never voiced any real reason for his reservations. Meredith's excitement about having her new husband working in the family business, and Arnie's devotion to his niece had seemed to quell his doubts, whatever they had been. At least at first.

After Adam came on board, he proved his value time and time again, but Arnie still seemed to resist embracing him, not only as part of the company, but part of the family. Mason and Annie had speculated that Arnie felt some territorial jealousy toward Adam, because the boy was nothing short of brilliant, and had presented an unending stream of ideas to streamline and improve virtually every facet of manufacturing, warehousing, distribution, and marketing. But Arnie had put on the brakes, and kept them on, when it came to Adam Pembrook.

Neither Mason nor Annie understood their partner's attitude toward their son-in-law. However, that part of the company was Arnie's arena, and as partners, they had always respected the boundaries between the creative side and the operations side. Still, over the years he and Annie had both offered diplomatic support of Adam's proposals and suggestions on occasion. Arnie's response had always been a curiously disproportionate pique that almost always escalated into a few tense moments of confrontation erupting between him and his sister.

Adam Pembrook had truly been the only serious point of contention between the partners over the years. They had always operated in somewhat remarkable harmony.

They had adopted a passage of Scripture, Ecclesiastes 4:12, as a motto early on: *And if one prevails against him, two shall withstand him; and a threefold cord is not quickly broken.* It had proved itself to be true, until Annie's death had severed that threefold cord.

Mason said at length, "I'll talk to Arnie. Honey, I'm sorry this has been going on and I haven't been there to help. Maybe I can do something." But he seemed at a loss about what that might be.

Meredith could see that her dad was not confident about changing her uncle's attitude toward Adam, and she hadn't expected him to.

"Really, Daddy, I don't want you to do that. Uncle Arnie and things at work are just part of it. Adam and I have bigger problems than that to try to sort out. What I'd like for you to do is keep the kids up here for a few days so we can have some time alone together. I know that's a lot to ask, but—-"

"No it isn't. I would love to have them here with me. I've missed them both. It'll be good for me, and maybe you and Adam can find a calm place in the storm. All marriages have their stormy times, you know."

Mason continued, "You said there are bigger things. Anything you want to talk about?"

"Well, you know I've told you Adam has always been closed about his past...his childhood. Secretive. It even makes him angry to be asked about it. He refuses to talk about anything before college. It seems like over the last few years that there's something that just continues to trouble him. And the only real problem he's had since we first met is trying to earn Uncle Arnie's respect. Everything else has been good. Great, in fact."

Mason watched his daughter, knowing how much better Annie would be at this. His eyes scanned the trees around them, wishing for a glimpse. But there was nothing.

"I've wondered if maybe it stems from his childhood. I think if he would just open up to me about some of that, maybe it would help. He seems to have, I don't know, just a lot of anger that I think he has sort of bottled up. I always thought it was just about Uncle Arnie, because that's all he would ever talk about that bothers him. But I think there's something else, and he just won't talk to me about it. I'm going to see if he'll consider seeing a counselor."

What Meredith was not saying was that Adam had always been impatient, but now he had begun to exhibit a temper that was both short and fierce. Over recent years he had verbally lashed out several times at her, but on one recent occasion, Adam had appeared to struggle to restrain himself from physically striking her. It had been her own instinctive flinching from the coming blow that had seemed to have awakened him to what he was doing.

He was genuinely remorseful, and had apologized with what seemed to be deeply grieved sincerity. Nevertheless, since that time Meredith had been afraid. More afraid for the children than herself. Afraid for Andy in particular, because his serious nature made him appear almost sullen at times, and that attitude seemed to inflame Adam's temper.

She was apprehensive about confronting Adam, but convinced that it was the only thing she could do. She would try. She had to try to get him to talk to her.

And she had resolved that she was going to talk to Arnie Warner herself. She loved and respected her uncle second only to her father, but he was wrong about Adam, and she was determined to tell him that.

She had not intended to tell her father about that part of her plan, but his restored accessibility made it easy to open up to him, just as she always had, and before she realized it, the words were out of her mouth.

"As far as Uncle Arnie goes, Dad, I think I want to talk to him about Adam. I never have had the courage to ask him what his problem with my husband is, but it's become obvious that he has one. Do you have any advice about how to approach him?"

Mason studied his daughter for a moment, and recognized that she had a measure of gravity that he had not acknowledged before. He had no doubt that she could hold her own with Arnie, if this confrontation with her uncle should be difficult.

"Arnie loves you, Honey. You know that. You can just talk to him. Maybe he'll level with you. I really would be happy to drive in and have that conversation myself. It may be that—"

Mason was interrupted by a high-pitched scream from below. The sound carried clearly from the lake up to the clearing in the woods, and both he and Meredith were up and scrambling down the bricked path in panic when they heard a second scream that both recognized as a terrified Macy.

Then the rising strident voice of Andy followed, "Macy! Macy! Mom! Grandpop! Mom!" Mason bolted out of the woods near the lake shore with Meredith a good twenty paces behind.

Mason took in a stricken-looking Andy huddled protectively over his little sister at the edge of the water. Macy was wet and crying, and he was caressing her shoulder and talking in a low consoling voice, his face resting on her dripping blonde ringlets.

"Is she alright? Andy? Is she okay?" Mason asked as he dropped down beside them in the sand.

"Are they alright, Daddy? Andy? Macy are you hurt?' Meredith shrieked as she fell on her knees by Mason and searched their faces for something. Anything. Her heart was pounding in her ears.

"She's fine now, Mom," Andy said with a new note of maturity in his voice as he released Macy to their mother's frantic inspection, and a relieved embrace. Macy couldn't seem to quit crying, and Meredith rocked her gently in her lap.

"I'm sorry I scared you, but she scared the crap out of me."

Mason, in his relief, almost laughed at his grandson's comment, but fought it back. The boy was still white and shaking.

Exhausted from the sudden dash down the hill and the anxiety, Mason reached over and put his arm around Andy and pulled him close, and between gasps of breath he said "It's okay. I got my exercise for the year. What happened?"

"Macy woke up and went outside. I didn't hear her go out. I was busy drawing. She decided to go for a swim. But she can't swim."

"I wasn't going swimming by myself. I know that's not allowed. My hat blew in the water. I was just wading out to get it," Macy said between stifled sobs. And then the water went over my head and I had it in my mouth and nose and I couldn't call out. And I—-" Renewed sobs caused her words to come out raspy and thin. "And it hurt in my chest so bad. And then that mean duck started biting my hair!"

"What? A duck was what?" Mason said, then looked at Andy for confirmation.

"Yeah, that's what made me come outside. This duck was going crazy, quacking really loud, flapping its wings and pecking at something in the water. Then I saw Macy's head come up. The duck had her hair in its mouth. It looked like it was trying to fly away with her."

Mason and Meredith's eyes met.

"And when I got to her, it let go and flew away," Andy concluded.

"It pulled my hair really hard," Macy whimpered.

"It sounds like she saved your life," Mason said, looking again at Meredith with raised eyebrows and a shrug. "It just might have been Poofannie," he added.

"Dad, I don't know—-" Meredith gently protested.

"Well now, maybe these kids need to hear about Poofs. Their grandmother and I made up some pretty wonderful stories about them, and I would love to tell them those *Pooftales* while they're up here with me for a few days," Mason said with a grimace as he stood up. Then he added, "Macy, I haven't run that fast since I was in the Army. I was pickin' 'em up and puttin' 'em down coming down that hill. Felt like I was in the Olympics. You should have seen me go! Zoom! I was jumping over stuff. I mean I was flying down through those trees!"

"I saw you. You left me behind. I don't ever remember seeing you run like that, Daddy," Meredith laughed.

Macy and Andy both giggled, relieved that the tension had passed. But Meredith had still not regained her color, and Mason saw her jaw tighten and tears well up as she picked Macy up to carry her into the house, with Andy walking alongside, his arm around his mother's waist. Mason knew she was thinking about the tragedy that might have been.

He turned and looked out over the water, looking for a duck, see-ing nothing but the gentle waves. But he knew it had been Annie. What duck does something like that. Macy would have surely drowned otherwise.

"You saved our little Macy, Sweetheart. I'm glad it wasn't time for her to become a Poof too. I don't think we could have taken that." Mason continued to look out over the water as he said a word of thanks to God for allowing Macy to be saved. He thought about that look of lost sadness he saw when Meredith realized she might have lost her bright little daughter that day, and his own eyes spilled over. Once more he thanked God for what Mason knew was a miraculous rescue.

23
1991

• • • •

MEREDITH KNEW THAT her husband was expecting her home late Sunday evening. She called Arnie Warner from the cabin shortly after 2 o'clock, knowing that he should be home from church, and his weekly luncheon with friends after the service. Arnie was such a creature of habit that one could set a watch by his daily routines.

"Hey Mareseatoats!" he said, using the nickname he had given her as a child. He never called her that at work. It was nice to hear the affectionate note in his voice.

"I thought you were down in the Ozarks with your dad," Arnie added, and then with a note of concern, "Is everything alright?"

"Everything's fine. We've been having a really good visit. I'm about to head home though, and I was wondering if I could stop by your house for a minute."

"Sure, but I'll see you at work tomorrow, right?" Arnie answered, not disguising his curiosity.

"Well, that's part of what I wanted to talk to you about. Are you going to be there? Do you have plans?"

"No, I'll be here. I'll see you around five?" Arnie asked, still sounding like he wondered what was going on.

"Probably more like half past. I've still got to pack. That won't take long. I'm leaving the kids with Dad for a few days."

"Oh really? Well that'll be great for him, I'm sure."

"See you about five-thirty, Uncle Arnie. Love you."

"Love you too. Be careful on the road."

Meredith carried her suitcase downstairs. "Okay guys, I'm leaving. Mind Grandpop, and don't be crazy."

Andy and Macy had both staked out spots in the living room floor with their books, and Meredith went from one to the other planting goodbye kisses, hugs, and admonitions about getting near the water without Grandpop there. Then she went outside where Mason sat in the porch-swing looking out over the lake.

"I'm ready to go, Dad. You're sure this is okay?"

"Oh goodness yes. You know it is. We'll have fun."

"About the Poof thing..." she began.

"Don't worry, I'm just going to show them some of the figurines your mom and I did, and tell them the stories that went with them. I won't have them out sitting around talking to birds," he said. "But I may teach them that little song," and he began to sing jauntily, "*Be kind to your fine feathered friend, cause that duck may be somebody's mother...*" and then he laughed playfully.

"Somebody's *brother*," Meredith corrected dryly.

"This morning I'm pretty sure it was Mother," Mason answered, still smiling.

"Well, I'm thankful for that fine feathered friend, I know that much." Then she put her arms around Mason and added, "It's been good to see you smiling, Daddy. I've missed that. And it was good for me to have you to talk to. I'll call you and let you know how my conversation with Uncle Arnie goes. And please don't let them get near the lake without you."

"Don't worry, Sweetheart. They'll be perfectly safe here with me. We're going to have fun."

Meredith went back inside and made another round of goodbye kisses and hugs. The kids remained on the floor amid their rubble. Mason waved her off as she rumbled under the *Reviresco* sign, praying a quiet request for her protection, and for a good outcome from her meeting with Arnie. He couldn't help feeling guilty that she was having to deal with something he should have put to rest a long time ago.

Back in the house, Andy caught him off guard.

"Grandpop, what are Poofs? I heard you telling Mom you thought we should know about them," Andy said without looking up from his drawing.

"Yeah, you said the duck that pulled my hair was Poofannie. Who's Poofannie?" Macy chimed in. "A crazy duck that flies around picking up little girls by their hair and quacking and flapping its wings like——" at which point Macy threw herself into a frenzied impersonation of both herself and the duck, complete with sound effects and whirling choreography.

"Macy! Holy cow! Knock it off!" Andy said irritably. "You stepped on my paper!"

Macy fell to the floor with a final wailing quack and said, "Sorry Andy, I was getting carried away." She erupted in a peal of laughter, and even Andy had to smile at her joke.

Mason thought, not for the first time, that Macy had inherited her grandmother's quirky, irrepressible sense of humor. But it was the first time the thought gave him a comforting sense of peace, rather than sending him into a paroxysm of rekindled grief.

"As I was saying, before I was so rudely interrupted by my quacking sister," Andy groused, but with a smile, "What are Poofs anyway, Grandpop? I heard you call that duck *Poofannie* too."

"Well, I said it *might* have been Poofannie," Mason said, going over the tall bookshelves that covered one wall of the big family room. Lighted cubicles divided the numerous books on the shelves. In each cubicle, was displayed a figurine that Mason and Annie had created over the years. It was a collection of their personal favorites...the first pouring of each piece.

He picked up one and turned it carefully in his hands, smiling and chuckling softly to himself. Returning to his chair, he sat the porcelain piece gently on the side table.

"Now this is Poofannie," he said pointing to a beautifully realistic red cardinal that appeared to just be rising off a jagged branch on which the bird had been poised.

"I thought Poofannie was a duck," Macy said.

"Poofs can poof into anything they want to be, but their favorites are things that fly," Mason answered.

"Don't interrupt, Macy," Andy said.

"When I need to understand stuff, I got to ask questions," she replied.

Mason then pointed out the two bumblebees that were also launching in different directions from the branch, "And this is Poofarnie, and up here is Poofernando."

"Poofernando?" Macy said, drawing out the last syllable and rolling her eyes comically. "Poofernando!" she said again with a giggle, clearly liking the sound of it.

"Macy, you're an idiot," Andy mumbled absently, still focused on his drawing.

"No she's not, Andy. She's just a nutty little monkey and can't help herself. Don't say mean things to it." Mason swept Macy up into his lap and said, "But I can't tell you the story if you keep running your little monkey mouth, so hush and listen."

He squeezed her and kissed the top of her head, with the sudden thought that it was the very spot where the duck...Poofannie...had latched onto their granddaughter's hair, and very likely saved her life. He kissed the spot again gently.

"Now, these Poofs were once regular people..." he began. Both kids were enthralled as Mason told the story of the Poofs that saved the little boy from being run over by the speeding automobile.

"Poofernando got squashed on the windshield?" Macy asked, horrified.

"And smeared by the windshield wipers," Andy added. "That's what he said, Macy."

"But he was okay," Mason said.

"Okay? Okay? He was squashed like splat!" Macy said, wide-eyed, smacking hand on the table dangerously close to the figurine.

"Careful there, Macy. That is a very special piece of work. It is the very first figurine your grandmother and I did together, and that was the first story about the Poofs."

"Poofs for real?" Macy asked.

"Of course not, your knucklehead. It's just a story," Andy answered.

"But Grandpop said the duck was Poofannie. And she saved my life just like Poofannie, Poofarnie and Poofernando saved your life in the story, when you were chasing your ball into the street," Macy said.

"Whoa! Who said that was me?" Andy said.

"Poofannie is Grannie. Don't you get it?" Macy said, as though it was the most obvious and natural thing in the world. "And now she's in heaven, so she can poof into anything she wants to be," she raised her hands and her eyes were wide and bright.

Jumping down from Mason's lap Macy said, "We gotta go outside Grandpop. We don't want Grannie to have to poof into a bug or something so she can come in the house. Let's go outside and see her!" And with that Macy went tearing out the screen door into the fading afternoon light calling, "Grannie! Where are you? Poof-grannie! Here I am! It's me! It's Macy your granddaughter!"

Mason felt a little chagrin as he got up to follow her out, but the chiding look Andy gave him, as he trotted around him and out the door behind his sister, made him wince. He had tried to make it just a simple story, but Macy was more perceptive than he had imagined. The idea of Poofs seemed completely plausible to her.

Andy caught up to his sister well away from the house and said in a furtive whisper, and with a tone that sounded more like his mother than he could realize, "You're going to upset Grandpop! Don't be acting stupid and yelling for Grannie. It was just a story."

Macy kept looking all around in wonder, "I know that was a story, but Poofs are for real because Grandpop said that duck saved my life, and it was Poofannie!" Whirling back to him, waving her hands emphatically, palms up she said, "*Poof*-guh-rannie!" Then she whirled and dashed away calling musically at the top of her lungs, "Poof-guh-rannie! Poof-guh-rannie! It's me your granddaughter Macy Marie Pembrook!"

"Macy stop that!" Andy called out after her. "It's just a story. Grannie is in Heaven, she's not a stupid duck or something."

Mason got to him just at that moment and the boy didn't meet his eyes, instead continued to look after Macy as she dashed around the edge of the woods calling out through a bright, expectant smile.

Mason's brow furrowed, and he realized that it was Andy who was feeling confusion and needed reassurance. He said, "Of course she's in Heaven, Andy. But for years Grannie and I talked about what Heaven might be like. As we worked on the figurines we sell at the company, the idea of Poofs came to us. Then we began to wonder if that might really be the way it worked."

"The way what worked?"

"The way God worked. The way Heaven works," Mason answered. I have an idea. I want to show you kids something very special," he said. "A very special place."

He had been watching Macy and she was near the path up to the fountain. Mason called out, "Macy, wait right there. We're going to take a walk."

24

1991

• • • •

OF COURSE, THE FOUNTAIN enthralled both children. There was a magical feel about the place, and they sat on the benches together watching birds flit in and out among trickling water on the branches and vines of the sculpture.

Mason chose not to tell them about Annie's ashes being sealed within the sculpted dove. He didn't want to have to explain cremation to Macy on top of everything else. But it seemed that he didn't have a choice but offer further explanation about Poofs.

As they had been walking up the bricked path to the fountain, Mason was considering what his approach should be. It seemed that the best way was to simply be honest with them, and so he was.

"You kids know that I have been very, very sad since we lost Grannie. She was the love of my life, and I've felt really lost not having her with me. It's made me think a lot about Heaven, and what it's like where she is," Mason began.

"I tried to envision her in a white robe with a bunch of other people just singing around the throne of God, or walking around in a place more beautiful and perfect than we can possibly imagine, but that really didn't give me much comfort. And I really needed some comfort." Mason was pleased to find that it was so easy to talk to his grandchildren like this.

"Then one day I was sitting out on the patio at the house in town, and this bird flew up and landed close by in a tree. It was a beautiful red cardinal. Well, cardinals had always been Grannie's favorite. As I looked at that bird, of course Grannie came to mind, and I began to think about all the stories we had come up with as we worked on our sculptures together."

186

"Stories about Poofs?" Macy interrupted.

"Yeah. Stories like the one I told you today. We made up those stories together, and they helped us make the sculptures special, because we had those secret stories about them that nobody else knew."

He looked at Andy and said, "You know, Andy, when you're drawing those battles with dragons and knights and all that wonderful stuff you love to draw, aren't you thinking about the story? Why they're fighting, and maybe things they're saying?"

"Sure," Andy said. "All the time."

"And that's what makes it fun, right? Well that's what Grannie and I did with our work. It made it fun, and somehow those stories sort of made their way into the sculpture, and that made them more interesting."

"Then we began wondering if that might really be the way Heaven is. It's in the Bible that those of us who have come to faith in Christ..." He looked at Macy and clarified, "If we believe in Jesus, then we get to be with Him in Heaven after this body quits working. And we get a new body that's way better than this one, and we can do a lot more things in it than we can in these."

"We get super powers?" Macy asked, eyes wide.

"Well, I don't really know what we'll be able to do, but a whole lot more things than we can do in these bodies," Mason said with a smile.

A bird suddenly got their attention, calling loudly from the edge of the fountain. It was a brilliant blue jay, and they all watched it plunge into the top basin and burst out again, shaking off the water and noisily repeated its distinctive throaty call.

Mason's eyes remained on the bird and both children looked at him, and then at one another as their grandfather continued, "Well, Grannie and I started thinking, what if our new bodies could actually *poof* into something else? What if it was really possible that after we die, we get to poof into anything we want to be, anytime we want to, and people we love could see us that way?"

"That's what I was thinking about while I sculpted this fountain, and that dove that's mounted there on the top basin."

Andy said, "Yeah but Grandpop, if you're in Heaven, where everything is perfect, why would you want to come to earth and be an animal or bug or something?"

"I've thought about that, and here's what I believe. I think when you love someone, like Grannie loves you and Macy, and your mom and dad, and Uncle Arnie, and me, even if you're in Heaven, there may be times that you just want to look in on them. Just be where they are, you know? See how they're doing, and what's going on in their lives. Now, the rules have to be that you can't talk to them or anything. That would cause all kinds of turmoil. But what if it would be enough to just know that they saw you when you were there?

"Like that beautiful blue jay there in the fountain," he said. "Now if it were possible that that jay was really a bird your Grannie has poofed into, so she could be up here with us, don't you think she would love to know that you see her there?"

Macy whispered excitedly, "Is that Grannie, Grandpop? Really and truly?"

Mason glanced at Andy, who was looking fixedly at the jay, a small, sad smile playing at the corners of his grandson's mouth, while his large green eyes suddenly brimmed with tears.

Mason said, "I don't know. But if it is, doesn't it make you feel good to think that she is right here with us? She can see us, and we can see her?"

Both children and Mason watched the jay intently for a moment, then it suddenly burst out of the fountain and darted among the oaks and hawthorns, becoming a flash of blue weaving in and out of the trunks of the trees. A series of raucous squawks eventually blended into the symphony of birdcalls from the surrounding forest.

"Why'd she go away?" Macy asked in a plaintive whimper. "I liked her being here with us."

"Me too, Macy," Mason said looking at Andy, who was still looking pensively at the fountain. "And that's just it. It makes me feel better...a lot better...just to think that maybe that was her, and she wanted us to see how cool she looked in those bright blue feathers, and how great she is at flying." He had to stop for a moment as he felt that too familiar tightness in his throat, then said, "It makes me happy. And it makes it a little easier to be without her."

They sat awhile longer in silence, listening to the trickling water, and though they didn't say it, all were hoping the jay would return. Mason realized the light was beginning to wane, so he stood up. "Well I'd better get us some supper going," and the kids began to follow him down the trail. A loud squawking stopped them all, and they turned as one to peer back into the clearing. The squawk came again from the unseen jay.

Macy said through a broad grin, "G'night Poof-grannie. See you later."

Mason didn't see it, but Andy too looked up into the trees and quietly whispered, "Bye, Grannie. I really miss you."

25
1991

• • • •

ARNIE WARNER COULDN'T remember a time in years when his niece had come alone to his house. He was puzzled, and a little apprehensive. He might have guessed it was to talk about her concern for her dad, but she had been with Mason when she called. He suspected it was about work, and if so, it was likely about Adam.

Arnie frowned. Adam Pembrook was a puzzle he had never solved. Arnie knew the man's history. Now he was the only person alive who did. Arnie had attended the funeral for his old friend, Joe Kitchens over in St. Louis last fall. Lung cancer. Stinking cigarettes.

Arnie had driven back thinking about the way Joe would ask how Adam was doing every time they had occasion to visit. One day not long after Meredith married Pembrook, and he had come on board at Warner & Crewe, Joe had stopped by the office. He asked Arnie to introduce them, and seemed genuinely taken with the young man. It was unusual for Kitchens to express that kind of interest in anyone. He was typically a pretty aloof fellow.

It had irritated Arnie, for some reason, that Joe was such a fan of Adam Pembrook. Everything the investigator had discovered about the boy's past spelled potential trouble. The guy was living a lie, and he had never confessed the truth, even to Meredith, as far as Arnie knew.

Adam's father had been a thief and a scoundrel. He was an abusive drunk, and while Arnie felt sympathy for the idea of a little boy trapped in that kind of situation, that boy was now married to his niece, and knee deep in Warner & Crewe's business affairs, against Arnie's better judgement.

THE UNDENIABLE POSSIBILITY

191

Arnie believed in the science of genetics, and as bright as Adam Pembrook may be, he was still Freddy Finger Junior...an imposter and a liar with an agenda. A ticking time-bomb.

Meredith rang the doorbell and Arnie answered right away. He still had on the slacks, shirt and tie he had worn to church. He hadn't even loosened the tie. At least he had taken off the suit jacket. It was things like that, which gave Meredith pause when her parents talked about how much she was like her uncle.

Looking at his smile and the light in his eyes upon seeing her, the confrontation she had envisioned for the past three hours of driving alone seemed to melt away, and the coil of tension inside her seemed to relax a bit.

They hugged and he ushered her into his den. Arnie's den, which seemed more like an old-world library, had always been one of Meredith's favorite places on earth, with its smell of old books, leather, and her uncle's cologne, tinged with the lingering aroma of cigars, his badly kept secret vice, which he indulged only at home, and usually only alone. The masculine, nostalgic scent of the room was enough to take her back in time to many evenings spent there with her uncle when she was a little girl. The smell of Uncle Arnie's wonderful hot cocoa was all that was lacking.

Arnie Warner was an enigma. He had impeccable taste, and a very distinct sense of style, evident in the décor and artistic appointments of his home, and particularly manifested in the meals he prepared and served. In contrast to that, aside from the predictably utilitarian dark gray suit, white shirt, and muted striped tie, judging by his bearing and demeanor, he would have blended better among a group of truck drivers at the counter of a roadside diner than at a country club soirée with international corporate colleagues. That incongruity was strangely most evident in his own home.

"You left the kids with Mason at the lake. I'm sure that will be good for him. How is he doing?

"He's doing better. I think this time there has been what he needed. He's grown a beard," she said laughing.

"A beard? Oh goodness."

"And he's been working on something, but I'll let him tell you about that. You should go down one weekend soon. You need to see what he's done."

Meredith was surprised at how easy it was to slip into this light-hearted banter with her uncle, as though nothing was wrong between them. Purposely, she nudged the conversation toward the reason for her visit.

"The kids love it there. They hardly noticed when I left. I thought it might be good for him to have them for a few days, but also, I needed a little time alone with Adam." She took an offered seat in an over-sized leather chair near the fireplace.

Arnie's eyes narrowed, but he didn't offer a response, asking instead, "Would you like something to drink? I need to check something I have in the oven," On his way into the adjoining kitchen he added, "I have a nice bottle of wine I planned to open for dinner. We could try a sip now if you'd like."

"Sounds perfect. I thought I smelled something wonderful when I came in." Arnie was an extraordinary cook. He had hosted the family Thanksgiving and Christmas dinners all of her life, and they were always exquisite meals. Before deciding on business, he had toyed with the idea of becoming a chef. He had the gift, but in the end, he chose to make it a hobby. It was a hobby everyone who knew him encouraged.

She heard the oven open briefly, then close again and then the pop of a cork coming out of a bottle. "Cornish game hen. Remembered it was one of your favorites, I put in two, just in case you could stay for dinner with me," he called from the kitchen. A moment later he was back in the den with two full wine glasses.

"That's a sip? I may have to stay for dinner to sober up," Meredith said, again surprised by how easy it was to be light-hearted after driving over a hundred miles blaming her uncle for virtually everything wrong with her life.

"I detected a little ominous tone when you said you needed some time alone with your husband. A good Merlot goes well with ominous."

"You've always been able to read me. It is pretty grim, I guess. I want to try to get Adam to take a couple of days off with me. There are some things we need to work through. It's hard for me to admit it...especially to you." She let those words hang in the air for a moment before going on. "Adam and I are having some trouble. I was hoping we could just get away from everything here for few days."

Arnie swirled his wine in the glass and took a thoughtful sip. "I'm sorry to hear that you two are having trouble, Meredith," was all he could think of to say. Then, as though he had just realized what she had said, he asked, "Why is it especially hard to admit that to me?"

Meredith had driven the winding roads back from the lake rehearsing this conversation in her mind. Dreading it, but knowing it was imperative. She had tried to think what would be the best way to approach him. In the end, she decided to simply trust her uncle's love for her, and the close relationship she had always cherished with him.

She looked at him squarely and began. "Uncle Arnie, you know how I've always felt about you. I've always been able to talk to you, sometimes about things I didn't even tell Mom and Dad. Right now, I really need to be honest with you."

"You always can be honest with me, Meredith," Arnie answered. "Always. About anything."

In a quiet voice she began, "This is going to be hard to say to you, but a lot of our problems stem from things at work. Things that have to do with you." There was a long pause as she worked to relax the quaking she felt in her voice. "Adam has never been able to gain your trust or support. He knows that you never have liked him." She added, "I know it too. I always have, even when we were dating."

Arnie crossed his legs and studied the dark liquid in his glass. He was unaccustomed to not being able to meet someone's eyes, but he was afraid that they would reveal too much to his niece.

"He and I used to talk it about it all the time. He would do everything he could to make you see his value, and Uncle Arnie, you've just refused. You've refused to give him anything."

"Everyone knows. I talked to Mom and Dad about it years ago. I know they tried to change your attitude about him. Mom told me that she didn't understand it either, but to give you time, and Adam's work would speak for itself. And it has," she said, her voice growing a bit more plaintive, "His work does speak for itself, but you haven't given an inch."

"Uncle Arnie, you are the champion of every employee at Warner & Crewe...except Adam. You never fail to look for an excuse to acknowledge excellent work or ideas to make us more productive or profitable. Unless they come from my husband." Meredith's tone had become progressively more impassioned, and now it took on an accusatory note, bringing Arnie's eyes up to meet hers with a steely look she had seen, but never before directed at her.

Meredith didn't shrink back, but moved to the edge of her chair, leaned in toward her uncle's challenging presence and said forcefully, "You've hardly spoken to him for almost thirteen years. You treat him like he's invisible. And the sad part is that you were the one he most wanted to impress. He wanted to earn his place. His sole ambition was to become your right arm. To learn from you." She fell silent, but continued to hold Arnie's now defiant gaze.

Arnie said nothing for a time, and the realization struck him that this was his adored Meredith, the closest thing he would ever have to a daughter, and he had caused her to challenge him like this. He knew every word she said was true. His look softened.

Instead of denying the truth of her words, because he could not truthfully do so, he asked in a low, controlled voice, "What does this have to do with your marital problems?"

Meredith blew out a sigh of disbelief, "Everything, Uncle Arnie. Our whole life is wrapped up in the company. We both work there. We both work for you. You treat me like a princess, and you treat Adam like you've caught him robbing the till or something."

A small sob caught in her throat and tears welled up in her eyes, but she blinked them back and went on with determination, "We go home and I'm in the middle. I'm trying to defend you, because I don't want to agree with what he's saying about you. But everything he says is absolutely true. If I say anything in your defense, I'm not being supportive of my husband, and it escalates. And now it has gotten so much worse."

"Worse?"

"It's changed since Mom died and Dad retired. They're not there to help defend him to you. To make you consider his suggestions. To be a buffer, I guess," she said, feeling her cheeks redden as she stepped directly into the issue. "Adam thought that he could step up and help you through this awful transition, and that you'd finally see what an asset he could be for you and for the company. He has been so excited about this new technology he's been researching, and what a breakthrough it could be for Warner & Crewe." She caught a glimpse of the dismissive look that Arnie quickly masked.

"Everyone was worried about Dad and me, but Adam could see what losing Mom was doing to you, and he thought he could help you get your feet on the ground by showing you that the company's best days are not in the past, but on the horizon. Adam thought he finally had something that would make you see what he brings to the table. He worked like crazy on that proposal, and you know what you did?"

Meredith's voice caught as her throat constricted. Finding it again she said, "You all but threw his proposal in the trash with hardly a glance. He says you treated him like a moron." And then Meredith lost her composure and began to sob.

Like a moron. The words leaped from Arnie's memory. The family that Pembrook claimed had abandoned him in Tulsa had named the boy "Moron." But in the next moment Arnie was reminding himself that the whole story about the family was a lie. It was all total nonsense. It was just another layer of obfuscation to hide the real truth about the man who now called himself Adam Pembrook.

Adam had indeed been pushing harder than ever these past months, and it was true that Arnie had shut him down, tossing his suggestions aside. But what Pembrook had suggested would change the company radically, and Arnie had no intention of seeing that happen to the business he, Annie and Mason had built from scratch.

Arnie was belligerent in spite of Meredith's tears. "Adam's proposal would have us competing with our retailers, and those people are our customers. They have made this company, and been faithful to us for decades. I'm not about to go around them directly to the public with this computer thing he's pushing. Maybe that's going to be viable sometime in the future, but—-"

"I'm not here to try to get you to reconsider the proposal, but Uncle Arnie, that isn't the future. It's here now. People are already beginning to make purchases directly on their computers at home. It is going to be huge, and it could be what saves Warner & Crew."

"Saves?" Arnie spat the word.

"Yes, saves. Adam and I worked together on that proposal. I did a five-year detailed analysis of our sales weighed against our top name competitors, and a cumulative of the smaller players. I am seeing that our market share is beginning to slip, and we're losing it to the small, independent companies. That tells me we need to change the way we do things...our product line, and the way we market to the public, fulfillment, customer service. Change everything. Warner & Crewe can either remain an industry leader, or fade into a nice old company that used to be something special," Meredith said with a tone of authority that Arnie had never heard from her.

"And you and your husband are the ones to take us into this bold new era?" Arnie asked with a caustic edge.

Meredith took a sip of the wine and considered just how strongly she wanted to state her answer, then sat the glass on the table, leaned forward, cupped her hands over her knees, and looking directly, and defiantly into her uncle's eyes said, "Damn right we are."

Arnie blinked, taken aback, and finally said, "And I'm in the way."

"It doesn't have to be like that, Uncle Arnie. Let Adam and I be your partners. We're going to be inheriting the company. Mom's gone and Dad's not coming back. Warner & Crewe has already changed, whether any of us like it or not. The world is changing with this new era in business. And here we are. Adam and I are educated, committed, we know this company inside and out."

"You don't own the company yet, Meredith. And Adam Pembrook certainly doesn't. He would have us producing Warner & Crewe products in China. Our employees have always been our greatest asset, and he would like to give half of them their pink slip. I have watched good men and women walk out of that building with their final check in hand, not knowing where they were going to find work. I will not allow that to happen again."

Meredith answered hotly, "I've heard that story, Uncle Arnie, but this isn't my grandfather selling his company to the Japanese. This is just change. We're not causing it, we're responding to it. Adam doesn't want to let anybody go, but if our numbers continue to decline, we have to." Meredith drove her forefinger into her palm as she forced her argument. "Or we have to find a way to increase our market share. That's what Adam's proposal was all about, and you dismissed it out of hand."

She took a breath and calmed herself before continuing, "But you can relax. He's given up. You won, Uncle Arnie. Adam's done. You have refused to give him even an ounce of encouragement or respect. And this latest thing has...I don't know what it's done to him. But I just know he's through trying to win your regard, and he's not listening to me anymore either."

"I have to check on my dinner. Excuse me." Arnie got up and walked stiffly from the room.

Meredith took a long drink of the wine, then taking the glass with her she stood up and followed Arnie into the kitchen. He was taking the baking dish out of the oven, but dinner together seemed incongruent with the turn their conversation had taken. She stood and watched him, not speaking.

"Two almost identical birds, both very hot," he said with equal measures of sarcasm and dismay. "So you think I am the sole source of your marital distress."

"It's your attitude about Adam that puts me in the middle. There are other things I don't understand, but if you would just try to give him at least the benefit of the doubt, maybe we can..." her words trailed off.

"Do you love him?"

"Uncle Arnie, how could you ask that? I loved him from the moment I met him. He was so brilliant and driven. So smart I could hardly understand what he was talking about. He could have gone to work for any of a thousand companies, but he knew that I wanted to continue this wonderful business that you and Mom and Dad built. He never even applied anywhere else. He just made my dream his own. And ran right smack into a wall."

"A wall named Arnold Warner. I think you've made that point clearly," Arnie said as he chopped a salad. "I am trying to process all of this...fairly. So may I ask you some questions about your husband, without you turning this back to me and the way you think I have mistreated him?"

"Sure," Meredith answered in a pinched tone.

"How much has Adam told you about his childhood?"

A bit defensively Meredith answered, "His childhood? What does that have to do with anything?" Her uncle's question had struck a nerve.

Arnie just looked up through his eyebrows as he sautéed asparagus sprouts, until Meredith relented and stammered, "Not much. He doesn't like to talk about it. His parents died when he was young. His grandparents died before he came to college. He has no other family but us. We're his whole world, Uncle Arnie."

Arnie said, "Would you get me two plates and salad bowls, and put out the silverware?" Meredith knew where they were kept, having helped her uncle set the table for family dinners all her life.

Arnie pondered whether to divulge what he knew of Adam Pembrook's real history as he assembled the risotto, small game hens and asparagus on the plates and divided the salad between the two bowls. Arnie always served his guest's plates filled, and his presentation would rival that of any fine restaurant.

As she returned to the kitchen, having laid the table in the precise way she knew Arnie preferred, Meredith said, less indignantly than her earlier response, "I've thought a lot lately about Adam's childhood. I've wondered if perhaps—" She tried to find a way to avoid anything about the outbreaks of rage that had begun to occur. That was the last thing she would want her uncle to know. "He just had so much loss in his life when he so young. It had to have scarred him, but he made it clear a long time ago that he will not talk about his parents or his grandparents. It's just too painful for him. He says he lives in the present, not in the past. But I think maybe his past haunts him. I don't know, but something is going on beyond his frustration with...work," she said, consciously not saying, *with you.*

Arnie raised an eyebrow and carried the plates into the dining room. "I don't think burying it is a very healthy way to deal with things that were obviously traumatic. Why would you think he is having some issues that stem from that time of his life?"

"Losing Mom and all this upheaval has changed him...changed us. My heart aches for what we had at first. It was so wonderful. We were going to be this amazing business duo, blazing new trails in all the exciting expanding markets, but since none of that has worked out like we'd hoped, he just has a lot of pent up frustration." She was carefully choosing her words. "It isn't good at home. Not for me, and not for the kids. I'm scared that it's going to...escalate."

Meredith paused for a moment, then heard herself say, "Something has to change. Something has to change, Uncle Arnie, or I'm going to leave Adam." The words were out before she knew it, and once said, they seemed to breach the dam that had held her emotions in check for months. The cry came from the depths of a sorrow that had engulfed Meredith from the day her beautiful, funny, relentlessly creative, irrepressibly *alive* mother had suddenly vanished from her life, taking her dad with her in so many ways, leaving a vast gulf in their only child's life. And then, when she needed Adam most, her husband had descended into some private hell that he refused to share. She was alone, with the love she had thought would last forever growing so dim that she had begun to wonder if it had ever been real at all.

The words Meredith sobbed were almost unintelligible, "The kids won't understand! My mom's dead. And Daddy is...I'm losing everyone I love, Uncle Arnie. I don't know how to help Adam. He won't let me. And I'm going to lose you!"

She collapsed into one of the dining chairs and Arnie leaned over, embracing her awkwardly, giving her a linen table napkin, and saying, "You're not losing me, Mareseatoats. And you haven't lost your father. He's just having a hard time adjusting. He'll be himself again."

"I know. He's getting better. He really is," she said. "But I will lose you, Uncle Arnie. If I lose Adam, I will lose you too."

Then Arnie understood, and his eyes filled with a deep sadness as he said in a husky voice, "You mean that I will lose you." Then drawing her close he said, "And I can't let that happen."

"Uncle Arnie, I don't know if it can be fixed," she answered as the wrenching sobs began to subside.

Arnie pulled her into his shoulder, holding her as she cried softly. He was looking beyond the room, and with a clarity that Arnie couldn't explain, he was seeing a dirt-caked, terrified little boy facing a raging drunken father. Somehow he knew that Freddy Finger was still terrorizing his son.

They sat for awhile longer, then left the cold dinner untouched and went back to sit in the den. Arnie was pondering something while Meredith sat staring into the empty fireplace, numb and spent.

He finally broke the silence, "I miss your mother too, you know. And Mason. The three of us together were unstoppable," he said with a sad smile. "When I talked to our father about our plans for the ceramics factory he thought I was a fool. He didn't mince words about it either. Your grandfather was not a pleasant man."

Meredith didn't answer. She had heard bits and pieces of the stories of his unpleasantness over the years. Her grandfather's negotiation with a Japanese corporation in the fifties had led to a highly profitable merger, followed by his sudden departure to facilitate transition of production to the Tokyo operation. That event was immediately preceded by his closing the venerable Kansas City ceramic insulator factory and leaving its employees jobless without warning. All they received were mumbled words of apology from his fresh out of college son, who was left with the task of handing out those final paychecks.

His father's transitional position in Japan became permanent, and Meredith's grandmother's temporary separation from her husband became abandonment, leading to the former society maven's rapid descent into an abyss of depression. Her impenetrable walls of bitterness resulted in just as much distance between their mother and her dismayed children as they faced from their father on the other side of the world.

In the meantime, Arnie Warner had reassembled as many of the former factory employees as the newly formed Warner & Crewe could afford, and over the years had continued to make places for others as the company's success grew. The three partners faced every business challenge with the brash confidence of youth and ignorance, and had succeeded in no small part because of Latham Warner's dismissive affront when he looked over his son's carefully crafted business plan.

Arnie Warner would have moved heaven and earth to make Warner & Crewe succeed after his father tossed the barely acknowledged presentation back across the table and pronounced the money spent on his son's education a *waste*.

Arnie held Meredith's shoulders and gently looked at her and spoke. "I have to think about all of this. You know I want the best for you, and I never want to see you unhappy like this. You and Mason and the kids are all the family I will ever have, and if—-"

Meredith cut him off. "Do you not hear yourself? Adam is part of our family. He is part of your family. He is my husband. He's the father of my children. And we are the only family he has. What did Adam ever do to deserve the way you treat him?"

Arnie said nothing, but the look in his eye hardened as Meredith pressed him with the unexpected renewal of fury.

"Tell me! If there's something he has done or said that I don't know about, then you need to tell me what it is, because I promise you, Uncle Arnie, I have never seen him doing anything but try his best to strengthen and build Warner & Crewe." Meredith stood up abruptly when Arnie continued his stoic silence. Defiantly she waited. When the silence grew uncomfortable she said, "You can't. You cannot tell me one thing he has done, can you?"

Then with a vehemence Arnie did not imagine her capable of, Meredith pointed at him and said, "Thirteen years you have been watching my husband...my *husband*, Uncle Arnie...looking for something you could blame him for, something to justify your opinion of him, and for all that time you have not been able to find one thing. Not a single thing!"

Her eyes were blazing now, and she tossed her head as she repeated, "Not one thing! And you know why? Because there is no reason! And if there is no reason then I have to conclude that you're a whole lot more like my grandfather than you ever realized."

Meredith picked up her purse and turned to leave. Arnie still sat. She turned at the door and came back.

"What you said earlier. You're right. If you don't do something to fix this, whatever your problem is with my husband, and take this pressure you've created off my marriage, so maybe, Adam and I will have some chance of salvaging our life together, then yes...yes, you will lose me. And that will break my heart, Uncle Arnie, but you know what? It's broken already." And with a sob she whirled and almost ran to the front door, slamming it behind her as she left.

Arnie sat in the leather chair where Meredith had left him, his fingers tented under his chin, staring coldly into a murky void that was the future of Warner & Crewe and the world Arnie Warner had so meticulously crafted. The image of his father's face floated among the various phantoms in that vision. No one had ever accused him of being like his father. Latham Warner was the last man on earth Arnie wanted to emulate. Meredith's words kept coming back to him, and his stomach rolled each time. If her intention had been to wound him, Meredith could not have chosen a better weapon than those words.

First he had lost Annie, the sister he adored. More than adored. His twin, although so different in temperament and talent, yet in a way that no other person could, she had made him feel whole. That was something Arnie had never realized until she was gone, and he found himself suddenly, and despondently incomplete.

From childhood Annie's raucous sense of humor had all but required her brother to be sensibly sober. Annie's sparkling creative vitality had made Arnie's methodical monotony palatable to everyone, even to himself. She had been a splash of vivid color against his somber tones of gray.

As painful as his own grief had been, Arnie knew that Mason was experiencing a far deeper sense of loss. But Mason had simply walked away...away from the company, away from him, and even from Meredith and the kids, leaving Arnie to deal with all of it alone.

He heard himself mutter, "Now look what I've done," and he shook his head. After a longer time than he realized, he got up and carried the untouched dinner into the kitchen and scraped it all into the garbage. The bottle of wine was empty when he finally turned out the lights and went to bed. It had been a long time since Arnie Warner had over-indulged in anything. He lay there for a moment, angry with himself, the room spinning every time he closed his eyes, wondering how anyone made a habit of such a thing, as he finally drifted off into a troubled sleep.

He dreamed about a drunken Freddy Finger fishtailing off the highway and lurching onto railroad tracks, racing against the mass of hurtling black steel that ripped both the truck and its worthless owner in two. In his dream, Arnie stood on the dirt road, caught in the headlights of the doomed truck as it came across the tracks...the last thing Freddy Finger would ever see.

26
1991

· · · · ·

THE PHONE RANG AFTER their third round of Wahoo that night. Mason answered.

"Dad? How's it going with the kids?"

"Great. Macy just beat us at Wahoo. How'd your talk with Arnie go?"

"Not good. Not good at all, Daddy." Mason could hear in her voice that she was struggling to maintain her composure, and he squeezed his eyes closed in dismay.

"What happened?"

"I don't know. I guess I just had so much resentment stored up about the way he's treated Adam that when it started spilling out, I just couldn't stop. It was awful, Daddy. I think I said way too much."

"You didn't resolve it before you left."

"Oh no. No, I pretty much told him to fix it, or my relationship with him was over," Meredith said ruefully.

"Meredith, surely that's not what you said."

"Oh it is, Daddy," and then went on to recount as much of her confrontation with Arnie as accurately as she could remember, ending with, "And then I stormed out of his house and slammed the door."

"Whew," was all Mason said.

"I don't know how it can ever be the same, and that's just the thing. Everything in the world has changed...and I hate all of it," Meredith said as she began to cry, and through her tears said, "I've just made it all worse." Through a sob she managed to say, "Daddy, I don't know what to do."

The cabin phone was in his small study. Mason pushed the door closed and said, "Well, sweetheart, you compose yourself so you can talk to the kids, and I'll be there tomorrow to see what I can do to help. I should have dealt with this a long time ago. I am so sorry that I didn't, but your mom always—-"

Meredith interrupted, "She was in the middle for a long time, running interference. She kept all of this from boiling over. Well I'm no good at it. I proved that tonight. I hate to have to ask you for help."

"You didn't ask. And it's my job, I should have already handled it. It was just easier to smooth it over," Mason answered, and then added, "Easier for us, but not for you and certainly not for Adam."

After a brief pause, in which Mason Crewe effectively came out of retirement, he said, "You stay at home tomorrow and I'll drop the kids by about ten. I'll deal with Arnie."

"Daddy, Uncle Arnie was very reasonable. It was me that got out of line."

"Did you say anything that wasn't true?"

"No, but I was terribly disrespectful," Meredith answered. "I owe him a apology for that."

"Arnie was not innocent in this. After the smoke clears you may want to talk to him, but for now, it's just fine for him to stew in his juice. I'm still a partner in that company, and I have a thing or two to say about how it's run," Mason said with a tone that Meredith hadn't often heard him use.

"And do you have a copy of Adam's proposal that you could give me when I bring the kids by the house?"

"I have a copy," she answered, but then with some hesitation added, "But, Dad, I'm not sure Adam would want you to—-"

"Like I said, I'm still part of Warner & Crewe. In fact, I believe I'm still president of the company. I think it is within my purview to ask to see a copy of a proposal that could redefine the way we do business. So, I want you to have a copy waiting for me," Mason said with finality. And then with a slightly lighter tone he added, "Now you're off the hook."

"Now, I'm going to put the kids on the line. You rest tonight, and don't worry. I've got this. I love you, sweetheart."

"Love you too, Daddy."

"Kids, your momma wants to talk to you," Mason called.

Macy darted across the family room and grabbed the telephone receiver from Mason's hand, and gleefully blurted, "Mommy we saw a beautiful bluebird today, and it was Grannie! She had poofed into a bluebird just like she poofed into that duck when she pulled me out of the lake!"

Mason squeezed his eyes shut and grimaced while Andy padded across the floor in his sock feet muttering, "Grannie pulled your head up out of the water. It was me that pulled you out of the lake, weirdo."

Mason smiled in spite of himself.

After the kids got off the phone, complaining about the news that they were going home the next morning, Mason surprised himself when he answered, "Well there's some things at work that need my attention, you guys, so it can't be helped." He never thought he would be saying anything like that again, then added, "You'll be coming back up here with me soon, I promise."

Then he picked up the phone and called his long-time housekeeper in town and asked that she put things in order for his return, and to expect to resume her former schedule. Her elated response kept Mason on the phone for some minutes. Finally hanging up, he called Otto Ericsson to tell him to check on the cabin, as he had since they had first built it.

When Otto asked when Mason would be returning, he admitted that he didn't know. Until that day, Mason had been seriously entertaining the notion of selling the house in town, and suddenly that idea was off the table. It was obvious now, that he had left the company prematurely, and neglecting his responsibilities there had led to this situation. He had indulged himself for the better part of a year, and now his daughter, Adam, Arnie, and even the children were paying the price for that indulgence.

With the phone calls out of the way, and having decided against calling to inform Arnie of his intentions, Mason told the children that they needed to bathe and get their things gathered and packed, because they were going to be getting an early start for home in the morning.

He did a load of laundry before bedtime, and bagged up the leftovers that had accumulated in the refrigerator. The whole time he worked through the short routine of cleaning and preparing to close up the cabin, he was thinking about the situation with Meredith, Adam, and Arnie, and how he would approach the problem. As he pondered that, some other things occurred to him, and Mason realized there were many things he had not yet fully processed.

It genuinely surprised him to think that his absence had such an impact. He had always thought of the company operations as Arnie's territory, and had respected those lines. Annie had always been completely immersed in the creative aspect, deliberately and confidently leaving everything regarding policy, employees, manufacture, distribution, and the million other details of operations to her husband and brother.

When they had formed the partnership, Mason was not involved in the creative, or as Arnie preferred to call it, the *product development* side. That was totally Annie's arena. Mason had worked from one end of the company to the other, wanting to learn the business as Arnie had, from the inside out. Of course, Warner & Crewe's product line was vastly different from the ceramic insulators that Arnie and Annie's father had produced, but the processes were essentially the same. Mason set out to learn everything, and did. It was only later that Annie drew Mason into the studio with her, and the creative work had taken virtually all of his attention from that time on.

Virtually all. Mason could see now that his and Arnie's communication was so effortless, that he had never fully recognized its contribution to the overall health of the company. As Mason thought back, he could envision a thousand times the two of them had hashed out one thing and another about everything from raises to buying new equipment. He and Arnie, in their way, had worked together very similarly to the effortless way he and Annie had worked.

The few times there had been a clear difference of opinion among the partners, they came between Arnie and his sister. Mason was always the mediator. And as Mason thought about it, the only instances of that happening seemed to revolve around their son-in-law.

Mediation had not been the right course. Mason should have stood firmly with Annie, and with Meredith, in support of Adam. He could see it now. Some resolution would have been far easier to accomplish at the beginning.

Latham Warner had been eager to get rid of his defunct factory and its dated equipment, and all but gave it to his son and daughter's fledgling company. Perhaps because of that, even though Warner & Crewe was, in every other way, a new business start-up, Mason had felt always that it was more Arnie and Annie's company than his. When Annie was gone, it had seemed vaguely that his claim to Warner & Crewe died with her.

It dawned on Mason that he was thinking clearly, and feeling more like himself for the first time since he had received that horrible call informing him of the accident that had taken Annie away from him. Once again, he could see everything in that clear, balanced way of his that, unbeknownst to him, his wife and brother-in-law had always recognized as the real key to Warner & Crewe's success.

Both of them had counted on Mason to be able to see what they were missing. At the same time, it was his utter confidence in each of them that had given Annie and Arnie the assurance to do their jobs with a certainty of success, that was, in itself, the very substance of that success.

Mason had never known that, but as he packed the car and got the children settled in for the three-hour drive out of the Ozarks and back to the city, it all laid itself out before him. By the time he pulled up in front of Meredith and Adam's home, Mason had fully reclaimed his partnership in Warner & Crewe.

"Did Adam go in to work?" Mason asked Meredith as the kids trundled their bags off to their rooms.

"Yes," she answered simply. Then with some hesitation asked, "Dad, what is it that you are planning to do?

Mason ignored her question and asked, "You have any coffee made?"

They sat in the breakfast nook just off the kitchen and Meredith poured him a cup of coffee. She was a little startled by the change in her father's demeanor. The focus and vitality, and even the strength and timbre of his voice gave the impression of a much younger, more vigorous man than she had left at the lake.

Mason began, "I first thought I would just come have a face-to-face with Arnie about this issue and get it straightened out, but as I've thought about it driving up, I realize that I've been invisible for almost a year now. I can't expect to just waltz in and do that. This may take a little time. I think I'm going to invite Arnie over to the house this afternoon."

"Daddy, just having you back will make all the difference."

"Well, it may get worse before it gets better. Arnie may not like the intrusion after running the show by himself for this long," Mason said. "We'll see. But I think you and Adam may need to be out of the equation for a few days. Anything going on that you can't leave?"

"I had been planning to be away, so I'm caught up on things there. I'll talk to Adam," she answered, then remembered something.

"Oh Dad, you wanted a copy of Adam's proposal. I've got that for you."

Meredith left the room briefly and returned with a manila folder containing a thick sheaf of papers.

"Great," he said, taking the file. "I need to go. I still haven't been by the house. Need to change clothes, get a haircut probably."

"I hope you keep the beard. I really like it," Meredith said as she brushed a hand across his whiskered cheek. "And call if you need any clarification on the proposal. I hope you like what you see. We worked hard on it."

Mason got up and called to the kids. After hugs and promises of going back down to the lake again soon, and a reassuring kiss for his daughter, he drove directly to the barber shop. He kept the beard.

Pulling into the driveway, looking out over the perfectly manicured lawn, Mason experienced a strange feeling of unfamiliarity. The proportions of everything seemed skewed. Smaller, larger, he couldn't tell. Just unfamiliar. His housekeeper's car was there, and Mason was glad. He hadn't been looking forward to walking into the empty house again.

"Mister Crewe, is that you?" the maid called out with genuine warmth in her thick accent as he stepped in from the garage and called her name. She met him at the kitchen door smiling, and took both his hands in hers when he had sat his suitcase down. "And a beard now! You look very sophisticated, Mister Crewe. Like an adventurer in a movie."

Pulling him into the kitchen beaming as she said, "I have missed you. Coming to this big house all empty makes me so sad. I am glad you are home. Everything is ready for cooking, for sleeping, all clean, and the pantry, freezer and refrigerator all stocked up for you. I was just doing finishing touches," she said as she fussed with a couple of fresh-cut flowers in a vase on the counter.

"Celia, it all looks great. Thank you so much for keeping every-thing in such good shape. We've always been able to count on you."

Ignoring the compliment, the housekeeper said, "I made you a casserole I know you like, and apple pie so you don't have to cook for yourself tonight. Just heat it up in the oven."

Mason thanked her warmly and listened patiently as she passed on a deluge of news about her children and grandchildren. At length she untied her apron, collected her things and left. Mason carried his suitcase through the too quiet house and back to his bedroom.

It was early afternoon, and Mason hadn't had lunch, so back in the kitchen, he scoured the refrigerator and found that Celia had in-deed stocked it fully. He made a ham and cheese sandwich, opened a bag of chips, poured a tall glass of milk and took it all, along with the copy of Adam's proposal, into his study. He settled down to read, chewing absently as he pored over the meticulously prepared docu-ment.

He rummaged through a desk drawer, found a pad of yellow sticky notes and jotted questions on them, pasting those to the edges of the pages. The questions were primarily about technical aspects of making electronic sales transactions.

The concept of such technology was astounding to Mason, and exciting. It was obvious that Warner & Crewe products were a nat-ural for this new way of doing business. Adam and Meredith had made the case beautifully, and comprehensively. It was ridiculous that Arnie had dismissed the proposal without consideration. Ridiculous that he had dismissed it at all.

There was a documented slip in sales for the figurines. New prod-ucts needed to be developed, and new avenues of increasing their marketing reach had to be explored. The investment was minimal, relative to the potential. It was exactly the kind of thing Arnie Warner should have been all over for the sake of the company's financial sta-bility. But he was throwing up roadblocks. *Why?*

Clearly it was because Adam Pembrook was the one pushing for it. Even Meredith's collaboration on the proposal had held little or no sway.

After going through the proposal front to back twice, he had removed most of his questions. They were answered in the text of the document, Mason realized. He had just missed it the first time, being unfamiliar with the new digital jargon.

Sitting back and taking off his reading glasses, he realized a new appreciation of Adam Pembrook's genius. And he took particular satisfaction in knowing that Meredith had contributed the marketing data, which was impressive and convincing. Mason sat at the desk pondering the rather amazing pairing of the very specific abilities that the company would require to take the business forward in this new, and rapidly changing business environment.

He knew that returning to a role at Warner & Crewe was important, but it would be short-lived. The opportunities this technology presented needed to be explored by younger, more innovative minds. He and Arnie both needed to usher in this change and retire to a role of prudent counsel and guidance.

Mason had a hard time envisioning Arnie Warner accepting such a role. Particularly since it meant placing Adam Pembrook in the chair his brother-in-law had occupied zealously for so many years. He cupped his hand under his chin and allowed various scenarios to play out in his mind.

Finally coming to a decision, he picked up his lunch dishes and took them back to the kitchen, picked up the wall phone there and dialed Warner & Crewe's office number.

Arnie's long-time secretary, answered, "Warner & Crewe, this is Maureen. How may I help you?"

"Maureen, this is Mason Crewe. How're you doing?"

"Mister Crewe? Oh it is so good to hear your voice!" and the conversation went on much the way his earlier one with Celia had progressed through the status of children and grandchildren's lives.

At the first polite opportunity he interrupted and asked, "Is Arnie available?"

"He's in his office, Mister Crewe. Hold on and I'll transfer you. Sure nice to hear your voice. We all miss you around here. It's not the same without you," she said.

Mason smiled and said, "I'll see you real soon Maureen."

He was on hold for longer than he expected. When Arnie finally answered, his voice was subdued. Not quite terse, but close.

All he said was, "Mason."

Mason matched his tone, "Arnie, I'm at home. You think you can you break away and come over to the house?" For just a beat Mason hesitated, his inclination being to add something to make the invitation sound casual. Non-confrontational. But he respected his brother-in-law too much for that, so he added, "We need to have a conversation."

Arnie hadn't anticipated Meredith involving Mason, but she had been very upset when she left his house. He didn't have to ask what this meeting was about. He knew.

"Yeah. I'll wrap up and be there at..." he checked the time on his wristwatch, "Three-thirty."

"I'll be out on the patio. Come on through. I'll put on some coffee."

• • • •

ARNIE HUNG UP THE PHONE. *Have a conversation.* How many times had he and Annie joked about Mason using that phrase? It was Mason's unconscious *tell* like those gamblers were said to have. Everyone knew what it meant. Mason Crewe was ticked, and although Mason always worried that his approach was diplomatic to the point of being too generous to the offending party, everyone knew that when Mason Crewe uttered that phrase, there was a mine field just beyond the genial confines of the *conversation.*

Arnie had been invited to *have a conversation* with Mason just a handful of times over the course of their partnership. Only one time had he pressed it from conversation to the point of confrontation. Until that day, it had been difficult for Arnie to envision the witty and whimsical, artistic Mason Crewe as the battle-hardened, decorated combat veteran who hadn't flinched at leading men into deadly conflict.

Arnie made a couple of notes and straightened things on his desk. He realized that he was dreading this *conversation.* Dreading it because Arnie knew that his attitude about Adam Pembrook was grossly unfair, if it was only about the quality of Adam's work. He was bright. More than bright. Arnie had never questioned that. And motivated, without a doubt. But motivated to what end? That had always been Arnie's question. What was Adam Pembrook's agenda?

Arnie selected a small key from his key ring and unlocked a lower file drawer in his desk. At the back of the drawer he found a thick, brown accordion file. He pulled it out and untied the attached cord that wrapped around and secured the flap closure. Pulling the contents out and looking at the folders filled with pages of handwritten notes, he envisioned the craggy face of his old, recently buried friend, Joe Kitchens. The notes read and somehow looked just the way Joe talked. Easy-going wording, punctuated with bold strokes and dashes that communicated an impatient, low tolerance for nonsense. Arnie would miss Joe.

He opened the top folder in the pile. It was an overview and analysis based on Joe's background investigation of Adam Pembrook. Joe had been conflicted in his conclusions. He had compiled evidence that suggested Adam Pembrook was a pathological liar with genius level intelligence. One consistency that Pembrook demonstrated from childhood was exceptionally patient cunning, that Kitchens identified as *potentially* criminal. Question marks punctuated that assertion.

That had been enough for Arnie Warner. The boy had invented two distinct histories for himself. The first at only twelve years old, when he surfaced in Tulsa, Oklahoma, having successfully stashed a very significant amount of his father's cash, much of which was likely stolen money. The second was six years later when he retrieved the hidden money and presented himself as the sophisticated, orphaned only child of an affluent Tulsa family who had left him amply provided with a trust fund.

In Arnie's opinion, that was when Adam started on a path to identify Meredith Crewe, and thereby her family's company, as his next layer of manufactured legitimacy.

When Kitchens had submitted his final written report, Arnie had skimmed over and chosen to ignore the footnote to his observations that Joe Kitchens added.

He read it now.

In that footnote, Kitchens offered his opinion that Adam Pembrook was a brilliant young man who had suffered medically documented long-term physical abuse, and likely an even greater degree of psychological abuse from infancy to approximately twelve years old.

In Kitchens' opinion, Adam had demonstrated extraordinary re-sourcefulness in taking responsibility for his own welfare at a very early age. He had further demonstrated character in earning out-standing scholastic achievement from the moment he emerged from that violently abusive environment. There was no evidence of unprin-cipled behavior that would disqualify Adam Pembrook from consid-eration as an employee of Warner & Crewe.

On the contrary, Kitchens concluded that he was a highly moti-vated, impressive young man who seemed to richly deserve an oppor-tunity to build a life.

There was a knock on the facing of his open door and Adam Pembrook stepped in and asked, "Got a minute?"

Too quickly, Arnie closed the folder, gathered the others, and turned to put the stack on the credenza behind his desk. Then he stood up.

Adam said, "If you're busy, Arnie, this can wait. I just wanted to make an appointment with you. Set up a time when we could talk."

Brusque, his composure ruffled by Adam happening in on him with that particular file open on his desk, Arnie snapped, "What about?"

Adam just looked at him for a moment, then with a shake of his head, his eyes never leaving Arnie's face, he said, "You know what? Never mind. There's no point." Adam wheeled and started down the hall.

Arnie was still standing, still staring at the door when Adam reap-peared, his face flushed above the starched white collar, and his blue eyes flashed cold as he closed the door behind him with a slap.

"No. No, Arnie I'm not walking away this time. For thirteen years of my life I have been walking on eggshells with you. Trying my best to prove myself to you. And you have treated me like a moron from the day I walked through that door. You've treated me like an intruder. And I am sick of it." Adam wasn't loud, but his rage was growing as he spoke.

"Forget that I'm part of your family. That ought to be easy. I never have been, as far as you're concerned." Adam paced and stabbed the air with his finger. "You know it's funny Arnie, but Mason and Annie accepted me, and I think they genuinely cared about me. Mason never has acted like I wasn't good enough for Meredith. Annie certainly never did. But man, you have. From day one. Not good enough for her, not good enough for this company, and not good enough for you."

Adam put his palms on the desk and leaned across toward Arnie, staring directly into the older man's eyes without a hint of deference or respect remaining. He had always known if he allowed himself to begin, there would be no salvaging anything, so there was no reason to hold back the flood any longer.

But as Adam spoke, there was an inner assault of long suppressed images that fueled his outrage, and in those images he saw Freddy Finger's grease-blackened hands in a vise-like grip around his thin arms lifting him into the air. He felt the hot breath and spittle as the Moron spat a string of filthy words into his face. Words carried on the sickening stench of cheap liquor and rotting teeth. He felt his small body being flung across empty space and heard the loud pop and shattering glass when his foot smashed through the television. He saw just a flash of the drunken face distorted in rage as a broad fist curled. The image seared into his memory in that lightning-fast millisecond before the knuckles slammed into his face, and the scrawny, underfed twelve-year-old received the ironic mercy of unconsciousness that lasted long past the frenzied punches, slaps, and kicks that followed.

Adam knew that he could not give himself over to that same uncontrolled rage. But he also knew it lurked there inside of him, pushing, pressing, looking for the opportunity to spring free and wreak havoc upon his carefully constructed life. It looked just like the Moron. It felt like him. It smelled like him.

Adam struck the desk hard with the palm of his hand, "But forget all that. Let's just talk about my work. I have given you...not Warner & Crewe, but you, Arnie, everything I had. I had a lot to offer this company, but I came in expecting to have to prove myself to you. I wouldn't have had it any other way. I didn't expect you to do me any favors. I knew I was going to have to earn your respect."

"So I had a high grade point in college. Honors graduate. I know that doesn't mean squat if you don't have the ability to deliver in the real world. Well I delivered, Arnie. I have given twice as much as you expect of anybody else. Time, absolute commitment, sheer work. I have not slacked off for one minute in thirteen years."

"And the thing is, Arnie, you know it. You damn well know it. And it counts for nothing with you. If this was just a job to me, I would have quit and walked away years ago, but you see, I'm married to this company. I made a commitment to Meredith. But I didn't bargain for this. Thirteen years is long enough to put up with you."

Adam took a breath and Arnie took the opportunity to say, "You need to sit down and get control of yourself."

"Don't talk to me about controlling myself. I have been controlling myself for as long as I can remember. You can't imagine what kind of control I—" Adam stopped, squeezed his eyes shut, breathing in a shallow pant.

"You know what I wanted, Arnie? What I wanted more than anything? It wasn't money, if that's what you're thinking. None of that matters to me. No Arnie, I wanted a place to belong!" He stopped, gulping air, then said again quietly, "I just wanted a family."

"You have a family," Arnie began. "You have Meredith and the..."

"I wanted to show you who I really am!" Adam almost sobbed.

"I know who you really are," Arnie said evenly. He watched Adam's face carefully as he continued, reciting the fictional past of

Adam Pembrook. "You came from a good family. Meredith says your parents were killed in an accident when you were a boy. Your grandparents took you in, and they both passed away, just before you came here to college."

The look on Adam's face stopped him. It was a cold, piercing gaze, his voice was low and menacing as he leaned in close enough that Arnie felt the hot breath in his face when Adam said, "And you know as well as I do that every word of that is a lie."

Neither of them said anything for a time. They stared at one another steadily until Arnie finally said, "Then why don't you tell me the truth, Adam?"

Adam didn't answer immediately, but his eyes remained locked with Arnie's until at last he said, "I know you run background checks, Arnie. You're bound to have run one on me. The information isn't hard to find." He stood up straight, backed away from the desk. "You know I have no family. I grew up in Carthage Creek Children's Home in Tulsa, Oklahoma. I was abandoned. I don't know who my parents were. I don't know my birthday. I don't even know my real name."

Arnie stood gravely looking at Adam, wondering why, when given the opportunity to tell the truth, Adam had chosen instead to lie. He started to ask, but thought better of it. Arnie finally responded, "Have you ever told Meredith?"

"No,"

"See I don't understand that. That's nothing to be ashamed of. Nothing you should hide."

"You're right, Arnie. You can't understand it. No possible way. Not for you." He looked down at the carpet between his feet and shook his head slowly. "I said a moment ago that I wanted you to know who I am, but you've been telling me who you think I am since the day I came to work here." Adam raised his eyes to meet Arnie's. "Nobody." Then Adam turned abruptly for the door, and said on his way out, "You're not the first person to tell me that, but I promise you will be the last."

Arnie sat down heavily and stared at his desktop. First Meredith, now this with Adam. And Mason was waiting for him. He gathered the papers back into the accordion file, tied the string around it and slid it into his briefcase.

Maureen looked at him anxiously when he stepped out of his office. It had been impossible not to overhear Adam Pembrook. In all the years she had been Arnie Warner's secretary, no one had ever spoken to him like that. She had never heard any exchange remotely that heated at Warner & Crewe.

"I'll be out the rest of the day, Maureen," was all Arnie said as he left.

• • • •

MEREDITH HEARD THE garage door. She was immediately apprehensive, because it was almost two hours earlier than she expected Adam. He was never home early. Never.

Meredith left the office in time to pick up the kids at school every day. More often than not, she had to delay dinner until Adam arrived. He worked long after everyone else had left the Warner & Crewe offices, claiming that those last two hours were his most productive, with everyone out of his way.

Her husband was a solitary man. She often thought that he would have been happier single. She knew he loved the children, but he was rarely engaged or affectionate with either of them. Especially not with Andy, and recently Meredith had thought that was becoming sadly obvious.

As for her, she consciously avoided thinking about the distance that was growing between occasions of intimacy with her husband, and the increasing distance between the two of them when they did occur. Everything in their relationship seemed to be woven from obligation, rather than need or desire.

When they had met, she thought Adam was mysterious, and that attracted her to him. He was so intelligent and well read, great car, great clothes, great hair, and yet there was something about his manner that was at odds with the so well put together exterior. Something awkwardly charming.

He was so good-looking and smart that she had expected that arrogant, privileged frat-boy manner that they all seemed to cultivate. It had amused and intrigued her that Adam seemed so...innocent. That was the word she had used at the time. He certainly wasn't like most guys. It was as if he had studied how to be charming, reading up on the various aspects of dating and social interaction, then put what he had learned into application.

She had joked with him once, asking if he was really an alien that had just landed on Earth, and was learning our culture and exploring our vulnerabilities. Or maybe a Russian spy. He laughed, but Meredith could see that Adam hadn't liked the teasing.

The mystery that had been so intriguing about Adam Pembrook in the beginning, over the course of their marriage had solidified into an impenetrably opaque wall. Meredith had long thought it was there solely to keep her out. She had now begun to suspect that Adam had built it with that dogged thoroughness of his, in order to keep something in. Something frightening that had begun to find its way through.

The door from the garage opened after a moment, and Adam walked into the kitchen where Meredith waited. He was looking at the floor, and glanced up, seeming almost startled when Meredith spoke.

"You're home early."

"Yeah. A thing happened between Arnie and me. I just left. I had to get out of there," Adam said. Then added vaguely, "I don't know, Meredith."

"What do you mean? What happened?"

"I don't know. I just sort of lost it. I said some things that I probably should have said a long time ago. Or maybe I never should have said them. I just should have gone somewhere else." After a moment's pause he added, "That may be what I have to do now."

"Tell me what happened."

Adam related the incident, omitting only the part about his fictional past. Meredith pictured her uncle's reaction, knowing that he had heard almost the same words from her own lips just the night before. And she felt certain that he would hear something very similar again when her dad spoke to him.

Before she thought, the words, "Poor Uncle Arnie," were out of her mouth.

Adam, for just a moment looked stricken, and then Meredith saw the rage ignite behind his eyes.

"Poor Uncle Arnie?" The veins stood out on his neck and the handsome suntanned face deepened to almost purple, and it twisted in fury as he advanced on Meredith in two quick strides. He clenched his fists at his sides and leaned in to within inches of her face, spitting out the words again, "Poor Uncle Arnie?"

"Adam, listen to me. I just meant—"

"I can't believe you, Meredith. Poor Uncle Arnie? You've been right there. You've seen it. I thought at the very least I had your support. If I don't even have that...if my wife doesn't even believe in me, what's the point?" He whirled away and threw out his hand in a vicious thrust, the back of his hand coming close enough to Meredith's face that she felt the wind stir against her cheek. She flinched away violently, slipped on the tile and fell to the floor.

Both kids, hearing the commotion, had come running to the kitchen. From the angle where they stopped, frozen in the doorway, Andy thought the blow had landed and he shrieked, "You hit Momma!"

Macy had seen it too. She burst into tears, shrinking behind and clinging to her brother's waist.

Turning, horrified by the terror she saw in her children's faces Meredith cried. "Honey, Daddy didn't hit me." She scrambled across the floor to them, and on her knees gathered them up into her arms. "He wouldn't hit me. I just slipped and fell down."

She looked back over her shoulder. Adam stood ashen, looking as though in the next instant he might bolt from the room. Meredith extended her hand to her husband, beckoning him to reassure the children. She could feel Andy pulling away as Adam slowly came across the kitchen toward them, but Meredith held him fast.

Adam stood, his hand over his mouth, looking down at them, and then he dropped to his knees beside Meredith. Tears filled his eyes as he gently placed the other hand on his wife's shoulder.

"I'm so sorry. I lost my temper, but kids, I would never hit Mom. Never, Andy, I promise."

Andy's frightened eyes hardened. It was a look Adam had seen before. He had seen it in his own reflection in the old cracked mirror on the wall over the sink in a filthy junkyard shack. In that moment, a fragment of Scripture quoted in a sermon that he had heard years before came to mind. The pastor had preached that the *sins of the father would be visited even on the third and fourth generation.* And the man had quoted a similar passage from three or four different places in the Bible to drive home the point.

It had been the most hopeless message Adam had ever heard, and that had been the last time he had been to church, other than the obligatory Easter and Christmas services with the whole family.

Now, in his mind he heard those words quoted again, but this time uttered in the guttural snarl of Freddy Finger, peppered with obscenities and punctuated with the Moron's mocking bray of laughter.

29
1991

• • • •

MASON'S DRIVEWAY LED around to a garage that was separated from the house by a covered walk, and an entrance to the back garden. It was a delightful place, beautifully landscaped and designed to erase the pressures of business and life. Arnie parked and took his briefcase from the seat beside him. There was a doorway that opened to a stone path winding through a copse of trees, offering a glimpse of the patio and the glistening pool beyond.

He always expected to see Annie back here, her unruly curls framing her smiling face under a big floppy hat, gardening tools in hand. He glanced over at the greenhouse built onto the inner side of the garage and wondered if her plants still flourished.

Mason was sitting under the shade of an umbrella at a table beside the pool, looking brown and fit, and sporting a close-cropped full beard. He looked up and closed a manila folder when he heard Arnie approaching. He stood and greeted his brother-in-law with genuine affection and more vitality than Arnie had seen since Annie died.

"I like the beard," Arnie said. "Very Hemingway. You look good, Mason. More like yourself than I have seen you look in a long time."

"Well, I think maybe I'm getting my legs back under me. I'm going to miss her every day, but I know, you do too. So does Meredith, and Adam and the kids. Annie was a wonder," and glancing up to the treetops he added, "And she still is." Mason gestured toward the table. "Have a seat. Can I get you anything? Coffee? Soda? Tea? Celia has me all stocked up."

"Nothing right now, thanks," Arnie said, and then segued directly to the obvious issue by adding, "But I may need a stiff drink after this." He sat down with a rueful smile, and met eyes with Mason.

"Arnie, you and I have been partners for a long time. And we're more brothers than a lot of guys joined by blood. I have more respect for you than anyone I've ever met. So we can work through this," Mason said evenly.

Arnie didn't reply.

"Meredith kind of came unwound at you last night, I gather," Mason began. "She gave me a pretty good account of what she said to you. She feels terrible about it, but I asked her if she said anything that wasn't true. Do you think she did?"

Arnie looked down and scratched his chin absently. "No. No, everything Meredith said was right. And just before I left the office, Adam laid into me with pretty much the same grievances."

"Really? What brought that on, because I don't believe Meredith told him about her conversation with you."

"I'm not sure what set him off, but I can tell you that no employee of Warner & Crewe has ever spoken to me like that. I thought he was going to quit there and then. I'm not sure he shouldn't have. Or that I shouldn't have fired him," Arnie said with some heat, then added, "If he wasn't your son-in-law I would have."

"Did he accuse you of anything you haven't done?"

"That's not the point. Look, Mason, you know me. I have one priority, and that is what is good for the company." Arnie stood up and walked toward the pool and said with his back to Mason, "Everything Adam said was true. Everything Meredith said was true. Yes, I have had my hand in the boy's face since the day you and Annie made it clear that you wanted him hired."

"You didn't want to hire Adam?"

Arnie turned back toward Mason. "No I didn't want to hire Adam. I thought it was a bad idea. I didn't trust him then, and I don't trust him now."

"So why didn't you just level with Annie and me about all this right at the outset?"

"Aw come on Mason, what was I going to do? Meredith was walking about a foot off the floor over this guy. Annie was too. And the two of you acted like his resumé was the greatest thing you'd ever read. I'm supposed to say *no* to that? Suddenly this kid was the future of Warner & Crewe."

Now Mason stood and walked over to face Arnie squarely, taking the manila folder that contained Adam's proposal with him. "Well Arnie, I've been going through Adam and Meredith's proposal, and partner, those two absolutely *are* the future of Warner & Crewe, if it's going to have a future at all."

Mason waved the file and said, "The two of them have created a business plan that will take the company from what we started, to something you should be leaping to embrace. But you're not." Mason stopped and let the words hang in the air.

"You're not. Why not? Do you have a plan, Arnie? Do you have an answer for the independent gift stores that are closing, one after the other across the country? Those stores have been our livelihood. Our conduit to the market. Do you have an answer for the glut of cheap imported figurines that sell for ten percent of the price of ours?"

Arnie said nothing as Mason walked back and sat down at the table. "See, Arnie, I think the problem is that you don't have an answer, and Adam does. It seems to me that you've spent the past thirteen years trying to prove that your first impression of this boy was right. Meredith said you hardly looked at the proposal. You all but threw it in the trash right in front of him."

Arnie blew out air and walked back to join Mason at the table, throwing himself down into the chair. He shook his head, looking at the ground for a long time.

"If you want, I can quote that proposal line and verse, I've worked through it so many times. Your son-in-law has tried to re-invent our company based on the whole world embracing this new way to shop. Yes, this computer web thing may become everything he claims, but I don't know that, and neither does he. Nobody does."

Mason said, "Why not discuss that with him, and with Meredith? Let them explain what they're seeing that you may be missing. Why let them both think you tossed it aside without a thought?"

Arnie thought for a moment then answered, "Mason you and Annie haven't been here for almost a year. I lost my partners. I lost both my partners, and that's taken a little getting used to. Now I'm sure my decisions haven't all been good ones. And I guess maybe I do feel a little like all that I have left is being wrestled away from me."

Arnie Warner was not a man to expose such obvious vulnerability. Mason sat gravely, stung by the realization of the burden he had inflicted upon Arnie by simply walking away from his responsibilities at their business.

After a long moment, Arnie continued quietly, "Mason, I never bargained to be partners with your son-in-law. You and I started this company together, and I have always been able to be honest with you about everything. Every issue, except Adam Pembrook, and I've been over a barrel about him from the very first. He has been a wedge between me and all of you. He's been a threat to the company, and a threat to our relationship."

"What are you talking about, Arnie? A threat? How is Adam a threat? And what do you mean you're over a barrel?"

"I know things about Adam Pembrook that nobody else knows. I have from the very first, and I've had to keep that to myself, because to reveal it...to expose him could have cost me my relationship with my sister, with Meredith, and with you."

Mason started to protest, but Arnie cut him off, holding up his hand. "No, listen to me. You all thought Adam was Prince Charming...intelligent, good-looking, ambitious, the whole package. He had this heart-breaking story about his childhood...losing his parents, then his grandparents. Alone in the world, and every one of you embraced him and that story completely, without question." Arnie paused before plunging into the rest. "Well I had questions. And I got the answers."

"I knew the truth, and the truth gave me a lot of trepidation about that kid, and yet for me to even express a doubt about his character, or to lay out what I knew about him would have caused a rift between us that would have affected everything. I simply was never willing to take that chance."

"Mason, you know how I love Meredith. I can't imagine loving her more if she was my own daughter. I was just afraid that if—" Arnie had to stop when a sudden tightness in his throat caught him off guard. He regained his composure before he continued, "And now for all that, look where we are."

"This mysterious thing you know, that nobody else knows about Adam," Mason said flatly, "I suppose you had Joe Kitchens dig all this up?"

"Yes," Arnie answered, picking up his briefcase and pulling out the accordion file.

Mason glanced at the file in Arnie's hand and asked, "When was that?"

"I called him right after Meredith introduced Adam to me. Something about the boy struck my radar wrong. It was obvious that Meredith was more than smitten. I felt like I needed to know."

"But I didn't?"

"I thought you and Annie would have considered it stepping over the line for me to be paying to have a kid she was dating investigated." Arnie paused and shook his head, "And it was over the line. I knew that, but then everything happened so fast between them. They were suddenly engaged. Married. Then you and Annie put him up for a job with us. What was I going to do?"

"You could have told us, and let Annie and me, her parents, decide how to deal with it."

"Mason, I didn't want to ruin it. Meredith was glowing, she was so happy. So were the two of you. And then in no time she was pregnant with Andy. There was never a time."

"And besides, Mason, I hoped I was wrong. I hoped that Adam would eventually reveal the truth about his past. If he had just been forthcoming, at any point, but he never was. So all of you were right...I never trusted Adam. I believe I had sufficient reason not to."

Mason said, "Maybe the time was never right for him either. Did you ever think about that?"

"Mason, Adam stood in my office not an hour ago and told me that every word of the story he told Meredith about his childhood was a lie."

"Really? Well then it sounds as if he——"

"And then he stood right there, flat-footed, and told me another lie. So my question now is why is he still trying to hide the truth? Here's his chance to admit who he really is, but instead...he lies through his teeth to me."

Arnie pulled the manila files out of the old accordion folder, but Mason said, "You can put those up. I don't want to hear it."

"You what?"

"I don't care what happened before Adam married my daughter. What I know, is that she loves him. I know he loves her. And he's a good father. And I know he is an asset to Warner & Crewe and he always has been."

Mason continued, "You mentioned Adam's resumé. I remember that resumé. It had letters of glowing recommendations going all the way back to his high school principal and the grocery store where he worked when he was a kid. He had multiple scholarships, top of his class in high school, top of his class in college, and in grad school. Good grief, Arnie, whatever is in that file of yours, it's obviously something that Adam wants to leave buried in the past. I'm guessing it was something pretty horrendous, but whatever it was, it happened when he was just a kid. A kid, Arnie! That does not define who he is today. You need to let it go."

The two men sat looking defiantly into each other's eyes for an uncomfortable time before Mason added in a strange, hollow tone, "Arnie, do you have any idea how many men I killed before I married your sister and became your partner?"

Silence hung in the air before Mason went on, "I'll just tell you about one. I chased him down. He had dropped his rifle and he tripped on the rocks trying to scramble up a hill to get away from me. He had just managed to get his sidearm out when I caught him and I drove my bayonet through his throat. He couldn't have been more than fifteen years old, Arnie. And I can still see his eyes."

Mason's face had gone ashen as he relived the scene, and he finally managed to say, "I have more I could tell you about. I never told Annie. I've never told anyone. Arnie, some of us have things we have to leave buried, or they will bury us. You're a fortunate man to have the luxury of not living with such a burden."

"My father helped me to see that who I am is not based on the terrible things I did in the war, but on who I am as a child of God. That was the new identity I adopted. Maybe instead of holding that file over Adam's head, you should judge him based on the identity he has chosen," Mason said, then nodding toward the folder still in Arnie's hand he added, "And burn that."

Mason waited, but Arnie made no reply.

"And by the way, you have not lost both of your partners. I'm back as of now."

"You say that almost like it's a threat," Arnie said.

"Now I'm a threat?"

"Mason, I just meant you sounded a little hostile."

"Arnie, I appreciate you giving me this time to get my feet on the ground, but it hasn't been fair to you. We both lost Annie, and it's been hard. Maybe this is a good thing, because it's made me realize that I have unfinished business here. I'm not going to stay forever. I'm happy down at the lake. That's where I want to live, but let's get this thing resolved...if only for Meredith, and Andy, and Macy's sake."

Mason and Arnie continued in stilted conversation, decompressing from the confrontation, and eventually warming to one another's company again. Arnie brought Mason up to speed on various recent events at Warner & Crewe, but they avoided the subject of Adam Pembrook. It was an awkward conversation, compared to the transparency they had always enjoyed with one another. Both had things they would like to say, but were purposely leaving those things unsaid, a restraint born of absolute trust and deep respect for one another.

Arnie was glad for the news that Mason had decided to return, even though he knew it was in response to what was being characterized as a problem that he had caused. It was clear that he had dealt with the whole issue of Adam Pembrook poorly from the outset, but he was going to have to take some time alone to think over some of the things he had been pummeled with over these two days.

They eventually heated Celia's casserole and Arnie put together a salad, whipping up a vinaigrette that Mason insisted Warner & Crewe should start bottling and selling with their line of salad bowls. Both were glad to have the unpleasantness fade, and Arnie in particular found himself thankful to see Mason more engaged and present than he had been in almost a year. He missed Annie terribly, but he had grieved just as much over Mason, watching his best friend wither in loneliness, when he had so much love and life left to enjoy.

Arnie silently gave thanks as he sat down to eat with Mason at the table by the pool. He thanked God for the problem that had stirred life back into Mason, and asked for a solution that would repair his relationship with Meredith.

Arnie and Annie had not been raised with faith. Their mother professed to be a Christian, but their father, until he eventually left, never worshiped anything beyond his own accomplishments in business. Mason had brought his trusting relationship with Jesus along with him into the family. He made sure everyone got to know Him.

After savoring Celia's casserole, Mason went inside and came back with two cups of strong coffee and a couple of good cigars. Sharing the indulgence with his brother-in-law out under the stars after a surprisingly good meal was a pleasure. As only close companions may, the two sat in comfortable silence, each enjoying the sounds and aroma carried on a gentle summer breeze. Mason heard the distinctive clicking chirp of a cardinal and smiled.

Arnie leaned forward in the patio chair resting his forearms on his knees, looked over at Mason choosing his words carefully, "This is probably the worst possible time to bring this up, in light of what's been going on the past couple of days, but it's something that's been on my mind for quite awhile and I've really been wanting to talk to you about it."

Mason settled back into his chair, crossed his legs and leaned on one elbow, raising his hand to cover his mouth under a cupped palm. Arnie had seen the pose countless times over the years. It was his partner's way of saying, "Okay, go on. I'm listening," without saying a word.

Arnie leaned back and took a sip of his coffee, and without further preamble, which was always his style, he began, "I'm sure you know that my will leaves my share of the company to Meredith, but I'm thinking I may change that." He paused and then added, "You have to trust me, this has nothing to do with this." He made a chaotic gesture with one hand, which Mason understood. "I've been thinking about doing something different. I guess it's been running through my mind ever since we lost Annie."

Mason was surprised. He and Arnie had never talked about the disposition of his shares of the company, but he had no other heirs, and he certainly loved Meredith as his own.

In Arnie's estimation, his niece had always been utterly without flaw or shortcoming. He had been certain of that from the moment he walked into the hospital room to see his sister's tiny toothless, red-splotched baby girl for the first time.

Annie used to joke when her daughter would ask for some special liberty that she would have to "ask her daddies first." Mason had always been generous to share his daughter with her uncle, and delighted in the way Meredith could bring out the playfulness in the otherwise cranky and gruff bachelor. As far as Mason knew, the conversation she and Arnie had the previous evening was the first instance of a cross word between them.

He had just always assumed that Meredith would end up with the full ownership of Warner & Crew when the three of them were gone. Meredith, and her husband Adam, would own the company.

With his hand still cupped over his mouth, Mason answered, "And what is it you're thinking?"

"I've been thinking about leaving my third of the company to our people when I die. Meredith will naturally inherit both Annie's share and yours. She and the kids are never going to hurt for money, regardless. I've always thought we should have worked out a way to transfer some ownership position in the company to the ones who have been with us for such a long time. Of course, it would be better if it were while we're still around to guide them. But we have virtually treated them all like partners for years. We've consulted them about every expansion, every equipment investment. It isn't like they don't know the business inside and out already."

"I think I may have a better idea," Mason broke in, sitting forward in his chair. "Why don't we give our employees Annie's third? And instead of waiting, why not do it right away? You know what she'd say."

"She wanted to give them half the company the first year we made a profit, remember? She'd love the idea, Mason," Then in the next moment he added, "Do you think Meredith will be alright with it?"

"You know she will be."

After a long pause Arnie said, "You know there's one person who won't be."

Mason just looked at him, and after an awkward moment he stood and picked up his cup.

"You want some more?

Arnie just raised a palm in answer, and Mason said, "You know you're going to have to figure out a way to make peace with him." He turned and walked away, leaving Arnie deflated.

• • • •

ARNIE HAD BEEN GONE for an hour or so when Mason's phone rang. He was in his study, going over the proposal again, and jotting still more notes and questions.

It was Meredith. "Hi Dad, is Uncle Arnie still there?" she asked, her voice low, clearly trying not to be overheard.

"No, he's been gone for awhile. It went pretty well, I think," he said, anticipating her question. "I gave him some things to think about. I really believe he wants this thing resolved. Certainly with you, and he knows if that's going to happen, he has to come to some resolution with Adam. I'm guessing Adam told you they had quite a scene today."

"Yeah. He's going to take a few days off with the kids and me. He was so upset when he came home this afternoon. I've never seen him like that."

"I think it's a good idea. Like I told you, having you two out of the line of fire for a bit may be the best thing for everybody. I'm glad Adam is willing to take some time off and just be with you and the kids."

"Honestly, the bigger issue may be convincing him to come back," Meredith said.

"After going over this proposal that you two put together, I can tell you that the company absolutely needs Adam," Mason said. "Arnie and I will come to an understanding about all of this."

After they hung up the phone, Meredith was grateful for the encouragement her dad provided, and she wanted to believe him, but the picture of Adam's face as he had stormed across the kitchen toward her, kept coming back into focus. She was sure that he had been

237

about to hit her. It had terrified her, and she thought now that, unless something changed drastically, it was only a matter of time before he would, no matter what he was promising now.

She stared out the bathroom window as she tried to pray. She thought she should pray. People were always saying that was the thing to do in desperate times, but her thoughts kept straying from her prayer to a vision of herself and the kids alone in the house. Adam gone, living somewhere else, maybe even in another city, and the awkward, painful moments when he would come to pick up the kids on weekends, or worse. Maybe he would leave and never see them, and she envisioned their faces...their precious little faces sad and confused.

Then the awful scene in the kitchen replayed in her mind yet again, just as she knew it would in theirs. Perhaps it was tormenting them even now as they lay in their beds. *What was it she had seen in Andy's eyes when she tried to reassure him as she tucked him in? Betrayal?*

Meredith believed it, whether that was what her son was feeling or not. She and Adam had betrayed their trust, allowing this, whatever it was, to invade their lives and destroy their happiness.

Her mind was in turmoil, and had been for the past year, if she was honest with herself. That was the problem. As pragmatic as she was about business, in personal matters Meredith had always been inclined to focus on the positive, and ignore the negative all too easily. It was a quality that made her a delightful child, a supportive friend, a model wife and mother, but now she found herself unable to deny that she was, and had been for a long time, a desperately unhappy woman.

As Adam's frustration at work grew, he distanced himself more and more from her. No matter how she tried to sympathize and support him, his fixation on her uncle as the enemy had somehow grown to include her.

Adam seemed to become infuriated by everything she said, even when she was attempting to encourage him. He had always had a quick temper, but until this past year, he had controlled it, and had always been remorseful when it would flare up. But now, in a heartbeat he could be in a rage. And it was getting worse. Much worse.

Meredith had been dismayed by Arnie's dismissal of the business proposal that she and Adam had worked on together, but she had warned Adam throughout the research and preparation that Arnie was going to be against it. She knew her uncle would fight anything that included employee layoffs. Adam had been infuriated by her warnings.

The proposal was a line in the sand, as far as he was concerned, and in her attempt to be realistic, and pose what she knew would be Arnie's objections, she found herself on the wrong side of that line, standing with her uncle in Adam's view.

And then, before he could make the proposal to the partners, her mother had been killed and her dad, in his grief, had turned his back on the company. Adam had waited for Mason to come back, for things to resume some normalcy, but it became obvious that Arnie Warner was going to be the sole decision-maker at Warner & Crewe.

Meredith understood her husband's frustration, but she didn't know what to do about it. He could not tolerate indecision, not taking action. He loved to plan, but when the plan was made, he wanted to execute. The time for thinking and talking was over. Resistance and obstruction were the enemies of progress, and Adam Pembrook was wired for progress. He loved the process, and his vision was clear.

He was convinced that there had never been an opportunity for business like the one on the horizon. Adam was certain that the fuse was already lit on a new era in commerce, and every day that Warner & Crewe delayed implementing his recommendations was destructive to the future of the business.

For almost a year he had been frustrated to the point of distraction, having to sit on his hands and watch his predictions being confirmed in businesses in America and around the world. Warner & Crewe was stagnating, and missing its chance to be in front of the wave.

Meredith allowed herself to contemplate what her life and the children's might be like without Adam. She hated the despair that she knew it would bring, but she knew that would pass, just as it had after her mother had died. It would fade to vague unhappiness. She could deal with being unhappy. One of her best friends from college had spent the past three years watching her mother fade into the oblivion of dementia. She knew a couple at church that had a daughter, just a little girl, dying of cancer, and they had no hope. She recognized that her unhappiness was nothing compared to that. Her situation was not hopeless. The thought of those people made her feel selfish and small.

It was that line of reasoning that Meredith always used to regain her footing and push on, but she could not bear to watch her children learn the grim skill of coping. She would not stand by and watch Adam turn Warner & Crewe into a battleground. Not when her father and uncle were being cast as the enemy. They had both been through so much, coping with losing her mother.

Meredith believed that she alone knew what Adam Pembrook really was becoming, and since it was she who had been his avenue into their world, it was her duty to fix it. She simply had no experience dealing with the confrontation that lay before her, and it was unavoidable. No, that wasn't true. She had been successfully avoiding it for months. She could have continued to avoid it.

There was no way she could confront this situation without changing everything. But in her heart, she knew that changing everything was exactly what she needed to do. The episode tonight was confirmation that Adam was losing his grip on something that threatened to lay waste to their whole world.

Overwhelmed, Meredith stepped into the shower and turned on the water. Masking her urgent whispers with the sound of the shower, she tried again to pray, "Lord, I don't know what to do. I don't know what to ask for. I don't know if...I don't know if I love my husband anymore." Then, her voice pinched into a sad silent wail, as the words echoed within, *And I don't know if he ever really loved me.* Through her tears, in great gasping sobs she said, "Oh Mom, I miss you so much. I need you so much right now."

31
1991

• • • •

THE NEXT MORNING ADAM was up early, and glad to not be going to work. He agreed with Meredith that he needed to take a few days off. He wasn't interested in seeing Arnie Warner yet, if ever.

What Meredith did not know, and what was making his frustration even worse, was watching people with lesser minds than his embracing this new technology and creating what he believed were potential empires, while in his mind he stood by, chained to a staid and prosaic old company that sold sweet little porcelain figurines to old ladies.

He had begun to resent Meredith for her dogged determination to preserve the family legacy. It was business, and such sentimentality was an encumbrance. Adam saw all of his work thrown away. The years of preparation leading to this opportunity, and he had walled himself in at a company that was destined to fade away, unless it could be transformed into something altogether new. Arnie Warner saw him as a usurper, when he should have seen him as his best hope.

Over the last year the discontent had grown to resentment, and eventually acrimony had taken him over. Every private moment he had, the whole thing seemed to wash over him, and Adam found himself venting his exasperation in imagined confrontations with Arnie Warner and with Meredith. Every headline in every business magazine seemed to mock him.

He felt stupid for trying to rescue a company that was destined to die on the vine. There was only one good reason to do everything possible to preserve it. If Arnie Warner would open his closed mind and listen to him, Adam could prove to him how Warner & Crewe's sterling financial position could launch any number of other businesses

242

that had a genuine opportunity to thrive in this exciting expanding business climate.

But there was now something far more important at stake than Warner & Crewe. Adam knew he needed to spend some time with Meredith and the kids. It had been two days, and things were still strained, particularly with Andy. He had been giving Adam a wide berth since the incident in the kitchen.

It grieved Adam to know what his son was feeling. He remembered that feeling. *Stay out of his way. Keep quiet and maybe he won't notice you.* Then he realized that there was a huge difference. Andy loved him. He trusted him. Adam had hated the Moron. He still hated him. And that's when he realized that what his son was feeling was worse. Much worse.

He decided to take the kids out for the day. A big pancake breakfast followed by a trip to the mall, the arcade, whatever struck their fancy. Anything to put out of their minds the memory of their dad backhanding their mother.

Even though he hadn't actually struck her, and Adam had played it off as a gesture of frustration, he knew that it had been only a last second wave of horror and force of will that had stopped his hand. In that flash of anger, he had wanted to hit her. He had intended to hit her, and that realization scared him to death and filled him with self-loathing.

Andy sat rigid and silent up front with him. Macy, in the back seat, was not her usual chatterbox self. Adam glanced up at the rear-view mirror, which was canted in such a way that it was his own eyes he was seeing. But they weren't his eyes. They were the Moron's eyes, and the hate they reflected back to Adam bored into him.

At that moment Macy caught just a glimpse of a large yellow butterfly floating out from the roadside, and in that instant her lips pursed to shriek, "Grannie!" just as the butterfly was obliterated into green goo and fluttering yellow shards of wings, laced with delicate black markings, squarely in her daddy's field of view.

"Macy! My gosh you scared me to death!" Adam barked as he pushed the windshield washer, and the wipers began to smear the voluble remains of the butterfly in an arc across Adam's line of sight.

"But it was Grannie, and we smashed her!" Macy cried.

Andy scolded her, "That wasn't Grannie, Macy. Shut up. It was just a regular butterfly."

"You don't know! It might have been her. Grannie could have poofed into a butterfly just like she poofed into a duck and saved me from drowning in the lake! It might have been!" And with that, Macy dissolved into sobbing wails, "It's just like in Grandpop's story! Grannie smashed herself into our car to save our lives."

The wipers and washer fluid served only to take the mess on the windshield from opaque to a translucent smear before the fluid ran out, so Adam stopped at a gas station and got out to get it cleaned up. Macy's lament had reduced to sniffles by the time he got back in the car.

"So what's this story that Grandpop told you, Macy?" Adam asked, trying to not sound too sharp.

"Just a story about a bird and bees," Macy answered.

"About what?" Adam asked, looking at his little daughter's earnest face in the rearview mirror.

"I'm sorry I screamed and scared you, Daddy. I just thought that butterfly was Grannie, like in the story. I'm sorry."

Fear. Adam heard it in his daughter's sweet little voice, and it broke his heart.

He let the subject drop until they had stopped for breakfast at the kids' favorite pancake place, where, after some gentle assurances that he had merely been startled by her scream and wasn't angry, Adam coaxed Macy into telling the story her Grandpop had told them. With exuberant dramatics, she related the story of Poofarnie,

Poofannie, and Poofernando saving the little boy from being run over by a car by poofing into a bird and two bumblebees. She supplied all the details from Mason's rendition and added a few of her own embellishments.

"That's why I thought that butterfly might be Grannie, because Poofs are dead people who love us and they poof into birds and bees and stuff so we can see them. And sometimes they do things like save our lives."

"I thought it was angels that were supposed to protect us," Adam said.

"Well, I don't know all the rules. Grandpop said there are rules for poofing, but we don't know them until we kick the can."

"Kick the bucket," Andy corrected. It was his first contribution to the story. "It means when you die."

"You said something about a duck that saved you from drowning in the lake?"

Macy's eyes widened, "Yeah! It was Poofgrannie!" And she went on to tell the story, which Andy reluctantly corroborated at his father's urging.

Adam's jaw clenched, as he listened, but he said nothing other than praising Andy for rescuing his sister, while wondering why Meredith had not thought their daughter almost drowning was something he should be told.

The tension between Adam and Andy lessened somewhat throughout the day, but Adam knew it wasn't gone altogether. It would take time, and even then, the memory of it would be stored away in the recesses of Andy's mind forever. Evidence.

The guilt was like a physical ache as Adam watched the children going from game to game at the arcade. He had a clear vision of himself as one of those fathers who picks his kids up for the weekend, according to whatever custody terms a judge decrees, and tries to make up for not being around with pathetic indulgences.

How had this happened? How did everything get so far out of control?

The phrase wormed its way into his mind again. *Sins of the father.* And that same feeling of helpless dread returned. The same feeling he had when he had first heard the minister issue that hopeless verdict on his life.

Sins of the father, even to the third or fourth generation.

Adam looked at his children...his sweet, innocent, beautiful children. But that was the thing. They were his children, so they were the Moron's grandchildren. Were they destined to destroy their own hope for happiness and fulfillment too, just as he seemed to be doing now? Was there any way to stop it? Would it be his face they would see leering and laughing from this abyss he was descending into. Would it be his mocking voice luring them into one of their own?

• • • •

MEREDITH STOOD OUTSIDE the door of her husband's study. He had pushed the door closed, but it hadn't fastened, and had remained open just enough that she had heard him from the den. Adam was clearly angry about something, and obviously talking with someone on the phone. She stopped in the hallway when she heard her father's name.

"Mason Crewe is losing his mind. He thinks birds in his back yard are his dead wife. He talks to them. He's telling my children that she turns into things and visits him. A butterfly smashed on our windshield today and it sent our daughter into hysterics, thinking we had killed her grandmother."

Meredith squeezed her eyes shut tightly as she listened. She had already heard this rant from her husband, but now he was telling other people. He was openly accusing her father of being insane. A tear streamed down her cheek as she tried to think of some way to stop it.

"He is incompetent to make this kind of decision. This will ruin the company and it cannot happen," he said, sounding barely in control of his rage. Then he was silent for a moment, obviously listening.

Then viciously, Adam replied to the caller, "I don't care. I don't care. You find a way. You find a way to stop this, and I mean right now. I mean today, or I guarantee you, Warner & Crewe will be finding another accounting firm," he hissed.

After an impatient pause, Pembrook responded loudly, "Don't you presume to lecture me on what I have the authority to do, Parsons. Whose bright idea was this anyway? Are you the one that started this ball rolling? Are you? Arnold Warner and Mason Crewe are not giving this company away to the stinking employees. Now fix it," he shouted, killing the call and slamming the receiver down, seething.

Meredith squared her shoulders and started to go into her husband's study, but hesitated. Hearing the way Adam had spoken about her father she wanted to burst in and confront him. Instead, she gathered herself and tried to appear calm as she pushed open the door.

Adam stood with his back to the door, his hands on his hips, the muscles of his square jaw working as he gritted his teeth in anger. He spat out a staccato curse and whirled and glared at the intrusion.

"I heard you arguing with someone. What's wrong?" Meredith asked.

"What's wrong, is your father is planning to give away your inheritance," he said. "He's giving away Andy and Macy's inheritance!" He paced in front of the bay window that looked out over a large expanse of carefully manicured garden beyond.

He stopped suddenly and turned on her with an accusing tone, "Has he talked to you about this? Has Arnie? Did you know about it?"

"Adam, no. Just calm down and tell me what this is all about."

"Don't tell me to calm down, Meredith! I've calmed myself down every day, day after day, just waiting for the opportunity to bring this company into the twentieth century. And now this. They're giving it away!"

"Dad hasn't said anything about giving anything away, and we talk every day," she said. "Please, just sit down and tell me what you're talking about." Meredith walked over and put her hand on her husband's shoulder.

Adam shrugged away from the touch and sat down at his desk. Meredith took a seat on the edge of one of the dark leather wingbacks across from him.

"I called the accountant to get some current numbers, and to have him run some projections. I thought since I was here at home I would update the proposal and get ready to take one last run at Arnie with it, now that your dad is coming back on board. I was thinking maybe…maybe there would be a chance of some rational decision-making for a change." With a bitter laugh he added, "My great hope for rational decision-making is a man who thinks his wife comes back to visit him from the grave as a——" he bit his lip to stifle the obscenity that almost followed. "As a bird for God's sake."

"Adam, don't talk about my dad like he's a lunatic. We've already been through this. If you'd heard the way he——"

"What I heard was our daughter going into hysterics about a butterfly hitting the windshield, Meredith! That's some pretty crazy crap, if you ask me, and I mean what I told you. I do not want the kids left alone with him again."

"Adam, you can't."

"I can't what? Protect our children from being traumatized every time they happen to see an insect being killed? Being humiliated at school because they have conversations with birds like their grandfather?"

"And if that's not enough, Meredith, now he's trying to give away the company! When I called Parsons, imagine this, our accountant just assumed that I would know about a change of ownership in Warner & Crewe. He was almost as astonished as I was that your dad had not informed us that he is planning to transfer ownership of a third of the company, your mother's shares, to the employees. A third of the company!"

Parsons tried to clam up and not tell me anymore about it when he realized I was in the dark, but I wouldn't let him. I finally managed to get it out of him that they have Parsons working on a seven-year vesting schedule, but that's ridiculous, because most of them will already be fully vested as soon as the thing goes into effect, because they've been with the company forever. It's millions of dollars of your money and our kids' money that they are just——" He stopped and choked back another obscenity before continuing, "That they're just flat giving away."

"It's not our money. It's their company and they can do whatever they——"

"No! No they cannot!" he spat, rubbing his hands over his face. "We're going to be the ones dealing with all these people. They'll be our partners." Then he stopped and in a caustic tone amended, "I mean they'll be *your* partners."

"Adam, don't."

"They'll have a voice in how the company is run. Worse than that, do you think they're going to keep working and building toward their retirement with a million dollars' worth of the company in their pockets?"

I'm sure Dad and Uncle Arnie have thought this through."

"Quit defending them, Meredith," Adam said, cutting her off. "Your dad suggested we both get out of the office for a few days? Take a little time to make up. I'm sure you've told him and Arnie all about our little scene in the kitchen."

Meredith didn't answer, recoiling at the fury she saw building. Unconsciously she backed away, watching her husband's face darken, the veins standing out on his neck and forehead.

Adam paced, seething and in a mocking voice said, "Take a few days, honey. Take a week. Uncle Arnie and I have a little project we're putting together. Be a lot easier if you and Adam aren't around to get in our way."

He whirled suddenly and Meredith started as he jabbed a finger toward her. "And not even a word to you about this? Their sole heir? Aren't you the least bit offended by that?"

"No. Adam. I'm surprised, I'll admit that, but I trust them. They're our family. They're not going to do anything that would hurt us. I'll go see Daddy tomorrow and I'm sure he'll tell me all about it."

"Meredith, it's your mother's share of the company they are giving away! This thing has Arnie's fingerprints all over it. He gets your dad to agree to give your mother's shares to the employees, then Arnie turns around and leaves his shares to them, and you end up as a minority shareholder. The employees will own two-thirds of the company. We'll be working for them!"

"Daddy wouldn't let that happen. The company is his and Mom's legacy to us, and to the kids. He wants it to stay a family-owned business, Adam."

Your dad doesn't care what happens to the company anymore. He hasn't cared since your mom died. And those *employees* are Arnie's family. We're paying to send every one of their kids to college, did you know that?"

"Of course I know that. That was not just Uncle Arnie's idea. Mom and Dad both love that they were able to do it. And the employees have to contribute to the fund."

"Oh yeah, they put in their twenty-five cents of every dollar. They're already the most coddled workers on the planet. Now they're going to own the company."

"Well, Adam, they've helped build it."

"It's a job, Meredith! They get paid. They can walk away free and clear without a moment's notice, and would do it if the offer was good enough. They have nothing at risk. No investment."

"Neither do we."

"Nothing at risk! Nothing at risk? You have no idea what I've risked to get where I am. You don't know the price I've paid!" Adam retorted with such vehemence that Meredith flinched and drew back.

Adam saw the reaction and gathered himself, and lowered his voice, "I have invested four years of undergrad, and two years for my MBA, and thirteen years of putting up with everything Arnie Warner dished out. He has treated me like an interloper since the day you brought me home to meet your family," Adam said. "I haven't had the option of walking away and taking another job. I'm married to this company."

"And that's a bad thing, Adam?" Meredith asked, taken aback, her throat tightening and eyes beginning to water in anger now. "Look around you. Warner & Crewe pays us pretty well. You're one of those coddled employees you're talking about. And so am I."

"Coddled? Really Meredith? No! You know what? I've had enough of this. Let them give away the company. Let them sell sappy, outdated figurines to a dying market until there's nothing left. Your daddy, your uncle, and you...good luck."

Adam opened his briefcase dumped the contents onto the desktop, spilling files and papers across the floor. "I am done here."

33

1991

• • • •

MASON PUNCHED THE INTERCOM button on his phone and answered with a cheerful, "Yes ma'am?"

"Oh Mister Crewe, it is so nice to have you back," Maureen said, the smile obvious in her tone. "Meredith is on line three for you."

"Thanks Maureen," and he punched the flashing button to answer the call, thinking he would rather be sitting on the porch looking out over the lake. "Hey honey." There was no answer other than a muffled ragged breath. "Meredith?"

"He left, Daddy. We had an argument and Adam just..." There was a long moment while she obviously struggled to continue, then finally she managed to say in a broken voice, "He dumped everything out of his briefcase, packed a suitcase. Mason ached listening to the sobbing that eventually subsided and ended with, "Adam left me."

"Honey...honey, it'll be alright," Mason said lamely. "Adam loves you and the kids, this whole thing—"

Interrupting, Meredith spat out a question that sounded more like an accusation. "Dad, are you giving Mom's share of the company to the employees?"

Before Mason could recover and answer she added, "Adam found out about it from Parsons. He called to get him to run some projections and Parsons said something about it to him. Naturally, he assumed we would already know about it."

Mason blew out a breath, "We're having Parsons look at it and give us some input on the how it impacts taxes and how the whole thing would work. It's just in the thinking stage right now."

"Don't you think this is something you might have at least——" Meredith began.

253

Mason interrupted, "We wanted to see what it was going to look like before we made a decision. I wanted to see the impact it might have on the company's bottom line. And I didn't want it to have any negative tax ramifications for our people."

"Well it's had a pretty big negative ramification on your daughter. I wish you had talked to us about this first. You know how fragile everything is. Everything *was* between Adam and me," Meredith said as she dissolved again into tears.

"Honey, I'm sorry. Parsons was supposed to put this thing together and get back with Arnie and me. I was going to discuss it with you as soon as I understood it well enough to talk about it. It takes me awhile to digest all that tax jargon."

"That's why you have Adam, Dad! He understands all of that. He speaks that language. Maybe that's why Uncle Arnie wanted to keep Adam out of it, because he could see what is really going on. Dad, if you do this, there's nothing stopping Uncle Arnie from leaving his own shares to the employees too. He's so convinced that Adam is trying to take over and get rid of his *precious people*, it wouldn't surprise me if he came up with this plan to tie his hands."

"Meredith, it was my idea to use your mother's shares."

"Was it, Daddy? Or did Uncle Arnie manipulate you into it." Meredith checked herself, sensing that she was crossing a line. "I just don't understand why you had to do this right now, of all times."

Mason chafed at being questioned like this by his daughter, but he managed to say in a reassuring tone, "We can talk about all of that later. Nothing is happening immediately. We're simply exploring the possibility. And I can assure you that Arnie did not manipulate me into anything. I'm not that far gone yet."

Mason said it with finality, but at the same time he was thinking back over their conversation and wondering if Arnie may indeed have been working a strategy to limit Adam's eventual power in the company, and protect the employees from changes and cut-backs he might want to make. Mason had a suspicion that he may well have played into Arnie's hand, and a flush of anger came over him at the thought.

"The issue right now is you and Adam," he added after a moment. "Where did he go, do you know?"

"No, but I thought he might come to the office. You should be prepared for...well, I don't know what he's going to do. I've never seen him like this," Meredith said. Her voice sounded distant and hopeless.

"I'll call you if he comes here. Let's just take this as it comes. Don't let yourself start agonizing about things that may not ever happen." Mason closed his eyes and his heart grasped for the words that would give his daughter some measure of comfort, and he heard himself saying, "You're not alone, you know. The Lord is right here, even in this painful moment. Don't you think?"

"Then why did he let this happen, Daddy? Why is God letting my marriage be destroyed? Why would He let this happen?"

"I don't know the answers, honey. I don't. And I've asked that same question a thousand times this past year. All we can do is trust that the Lord sees a lot farther down the road than we do."

Mason felt own father's words surface, gleaned from the hundreds of sermons Mason had heard him deliver over the years, "Honey, people talk about having faith, or believing in God, and all they're really saying is that they believe that God exists. Real faith is trusting the heart of God to be not just interested, but actively involved in your life."

Mason hoped he wasn't saying too much, but he went on, "You know that Jesus is the embodiment of God. Fully God, but He is also a person. A person that you and I can believe in, we can trust, and have absolute confidence that when we don't know...He does. He knows why. He knows you, He loves you, and doesn't want to see you hurting any more than I do. He sees the outcome. And He's got the whole thing firmly in hand."

When Meredith didn't respond, he added, "Honey, you can trust Him."

"I'm trying to," she answered.

When Mason hung up, he went immediately into Arnie's office and closed the door. He laid out the situation, excluding Meredith's speculation about the disposition of his partner's share of the company. Arnie looked ashen when he had finished.

"This is my fault," Arnie said into the desktop.

Mason didn't say anything for a long time, which his brother-in-law took as confirmation that he agreed. At length Mason did offer some consolation, saying, "Well, there's a lot of things going on under the surface with Adam. The guy never had a dad. I can't imagine growing up without my dad to turn to."

"I had a dad," Arnie said, "But he wasn't someone you'd ever want to go to with a problem. He'd hand you your head for being too weak to stand on your own two feet. And God forbid you should ever question him. Especially about his business."

"You know me, Mason. I've always wanted to be the kind of guy who stood up for his people. Got the best out of them because I gave them my best." Arnie walked to the window and looked out, seeing nothing. "I mean, I've always been willing to go to the mat for anyone who gave us their best effort. I've always tried to be...to be anything *but* what my father was."

Mason said, "You have always put the employees first. And I have to tell you, that's why I find something Meredith said very plausible, and very disturbing."

"If we transfer ownership of Annie's shares to our employees, and then later, should you decide to bequeath your shares to them as well, Meredith and Adam have only the shares that she will inherit from me, and that leaves the employees with controlling interest in the company."

The ticking of the antique grandfather clock at the end of Arnie's office seemed to assault the silence that hung between the partners. Mason didn't stir. Nor did Arnie. He continued to stare fixedly out the window until the clock struck the quarter hour, then he went back and sat down behind his desk without meeting his brother-in-law's eye.

Mason could see that something was playing through his mind. Something painful. He knew that his words suggested a betrayal of trust, and Arnie's reaction, or rather, lack of reaction, told him that the accusation was not totally unfounded.

Mason broke the silence and said, "Arnie, I'm not the one who has to fix this."

They heard muffled voices through the closed office door, and both looked up as it suddenly burst open and Adam Pembrook walked in and stood, his steady gaze icy, and his voice husky as he said with no small degree of defiance, "I'm glad you're both here. I have something I need to say to you two."

Arnie stood up, his eyes locked with Adam Pembrook's, and he said, "I'm afraid that will have to wait. You and I have somewhere we need to go." As he continued, he pulled something from a lower desk and placed it in his briefcase. "And we have to leave immediately. I was just about to call you." Then to Mason he said, "Adam and I should be back tomorrow...the next day at the latest."

Adam was so taken aback by Arnie's sudden air of urgency, that he said nothing as he watched Arnie step to a small closet and retrieve an overnighter and a garment bag. He nodded to the briefcase he had left sitting on the desktop and said to Adam, "Would you mind carrying that for me?" And then he walked out the door and said over his shoulder, "We need to leave now. We'll take your car if that's alright."

Adam looked at Mason, who was as puzzled as his son-in-law, but he consciously decided to feign being fully aware of the reason for their sudden departure. Clearly Arnie had something in mind.

Mason responded to the questioning look by merely saying, "Don't forget his briefcase," and he followed Arnie out the door.

As for Arnie, he was playing the whole scene by ear. He always kept a change of clothes and a bag packed, because business emergencies, on rare occasions over the years, had required him to catch the first available flight out. Arnie Warner liked to be prepared.

But that part was the only part of this scheme that he was prepared for. The rest of it, he was making up as he went along. Or following along, for it almost seemed to him that he was being run through a maze, and the only way out, required that he and Adam Pembrook were being drawn to confront something, and they had to do it together.

"Do you mind if I drive?" Arnie asked going to the driver's side door of Adam's car. "I'm not good at riding. Motion sickness," he lied.

"Sure. Can you at least tell me where we're going?" Adam responded, getting in on the passenger side of the car, still bewildered, but now growing genuinely curious.

Arnie ignored the question as he fussed with hanging his garment bag and putting the suitcase in the back seat. He noted, as he had expected, that Adam had his own packed bag and some other clothes on hangers, the result of his hasty departure after the argument with Meredith. He closed his eyes and offered a wordless, desperate prayer for what he was about to attempt to do.

Arnie closed the rear car door and was about to get in behind the wheel when a large black bird landed with a noisy squawk on the hood of the car. It pecked at the hood ornament, fluttered off onto the parking lot pavement, then back up to the hood, then down to the pavement, punctuating each movement with a harsh clicking squawk. It did it twice more before flying off to the south as the car pulled away.

From his second story window above the parking lot, Mason was watching Arnie and Adam loading up to leave. He saw the grackle's antics and with a quiet laugh, he relaxed his furrowed brow.

"Annie, you look like Lassie trying to get Timmy to follow her," he said with a chuckle, recalling the old black and white television show from the fifties. He reached for the telephone to call Meredith.

• • • •

WHEN THEY PULLED OUT of the parking lot at Warner & Crewe, Arnie had no idea what he was going to say to Adam Pembrook. He wished there was a way to have some time to think about it, consider the consequences, and plan an approach. That was Arnie's way. Outline it, define objectives, pros and cons, make a decision, then stay the course.

He was as taken by surprise as anyone, hearing himself rushing Adam into embarking on this completely unplanned, chaotic trip. He didn't even know which highway to take. Checking the fuel gauge, he was relieved to see that it was below half full. Stopping for gas would give him a chance to check a map.

"We're going to need gas," he said, pulling into a station just down the block from the Warner & Crewe factory.

"Where are we going, Arnie?" Adam said as the car stopped at the pump.

"I'll explain it all when we get on the road. Put this on the company card. This is business," he said as he got out and went inside, leaving Adam to see to the fuel.

Inside, Arnie found a map and purchased it, quickly noted the route, and realized this was going to be about a five-hundred-mile trip. He and Adam Pembrook would be in the car together for a long time.

His resolve was wavering. He looked over at Adam, who was fishing his credit card out of his wallet as the attendant washed the windshield. Arnie was just looking away when he caught some movement and looked back. That black bird, or another black bird had landed on top of the car. It was flapping its wings and had caught both Adam and the attendant's attention.

"Weird," Arnie muttered. And then wondered vaguely if a black bird sitting on the car might portend some doom. Then he brushed away the thought, because the doom was already upon them if he couldn't make this work. He took the few remaining moments apart from Adam to try to think about his approach, but gave it up.

I'll just have to wing it, he thought, then looked back out at the bird, still flapping its wings on the roof of the car, and laughed a little dismally to himself. *Time to tell Adam where they were headed.*

Arnie pulled out of the station with Adam staring at him from the passenger seat for a half a block, before he finally responded, "Tulsa? What's in Tulsa?"

"I don't know," Arnie answered. "I've never had occasion to go to Tulsa before, but you grew up there. That's why you're going with me."

"You want me to show you around?" Adam said a little sarcastically. "I didn't get out much, Arnie. The school, the grocery store where I worked, and the orphanage where I lived. That's about it."

Arnie turned onto the interstate and headed south, letting Adam's words hang in the air for a bit before answering, "Adam, I wanted a chance to talk to you. And I want to begin by apologizing for the way I have been toward you."

Adam said nothing, but his gaze did not waver. Arnie could feel it on the side of his face as he drove, searching for the right words.

"Everything you said a few days ago when you came into my office, and everything Meredith said when she laid into me at my house the other night—"

"What are you talking about?" Adam asked sharply. "What do you mean Meredith laid into you?"

"You didn't know Meredith came to my house when she came back from the lake?" Arnie glanced across at him.

"She didn't mention it."

"Meredith told me that you and she were having some problems in your marriage."

"Really? Good grief! We have no privacy to begin with and now she's telling you about our marital issues."

"Adam, the reason she talked to me, as she made perfectly clear, is because your wife believes that whatever is going on between you two is my fault."

When Adam didn't respond, Arnie continued. "As I was saying, everything she said, and everything you said was true. And for that matter, so is everything Mason said, because he's weighed in on it too." Arnie looked across at Adam, and saw confusion had replaced the flash of anger. And added with a sardonic smirk, "In fact, at this point Macy and Andy are the only ones in the family that haven't made it clear to me that I am an insufferable ass."

"Adam, as hard as it is for me to admit...and trust me, it is hard..." Arnie sat for a moment, the opposition within taking over his thoughts. *This is a mistake. You should not give in. You give in, and this guy will gut the company. It will be your fault. Your fault! It's happening all over again. They are going to think that you are just like your father.*

A highway patrol was parked ahead just off the roadway. Seeing it broke the destructive train of thought. Arnie checked his speed and let off the accelerator a touch. As they approached the patrol car he glanced over, then did a little double-take as he noticed a black bird on the light bar of the cruiser flapping its wings and hopping from one end to the other.

Another one. Strange...very strange.

Arnie looked across at Adam and continued, the voice in his head pushed aside, "It is really hard for me to admit, but you're all absolutely right. Adam, you've never given me any reason to treat you with anything but the highest regard, but I've denied you that.

I hope, before this trip is over, you and I can come to a new under-standing."

He looked across at Adam, who was now staring down absently into the floorboard, and added, "And I hope then we'll be able to start with a clean slate."

They drove on a mile or more in silence, Adam still looking into the floor of the car before he finally said, "You could have said all that at the office. Why are we driving to Tulsa?"

After thinking about it for a minute, Arnie shook his head and said, "Honestly, I don't know."

"There's not some business matter there?" Adam asked.

"Oh this whole thing is a business matter," Arnie responded. "You and I have some things to work through if we're going to save a company, and a marriage, don't you think?"

"My marriage is not your concern," Adam said hotly.

"Your marriage is everything to me, Adam." Arnie said, matching his intensity. Then after a moment, in a more subdued voice, he added, "You know I have a very small world. No wife and no children of my own. From the moment she was born, Meredith has been the most cherished person in my life. And now she thinks I've ruined her happiness." Then he added, "You know why I really wanted to take your car? Because I knew you already had your bags packed."

"Man, there are no secrets in this family," Adam spat out, shaking his head and looking out the side window.

"No Adam, there are a lot of secrets," Arnie said, "And that's been the problem."

Adam's eyes narrowed and he turned back, about to speak when Arnie said, "I want to tell you about my father. I've been thinking a lot about him over the last few days. I'm sure Meredith's told you a lit-tle about him, but she doesn't know the whole story. We've just never talked about it much. Nothing about him is a pleasant memory."

"He was all about himself and his business. He should never have married, and he sure shouldn't have been a father." Arnie paused for a moment, then looked over at Adam. "Well, he wasn't a father. Not like Mason. Not like you."

"He was good in business, but that's all. And even at that, it was making money he was good at. The people meant nothing to him. They were like the machinery, or actually less important than that, because he was willing to invest money in taking care of the equipment. He wouldn't invest a penny in taking care of the employees."

"When I was a kid, I worked every summer on the production line and filled in on the night crew when we had a big order and everybody was working overtime. I got to know those guys. I was the boss's kid, so I know they cut me a lot of slack, but I gained their regard over time, and that meant a lot to me. It still does."

"But I sure couldn't earn my dad's regard. He treated me just like he treated every other employee. I was invisible. He paid me the minimum, and no matter how good I got at the job, he never took notice."

"He was an arrogant, egocentric bully. Later on, our mother told Annie that he had been unfaithful innumerable times over the years. It humiliated her, because apparently, he made little effort to conceal his affairs. If she ever confronted him about it, he would buy her another diamond bauble. That was just a deeper assault on her dignity, because it felt like payment to keep his bed warm between trysts with other women."

"Of course, none of that was a surprise to us. Annie and I had figured out what he was when we were just kids. Everyone knew."

Arnie talked on for a long time, sharing several stories about his and Annie's faithless father, and the humiliation his behavior inflicted on his wife and children. At dusk he pulled into a roadside diner.

He cut the engine and sat there for a moment before saying, "I know that was a long tale. I could have just said that my father was a mean-spirited, evil man, but Adam, I really want you to understand why I am so devoted to the people at Warner & Crewe. And so protective of them."

"For those years we were in high school and college, our mother was mired in dealing with all that Dad was putting her through. Annie and I were pretty much on our own. Annie was always such a free and creative spirit. It always seemed to me that she didn't need anybody's approval or encouragement. I wasn't cut out that way."

"I busted my tail to show our dad what I was made of, but he couldn't have cared less. The fellows I worked with on the line could see the whole picture, I guess. They were the ones who encouraged me. The reality is, looking back on it, I imagine they were counting on me coming along and taking over the company, and being a better boss than my father."

"Those men, my friends that I worked alongside, oh they gave me thunder about my grades, politics, girls, my hair, you name it. In the process, they taught me about honor, taking pride in your work, and the dignity of doing a job well, just because it's your job, and not because you're trying to please a boss. Those fellows raised me."

Arnie stopped and swallowed hard, looking away from Adam, then continued, "And then when my dad sold the company and closed down the plant, he left me the job of handing every one of those guys their final paycheck."

"It killed me to do that, Adam. I hated it, and I hated him for doing that to them. And doing that to me. When we started the company, I got the chance to hire some of them back. I suppose I've spent the rest of my life trying to prove to them, and maybe to myself, that I am nothing like my father."

Arnie sat silent for just a moment, then said, "Well we'd better see if they have anything fit to eat in this joint," and abruptly got out of the car.

It was comfort food. Both ordered a breaded chicken-fried steak and mashed potatoes that were served with thick cream gravy over the whole thing. A little effortless stab at a salad in a bowl on the side was disappointing, but the steak was good.

They ate most of the meal in silence, Arnie happy for an excuse not to talk, and Adam glad not to have to listen. His mind was in a whirl, with everything Arnie had been saying taking him totally by surprise. The whole scene with Meredith was replaying in the background of everything he had been listening to Arnie say.

The waitress came around and they both went with her sassy recommendation, ordering cherry cobbler and coffee, then as she sashayed away, Adam said, "Excuse me for a minute." He got up and went out to the phone booth on the sidewalk in front of the diner.

He dialed for the operator and gave her the number, and heard Meredith answer and the operator ask if she would accept charges.

"Adam?" Meredith said when the operator had said to go ahead. There was a touch of alarm in her voice.

"Yeah, I just wanted to check in. This has been a pretty weird day."

"So I hear. Dad called and said you and Uncle Arnie left together on some kind of trip. Where are you?"

"Nowhere yet. We're on our way to Tulsa."

"Tulsa?"

"Yeah, I'm not sure what's happening, but Arnie is...I don't know. But, he's apologized and has told me that he's realized he has been wrong about me. He says he's wanting us to come to some kind of understanding. Make a fresh start. I don't know why we had to drive to Tulsa for him to say it." There was a long pause, and he added, "He told me about you going over and tearing into him. I guess that's what got this whole ball rolling."

"I should have done it ten years ago, or sooner."

Silence again.

"About this morning, I just wanted to apologize. I'm sorry. My temper has been...I don't know what's happening with me. It scares me, Meredith."

"It scares me too."

"You don't know—" Adam looked out across the truck stop parking lot, but the lighted interior of the phone booth obscured his view with his own reflection in the streaked glass. He turned his face away, but on every side he saw the same face looking back at him. Grim, accusing, glowering.

And then he heard the Moron's voice so clearly that Adam thought Meredith surely could hear it too.

No she doesn't know. She doesn't even know your real name. She doesn't know you grew up in a shack by the city dump. She doesn't know you stole my money! She doesn't know how you made all your little plans to kill your own father! How bad you wanted to kill me! You think I didn't know that? You think I didn't know you were spending every day looking for my money, and when you finally found it, all you could think about was how you could get away with murdering your old man? You think I don't know how you were thinking all the time about how it would feel to split my head with that crowbar. I knew it all! I was just waiting to see if you had the stones to try. I should have broken your scrawny neck and buried you out in the junkyard beside your stinking mother!"

Adam squeezed his eyes shut and said, "Look, we'll talk when I get home." Hanging up the phone he burst out of the phone booth, afraid to look back. Afraid to see the menacing face of the Moron reflected there.

He went back inside. Arnie looked up from the pie and coffee and said, "Everything okay? You look like you've just seen a——"

"Everything's fine," Adam cut him off. "I was just checking on Meredith and the kids. Cobbler any good?"

Arnie left him alone with his thoughts while they ate their dessert. Adam's color had been gone when he came back in from making his phone call, and Arnie assumed the conversation had gone badly.

As soon as they were back in the car, Arnie began again, "I want to talk about the business plan you proposed."

"Alright," Adam replied evenly.

"You and Meredith thought I dismissed it without any consideration. That is not the case. Far from it. As a matter of fact, I've been studying it ever since you gave it to me. Like I told Mason, I can quote it line and verse."

Arnie continued, "I didn't want you to be right, but I know you are. I knew it the day you presented it. I'm no idiot, Adam. I've been watching the numbers, seeing the market change. I realize the company is vulnerable, and we need to do something."

"Just not something I suggest." Adam said with a touch of defiance in his voice. "You know, Arnie, if you had just said that. If you had only said that you needed to look at it and think about it, instead of what you did. I seriously thought you were going to throw it in the trash right in front of me, just to make a statement about how little regard you have for anything I think."

Arnie sat for a moment, his eyes straight ahead on the highway before answering, "As I said earlier, Adam, I have been wrong in the way I have dealt with you, and I am freely acknowledging that." Arnie glanced across at Adam with a sharp look, "But Meredith is my partner's daughter. You are my niece's husband, and I do not have an obligation to explain myself to you, nor to Meredith for that matter, any more than I do to any other employee of Warner & Crewe."

"Now that sounds more like the Arnie Warner I know," Adam retorted.

"I'm just saying it's a business. It's not a democracy, and until you and Meredith are owners, you come to the table at my invitation. Mine and Mason's together, now that he's coming back to work."

Adam blew out air, glared into the night and said, "From what I hear, you and Mason are inviting the whole company to the table. If you make every employee of Warner & Crewe an owner, that sure sounds like you're trying to make it into a democracy."

"Again, Mason and I don't have to explain ourselves to you, but since you brought it up, I talked to Mason about bequeathing my third of the company to the employees. It was his idea to transfer ownership of Annie's third to them instead, so they could have the benefit now, rather than when I die."

"We have always treated the company like a partner, Adam. If we took bonuses or a profit share, we distributed an equal amount among the employees. This ownership transfer would merely assure that our policy would continue. They would be limited partners, with no hand in the operations. Not a democracy."

Adam asked, "What's to stop you from going ahead and giving your third to the employees as well, leaving Meredith with a minority of the company?"

"Do you seriously think I would ever do that to Meredith?" Then without waiting for an answer, Arnie continued. "When Mason and I started talking about this, and he suggested using Annie's share of the company for this new benefit package, it occurred to me that this could be a way I could live with some of the changes you are proposing."

Adam looked across and said, "You mean the employee cutbacks. If they're let go, they retain their shares, and receive whatever profit share we..." He stopped and pointedly corrected himself, "The *company* distributes."

"And they become fully vested if not dismissed for cause." Arnie confirmed. "So, although we will likely have to be cutting back, even those not close to retirement will have some ongoing benefits."

"Well, speaking as one of the employees, I can tell you they won't appreciate this like you think they will," Adam said. "Not when they get their pink slip. And it's still going to kill you to hand them that final paycheck, just like it did before. You won't feel a bit better, and you're fooling yourself if you think they won't resent you. You will have given away a third of the company for nothing."

"It isn't about what they think of me," Arnie said, although both men knew that was untrue. "But I'll take that into consideration. I'd like to think you're wrong."

"But you know I'm not," Adam said. And then thinking he had nothing to lose at this point, he added, "Your father closed down the company. There will still be people going to work every day at Warner & Crewe. Just not the ones that are laid off. To them, that will be worse than what your father did."

Adam could see the effect those words had, as Arnie recognized the truth in what he had said. "But Arnie, I am not advocating cutting back. The truth is, we will create a need to hire even more people if we diversify and expand our market. That's the whole point of my proposal. The lay-offs are inevitable only if we continue to lose market share and do nothing about it."

Adam took a breath and added, "Growing the company is the only way you can guarantee jobs for your people, but you can't grow the company, and you sure can't create new jobs and expand opportunities for them if you start giving pieces of the company away and eroding its financial strength."

The two were absorbed in debate and discussion for the remainder of the drive into Tulsa. The issue of foreign manufacturing alternatives was a main point of contention, but both made and conceded points as they traveled.

It was a new road that they were on, and as the two of them grappled with ideas about the future of Warner & Crewe, both were too immersed to step back and marvel at what was happening between them. It was only after Arnie pulled into a motel off the interstate and they were each settled in their rooms, that they each reflected, and both found themselves completely astonished by the events of the day.

35
1991

• • • •

THE CONTENTS OF JOE Kitchens' old accordion file lay spread across the small desk in Arnie's hotel room. He sat staring down at it, pondering the next step of what he hoped to do. He was struck by his own foolishness of keeping Adam's insightful mind at bay for so long. Everything Meredith and Mason had said to him now took on more weight.

When he had suddenly leaped into this, and all but tricked Adam into leaping with him, Arnie had only the slightest outline of a plan. It had been a thought that had formed in his mind in the aftermath of his confrontation with Meredith, in a moment when he had no small hostility toward her husband.

He had sat there after Meredith left his house and finished off the bottle of wine alone, fantasizing about exposing Adam Pembrook for who and what he really was, and forcing him to tell the truth for once in his life. Arnie had just enough alcohol in his system that night to indulge in gloating about proving himself right, and everyone who had attacked him, dead wrong.

The first time Arnie met Adam Pembrook, he had that visceral reaction that there was just something *off*. Something not right. And that instinct warned him off the boy. In every area of his life, Arnie was guided by careful thought, and facts he could weigh. He scrupulously rejected feelings, alone, as a barometer of truth, believing completely that emotions were simply too easily manipulated to trust.

But this discernment Arnie occasionally experienced, seemed to be more than a mere feeling. He had never understood it, but he had learned to trust and obey, as the old song said. He would simply step away.

Since stepping away from Adam Pembrook had not been an option, Arnie's response had been to go about gathering facts he could weigh. Here, over a decade later, he had those facts before him once again, but this time he would be able to add to that equation what he knew of Adam from his own experience over that same span of time.

He and Adam driving together, grappling with the challenges that faced Warner & Crewe had been a promising start, but it was a very shaky foundation, considering the confrontation Arnie had in mind to impose on the unsuspecting Adam. But those few hours of conversation with him, coupled with the things Meredith and Mason had said, though they had been very difficult for him to hear, had given Arnie a new perspective about this undertaking. Now, rather than looking for evidence he could use to prove that Adam was a threat to Meredith and to Warner & Crewe, Arnie was sincerely looking for a way to repair the undeserved damage he now realized that he had inflicted upon him.

With that goal in mind, as Arnie sorted through the file once again, the narrative presented a completely different picture than Arnie had formed in his mind all those years before, when his old friend, Joe Kitchens, had attempted to unravel the mystery of Adam Pembrook.

He found a carefully drawn map of Slaterville, and the locations Joe had noted were names Arnie remembered from Joe's account of the various interviews he had conducted. As Arnie studied the notes from those interviews he could hear Joe's rumbling voice, and see him looking up over half glasses as he told the story of the boy's life as he had reconstructed it.

Arnie found himself more than once squeezing his eyes shut and shuddering in regret over his own treatment of this boy who, by whatever means, had managed to extract himself from a quagmire of abuse and neglect. After a couple of hours, he still had only the sketchiest of plans and a strange mixture of both hope and dread of the day that would follow. Still, his resolve was unshakable. He didn't know how he would do it, but Arnie knew it was up to him to set things right.

He thought about praying, because he knew that's what he was supposed to do in situations like this, when he needed wisdom and help to do and say the right things. At least that's what everybody claimed to do. He knew Mason actually did it. He and Annie both had always been big on them all praying together about decisions they had to make. Arnie had bowed his head and gone along, but it was always Mason who did the praying.

He went and pulled back the drape and stood at the window looking out at the sky above the Tulsa streets. No stars. The lights of the city washed the skies black. Arnie remembered a conversation he'd once had with Mason years before, perhaps three years after they had started Warner & Crewe. It struck him odd now, that he couldn't remember what it was that had troubled him so much that he had sought Mason's counsel. He remembered that it was a personal issue, not business, and he remembered Mason's advice, and the conversation that followed.

Mason had said, "I think it's something you really need to pray about."

Arnie had been relatively new to faith at the time, and although he was certain of his belief, the whole *relationship* part of the equation evaded his grasp.

He mumbled some agreement in response to Mason's advice, but then checked himself. He needed something more definite than *you need to pray about it.*

Arnie asked him, "What does that really mean, Mason? I hear people say that at church all the time. I hear you and Annie say it, and I respect it coming from you, because I know you're anything but phony. I guess I'm just not a very good Christian, because when I'm alone and try to pray about things, honestly it just feels like I'm talking to myself."

Mason had said nothing in response, perhaps because Arnie was so closed about such matters that it was a surprise to hear him blurt out an admission like that. Or, Arnie surmised now, Mason had sensed that his brother-in-law wasn't really talking to him at all.

Arnie had continued, "I mean, if I'm talking to someone and they don't ever respond, what kind of *relationship* is that?" Arnie had been sitting on the sofa in Mason's office with his arms resting on his knees, kneading his fingers as he spoke. "Sure, I can imagine God saying things to me that I want to hear. I know that's what Lenny Brockmire does. And that just drives me nuts."

Lenny Brockmire was Warner & Crewe's insurance agent, and he was always talking about *God telling him* he needed to go drop in on Arnie Warner that day, and *God telling him* he should wear his blue suit that day, or to lay off potato chips.

"If God is as vacuous as that, I don't want Him bothering me any more than I want that idiot dropping in without an appointment and wasting my time, because he makes God sound a whole lot like Lenny Brockmire."

"I just want to know God is listening, and that He, I don't know, maybe gives me what I need to say or do about whatever's in front of me." At that Arnie fell silent for a time.

Finally, Mason thought it was time for him to speak. "You know all that you were just saying? That's how I pray when it's just God and me. That sounded like a prayer to me."

Arnie looked up. "You're kidding."

"No, that's pretty much the way I talk to God," Mason had said with a shrug.

"No *thees* and *thous*?"

Mason laughed, "No, I just talk to Him like I'd talk to my dad."

Arnie shook his head and said, "Well I don't think I could talk to God the way I'd talk to my dad if he ever left his Geisha girl to come home for a visit."

"Look Arnie, I don't know whether it's really the voice of God in Lenny's head, telling him to lay off potato chips or whatever, but that's Lenny's way of expressing his faith. Now I'll admit that I think that kind of talk probably puts a lot of people off, but on the other hand, do you have any doubt that Lenny Brockmire genuinely wants to do whatever God would have him do?"

Arnie answered, "Oh no, I don't doubt that, but it just bugs me that he acts like God telegraphs him a *To Do* list every morning or something."

Mason laughed again, shook his head and came around his desk and sat down with Arnie, "Look, I don't pretend to have the answers, but I am thankful every day that God gave me a dad who seemed to. I'm sure it's easier for me because of that. You and Annie didn't have that example, I know, but my dad has always been there to nudge me back on the path, and I think that's just how God does it too. A nudge here, and little push there, sometimes holding us back just for a minute, then letting us go."

"You don't hear *words* like Lenny Brockmire?" Arnie asked.

"No," Mason smiled. "My daddy always said if you'll delight yourself in the Lord, He will give you the desires of your heart, and that doesn't mean a million dollars in the bank." Mason looked at Arnie and said, "I just heard you say that all you want is for God to give you what you should say or do in this situation in front of you. The desire of your heart is for that to happen. So delight yourself in the Lord, Arnie. And then trust Him to give you the desire of your heart."

Mason had stood up and gone to the door, leaving Arnie on the sofa. He turned and added, "And then just like Jesus said to Simon Peter, "Get out of the boat." He had closed the door behind him.

A sharp noise snapped Arnie out of his reverie, and he looked down at the window sill in time to see a black bird peck the glass with its bill, flap its wings furiously, then fly into the darkness.

"Are you kidding me?" Arnie muttered.

36

1991

• • • •

ADAM WAS IN THE HOTEL restaurant, with coffee and a newspaper when Arnie came down the next morning. He looked up when Arnie spoke.

"Good morning. I'm just going to go ahead and check us out."

It had been a restless night for Adam. He had slept very little. As he attempted to consider all that had passed between Arnie and him during the drive, one scene after another had intruded upon his thoughts. Times when Arnie Warner had so blatantly exhibited his low opinion of Adam and his work, and Adam suppressing his anger and disappointment. And following those, imagined scenes of the confrontations that never occurred. Those washed over him one after another as he lay in bed, his teeth clenched, and his anger seething.

Then he would resist the rage he was feeling, and find himself replaying the scene from the night he came so close to hitting Meredith in front of the kids. He remembered it from his perspective, stopping his hand at the last second, and seeing Andy and Macy's horrified faces. The accusation in Andy's eyes burned into him. He saw the fear and heartbreak in Meredith's face, and hated himself for all of it.

And then the worst was seeing himself through their eyes, his eyes cold, mouth cruel, and hand raised. Then suddenly, gone were the gray slacks, crisp white dress shirt, and tie. In their place were oil-stained faded khakis and a filthy yellowed undershirt. The black wingtips buffed to a high gloss were replaced by leather brogans caked with black grease. A short-billed cap that stank of sweat and oil was pulled down and shaded the eyes, but they blazed out of the shadow in a drunken challenge.

They glared out at him, and focused. The corners of the half open mouth raised in a disgusted sneering smile, and the Moron's voice traveled through time and the grave, "You little——" and the filthy name he'd always used for his son struck Adam with the same venom as always. "This is the way it's done." And he saw Meredith's head snap back as the back of the Moron's hand slashed across her cheek, then blazed across again, slapping the opposite side of her face, leaving a bloody smear from her mouth and nose. He saw a fist draw back, and his stomach recoiled in a spasm as he saw his wife double up over a vicious blow that raised her feet off the floor and she fell back across the breakfast table and lay still.

He watched in horror as Andy ran to his mother. The Moron turned to look at him and said, "Oh this is going to be fun. Just like old times."

Adam finally shook himself out of the awful vision, but that haunting phrase, *sins of the father,* echoed through his thoughts.

"I am not him." he spat out in a desperate whisper. "I am not him."

Arnie returned to the hotel dining room, sat and almost as soon as he turned the inverted cup over, a waitress filled it and placed a menu in front of him.

"So where is the mystery tour headed today?" Adam asked from behind his newspaper.

"We have some time this morning. You said something about showing me the place where you grew up. I'd like to see it," Arnie answered offhandedly as he unfolded and began to peruse his own paper and gingerly sip the steaming coffee.

"I have no desire to see that place again. Why on earth would you want to?"

"Was it that terrible?" Arnie asked in return. "Is that the reason for inventing the story about living with your grandparents?"

Adam was immediately uncomfortable, and just sat looking at the tabletop. Arnie lowered the paper and looked at him.

He spoke lowly, so the few people at adjoining tables would not overhear. "I want to know about you, Adam. You've said, and you're right, that I have treated you like you were nobody for all these years. I was wrong. It was unfair and I want to change the way things have been between us."

Adam was defensive when he answered, "And you think taking me back and looking at the children's home will do that?"

"I just thought if you could show me where you grew up, and maybe talk a little about that time of your life, it would help me understand you, and appreciate the challenges that you had to deal with."

Standing up, Adam said, "Arnie, you could never understand what I've had to deal with." Then downing the last of his coffee, he spat, "But fine, let's take a trip down memory lane," and he tossed a five on the table as he turned and stalked toward the lobby.

Arnie looked after him, blew out a breath through puffed cheeks, and whispered, "Lord, this is going to be hard." He gathered his things and got up.

In the car, Arnie again took the wheel. Adam had resigned himself to showing Arnie the orphanage where he had lived. It was obvious that the man was trying to reach out to him somehow, by making him confront a part of his life that he had attempted to hide when he went to college.

Adam directed Arnie to the interstate, which took them out just beyond the southwest edge of the city, then they exited and drove a few miles east on a narrow highway until they came to an entrance gateway. River rock pillars jutted up from stair-stepped rock planters on either side of the road, and the pillars were connected by a parallel arch of two black steel pipes high over the road. Thick metal letters welded between the pipes announced "Carthage Creek Home for

Children." A half mile or so beyond the entrance, Arnie pulled over and stopped on a hilltop overlooking rolling hills dotted with trees and cottages scattered over the well-tended acreage below. A cluster of administrative buildings surrounded a black topped tennis court.

Adam looked out and said with disinterest, "They must have a new benefactor. The tennis court is new."

"It looks like a decent place," Arnie said, uncertain of how to proceed.

"Look, Arnie. Here's the deal. I was a kid who grew up in an orphanage. In school here, we were *the children's home kids*, and the other kids, the teachers, the parents, they all looked at us differently. You could tell they all wanted to know what lurid story landed us out here, but nobody was willing to ask. I just wanted to leave that part of my life behind and start college fresh. Just a guy. So I made up a story."

"I think I can understand that."

"If I'd been a few years older, a little more mature, I probably wouldn't have done that. But I was eighteen years old, and had been..." He stopped long enough that Arnie looked across and noticed a curious wave of stifled emotion before Adam continued, "I wanted what every kid wants. I thought I deserved a different life, so I made one up."

He turned in his seat to face Arnie. "I thought about telling Meredith, I don't know how many times. But how do you say that?" He stared at Arnie for a second, then turned away and in a flippant voice said, "Oh by the way, Sweetheart, you remember that story I told you about how my parents died in a car accident, and my grandparents raised me, and then both of them died right before I came here to school? Yeah, well, I made all that up."

"She's your wife and she loves you. She would have said it didn't matter."

"What about her parents? What about her uncle?"

"I've known it wasn't true for thirteen years. If you had been forthcoming about your real past, maybe things would have been different between you and me," Arnie said, then very deliberately added, "There's nothing about your childhood that you should hide."

"What about Mason and Annie? Did they know?" Adam asked, still looking straight ahead.

"No. Only I knew," Arnie considered and then continued, "And a few days ago, when Mason decided to step into the fray, I started to tell him. You want to know what he said?"

Adam just turned his head and stared at Arnie evenly.

"He cut me off. Told me he didn't want to hear it. That whatever was in your past was your business, and everything he knew about you was honorable."

"I appreciate that," Adam said quietly.

Arnie took a breath, "So how did you come to live here?"

Adam looked at him hard, "Don't you know? Didn't your background investigator get that part of the story?"

Arnie didn't answer the question. Instead he said, "I can understand you wanting to leave the past in the past. But sometimes the past just won't go away. I've been hounded by the memory of my father and the things he did. Scared to death that I was going to turn out just like him."

He watched Adam's face, but it was an impassive mask, as Arnie continued, "Meredith hit a nerve when she came over and had her *conversation* with me. There are things nobody but Annie knew about the way our dad was toward me. She was the only one that saw it, and saw what it did to me. When I got out of school and went to work for him full time, I had so many ideas about ways we could modernize and expand our business, but he was highly insulted that I would dare to suggest that anyone, and especially *I*, could improve on his operation." Arnie stopped and stared out over the steering wheel. "Sound familiar?"

Adam didn't answer, but just sat staring into his lap as Arnie studied his profile, and found himself praying within, *"Please let this be the right thing. Please give me the right words to say."* Then aloud to Adam he said, "The very person I never wanted to be...that's exactly who I've become." He paused and added. "It makes me sick to have to face that about myself."

"Sins of the father," Adam muttered.

"But that's not who I am. I don't have to be him. If I'd seen it sooner..." Arnie paused and tried to structure his thoughts, but abandoned the attempt. It was no time to craft an argument. He said what came from his heart to his lips, and it surprised him. "I have an identity he did not possess."

Adam looked at him, but his expression was neutral.

"When Mason married Annie, he brought something to our family that we had never experienced. He brought his faith. Dad had just left, Mom was out the window dealing with all that. Annie had Mason, and even though we worked together, I was alone. And I needed something...some*one* to believe in. And I needed someone to believe in me."

"Mason introduced me to Jesus," Arnie said quietly. Then looked at Adam, who now appeared to be studying the grounds of the facility below with more interest than he had in what Arnie was saying.

"Mason just so obviously had something...*else*. When we were starting the company, he'd say just a word here and there, and we'd all have an occasional conversation that would end up being about how he wanted the Lord to be involved in our decisions. He didn't push, and I can't even tell you how it happened, but Annie and I both came to a point where——"

Adam interrupted, "If we keep sitting here someone's going to think we're out here stalking the kids or something. I grew up here, the people were nice enough to me, but this isn't like looking fondly at the beloved old home place or anything. I left this place the first minute I could, and I never intended to come back. If you're satisfied, I'd like to go now."

"Sure, Adam. We'll go," Arnie said as he put the car in gear and turned it to head out the gate. "There's just two more places I'd like to see while we're here...your high school and where you worked."

"Arnie it's a school and a grocery store, for goodness sake. What are you trying to do here? You've apologized for treating me like crap. I appreciate it. I accept your apology. I understand that you realize you treated me just like your dad treated you and that makes you feel bad about yourself. Okay, I get that, too. So now, why don't we just drive the three hundred miles back home and see if this new understanding we have makes a difference?"

Arnie absorbed the outburst and answered calmly, "Because it won't." He looked across at Adam. "We haven't gone far enough."

"What's that supposed to mean? Look, Arnie, Meredith and I have had problems. I've lost my temper with her and the kids a few times lately, but that was after I had spent all day, every day wanting to put my fist through the wall in total frustration with you at work. It's understandable that I would be a little intense when I came home and my wife was defending her beloved *Uncle Arnie*."

Adam's fists and jaw clenched as he tried to suppress the urge to lash out again at Arnie. "Look, I get what you were saying about needing someone to believe in you. Oh, I understand that completely. But now you're saying you're willing to start fresh with me. Okay, so am I." Adam said the words, but the tone was almost derisive.

He continued, obviously making an effort to sound conciliatory. "And Arnie, I think the problems that Meredith and I have had, we'll be able to work out now that this thing between you and me is resolved." He stopped talking and stared out the side window for a moment before adding with impatience, "So can we just head back now?"

"It won't be enough, Adam. It isn't just me that's been eating at you. Something else is going on. You're like a pressure cooker about to explode."

"And why wouldn't I be? Arnie, I walked out of my house yesterday with my bags packed. I came into your office ready to quit. I was completely resolved to leave everything I had...Meredith, my kids, all of it...and start over."

"Create another life for yourself." Arnie said flatly. Then added, "Again."

There was a long silence between them as Arnie drove. He glanced for a moment down at the road map on the seat beside him and then took a deep breath and asked, "Can you tell me about your life before you came to the children's home?"

Adam just stared at him.

Arnie didn't ask again, but very deliberately turned and met Adam's eyes. It was just for an instant, because Adam looked away, but in that instant Arnie knew that Adam was going to lie again.

"I was abandoned here in Tulsa when I was about twelve years old. I'm sure you know that, Arnie."

"Yeah, that's what I was told," Arnie answered, and after another silent prayer, which was nothing more than, *Please, Lord.*

As the interstate once again came into view, he asked "What do you remember about the time before?"

Blown out air and a shake of the head was his answer.

"Can you tell me, Adam? I'm sure it's hard to go back to that time, but I'd like for you to trust me enough to do that." Arnie paused and slowed the car slightly as they neared the underpass, "I'd just like to hear the story from you. I want to know about you, Adam. You've hidden all this stuff long enough."

Again, Adam blew out a sigh and said, "Fine." A deep breath and he continued, "There were these people. I don't think I was related to them, but I was with them as long as far back as I can remember.

They were trash. They were like gypsies, always on the move. I don't remember anything about it, but I know they made their living steal- ing——" Adam interrupted himself, "Wait! You were supposed to turn right at the access. Kansas City's that way."

"We're not going back home yet," Arnie answered as he acceler- ated under the interstate and up the access road to merge into the steady stream of trucks and cars hurtling toward Oklahoma City.

Neither spoke again for over half an hour. Adam was curious about Arnie's reaction to his brief, and incomplete recitation of the all but forgotten story of the family that had abandoned him. It was a story that he hadn't told since he was a kid, and it had sounded so outlandish in his own ears, telling it as an adult, that Adam marveled at the memory of the parade of police officers and social workers who had questioned him and apparently believed the tale.

It had seemed to agitate Arnie, but he hadn't asked any more questions, and Adam was relieved about that. He pulled his briefcase out of the back and was absently thumbing through various files, not really looking at any of them. He would occasionally look across at Arnie in disbelief as they continued farther and farther from Kansas City.

Arnie's stomach was in a knot as he thought about what he was going to do next. He had no idea what Adam's reaction was going to be. His thoughts were a jumble of inarticulate prayers, badly con- ceived speeches, and self-recrimination for the whole project.

Finally, Adam broke the silence, "This is getting ridiculous, Arnie. I need to get back to Meredith. She and I have things we need to deal with. For one thing, I need to tell her about the children's home. You're right, about that. There's no reason for her not to know. I should have told her a long time ago. Let's turn around and get back. We can be back in Kansas City before dinner. I feel like I need to see the kids and Meredith."

"And you think that's all you need to tell her?" Arnie asked.

"What's that supposed to mean?"

"I just think when you're telling her about the children's home that, you ought to be sure there's nothing else you've deceived her about," Arnie answered, then put on his signal, took the exit for State Highway 99, and turned under the underpass. But he didn't turn back up onto the interstate and head back toward Tulsa.

Instead he drove due south on the state highway and waited for it.

It took only a moment. Adam slapped his briefcase shut and demanded, "Now where, Arnie?"

Arnie took as long as he dared to answer, then took a deep breath. *Lord please let this be the right thing.*

"Adam, I'm taking you back to Slaterville."

. . . .

ADAM SUDDENLY LOOKED like a trapped animal. Arnie hoped there were no stoplights between them and their destination. There was no doubt in his mind that Adam would bail out of the car if he slowed down. But he said nothing. He didn't look at Arnie. He stared instead at the dash. Adam's eyes were fixed, his mind racing, his breath loud and erratic.

God I hate this man! He knows! He's always known. But how could he? How could anybody? I can't go back there. I can't. I won't! Nobody can make me go back there! Nobody!

The face of the Moron, the fist smashing into his stomach and the awful pain and panic of being unable to breathe, his scrawny stomach heaving, writhing on the filthy floor while the Moron stood over him and cackled. The shack, permeated by the stench of the Moron and the junkyard, with its circling buzzards...it all assaulted Adam's mind at once. Memories that he had been trying to keep at bay for twenty-five years. Images that he had been fighting to keep out of his mind more and more over the past months.

After ten miles of growing silent tension, Adam suddenly slammed the dash with the heels of both hands and twisted in his seat with such sudden ferocity that Arnie jerked the car over the center stripe of the blacktop as Adam burst out in a raw, retching voice, "Why are you doing this to me? Do you hate me that much? You don't know! You don't know what I lived through in this place! For God's sake Arnie!"

Arnie stared steadily at the road ahead, and gripped the wheel, looking resolute. Inside, he was anything but that. His thoughts echoed what Adam was demanding next to him.

What are you thinking? You've already ruined this boy's marriage and now you're going to push him off the deep end. Listen to him! He's losing it and it's your fault. Your fault! Are you not going to be happy until you've totally annihilated the guy? Well you're just about there. You have no idea what kind of horrors he endured, and you're about to rub his face in all of it. Bring it all back! It's going to kill him and you're the one doing it. You're no better than his father. No better than his father! No better than your father!

Arnie's pulse was racing and his palms were sweating. He realized he was slowly shaking his head when Adam's voice broke through.

"Are you even listening to me?"

Lord, help me.

"What are you hoping to accomplish here, Arnie? You want to prove to the world that you were right about me and everybody else was wrong? Are you trying to make me accept that I don't belong in your world? That I was born trash and I'll always be trash? Is that what you're trying to do to me?"

Please Lord...help me. Give me the words.

"No, Adam. No that's not what I'm trying to do," Arnie finally managed to say. "Just the opposite. Completely the opposite of that." He looked across at Adam, who turned away. "You're right, I don't know what you went through here. But I have an idea that whatever you've tried so hard to bury here isn't staying buried anymore."

"You don't know anything, Arnie! What do you think you are, some kind of psychologist? Some kind of preacher? Are you trying to save me, Arnie? Is that it? You want me to fall on my knees and repent or something? You keep trying to slip your little sermons in. Spare me, alright?"

"Look, Adam, I've realized something that you and I have in common. We've both spent our lives running from men that we don't want to be." No reaction from Adam, so Arnie plunged on. "But neither of us is our father, Adam. I'm not Latham Warner...and you're not Freddy Finger."

Saying the name seemed to suck the air out of the car. Adam's head involuntarily dipped like flinching from a blow, and his eyes squeezed shut. His lips were pressed together, jaws clenched, and there wasn't a drop of color left in his face.

"They have no power over us, Adam. No power other than what we give them. And that power has been destructive... to both of us. And now to Meredith and the kids, and to the company."

"Do you know why I never married, Adam? Why I've rarely even gone out with a woman?" Without waiting for an answer, he went on, "Because my father slept with every woman that came into his path. My mother endured that humiliation, that sense of worthlessness and shame time after time after time." Arnie was saying words that he had never uttered, and voicing thoughts that he had never allowed himself to face.

"I have lived like a monk my whole life, because I was terrified of being like Latham Warner. I let that man rob me of the kind of life Mason had with my sister, and that you have with Meredith."

There was a moment of silence while Arnie absorbed what he was hearing himself say, and then he added quietly, "He's been out of my life for forty years, and I'm just now seeing that I let him do that to me."

Adam said nothing, but Arnie could see that his hands were no longer balled into white-knuckled fists as they had been. Without thinking Arnie went on, "And at the company...I get it. I get it, and you're right. I'll admit that I have been so intent upon never being like him that I've lost objectivity about our people from time to time."

"Adam, I wish that thirty years ago Mason, or Annie, or anyone could have seen what I was letting my father do to me, and could have made me face it. It might have changed everything. I might have had a wife and a family...a son." The emotion caught Arnie completely by surprise. The last word came out thin and high as his throat constricted. Tears sprang suddenly into Arnie's eyes as the sense of loss engulfed him.

Arnie Warner could never remember crying in front of anyone since he was a child. Even when Annie died, he had held his grief in check until he was alone in his house.

He turned to Adam, heedless of the tears that coursed down his cheeks, "That is what I'm trying to do for you, Adam. I don't want to hurt you, but you have to face him and realize that you are nothing like him. Adam Pembrook is nothing like Freddy Finger. Never was, and never will be."

Silence fell between them. After another mile or more, Adam broke it with the quiet question, "What about the sins of the father? The Bible says the punishment for the sins of the father will pass on through three or four generations."

The question immediately brought to mind a long-forgotten conversation he had once had with Mason. Arnie marveled at the clarity of his memory of it, and how completely he had missed Mason's point all those years before. Missed that Mason had been trying to make him see it. Mason had tried to do just what he was doing now, but he had been too diplomatic. Too kind. Arnie had completely missed it...until now.

He began to draw from the memory, "You know, Adam, there's no doubt that you and I have inherited genetic traits from our fathers. And those may be passed on. It's something to be aware of, but it isn't a curse. It's just genetics. A predisposition that we do not have to give in to, because we have a choice."

"As for God punishing you and me for things our fathers did...there is no punishment for us. Not if we are in Christ. If there was, Jesus died for nothing. That curse is Jewish Law, Adam. Old Covenant Law. We live in Christ, not in Moses."

Arnie realized that he had no idea if Adam had ever expressed faith in Christ. He just knew that Adam needed to hear what he was saying. And so did he.

He looked over at Adam, whose eyes were straight ahead, unblinking. "Our salvation freed us of the curse, Adam. You and I, we are free of those two."

Adam didn't answer. His eyes were fixed straight ahead. He had seen the edge of a town looming on the horizon. Arnie braked and pulled the car over into the high grass that edged the two-lane highway. He got out and walked around the car to the passenger side and opened Adam's door.

"You take the wheel now."

Adam stood up and the two men were standing face to face so close that both could smell the other's after shave. There were no words. Arnie just stood there, his hands at his sides, prepared to take the punch, the profanity, or whatever Adam was about to throw.

Adam was pallid and his face was glistening with sweat. He suddenly pushed Arnie roughly aside as he scrambled down into the drainage ditch beyond the shoulder, then doubled over and heaved violently into the tall weeds.

Arnie quickly got in the car to give Adam time to recover himself. The accusations that assailed him turned his own stomach.

"What am I doing? I'm torturing this kid! This is the *place that he escaped from, and I'm making him go back there?* I don't have the right to do this! *I don't! I've been holding this over his head for his entire adult life, and he didn't even know it. He couldn't even defend himself! Why am I doing this? Why? Am I just——"*

A gray dove landed on the hood of the idling car, then hopped up onto the hood ornament, made a fluttering pirouette and faced Arnie, balancing atop the steel circle emblem.

For no discernible reason, Annie suddenly came unbidden into Arnie's mind. Just a moment snatched from his memory. One of a million similar times, but this one stuck, for some reason. She was in her studio, smiling as she worked. One of her clay-smeared smocks covered her clothes. She was smiling, it seemed, at the work...a sculpted dove on the turntable before her. Then she reached over and turned the clay head of the dove to face him, and Annie turned her own head, matching the bird's quizzical look.

The driver's side door opening interrupted the memory, and the bird flew away as Adam said, "Sorry about that."

"No, I understand," Arnie answered, still puzzling over the curious reassurance he suddenly felt.

"Do you? Do you really think you could possibly understand? What do you think you know about me, Arnie? You tell me right now...all of it. What do you think you know? How did you find out? And how long have you known it?"

Adam continued, still intense, but the nausea had drained him of the pent-up fury Arnie sensed earlier. "I think I deserve for you to tell me what you know."

Arnie was caught off-guard. The bird and the strange memory of Annie had distracted him, and Adam's sudden barrage of questions gave him no time to think. He had wanted Adam to confess his story, to tell the truth about himself, but Arnie didn't argue. He simply began to recite the facts as Joe Kitchens had related them to him.

"You lived there in Slaterville. You were probably born there, and maybe born at home, because there's no birth record on file. No marriage record either, so I don't know anything about your mother. Freddy Finger was your father. He had a towing service and garage. He was a good mechanic, but he drank a lot. He was foul-tempered, foul-mouthed, and violent enough that everyone gave him a wide berth, especially when he was drinking."

Arnie took a breath and looked at Adam, whose face was impassive. He went on, "You never attended school. He told people around here that your mother left him and took you with her. But you were seen from time to time when people would haul garbage out to the dump. You lived in a house near the entrance, and they would see you outside there."

"Your father got drunk one night and apparently tried to get across the railroad tracks before an oncoming train blocked the turn-off to the road where you lived. He was killed."

Looking up at Adam, he added, "And three or four days later you showed up in Tulsa. You had signs of long term physical abuse, and a story about being abandoned there by a roving band of thieves."

Arnie stopped talking and Adam just sat there for a time. Finally he said, "And that's what you've held against me all these years? My father was an abusive drunk, and when I saw him die in a horrible accident, I ran away?"

"Do you remember a guy named Len Coffey?" Arnie asked.

The name sent Adam reeling back through time. He could see himself hidden in the old well-house, watching the Coffey brothers through a crack in the door as they struggled to get the Moron's boat motor into the back of their truck.

"Yes," was all he said in answer to Arnie's question.

"He had a brother who was friends with your father, and worked for him some?"

"Yeah...his name was Floyd."

"He said that your father——"

"Look, would you stop with the *your father* stuff? Don't you get it? That was the whole reason I left. The whole reason I made up that story about the people I'd lived with. I was twelve years old. I lived on scraps. I'd hardly ever been let out of the house. If he ever heard that somebody saw me, he'd beat me until I was unconscious. Every time that happened, I thought he was going to kill me. I never wanted anybody to know that I came from...from that godless piece of trash. Ever! And now you're rubbing my face in it? Do you think this is going to make things better for you and me? Better between Meredith and me? What do you want from me?"

"I want to help you, Adam."

"Help me?" Adam was incredulous. "Help me, by making me face my demons? Arnie, I face my demon every day! Every time I look in the mirror."

Arnie had no idea if he was doing the right thing, the wrong thing, or what the result was going to be, but he plunged on, "Adam, you're a good man. A good husband and father."

"Not anymore I'm not."

"Look, here's what I thought. I've known about..." Arnie hesitated, trying to frame his words gently, "About your history here. Just enough of the story to put two and two together. I can't know what it was really like for you, but I have an idea. I know you were physically abused, and the people Joe talked to in Slaterville painted a pretty good picture of what kind of man Freddy Finger was."

"Joe?"

"Joe Kitchens. You met him once at the office," Arnie said. "A retired FBI agent who did background checks for us."

"Yeah, I remember him. So he's the one who dug up my past for you, huh?"

"He was a great investigator and a good friend. And for the record, he had a lot of admiration for you. Joe was the first one to tell me that I was wrong about you. I wish I'd listened."

"I guess a twelve-year-old didn't have much of a chance of outwitting a G-man," Adam said with a mirthless laugh. "I thought I had erased any connection. I'd love to know how he found out."

Arnie reached into the back seat and pulled the old brown accordion file out of his briefcase. He handed it to Adam and said, "It's all there. Joe was a thorough guy. Read it, destroy it, do whatever you like. I'm not going to hold it over your head anymore. From now on, as far as I'm concerned, you are Adam Pembrook. Everything you have ever exhibited to me has shown you to be a man of great integrity and extraordinary ability. I am deeply ashamed of how I have treated you."

Adam's face was pinched, his lips pressed together, his head down as the two sat in silence. Finally, gesturing toward the town ahead, Adam said in a thin voice, "What about this?"

"You're in the driver's seat. I thought it would be good for you to face this thing you have tried so hard to keep hidden from all of us. Maybe to realize that the vile man who abused you is dead. This place is just a place. It was just a chapter in your life. A horrible one, no doubt, but it happened, and you survived it. Not only survived it, but triumphed over it."

They sat in silence again for a time, then Arnie continued. "Adam, I read every word of that file again last night. I've read through it several times over the past few days. I wish I could take back the way I interpreted all of the information Joe put together, but I can't."

"My sense is that something deeper is going on. I can see how this place is affecting you, and nothing should have that kind of power over you. Maybe if you just faced it down."

Adam didn't respond, and after a moment Arnie said, "You can do whatever you want. If you want to drive into that town, I'm with you. If you want to turn around and go home now...I'm with you."

"Arnie, I've dreamed about this place night after night. I wake up in a cold sweat, and I think I'm back here, and I can hear him. I can smell him. And it's been getting worse. And it's more than that. I feel like it's him. He's still——" Adam stopped abruptly and again pressed his lips together, his eyes squeezed shut.

"I can't imagine what that is like, Adam. But Freddy Finger has no hold on you. Not anymore. The only power he has, is in your memory of those things that happened when you were a defenseless kid. Those memories can't be suppressed anymore. Maybe getting them out in the open will at least help put them into proper perspective." Arnie reached across and grasped Adam's shoulder. "I don't know what you will tell Meredith or Mason. That's up to you, and if you choose to not tell them anything at all, I will respect that, and I will never say a word either. I promise you that. But Adam, if you ever need to talk to someone, I'll be here."

Adam just made a stiff nod, and sat for a moment. He had held the folder in his lap since Arnie gave it to him. Now he placed it on the seat between them and put the car in gear. Arnie fully expected him to turn across the highway and head back to Kansas City. Instead, Adam headed into Slaterville.

• • • •

SLATERVILLE, OKLAHOMA had changed remarkably little in the twenty-five years since a twelve-year-old boy in ill-fitting, filthy clothes had sneaked under the tarp of a trailer at the same truck stop he now passed on the way back into that town. Adam could remember the oily smell of the tarp, and the thrill of fear and freedom he had felt when the truck started and pulled onto the highway.

They drove slowly through the town, but aside from the truck stop, nothing struck a chord in his memory. The Moron had rarely let him leave the house out at the dump. Arnie said nothing, but looked at the map that Joe Kitchens had carefully rendered, and tried to orient himself. That was easy, there wasn't much to the town, and the few landmarks Joe had noted were still there.

Adam turned at the solitary signal light in the middle of town, and Arnie looked up the block to where Pembrook's Grocery should have been. The sign on the building caught him by surprise, and he almost laughed.

"What?" Adam asked, hearing the stifled response.

Arnie said, "Oh I just saw that sign and realized that I could use a cup of coffee. What do you think?"

Adam looked at the building where the kind old Mister Pembrook had once given him a free candy bar, and whose name came to mind when he was deciding what his new name would be.

"*Coffey's Coffee*" he read aloud.

Arnie said, "Floyd Coffey died not long after you left here. This has to be Len's place," he said with a smile, remembering the way Joe Kitchen's had described the mechanic. He had told him that Len

Coffey had suggested that the two of them should open a place to-gether...*Coffey's Coffee and Kitchens' Kitchen.*

"Floyd and Len took over Finger's Garage. Then Len ended up with it. That's where Joe found him. He liked Len. Joe said the brother and Finger were friends, but Len was a good guy."

Adam pulled into one of the parking spaces in front of the glassed front of *Coffey's Coffee*. A row of red vinyl upholstered booths lined the window, just visible behind a table-height red and white checked curtain. There were a few pick-up trucks and several cars distributed among the other parking spaces.

As Adam and Arnie entered, several of the booths had people visiting good-humoredly with their companions and those at other tables, and a couple perched on swiveling stools mounted along a long counter. The conversation quieted for a beat while everyone looked to see who had joined their lively party, then resumed when it was collectively acknowledged that the two were outsiders.

They found a spot at a booth in a back corner, just as a compact man with close-cropped graying hair and a broad, engaging smile emerged through a swinging door behind the counter. He wore a long white apron, and wiped his hands on a towel tucked into the ties that doubled around his waist.

As he approached the table, he was already saying, "Newcomers! Welcome to *Coffey's Coffey*. I just took an apple pie out of the oven and a cup of Coffey's coffee with a slice of that, and a piece of cheese melted on top. Aw, there ain't nothing better! You know what they say, apple pie without some cheese is like a kiss without a——" He stopped in mid-sentence just as Adam turned and looked up. The smile fell and the little man's mouth remained open as he stared at Adam.

Adam looked back at a middle-aged version of the wiry little man he had last seen through a crack in the well-house door. He knew immediately what Len Coffey was thinking. He said quietly, "I'm his son."

Len Coffey expelled the breath he had been holding, and blurted, with something like relief and wonder, "Well I'll be dog!"

Coffey extended his hand, "Len Coffey."

"Yeah I remember you," Adam said. "And your brother, Floyd."

The handshake and the voice were warm, "Well what brings you back to Slaterville after all these years?"

"Just taking care of some business," Adam answered casually. "This used to be Pembrook's Grocery. I guess old Mister Pembrook died."

"Passed, oh goodness, years ago. I loved that old fellow. He was like a daddy to me. In fact, he gave me this place after he closed the grocery store. He helped me in a lot of ways. A whole lot of ways. Now how 'bout that coffee and pie? Gonna try it with the cheese? I'm telling you, that just makes it."

They both acquiesced, and he went back through the swinging door into the kitchen to retrieve their pie and coffee. It seemed that Len went everywhere in a spritely half-run. Arnie asked, "How did he know who you were?"

"I told you, I see my demon every time I look in the mirror. I look like him. I look *exactly* like the Moron."

Moron struck a chord in Arnie's memory. In Adam's story that he'd told as a child in Tulsa, the people who had him called him *Moron*. Meredith said that was how Adam had described the way Arnie had treated him...*like a moron.*

"The Moron...Finger?"

"Yeah that's what I called him," Adam said, "The Moron."

"You're about the age that he was when he was killed, right? Your last memory of what he looked like."

"I suppose so. I've never thought about it."

"And the older you've gotten, the more you look like him?" Arnie said. "Look, I'm not trying to let myself off the hook here, but don't you think that could explain some things?"

When Adam didn't respond, Arnie went on with his thought, "I've told you how I feel about being anything like my father. My fear of that has had a terrible impact on my life. I don't think I have ever realized how much it had cost me until today. And I do have some physical resemblance, sure, but nothing like you, apparently. That guy looked like he saw a ghost when he looked at you. If I saw Latham Warner looking back at me every morning when I was shaving, I can't imagine how that would have reinforced my..."

When Arnie paused, searching for the word, Adam completed his sentence, "Your hatred of him?"

Arnie met Adam's eyes for a moment, then looked away, "You and I have more in common than I ever knew, Adam."

Len Coffey's jovial arrival with their pie and coffee interrupted the moment, but as Coffey prattled merrily on about the merits of melted cheese on hot apple pie, which drew good-natured debate on the subject from some of his regulars, Arnie felt a welling up of something that had been long boxed up and put away somewhere in the deep internal recesses of his heart.

Arnie Warner had always been a man who saw what needed to be done and did it. He didn't second-guess himself, and he didn't waste time with a lot of pointless introspection. He just lived and worked. The two were essentially the same thing for him.

Arnie looked around and saw the smiling faces, and vaguely heard the light-hearted banter, and within himself he sensed the echo of some vague unlived life that seemed to stir and beckon.

A movement beyond the window caught Arnie's eye and he glanced out at the old-fashioned gaslight mounted on the edge of the sidewalk. He noticed a gray dove was settling on top of the globe of the light, and it seemed to peer somberly inside the coffee shop.

Arnie's sister came to his mind, and the countless times she had tried to coax and maneuver him into relationships with various women.

"Well what do you think?" Len Coffey's high-pitched smiling voice interrupted the strange reverie.

Arnie glanced with some surprise at his half-eaten slice of pie. He hadn't tasted a bite he had taken, but mumbled an appreciative, "Delicious."

"I was right about the cheese, huh?" Coffey said, looking over his shoulder with a sly chuckle at the former cheese critics.

Both Arnie and Adam mumbled their assent as they dutifully took bites, and Arnie realized it truly was a delicious pie.

"The wife makes the pie and I make the coffee," the little man said proudly. Pulling up a chair while adding, "You mind if I sit with y'all for a minute?"

The other patrons all began to leave as though on signal, with a variation of grateful and affectionate farewells to the smiling proprietor.

Seeing Arnie's look of surprise at the sudden exodus, Coffey explained, "That's a group that meet here for a Bible study every week. We'd just finished up when y'all came in." He looked at Adam and added, "We call it Mister Pembrook's class. That old man made a difference in a whole lot of people's lives. I'm surely not the teacher he was, but this group doesn't really need a teacher. Just like the Bible says, we have a teacher and a counselor right in here." He thumped his chest. "Of course, it's this part that's the problem." Then he thumped himself soundly on the side of the head, laughing. "Full time job for the Holy Spirit renewing this ole noggin, I'll tell you."

Len Coffey glanced down at their cups and hopped up to retrieve the pot from behind the counter and topped off both with more of the rich, strong brew. When he came back to sit down with them, he had his own cup.

"You know I've wondered whatever happened to you. Saw that Mercedes Benz you drove up in. Looks like you've done well for yourself. I'm proud you have. You had a pretty rough start."

Adam just nodded and looked down at his coffee and Coffey looked at Arnie, "And I didn't catch your name, sir."

Arnie offered his hand and said, "I'm Arnie Warner. I'm his uncle. We're in business together."

Adam glanced up with some surprise at both comments. Arnie looked at him steadily over a sip of the coffee.

And do you go by Fred, or——"

It's Adam, actually."

Oh. Oh, well it seemed like I remembered your daddy calling you——"

He called me a lot of things, Len," Adam interrupted. "I don't have any fond memories of him, or my life here in Slaterville."

There was an uncomfortable silence for just a moment, then Adam, looking around the coffee shop added, "No that's not true. I have one. One time Mister Pembrook gave me a candy bar. The first one I'd ever had. He let me pick out whichever one I wanted, but I didn't know which one to choose. He finally picked one for me."

"When I got home I hid that candy and would take just a little bite every night. I made it last for about two weeks. I had never tasted anything so wonderful, or had anybody ever be so...so kind to me."

Adam sat for a moment. No one spoke as he mulled over something. He had never allowed himself to think about his life before the children's home. He had forced every thought of that time out of his mind, and now they flooded back, but with a certain detachment that surprised him.

He could remember the smell of the Hershey bar, and unwrapping the foil wrapper, scared to death that the Moron would smell his treasure and take it. And beat him for having it.

He remembered all of it perfectly, but when he had told Arnie and Len Coffey, it felt as though he was talking about someone else's life. It didn't feel like it had been him at all. Adam marveled at the lack of connection he felt. He thought it should overwhelm him, but instead it was more like telling a story he had heard.

Len Coffey nodded, "Yeah Mister Pembrook was a sweet ole bird. He led me to the Lord, you know. My old man was a lot like yours, Adam. And Floyd was just like him. Two peas in a pod. Neither one of them ever had a thought about such things. After Floyd died I was alone. Mister Pembrook took me under his wing."

The wiry little man cocked his head and chuckled to himself, "Now that's funny. He took me under his wing." He shook his head at some thought he was having, then said, "Now, I know this is going to sound weird to you fellows, but my wife Lorna and I live here in the back of the cafe. We have a little patio out back there with a big ole maple tree in it. I get up about five in order to get everything ready for the breakfast run. Almost every morning in warm weather I wake up to the sound of this same ole bird just singing up a storm up there in that maple tree. *Okay Mister Pembrook*, I'll say to him. *I'm getting up. Good morning to you too.*"

He chuckled again, "When I just said that he took me under his wing..." He finished the thought with a shake of his head and a smile.

The crazy stories Mason had been telling his kids crossed Adam's mind, then he dismissed the thought and asked, "Len, maybe you can tell me something I've always wondered about." Adam paused for a moment, suppressing a sudden feeling of outrage that caught him completely by surprise. He asked at last. "Why didn't anybody do anything...about me? Take *me* under their wing. It's a small town. People had to know. I was never enrolled in school. I knew who you and your brother were, because you came out to our house a few times. I know the sheriff or whatever he was saw me. He followed the truck out to the house more than once when the Moron was so drunk he couldn't see. Mister Pembrook knew who I was, because we would come in here to buy things from time to time and I would come in when the Moron was too drunk to get out of the truck. I don't remember ever seeing anyone else, except the folks that came out to the dump. He made me run inside and hide if a car ever came over the tracks. Threatened to beat me to death if anyone ever saw me."

Adam paused and just looked at the now grim face of Len Coffey, whose eyes darted here and there, looking like he was trying to find somewhere to escape.

"Can you explain any of that? Why somebody didn't turn him in or something? Why did everybody in this town just turn a blind eye? I was just a little kid."

Len stammered, "I just remember that everybody was afraid of him. He was meaner'n scratch. Had an awful bad temper, and he didn't care. Freddy Finger didn't care about anything. And besides, he told everybody you lived with your mother somewhere else...I can't remember. He said you came down here for visits, but you lived with her." After a moment, looking at the floor, he added quietly, "Nobody really believed that though. People saw you out there all the time. There ain't no excuse."

"Do you remember my mother?"

"No," Coffey answered. "She was already gone when Floyd started working for Freddy," he said.

"Did you ever hear anything about what happened to her?" Adam pressed.

"Well, not exactly." Coffey mumbled then added, "So you didn't ever go live with her someplace up the country?"

"No, I never even knew my mother's name. One day she was gone. I can't remember much about her at all."

Len Coffey sat quietly, but he was nervously working his mouth. Adam sensed that there was more the little man wanted to say, and he was trying to frame the words in his mind.

"What?" It was more of a demand than a question. "There's something else."

"Oh, I don't know anything. Nothing for sure really. And I sure don't want to tell you anything that, you know, would be——"

"Just tell me, Len. That's why we came here. We came to get a few questions about my childhood answered. You're probably the only person in town that even remembers me. Help us out here."

"Well," Coffey hesitated, squeezing his eyes shut before plunging on, "My brother said one time when Freddy was drinking pretty hard he told him that—" The little man interrupted himself and said earnestly, "You say your name is Adam? Well this is a bad story, Adam. Are you sure you want to hear it?"

"I need to hear it."

"Well," he said swallowing with some effort, "At the time I didn't know whether to put any stock in it. My brother kind of liked making up stuff just to see how people would react. Especially me. I guess I was sort of gullible, and he was always feeding me a line about something or other. But I think maybe this time it was true, you saying you didn't go live with your mother after all."

"I'm sorry to tell you this, but he said Freddy was thrashing you, and your mother tried to stop him one time. Freddy was a strong guy. Solid muscle, rock hard, you know. Floyd said he bragged about this. Never would have said such a thing sober. He said he always wondered if he could kill somebody with just one punch. And now he knew. I think he must have done that to your mother. I never wanted to believe it." Coffey looked around like he wanted to escape rather than finish the story. "And then he...well he said he—"

"He buried her in the junkyard," Adam finished for him.

"You knew that?" Len Coffey was aghast, as was Arnie, who had sat silently observing the exchange.

"He threatened all the time to do the same to me. He said I was nobody, just like my mother, and he could do anything he wanted with me, and no one would ever even notice," Adam answered, his voice flat and eerily emotionless.

Coffey glanced at Arnie, and got the sense that he too was hearing this for the first time. He sniffed and said, "I don't know if you knew this, but a few years ago the city hired some company to come in and modernize the city dump. They did a bunch of excavation out there, and they found a human...well some human remains. Couldn't be identified. They sent it up to Oklahoma City and they said it was likely a female. At least that's what came out in the paper."

Coffey stopped to look at Adam's blanched face. "I thought then, that's got to be her. That's got to be Freddy Finger's wife. I told the police chief about what Freddy had told Floyd. Old Aubrey Barstow might have listened, because he knew Freddy Finger, but the new guy didn't pay no mind to me. He didn't last long. I can't even remember his name."

A sad, soft voice, haunted eyes, long limp curls of dark hair, faded flowers on the shoulder of her dress...the memories of her were like shards of shattered glass. They didn't fit together, and every one of them seemed to slice into Adam's heart as he imagined the bulldozer tearing and scattering her fragile remains. The faint memory of her cries when the Moron would hit her brought the blood to Adam's face, and his hands balled into fists.

Len Coffey saw the reaction, and sat nervously turning his coffee cup awhile before breaking the silence. "You know, there was a big fella that came to see me about you years ago. I's still out at the garage then." Len furrowed his brow and muttered to himself, "Now what was his name?"

Arnie said, "That was Joe Kitchens. He worked for us."

"That's right! Goodness, I hadn't thought about him in a million years. Coffey's Coffee and Kitchens' Kitchen," he said with a smile. "So, you must've finally got your money. You know Floyd went out there and tore that place apart trying to find it, but never did. I told him it was rightfully yours. I told him I was glad he couldn't find it. Made him madder'n all get out, but I told him. I'm proud you finally got it. I hope it was a tub full."

Adam looked confused. His eyes darted from Len Coffey to Arnie's face. As his mind raced to piece together what he was hearing.

"Kitchens told you he was trying to find me to give me some money?" Adam asked.

"Well, it was a long time ago. I can't exactly remember. He was asking me a lot of questions about you." Len said, thinking he had misspoken, "But he knew about the money your daddy had." He began to choose his words carefully, "The money Freddy had left you, and said that was why he was looking for you."

"Money he had left me?" Adam laughed mirthlessly and looked icily at Arnie.

Len Coffey sensed the sudden tension and hastily got up and said, "Well, it was a long time ago, maybe I've got my wires crossed. Shoot, I can't remember my name half the time anymore. Listen, I need to get back to the kitchen. It was sure good to see you, Adam, and I want to wish you all the best." Then as he made his way to the kitchen door, he turned back and said, "The coffee and pie is on the house, by the way. Come see us again. God bless y'all."

They sat for just a moment longer and Adam got up and walked to the door. Arnie followed. On the sidewalk Adam turned, "Is there anything you don't know? Do you know where I found the money *my father left me*?"

"In a brick-lined hole near the well-house. It was under an oil drum filled with water, with an Evinrude boat motor mounted on the side. It's all in the files I gave you."

"I can't believe this," he turned in a full circle and faced Arnie again. "So I guess you also know how much there was?" Adam asked, more astonished than angry now.

"No idea. Quite a bit, I imagine. Enough to pay cash for a new Corvette and put you through college and graduate school in style," Arnie answered without flinching.

"Well, at least I still have that shred of privacy left," Adam retorted as he walked back to the car. "I suppose now you want to go out to the old home place.

"Up to you. Completely up to you."

* * * *

THEY DROVE TO THE EDGE of town on a two-lane blacktop that ran parallel to a railroad embankment along the left side of the highway. About a quarter of a mile out, Adam slowed the car. A sign on the shoulder pointed out the entrance to the city dump to the left. Adam turned across onto a narrow road, then pulled up and stopped at a railroad crossing, complete with signal lights.

"*The Freddy Finger Memorial Railroad Crossing,*" Adam announced as he inched forward, the front wheels bumping across the tracks. He stopped the car straddling the rails and said, "The train hit him here. Half of the truck ended up right down there. The rest was over under those trees," he said as he pointed to a copse of trees fifty yards away at the bottom of the railroad embankment.

He slowly rolled on over the crossing and down the embankment, then up a long hill. "They've paved it. It was caliche when I was a kid."

At the top of the hill, Adam slowly pulled off to the right and parked, and got out of the car alongside a shiny chain-link fence that bordered a large rectangle of sparkling white crushed quartz. Isolated in the middle of the lot, painted an equally brilliant white, a small flat-roofed white concrete block building stood, with a much smaller block building standing off to its side. A large white sign affixed to the high chain link fence alongside the open gate announced *City of Slaterville Department of Sanitation*. The single blight, a faded brown sedan, sporting evidence of multiple minor collisions, sat conspicuously incongruent in the sea of glistening whiteness.

The whole scene reflected the afternoon sun, as both men got out and were assaulted at once by the putrid smell of rotting garbage and

310

decaying animal flesh. Adam looked around in some relief at the anticlimactic effect it had on him.

"This is where the house was. That smaller building must be a new well-house. It's all gone. Nothing is the same, except the smell...and them."

He pointed up at the buzzards, perhaps a dozen, all riding the thermal currents in a slow reel above the dump, a quarter mile down the other side of the hill. Adam stared at them for some time, then said to Arnie, "There's nothing here for me."

Arnie just shook his head in agreement, and both men got back in the car and turned across the pavement and headed back toward town.

After a few minutes Adam said, "I used to get on top of the house during the day. I'd lay up there and watch the buzzards. I hated the buzzards, because I always pictured them going at my mother's corpse the way I'd seen them tear apart a bloated dog's carcass. I was horrified by that vision, but I still envied the way they could fly. And sometimes I would see a hawk. I loved to watch the hawks, the way they would soar and swoop, so patient, taking everything in, and then suddenly they would just plummet into a dive after their prey. Amazing birds."

He fell silent for a moment more, then said, "When I would be up on the roof, I couldn't see the filth around me. Just the sky, and the birds. It was...pure."

"It didn't smell pure out there," Arnie said, sniffing at the sleeve of his shirt.

"You get used to it and don't even smell it after awhile." Then after a minute, he said, "Until you leave, and then you never stop smelling it. No matter how far away you go." He was silent again for a few seconds, then added, "And other people smell it on you too, just like you did, Arnie."

"That wasn't it at all. It wasn't where you came from that bothered me, Adam. Your story is both horrendous and amazing. You had absolutely no education, virtually no social interaction with anyone other than a man who terrorized you. Goodness Adam, he murdered your mother. You were just a little boy, and this monster threatened to kill you constantly. The most unhealthy environment that a person could be born into, and I know that I am aware of just the tip of the iceberg. I cannot fathom what you have endured."

"Coming out of that horrible situation, that hideous man's abuse, at only twelve years old, you crafted a life for yourself. You managed to completely erase all traces of your former identity."

"Clearly not all traces. You discovered it. Or your FBI man, Kitchens did," Adam responded.

Arnie didn't respond, but continued, "You managed to locate and safely conceal a fortune somewhere, and had the discipline to walk away and leave it there until you were old enough to retrieve it and use it." Arnie looked at him in wonder, "And you were Andy's age. Imagine him doing something like that."

Arnie didn't say anything for quite some time. Then he plunged forward, "And when Joe Kitchens told me about how you had managed to do all of that, do you know what I thought?"

Adam sat stoically behind the wheel.

Arnie said, "I thought, if he can deceive that many people, if he can be that cunning, and that patient...if he is such an exquisite liar that he could do that at twelve years old, there is no telling what a master of deception he has become as an adult. With your incredible intellect and education, and that kind of focused ambition, there would be no stopping you. No controlling you."

Their eyes locked for a moment as Arnie concluded, "And you were about to marry my niece, the sole heiress to Warner & Crewe, and be welcomed into our company, where I knew I would be no match for you. I couldn't do anything to protect Meredith, but I determined that I would not be taken in by you. I had to remind myself constantly that you were a deceiver, and just like drunks drink...deceivers deceive."

"I felt like my relationship with Mason, Annie, and Meredith were all being taken hostage by you. The company as well, because Mason, Annie, and I *were* Warner & Crewe. My hands were tied, because when it comes down to a choice between a daughter and a brother, a parent is going to go with the daughter every time. You were their daughter's husband. And before I could turn around, you were the father of their grandson. My relationship with the people who meant everything to me...all the family I have, Adam...would just be collateral damage to whatever agenda you had."

Adam stared straight ahead now, not taking his eyes away from the road. Arnie watched his face. The jaws didn't clench, Adam had a careless grip on the steering wheel. He seemed totally unaffected, which disturbed Arnie more than anything that had transpired.

Arnie had showed his hand. Every card. Now Adam seemed utterly calm. That was not the reaction he had anticipated, and it sent a chill through Arnie Warner.

When the car slowed, he looked out to see that Adam was turning in at the Slaterville cemetery entrance.

He sat silently as they drove through the maze of gravel lanes between plots, and out to an area beyond the marble monuments and curbed borders around graves covered over by neatly clipped grass, with splashes of color here and there where flowers had been deposited.

Farther on, bare brown dirt humps dotted the slightly descending grade, which kept the area discretely out of the line of sight of the more respectable mourners. Grassburs and goathead stickers covered the ground around these graves.

The car pulled to a stop, and still, neither of them spoke. Adam reached into the back seat and retrieved the accordion file that contained the investigation report that Joe Kitchens had compiled for Arnie thirteen years before.

He had not looked at it when Arnie gave it to him. He opened it now and pulled out the assortment of manila folders, each carefully labeled. He began to read.

Arnie watched Adam's face for some reaction, but saw nothing. He had been brutally honest about his suspicions, and Adam had not given the slightest indication that he had even heard him. A sick feeling came over him, as Arnie wondered if Adam Pembrook truly was everything he had always suspected him of being. He had never wanted to be wrong so badly in his life.

Joe Kitchens had organized the report with an overview and conclusions, followed by each step of the supporting evidence, meticulously documented in chronological order.

It read like a prosecutor's case file. Kitchens was the prosecution and Arnie Warner had been the judge. Adam flushed as the thought formed that he had been tried and convicted, and never was given the opportunity even to know he was being accused, much less to defend himself.

He read each entry thoroughly. Arnie sat silently looking out across the forlorn vista of untended graves, feeling like this was the most appropriate place on earth for this episode to end up.

He glanced over at Adam from time to time, but could discern nothing beyond the obvious. Most of it, Arnie had already disclosed. Adam's duplicity had been exposed years before, and he had been completely unaware of it.

It took a full half-hour for Adam to read the whole report. Arnie braced himself for the reaction.

Adam said nothing for a time, looking out over the grim landscape before them. He just slid each document back into the accordion file and tied its cord in a hard knot.

Then Adam said, "I didn't know he was a thief too, but I'm not really surprised. When I was a kid I thought it was just money he had saved from his work. Later on, I realized that it didn't add up. There had been too much there."

He looked at Arnie, "So you figured the apple didn't fall too far from the tree."

"I was afraid of you. It's as simple as that, Adam."

"Afraid?"

"Afraid you had targeted Meredith as your means of taking over Warner & Crewe."

"Do you still think that?"

"Honestly...I don't know that I was wrong."

Adam absorbed that comment, then sat for a time looking like a condemned prisoner, until at last he said, almost in a whisper, "I was going to kill him."

"I knew he had some money hidden. He bragged to me all the time about having more money than anybody in Slaterville, and how he was going to build a big, grand place down on Lake Texoma with that money. He didn't trust banks and he hated the government. He hid his money like he tried to hide me."

"I think the whole reason he kept me the way he did, was to keep me under the radar of any authorities. If Kitchens found no birth record, and I was never enrolled in school, I had no identification whatsoever. I was nobody. I didn't exist. He had the power of life and death over me, and he never quit telling me that."

"I haven't ever tried to figure out what his motive was for that. I suppose it just made him feel powerful. Whatever it was, he was a twisted, sick piece of trash, and when he was killed, his pathetic kid died with him as far as I was concerned. I didn't think I would ever have to face him again." Adam looked at the brown packet in his hands, "But he got the last laugh, didn't he?"

"I knew he would kill me sooner or later. He would hit me so hard. I look at Andy today, and I can't imagine it. What kind of monster does a thing like that to his own child?"

Arnie said nothing, and Adam continued, "I decided that my only chance to live was to find his money and run away. It took months for me to figure out where he hid it. I can't imagine how Joe Kitchens figured it out, but he was right. It was under that oil drum with his stupid boat motor clamped to the side. He would stand out there revving that motor, thrashing the water in that barrel, and one day I just knew that was where it had to be. It had to be buried under there."

"When I found the money, I realized that he would kill me just for finding it. If I took it and ran away, I knew he could find me. And then, I knew he would kill me for sure. The only way for me to get away from him, was if he was dead. At least that's what I thought at the time."

"I worked it all out in my mind. A lot of times he would be so drunk when he got home that he passed out before he could get out of his truck. He always drove with the window rolled down and his elbow out. When he'd passed out before, I'd seen him out there with his head lolled over resting on his arm in the window. He'd be out there until morning sometimes."

"I decided the best time I could do it was when that happened again." Adam looked over at Arnie, "I hid a crowbar under the porch, and the next time he came home and passed out in his truck, I was going to kill him with it. I would have done it too, Arnie. I would have murdered him at the first opportunity. And then I was going to try to drive the truck down and park it across the railroad tracks."

He went silent and stared out the side window at the ground beneath, before adding, "Ironic, huh?"

"I had imagined what it would be like so many times, that when that train hit him that night, it felt like I had actually done it. I truly wasn't sure I hadn't. I could see myself sneaking out the door and pulling that crowbar out from under the porch. I could feel that cold steel in my hand, and see the back of his greasy cap, and his head just lying there on his elbow waiting."

"I had practiced." A dry, grim chuckle sounded in Adam's throat. "I had actually taken that crowbar and smashed the tops of the wooden posts on the fence around the junkyard. I was trying to build up my muscles to be able to hit him hard enough to kill him."

He looked over at Arnie, whose face had lost its color as he listened to the story related in an emotionless monotone, "See, I knew I would have to hit him hard, and not stop, because he had hit me hard so many times, and it just knocked me out. I knew it was harder to kill somebody than most people think."

"When I dream about it, and I do all the time, or even when I think back, Arnie I swear I can remember swinging that crowbar. The sound of it hitting his skull, again and again. And I can remember how hard it was to push his body over, and getting up into that slick, bloody seat beside him, starting the truck and inching it down the hill and up onto the railroad tracks."

"Arnie, when I just read that the engineer saw him racing to beat the train, and saw him pull across in front of it——" Something like a sob escaped Adam's compressed lips. "That's the first time I've known for sure that I didn't do it. That I didn't kill him. I wanted to. I planned to. But I didn't. I thought I had. But I didn't."

Adam pushed out a ragged sigh, breathing like he had been running hard. Arnie just sat and let him collect himself, his heart aching as his own guilt hammered him within.

Adam's gasping abated and he again began to speak quietly, "When I had found his money, I took a hundred dollars out, and put everything back the way I'd found it. I thought that after I killed him, I would hide the money and buy some new clothes and a bus ticket somewhere. I knew people could buy tickets to go places on a bus.

But the more I thought about it, I decided I would just sneak onto the train, or a truck, so no one would be able to say they saw me leave. I wanted to disappear, and when I was found, I didn't want anyone to know where I had come from."

"Right after the train hit him, I went back to the house, but I couldn't go in. I just couldn't. I thought he would be in there waiting. I stayed in the well-house all night. The next morning, I saw Len and Floyd Coffey come and steal the boat motor. That was after Floyd tore the house apart looking for the money. I was scared to death they were going to find it, or find me in the well-house and turn me over to the sheriff or something. But they didn't. They were close though, when they took that motor off the oil drum."

"After they left, I dumped over that drum and got the money. Then I filled it up again, so the hole was covered. I don't know why, except I was just focused on the plan I'd been making for all those months, and I followed it through. It wouldn't work today, with computers and communication being what it is, but it worked then."

"I thought that the money was my only chance for a different life. But you know what I wanted more than anything? I just wanted to go to school. I wanted to learn. I wanted to have clean clothes, and sleep in a bed. I wanted to be anywhere but here. With anybody but him. I figured I would end up in an orphanage. I knew what orphanages were, because he was always saying that he should have put me in one. I just wish he had."

Adam started the car suddenly, and backed up the dirt lane to an intersecting track in the grid of cemetery roads. He then proceeded to a cluster of squat buildings near the gateway into the graveyard. The house appeared to be abandoned, but the nearby barn seemed to be in use. The caretaker no longer lived on the property as he had when Adam had last been there.

As the car pulled to a stop outside the barn, Adam said, "I hid in there for two days after he was killed. I knew the place, because the old tractor they had was always breaking down. He brought me along a couple of times when he came to work on it, probably just because he thought the place would terrify me."

Adam got out abruptly and tried the small side door on the corrugated metal building. It opened and he stepped in, only to emerge a moment later with a shovel in hand. Arnie was mystified, but asked no questions when, after placing the shovel in the trunk of the car, Adam got back in, backed out of the yard, and headed back the way they had come.

They stopped in the exact place where they had parked before, and Adam got out. He retrieved the shovel from the trunk and shocked Arnie by setting to work digging in the middle of one of the grave mounds. Arnie got out of the car, came around and walked up behind him. He read the small metal marker at the foot of the grave.

Freddy Finger
Born March 15, 1931
Died July 17, 1966

Adam dug a square of earth out of the center of the grave over two feet deep before stopping. His face and the front and back of his shirt were soaked with sweat. Leaving the shovel sticking up in the mound of freshly excavated soil, he went to the car and came back holding the accordion file.

He dropped the file into the hole and looked up at Arnie. "That's the third time I've had to dig that hole. The first time was when I hid the money. The second was when I came back and got it six years later. This time I'm burying Freddy Finger Junior and his short, sad life forever." He handed the shovel to Arnie. "Are you willing to let him rest in peace this time?"

Arnie took the shovel handle and met Adam's eyes, "Yes, absolutely I am." And then with no forethought, surprised himself by saying words he had never uttered, "Can we pray?"

Without waiting for an answer, Arnie bowed his head and began to speak, the words coming to him without effort, "Father, we are here to lay this boy to rest in your care. He sure didn't deserve the hard, brutal life he had, but I pray that the life he has now will be filled with so much happiness and fulfillment that all he has endured will fade away in comparison to the present and future blessings You have waiting for him. Thank you for preserving him, Father. I pray that the terrible past that has haunted him, and that I have held against him for so long, can be buried here, now and forever."

Arnie paused for a moment and looked up to meet the direct gaze of Adam Pembrook's penetrating blue-gray eyes, and continued to pray, giving no thought to his words. Later he would think back on the moment and know with certainty that the words were not his own at all. Arnie had always been painfully uncomfortable with the idea of praying aloud in front of anyone, but on this day the words flowed, not from his mind, but from the core of his being.

"Lord I thank you for bringing Adam Pembrook into my life. I know that he is acceptable to You. I pray that his heart can be opened to receive that acceptance, and that he can know that You offer him so much more than a new name, but an altogether new identity as a child of God in Christ Jesus. Free him of the guilt he has been unfairly bearing. Free him of the shame he has felt."

He glanced up again, and a movement drew Arnie's eyes to the top of a stunted tree visible just over Adam's shoulder. A gray dove had settled onto a branch and now turned to face Arnie, and once again, completely without reason, he envisioned Annie's face, her gentle smile and an approving nod of her head, haloed in tousled curls.

Arnie once again bowed his head, and felt tears pooling under his closed eyes, "Make Adam know that he is free of this man who hurt him so deeply, whose memory has continued to torment him. Help him come to a certain knowledge that he is Your child...a son who is loved, approved, and cherished, and able to live free of this burden that he had been bearing for so long. In the name of Jesus our Savior and Lord I ask these things. Amen."

Arnie pushed the spade into the mount of dirt and lifted it, then spilled the earth over the file that rested in the bottom of the hole. He was about to fill the shovel again when Adam grasped the handle and took it in hand.

Very quietly Adam said, "Thank you, Arnie. Thank you for everything."

Adam replaced the soil in the hole and patted it down with the back of the shovel. He then scooped up some dry dirt from a spot alongside the grave and spread it over the darker, moist soil. The grave looked undisturbed once again.

Few words were spoken as they replaced the shovel in the groundskeeper's barn and drove back into Slaterville.

Arnie checked his watch and said, "What do you think about stopping back by Len Coffey's place and grabbing a bite before we leave? And maybe another piece of that pie."

Coffey's Coffee was almost empty when they went back. They were returning to the booth that they had occupied earlier, when Len Coffey, in his usual hopping jog, burst merrily out of the kitchen.

"Well you fellows are becoming regular regulars! What might I do you for? The special today is a tuna salad sandwich, and I think we still have some left. Comes with chips, a drink, and a homemade dill pickle. It'll leave just enough room for pie. So whaddaya think?"

Neither one of the men could suppress the smile that Len Coffey's jubilant nature evoked. They looked at each other, and once again mutually agreed to the little man's suggestion.

When he brought them their drinks, on an impulse Arnie asked, "Mister Coffey, I hate to impose, but Adam and I have a private business matter we need to deal with right away. Do you have an office phone we could use for a few minutes?"

"Well sure thing. The office is just back here behind the kitchen. Follow me."

Adam looked up with some curiosity as Arnie stood up and motioned for him to follow. They passed into the kitchen, where a plump, pleasant-faced woman smiled at them from a counter where she was busy assembling their order.

"Honey, this is Mister..." Coffey began but then realized he didn't remember Arnie's name.

"I'm Arnie Warner, Mrs. Coffey. Nice to meet you. Loved your pie earlier today and just had to come back for more."

Coffey then said, "And this young fellow here is——"

"I'm Adam Pembrook, Mrs. Coffey. It's good to meet you."

Len Coffey looked confused for a moment, then he just smiled broadly, scratched his cheek and said, "Well I'll be dog." He continued to smile at Adam, his mind working as though he was putting together the pieces of a puzzle, and then he turned and did that little hop-jog toward the back of the kitchen, and the two men followed. Coffey called back over his shoulder, "Darlin' they're going to use your phone for a minute."

As they entered the small, neatly organized office, Arnie said, "This will be a long-distance call, but I'll reverse the charges, of course."

"No problem at all Mister Warner. Just make yourself at home. I'll just close the door so you can have some privacy, and we'll have those sandwiches ready when you're finished here."

"What's this all about, Arnie? What's so urgent that we need to handle right now?"

"It's just something I need to do, but I want you here with me while I take care of it," Arnie answered as he dialed for the operator. The operator answered and he placed a collect call. He had to repeat both the number and his name twice to the operator before the call went through.

Adam could hear the voice faintly through the receiver, as the call was answered and the charges accepted. The call was then transferred and Arnie was eventually connected to whomever he was calling.

"No, I'm not in jail, Gerald," Arnie laughed. "Listen I want you to draw up a change in my will." Arnie paused while Gerald Forsythe, his longtime attorney, obviously expressed some curiosity about such a call.

"Well it's a simple change. Just draw it up and I'll stop by the office tomorrow to sign it. I'll explain then, if you think it's any of your business," he laughed and then continued. "Here's what I want. You know I have Meredith down as my sole beneficiary. I'd like to change that."

Arnie looked up at Adam as he went on, "I want to take Meredith's name off, and replace as sole heir to my estate, including my share in Warner & Crewe, my nephew, Adam Pembrook."

A long pause ensued, while the attorney apparently voiced some opinion, to which Arnie replied, "I know, but this is what I want to do, Gerald. Just draw it up, and I'll be in tomorrow to sign it. Thank you, now I'm getting off the phone because your meter is running."

The whole time he talked, Adam was staring in stunned disbelief. And when the phone was hung up he said, "Arnie, you don't have to do that."

"No, I know I don't have to," Arnie extended his right hand and grasped Adam's shoulder with the other, "But yes I do."

EPILOGUE
Today

• • • •

ANDREW PEMBROOK CLOSED his eyes and listened to the sound of the fountain and the forest that surrounded the clearing. His memory shuffled though years and ages as he and Macy grew up, while Grandpop and Uncle Arnie grew old. The smells, the sounds, and feeling of it all gripped his heart. Even focusing on the good times, he felt an uncomfortable tightness in his throat.

He opened his eyes and turned to look at the old fountain. Above him, along the edge of the uppermost tier, were perched three sculpted birds. The wings of two touched, as one's beak dipped into the water, while the other stood upright and alert, appearing to be watching out over the lake beyond. The third was positioned slightly apart, its wings raised as though about to take flight. The bronze fountain and its three permanent residents quieted Andy's mind, and he sat for several long moments studying the variegated patina of the three birds, thinking about what was sealed within each one, listening to the trickling water. It comforted him. Grandpop had been right about that too.

The sudden rustle of wings brought Andrew out of his reverie. A large jay landed noisily opposite the sculpted doves, and with a quick glimpse around, it buried its head in the water, then jumped in and flapped it wings, sending a sprinkle of cold water across Andrew's upturned face. He jerked back and wiped his face with his hand, and with the sudden motion, the bird retreated to a low limb on a nearby tree. It shook its body and squawked noisily in his direction. Andrew smiled up at the bird, his thoughts turning, unbidden, to his grandfather.

Without thinking, he plunged his hand into the water and squeezed it into a fist, squirting a stream of water in the direction of the squawking jay, falling far short of its mark. It was a trick Grandpop had taught him when he and Grannie lived at the old house in town, with its big pool in back.

A clear, shrill series of rapid whistling calls drew Andrew's eye to a tree across the clearing, and within its branches he spied a red flash of a cardinal flitting from branch to branch.

Macy had told him not long ago that she had only vague memories of the old house now, which had to mean that her memories of Grannie were equally dim. Andrew regretted that for his sister. The memory of how Grannie laughed, or the games she invented to play with them when they were little, and especially the memory of the way her voice sounded, would be a precious thing to have lost.

It had been she who taught him how to identify various birds, he remembered, when a large thrush settled on the rim of the fountain alongside the sculpted trio, only to streak away when Andrew turned his head to look. Just a glimpse of the distinctive long curved beak was enough to bring back the memory of that page from her little *Book of Birds*.

The blue jay once again issued its loud throaty squawk, and began to flutter from limb to limb around the clearing that surrounded the fountain. It would stop and cock its head, looking at Andrew, seeming to dare him to try to squirt him again.

"That's hardly fair. Come down here and fight like a man," he heard himself say aloud to the bird. Then his handsome face took on a shamefaced grin and he shook his head, looking up at the jay, its brilliant blue feathers flashing across the deep greens of the wooded hill beyond.

"Now you've got me doing it."

He heard the bell ringing out from the cabin porch below. That meant Macy and her family had arrived. He heard the lilt of delight in his mother's voice as she called out the names of Macy's children. That's what she needed right now, to be surrounded by her grandchildren.

The past eight months had been so brutally hard for all of them, but that was only because there had been so much love.

The painful vision was cut short by the joyful sound of the twins squealing in unison. Andrew saw them streak across the end of the path below, dashing toward their cousins, their arms high in the air. So much love. So many good memories.

The thrush, the jay, and the cardinal all chattered and whistled as they flew away through the trees.

"Going to see Macy?" he said aloud with a small chuckle.

Andrew stood up and looked around him, almost with a feeling of expectation. There were other birds in the trees around the fountain, but *that feeling* wasn't there.

Poofs were such a strange and wonderful phenomenon. They had become woven into the fabric of his family over the years. It was their private comfort, beginning when they had lost Grannie. Then years later, Grandpop. And not long after that, sweet Uncle Arnie.

Another wave of tightness gripped his heart as his eye fell on the sculpture of the bird that sat slightly apart from the other two. Andrew recalled how his dad had wept as he sealed Uncle Arnie's ashes in the sculpture, and placed the bird on its mounting pins on the fountain, saying, "Poofannie, Poofarnie, and Poofernando. Now you're all together again."

His eyes fell on the second tier of the fountain, where two new mounting pins had been installed, and he found himself glancing again around the clearing.

Poofs had not been something they had been willing to share with other people. Warner & Crewe didn't need rumors about its founding family being a bunch of fruitcake eccentrics who believed their dead loved ones poofed into birds and butterflies and flitted around their back yards.

The twins weren't yet born when his Grandpop died, but losing him had naturally turned Andrew's thoughts back to the stories he had told Macy and him after Grannie had passed. They had all convinced Grandpop to write the stories down, and even to record some of them. He had thought then that he wanted his own children, should they ever have a family, to be able to hear those same stories.

Andrew now occupied his grandparents' old studio at Warner & Crewe. It was there, in the very place where they had created the stories and figurines that had launched the company, that Andrew had illustrated the children's books that had created such a phenomenal resurgence in popularity of the original figurines.

Poofs were no longer a family secret, and although there had been a ripple of religious backlash when the stories came out, it seemed that many people already had an inkling that their loved ones occasionally found a way to impart just a moment of comfort or encouragement when they seemed to need it most. Parents seemed willing to embrace and share such a sweet opportunity to comfort children who were faced with loss. And it seemed that adults received the uplifting message of the stories as eagerly as did their children.

Andrew was glad to know that people had embraced the idea, and received that precious fleeting glimpse through the veil, most often when they would least expect it. It helped make times, such as they were all facing today, almost bearable.

He recalled how Grandpop had said that the Holy Spirit had taken the form of a dove to give Jesus exactly that kind of reassurance when He had been baptized. Andrew had read those passages of Scripture many times over the years.

He looked around the clearing once again, then started down the path to join the family. He had taken only a few steps when he heard the unmistakable long, shrill call of a hawk above. He looked up and shaded his eyes against the noonday sun that burst through the canopy of treetops on either side of the path.

Suddenly Andrew remembered the countless times on their trips up here that his dad had pointed out a hawk above those same treetops and talked about how he loved to watch them as a boy, and had tried so often to imagine what it must feel like to be so free...circling and soaring among the clouds like that.

The hawk came into view, bathed in sunlight, wheeling across the ribbon of brilliant blue above the pathway, seeming to almost stop in midair, then plummet into a streaking dive, only to soar back to the heights in the next moment with another exultant screech.

"Dad..." Andrew said in a hoarse whisper, the tears springing to his eyes, his voice choked, his heart aching but utterly joyful, "Oh man! Oh man! Dad, just look at you!"

Please Rate and Review

THANK YOU FOR READING *The Undeniable Possibility*. This is one that was written from my heart. I hope you enjoyed it, and if you did, I would so appreciate having you join me in making sure many others have the opportunity to experience the reassurance I believe the story can offer.

Such a recommendation may help someone discover more than a story they will enjoy. My prayer is that *The Undeniable Possibility* may give you, and everyone who reads it, just a moment of comfort and encouragement in the midst of those inevitable times of sorrow.

If you enjoyed the book, I would be deeply grateful if you would go to my book page at Amazon.com and post a 1 to 5 Star rating (1 being lowest, and 5 Stars being the highest rating) for *The Undeniable Possibility*, and perhaps write a line or two encouraging others to read it.

• • • •

I AM WORKING ON A NEW book, based on my musicals *Bethlehem & Pentecost*, that we plan to publish in late 2018. If you'd like to sign up to become part of my advance reader group and receive a free advance copy of that and other books I write, please click on the link below.

• • • •

https://www.chippolk.com/arc

A Free Book

YOU MAY ALSO ENJOY my little Christmas novella, *Say Nicklaase, A Great & Wonderful Christmas Story*. It is an adaptation of my most popular musical. It is a whimsical, but touching Christmas story that will make you want to believe.

I invite you to read the following excerpt, which is the prologue of the novella. If you like it, there is a link at the end where you can get the ebook edition as my free gift.

. . . .

NICKLAASE ELLIFFE WAS a good man. He was very, very much more than a good man. He was a great and wonderful man, but that was not something he ever thought about or planned. Nicklaase just was what he was, like a carrot is a carrot or a goat is a goat. And he was never what he was not, which as it turns out, is harder not to be than one might expect.

With unruly snow-white hair poking out in every direction from under his cap, and curling over the scarf he wore tied around his neck, and a bushy white beard with a very distinctive handlebar mustache, Nicklaase Elliffe just looked like an old man to people who didn't know him. But he felt like a best friend to everyone who did. Even to children. Perhaps, especially to children.

Well, to be perfectly honest, there was one man who still saw nothing more than an old man, even after he got to know Nicklaase. But that part of the story comes later, after you know Nicklaase a bit better yourself.

Nicklaase Elliffe lived with his wife, Meena, in a cottage at the edge of a wood in Norpol Province. It probably made you shiver to hear that, because anyone who has never been there thinks it is always cold in Norpol Province. It is true that it does get very cold in winter, and the winters there are longer than in most other places. But spring and autumn

are beautiful and colorful, and crisp. And then, of course, there is sum-
mer in between, and in summer the sun comes out, coats come off, and
a sweater, cap, and perhaps a knitted scarf are all one needs to be toasty
warm during the day.

Both Nicklaase and Meena spoke with the accent unique to Norpol
province, and one of the very few things Nicklaase was particular about,
was the way his name was pronounced.

"Say Nee-klaase," he would insist. And if there was a child nearby,
and there always was, he would lift one up onto his knee and bounce
them until they erupted in giggles, repeating with him, "Nee-klaase!
Nee-klaase! Nee-klaase!"

The Elliffe cottage always had that warm and comfortable feeling
that smelled of peanut butter and chocolate chip cookies in the oven. Of
course, that was Meena's doing. Meena Elliffe was as sweet and soft and
warm as the cookies she baked. She was a relentless knitter and mender
of scarves, caps, sweaters and socks. And Meena was also a very good
reader of great and wonderful stories, and maker of hot cocoa that tasted
just like the laughter of children.

Laughing children always filled the Elliffe cottage, and spilled out
across the yard and into Nicklaase's shop, and the woods beyond. If
you ever heard it, then you would remember how Nicklaase Elliffe's big
booming laugh was always part of the chorus of the children's giggles and
squeals.

There was a gravel road that led from the Elliffe cottage over a hill,
and continued beyond a cluster of smaller buildings surrounding an
austere and very imposing gray stone, two-story building with two great
columns on either side of the entrance. The road meandered through the
valley past numerous other cottages that looked much like the Elliffe's.
They too were made of rough stone and stucco, with brown shutters and
trim, but only the Elliffe's cottage had a red door. And only the Elliffe's
cottage had that warm and comfortable feeling.

The road ended at a narrow, paved highway that led to a small town nearby. There was a gateway with a sign over the gravel road. In iron letters welded above, were the words "State Home for Children No. 13."

In the story, Nicklaase and Meena Elliffe are house parents at State Home for Children No. 13. But, they are much more than that. The Elliffe household shares the joyful work of making toys for all the other children who live in children's home cottages in their valley. The toys they make are distributed once every year, on Christmas Eve.

When an ambitious new headmaster forbids the gifts to be given to the children, it begins an unforeseen chain of disastrous events. The final calamity results in an opportunity for the Elliffes, and the children living in their cottage, to trust that the Lord can indeed work all things together for good.

I would love for you to have the ebook edition of *Say Nicklaase, a Great & Wonderful Christmas Story,* as my free gift to you. It's available right now at the link below.

• • • •

https://www.chippolk.com/saynickfree

Acknowledgments

THE PREMISE OF THIS story came to me in 1984, shortly after the tragic death of my nephew, Jeff. He was my brother, Glenn's, 12-year-old son. It took me over thirty years to find the words. Just as the final pages were being written, my eldest brother, Travis, also had the heartbreaking experience of saying goodbye to his son, who passed away suddenly at 53 years old. Bookended by my brothers' painful losses, this story has deep significance for me.

Through the losses of these two, and other loved ones over three decades of carrying this book in my heart, Robin, our children, their spouses, and I, much like Mason and Annie Crewe in the story, have been the only ones who knew about *Poofs*. We have all secretly treasured moments of gentle comfort when a bird, a squirrel, or a butterfly caught our attention, and inexplicably brought one or another of those dear ones to mind. Whether real or imagined, it was comfort and consolation for which we have each been grateful.

As I've watched others suffer painful losses, it has made me feel selfish, and guilty that I had yet to finish the book, and lacked the boldness to share what has been such sweet solace for me. I so hope that this story will enable those enigmatic occurrences to be shared, because the experiences are not unique. Given the conversations with the few people, in which I have recently confided the secret of *The Undeniable Possibility*, it seems that *Poofs* are already something of a universal, but seldom talked-about phenomenon. It should be joyfully shared.

I am blessed to have a great team of collaborators within my own family. For almost 43 years, Robin has been not only my adored wife, but my intrepid business and creative partner in every endeavor. She has been right there with me from page one of this book; my first reader, proofreader, copy editor, and willing listener as I have blathered on about *Poofs* for over thirty years.

Aside from unfailing belief in the dreamer she married, among her greatest contributions are two children, Jordan and Jency, who inherited their mother's intellect and unflinching honesty. Both have made huge contributions, from consulting, editing and cover design for the book, to the website and marketing. And like their mother, they brought two great members of the team on board. Cassie and Thomas married into the creative milieu that is the Polk clan, and have become trusted advisors and generous encouragers. My brother, Glenn Polk, was also a valuable part of the editing team, offering fresh eyes, and with his wife, Twila, provided encouragement from their personal perspective of having endured a devastating loss.

I am grateful to my son-in-law, Thomas Anciso, for his experienced insight and counsel about the combat scenes depicted. I am also indebted to Robin's grandfather, the late Horace Salter, who in 1977, privately shared with me his horrendous ordeal of being mustard-gassed, and held prisoner during the first World War. I considered his confiding such remembrances to me a profound privilege, and attempted to faithfully convey some sense of the horror of his experience.

I am grateful to my friend, and former FBI Special Agent Joe Cook, for his advice and counsel regarding realistic investigative procedures, as well as combat scene realism.

And finally, this book pays a certain degree of homage to orphaned and abused children. Our kids attended a small school with many children from a local children's home. Imagining the agonizing circumstances that resulted in their placement in those facilities touched our hearts. They so needed love, a sense of belonging, and an identity apart from the one imposed by their circumstances. My memory of them had much to do with the depiction of Freddy Finger, Jr.'s painful life.

January, 2018

About the Author

CHIP POLK HAS PENNED twenty-eight gospel-based stage plays, five of which are musicals. He has published a novella, *Say Nicklaase, A Great & Wonderful Christmas Story,* and his first full length novel, *The Undeniable Possibility.*

He is also a singer-songwriter and pianist, with four albums released to date, and a soon-to-be released collection of all original piano compositions. Chip performs in concert, and his plays are produced year-round at Ragtown Gospel Theater in historic Post, Texas.

Discover links to his books, plays, music, concert booking and other information about Chip Polk and Ragtown Gospel Theater at http://www.ragtown.com[1], and at http://www.chippolk.com.

You may email him at chip@ragtown.com. Follow him on Facebook and Twitter @ChipPolk. Chip and his wife, Robin live in Ransom Canyon, Texas.

---

1.   http://www.ragtown.com

Copyright

The Undeniable Possibility

53231529R00202

Made in the USA
Columbia, SC
14 March 2019